Action Not Words

A journey from chaos to calm

CHRISTINE EMMA CAREY

Paperback: 978-1-968667-66-5
Hardcover: 978-1-969919-53-4
eBook: 978-1-968667-67-2
Library of Congress Control Number: 2025918688

This is a work of fiction based on actual people and historical events.

Ordering Information:

Prime Seven Media
518 Landmann St.
Tomah City, WI 54660

Printed in the United States of America

*To my husband and all of our children who
live daily by the title of this little story.*

Table of Contents

"And at home by the fire, whenever you look up, there I shall be - and whenever I look up, there will be you."

Gabriel Oak.
From 'Far From The Madding Crowd."
Thomas Hardy

Chapter 1

October 1918

John looked up at the church tower clock which was facing west, catching the last of the failing light of this October day and, pointing at it brusquely and silently to his fellow officers, he pulled out his pocket watch, as did the others, and checked the time on its cracked and worn face. Perhaps that was an apt description of his own face after this grim and unforgiving climate on the Front in the dying days at the end of this bitter conflict. He was body weary and losing concentration too easily, especially by this time of day. His head was heavy with grief for the deaths of the men he had known. He had witnessed the fear and desperation of those who were still fighting on; those who had been lucky enough to come through so far. And it was wearing him down. It was a fight in itself to keep strong and sure as a captain among his men tonight.

A sudden shudder caught him as the damp chill of dusk crept under the collar of his greatcoat. The nights were drawing in and there wasn't much clear light left. He needed to stay focussed.

He checked again:1900 hours. Everyone synchronised. Each officer had received the same instructions. They were time-ready for tomorrow. Now to distribute rations, shovels and rifle grenades to each soldier and to give them their instructions, as described in their own battle orders, signed off by Second Lieutenant Beresford of the Cheshires.

How familiar the routine was. Firstly, the briefing, then the synchronising of timepieces; the following of orders and then the reality. Every single man, whether quietly and inwardly, or loudly and vociferously, demanded to know when it would all be over. They said, whoever the hell <u>they</u> were; it would soon be all over. The Germans were weak and hungry and they could not uphold their numbers. They were running out of ammunition. Morale was waning on both sides it was true, but even now after these four years, the British Army was well catered for in all senses. Never mind, end of the war or not, this was an important battle, just as every single other had been before it, and they were determined to be the victors.

The officers dispersed towards their own companies to begin the task in front of them. They had three hours to organise themselves before moving towards the Line.

There was some time to kill. They needed to wait for the tanks to go through to clear the route along which the soldiers would go. It was only a short trek admittedly, but as always happened, there were tanks ahead checking for any unforeseen danger - buried shells and other ammunition, not to overlook the possibility of the enemy lying in wait!

"I reckon the time for action will be first light sir," suggested a young lieutenant of 'A' Company. "At this time of year? Don't get your hopes up lieutenant! There's no decent light before 07.00 at least. No, I dare bet that we'll begin manoeuvres while it's still dark. But let's wait to be informed of zero hour," said John grimly.

Onward they marched, checking the coordinates on their maps by torchlight as the evening wore on. There was cloud, and that provided ideal conditions for marching forward to enemy lines. The rhythmic trudging sound of the men as they advanced towards their positions was uplifting for company spirit. The regular, controlled and determined footsteps of men who knew that their fate was fragile and uncertain, but the cry of "Let's get these bastards, lads" was always lodged in every soldier's sub conscious as each time, the battle approach was made.

It was just a short march to their positions, where they would wait for manoeuvre instructions through the cold October night, after they had dug themselves in - again- as they had so many times before. The waiting was agonising. It was the most challenging time for every man, as they exchanged tobacco and sang softly without breaking night silence, in order to pass the time. At least there was a decent ration to tuck into. The food was not what mother would make, they would smirk, but it was filling and energy giving and eating it always passed the time.

As always, John was outwardly calm. He took his role seriously and did not allow himself much time for relaxation. His head was filled with grief and sadness, to which he never admitted nor submitted. He rarely indulged in light or frivolous chatter, nor did he share the jokes that flew around between his fellow officers. He was empathetic but focused and he was quick to understand orders and quite simply, obey.

Not standoffish though, he would usually position himself on the edge of the command post, listening to them all, whilst drawing in some pleasure from his pipe, quietly reflecting on whatever the current situation happened to be, or on the people he had left behind.

It was easy to see how everyone who met him, admired him for his cool and measured action and his sensible nature. Not being the type to talk about himself, very few people knew his origins. When was there time for such chit chat anyway? There had never been the luxury of time now, and definitely not in his early years. He was always too busy, helping out on the family sheep farm in the wild hills of Cumbria. At the same time, he shone at his school studies and attended grammar school and he was such an accomplished sportsman that he was captain in both school and university football and cricket teams. Then on to Manchester University, he gained a First in Mathematics and Physics. There was no doubt, his upbringing and a sharp brain had shaped his outlook, his attitude to life and his straight and sensible application to any task that he faced.

These were clearly the essential attributes of an army officer, leading by example to inspire and motivate the troops and so, he entered the Cheshire Regiment, after initial training in 1916 and became a Captain.

"Action Not Words!" he would say.

"Get the job done!" he would add.

And he did.

23 October 1918

John was brushing the splattered mud marks on his uniform. They had barely dried out, but needed to be smartened up for the next call. He gained quiet satisfaction in painstakingly smartening his appearance before each battle. It was a form of ritual that prepared him mentally for the challenges he was yet to face. Perhaps it could have been a strategy for delaying the inevitable ghastliness and horror they were all likely to encounter in the following hours. His thoughts tumbling around in his mind were interrupted, as the runner appeared at the command post, breathless and smelly. His khakis were splattered and stained, but his fresh plump cheeks were shining red in the gaslight and he panted with energy and a sense that things would now be happening.

"Zero-hour message sir," he announced as he saluted.

John pulled on his battledress jacket saying, "Thank you, sergeant. Good timing man. We are ready." John unfolded the neatly scripted memo and read it slowly.

"04.30 hours"

He had just 85 soldiers and artillery in his company for this manoeuvre. The numbers were dwindling but the three other companies that would strategically work together, as detailed in the Orders would strengthen the advance and overpower the enemy. He was far from feeling discouraged.

As the sergeant had run past the troops, who were now dug down and dozing, there had been a flurry of movement. They knew that this runner was delivering the message that would be the last and most important detail for this attack. Several called out words of mock encouragement although you could detect the undertones of doubt and fear as well. Understandably, the lads were weary and lacked energy at this unearthly hour, but a sense of humour and the ability to find the funny side of things was a great skill they had all seemed to have developed, for keeping each other's spirits sharp and uplifted.

"Letter for me is it Sarge?" called out one.

"Who'd want to be writing to you?" cried out another.

"Mother's missing you?" joined in a third.

The banter stopped as John stepped forward to address his sergeants.

"Over here, men. Now listen carefully. We can't make any mistakes today. No room for error. Here are the final instructions."

Quietly and firmly, John outlined the strategy before them defining the objectives and the limits. These had come through from British HQ since he had received the first Battle Orders.

Briskly directing the gunners to position, he then indicated to each of them the positions they would take. He had been informed by now that his men would fight alongside the Bedfords and the Lancashire Fusiliers, and this would boost the obviously depleted numbers in his company and help lift the morale of them all.

Then at the command, it was every man over the top and into no man's land, on their scrawny bellies, keeping low and stealthily creeping forward. They all knew what to do. It was a routine strategy and they cursed and swore as they assembled.

The iron grey sky was smouldering with glimmers of orange behind the October clouds, proving that battles along the Frontline were already underway, together with the continual thunder of cannon fire and thousands of troops would be attacking each other. Kill or be killed growling in their throats, fire in their eyes and fear in their hearts.

With aching arms and cricked necks, they followed orders:
"Load!

Aim!

Fire!"

Again and again, without hesitating, they continued. Even when someone fell, the orders were to carry on. If you were alive, you fought, no matter what. They were the orders. There were severe consequences for those who got involved and allowed their emotions to surface. There were medics to sweep up the injured anyway. They had their own orders. The dead would be left where they fell. "Action!" his sergeants roared, echoing the tactical expression used by the officer in charge as they skidded through the greasy mud underfoot, taking up new positions to shout orders at young corporals who were disorientated and confused. These lads lacked experience and had not had time to toughen up, having been called to the Front at this late stage in the war.

The Stokes Guns were heavy and complicated for positioning and loading. The gunners were skilled and slick but were deafened by the noise of the firing. Later, most soldiers discovered that they had impaired hearing caused by the constant barrage of gunshot they experienced every day and every night. These gunners did have some experience and were lined up to form a strong line of defence. Communication had to be intuitive and through gestures. It was no good trying to talk above the deafening cracks and bangs of relentless, persistent firing. They were the 'here today gone tomorrow' mob - an apt description of the gruelling risks they took manning these monster mortars.

As with every other battle that John had been involved in, the sulphur stench of gunfire, acrid smoke and rotting flesh of soldiers who had fallen before them, made him retch, but by now had just managed to control himself by looking out towards the horizon. Disorientated often, at this moment, he wondered what did lie beyond that horizon - and this averted the retching reflex but never failed in personalising and disturbing his mind for just a moment. Today, as with all the others, he marched along the Company front shouting out encouragement and boosting them. "Aim and fire, aim and fire. Never give up. You're doing great. Grand work." He repeated these words of encouragement, over and over again, as he walked the line.

Then he looked back and to his horror lay a trail of dead and injured men. "Oh, dear God," he muttered, realising that the enemy gunfire had been rapid and accurate. The casualties were beyond numbers that they had imagined.

This certainly applied to this battle, in particular. This was the one they all expected would be harsh, bitter and frenzied. But not like this! All along the front the fighting had been even more vicious and intense during the last few days, as the rumours of a truce were rumbling round. Suddenly, he was angry and his contempt for the danger which they were all in, punched him deeply inside. This he defied, would not be a battle lost.

"We're not losing this bastard," he screeched to himself and then turning to the gunners he yelled, "Cover me! I'm going over!" and he took speed along the line and over towards the enemy.

Then others followed a short distance behind, moving swiftly, keeping low. Blind with belief, they were confident the captain knew what he was doing. He had a reputation for doing the right thing and the soldiers would always follow instructions to follow orders, without question; without doubting.

He strode firmly across the ocean of mud, making an arc through the dead contorted bodies of English and German soldiers lying where they had been slain. There in front of him was the profile of a lone enemy soldier whose metal helmet had slipped over his eyes as he looked down to load his machine gun. Two men beside him were seriously wounded, totally incapacitated. John grabbed the lone one from behind; his left arm gripped tightly around the soldier's neck and simultaneously he slammed his right hand over the man's hand, forcing him to drop his gun. The soldier was gasping, struggling to breathe and was so weakened through lack of food and sleep and orders from his own officers, that he buckled and submitted himself. Silently, mercilessly, John snatched the machine gun from him and aimed it towards the man's chest.

"Get up!" he growled. "Move!"

Hearing the anger, and feeling the pain from John's iron grip, the soldier, confused and dazed, scrambled to his feet, as John prodded him in the back. "March!"

In front of him were other German soldiers, slumped with fatigue, and exhausted. They appeared to be bereft of ammunition at that moment. Instinctively and moving fast, John shoved the man towards his compatriots who stared back at him in disbelief. They were helpless and it would be useless to retaliate.

Bewildered, they were asking themselves what was happening. An ambush without a single shot being fired? This was unheard of in their camp.

Completely surprised now by these events, they froze in uncertainty and fear. Warfare, to these soldiers was a 'dog eat dog' mentality and John kept repeating his orders. "Move!"

He pushed the captive in front, and indicated to the men to rise, otherwise they would witness a bullet shattered body before them. One by one they moved their bodies, without saying anything, scrambling awkwardly to their feet in the slime; spilled blood and gore in the mud beneath them.

Then closing in behind him without a sound, four English soldiers appeared in the shadows of John's determined advance.

"We got yer back sir," they whispered hoarsely.

"Just follow me, dammitt. Aim at 'em. Don't fire. They're POW's now," he barked as he cocked the latch on his gun, aiming towards each individual enemy soldier menacingly. One by one, they meekly gave in, following the actions of the man before him. Beneath their filthy faces they were ghastly white with fear. Confusion and dread for what was going to happen next was so apparent in their compliance and submission.

"Poor bastards 've given up, haven't they?" muttered one of John's men, as they closed around this growing number of the living enemy.

"Shut up soldier, and group them now because I'm going to threaten attack here," snapped John.

"We've got forty odd Germans here; I'm not losing them now."

Across no man's land they trudged, slowly and deliberately toward the English line; the enemy soldiers with hands behind their heads all hanging forward, overpowered and admitting defeat.

The message had been given to command that there were prisoners on the way and so one area of the trench was cleared and they were roughly pushed towards it.

"Get down! Stay down!" John bellowed, as he handed over to two other officers to deploy some guards until they were removed from the trench space.

"Good work men," John called out gruffly, as he turned towards them. "Couldn't have done that without the back up."

Slowly, he turned towards the command post of his tiny billet within and flopped down wearily, cradling his head in his hand.

"Christ! Did I just dream that episode?" he thought.

Someone passed him a tin mug of hot sweet tea and a tot of rum. It was the soft voice of his lieutenant.

"Sir, that was incredible! Are you okay? You'll be wanting this after that palaver!" said the lieutenant offering a familiar tone.

"Thank you, Jack," he responded in a daze, pulling at his boot laces to loosen them.

"We've covered you, and jolly well done Captain - for now. That was great work. Take some time to collect yourself," spoke Major Longden, looking up from presenting his daily report for the stenographer to deal with.

There was an obvious atmosphere of admiration for the action of young Captain Bland, and although words were few, he felt a small sense of relief that his spontaneous action had been acknowledged. Suddenly, he felt trembly and weak. Aftershock, he thought.

He pulled out his pipe from his safe box and stuffed the tobacco into its bowl, lit up, puffed gently and breathed. This would surely soothe his heartbeat and restore his composure.

"Herding sheep," he pondered whilst alone. That 'palaver' as Jack had called it, had referred to the risks involved in ambushing the enemy in such numbers on his own, but he was aware and was clearly impressed with such daring.

"No difference," he reflected, as the events of the last hour flashed through his mind like some cine film flickering. John of course had used exactly the same approach as he had over the thousands of times he had herded a flock back on Shap, just himself with a couple of collies. He'd been shown how to go about it by his father since he was ten years old.

Pacing across the heather with his roughhewn crook he would whistle and stride towards the strongest ewe. Then calling out instructions to his dogs, once he'd got the measure of which he wanted and where he wanted them to go, they would move them. Usually to fresher grazing. Such docile creatures could be easily panicked, but Snip and Dolly were well trained, rewarded for good work and knew exactly how to earn a good meal and a rest at the end of the day.

He hadn't given it a second thought when he saw this gaggle of disorganised and shabby soldiers. They were an easy challenge to be honest. When he saw their ashen faces and their haunted and hungry eyes, he saw those sheep on the craggy Shap moors.

Nevertheless, he was well aware that if just one of the crazed enemy soldiers turned hostile and nasty, they may do something reckless and risk the safety of his men. Once he had made the first advance, it was imperative to see it through.

A ruthless and aggressive side to his character surfaced from somewhere and on reflection, sometime later, it shocked him that he was capable of such. But he had only one chance at this brave, unplanned assault and if it went wrong, his own life would go too. And those men just behind him, watching his back, would see him fall… and fail.

That was enough rest time. Ten minutes was a luxury. He knocked out the spent tobacco and returned to the trench to hail the company to retreat. His legs felt weak and unsteady, another indication that his adrenalin had been gushing to strengthen his determination to see that the ambush had been successful. He bent down slowly to tie up his laces again, and, back to real time.

Pulling at his jacket ensuring it was correct, he straightened himself up and commanded the return of the troops. He wasn't a big chap, standing five foot three inches at best, but his height didn't seem to be a disadvantage because his presence and his formal manner radiated strength and credibility. His good looks, with dark blonde hair and grey- blue eyes that held a calmness of spirit and reassuring self-belief, gave him the stature and build needed when in charge, directing, motivating and leading. As he looked across towards the horizon, he could hear the same commands being issued and repeated by fellow officers as they scanned the skyline for movement of soldiers.

"Retreat, retreat."

No one seemed to be returning.

Questions raced through his head. No one there? What the …where were they?…. Come on! For Christ's sake boys! Show yourselves. He muttered over and over in his agitated state.

Eventually, after a long and agonising wait, a few shadows limped over the top. They were heavily wounded, carrying each other across the wretched ground. It was brutally clear - there had been massive losses.

Indeed, this was heavy loss, greater than any of them had expected. So much for this being regarded as a straightforward strategic attack. The orders had come through clear and simple. The Germans had suffered such a crushing defeat down the line. They were known to be weak and tired by now. This should have been a straightforward victory for the Cheshires and the Bedfords who had been joined by the Lancashires, the Manchesters and the King's Artillery in a coordinated assault.

It was a scene, that would not be better or worse than the news that had been reported, of other battles. And like so many of the other battles fought in this wretched war, it was horrifying and incomprehensible for those at home. Yet again, the press men would be reporting the same stories of gunners who had perished, and rifleman who had fallen, many of whom would be unidentifiable and remain unnamed.

There was a formula for reporting at this stage in the war. The details of the horrors never reached the loved ones of those who had been lost in the name of freedom. There would be no reporting of the screaming as they were hit; the crying of "Mother I love you!" and "Don't leave me alone!" uttered in their last dying breath of suffering and pain. There would be no visual reporting of irreparable wounds, and the collapsed state of dying young soldiers falling over their weapons, being left there to perish in excruciating agony.

John gritted his teeth as he marshalled the survivors into the ditch, firmly cupping a shoulder here, a light tap on the back of a limping person passing there. Praising them for all their labours and all that they had achieved, he kept it straight and simple. There was no room for sentiment and emotion at this stage. That would only serve to weaken and stir up feelings of loss, the fear and self-belief in them all. He included himself and his fellow officers in that philosophy. No place for emotion and sentiment he would keep repeating quietly to himself.

He left them to their own devices, such as was possible in these grim surroundings. He returned to his own space, dropped down on an empty artillery box, and, knocking his cap from his head he bowed his head in his hands and prayed.

Then, looking around, he realised there were only three other officers who were likewise in shock and confusion at the extent of the loss of life, and now, were unprepared for next orders.

"Heavy losses Men," he sighed, as he rose to face them. "We need to do some head counts here and establish our numbers. Let's get moving and reconvene in 20 minutes to report back. We need to do some urgent reorganising and reconfiguring of each company. No time to lose."

11 November

"Captain… sir, some urgent news is coming through. You are needed here to receive it personally. There are orders to bring you to the phone," announced the radio controller, and down the radio line came the statement from a colonel. John did not catch his name through the crackling reception and the noise of shell fire and gun noise from behind.

"This is an important announcement. Ensure that this message is received by all NCO's and senior officers.

"*On the 11th November 1918 at 11.00am Central Europe Time an Armistice Agreement was signed by the Allied Forces. Orders from General Foch are as follows:*

> "*Hostilities will cease on the whole front as from November 11at 11o'clock. The Allied Troops will not, until further order, go beyond the line reached on that date and at that hour*"

The message continued,

> "*Convey message to all company soldiers and await further details, due imminently. Write down this statement that you are now ordered to use to inform the troops.*"

With slow steps and feeling numb in disbelief, John turned towards his fellow officers and repeated the message that he had written down. They knew it was good news from his flushed and sweat beaded brow, but in a strong and clear voice he declared,

"The Great War is over. We are now ordered to present the message to the troops."

He read out Foch's statement, as recorded by radio control and his fellow officers wrote feverishly in calm disbelief, that this was it. This was ceasefire. They could go and inform those men lying out there in the dirt and blood and spew, that there would be no more fighting, that they could prepare to go home to their loved ones. The trucks would be rolling out to collect them anytime now.

"It's all over, thank The Lord," they all sighed.

After 23 October 1918, John's family learned of his heroism.

"Lieutenant Bland The Cheshire Regiment Awarded the MILITARY CROSS for: -

> *Conspicuous gallantry and good leadership in the attack on Beaurain N. Of Le Cateau on 23rd October 1918*
>
> *His Company suffered very heavy casualties on the march to and in the assembly positions.*
>
> *On every occasion he showed the uttermost contempt of danger, rallying his men and walking along his company front to inspire confidence.*
>
> *After he captured single handed an enemy machine gun and took 27 prisoners by sheer skill and coolness, advancing them from behind and taking them by surprise.*
>
> *He also helped and assisted in re-organising the Company which had lost all its officers and most of its N.C.O.'s*
>
> *He collected men of other companies and formed them into original parties.*

> *His courage and skill won the admiration of all who saw him and there is no doubt that it was mainly owing to him that the Battalion gained their objective in spite of heavy casualties which exceeded 40 per cent of those who took part in the advance."*

Extract from the LONDON GAZETTE

No one had any idea of the atrocities John Bland had seen, just as so many of the soldiers who returned. They vowed that they would never speak of the horrors and the suffering of that time in battle. He himself never divulged any detail of his particular act of bravery that had been recognised and had been awarded him through the Military Cross.

The only information anyone had, throughout the two generations who were alive during his lifetime, was through this newspaper article, and a skilfully calligraphed citation of his award for bravery.

Chapter 2

After The War

There are so many unfinished things I have to do, Mother. I really must go back over there," John stated quietly to his family in the parlour back at Whitemoor Farm. It was already the end of November 1918.

"I have met someone over there whom I would now like to see again."

They were finishing afternoon tea with today's scones and yesterday's tea bread and all that remained were the crumbs on their lace doilies. He gazed at the familiar blue design of the willow pattern on now empty tea cups and saucers, set out on the table in front of them. They had been in the family for generations and their familiarity was as much of a comfort as the family members who were gazing back at him.

There they all sat. Mother, always initiating conversation; Father, always listening, rarely contributing; Willie, always hungry and therefore just eating; Anne, quietly composed and with a steady smile like himself and Emma, the bossy one who always claimed she was right. He felt close to them all in different ways and yet he was determined and unstoppable and he longed to stride forward to meet new challenges.

"And who might that be?" enquired his mother who, understandably was anxious that her son would be leaving them again and slightly worried that he would not return. She also had a mother's intuition that a woman was involved.

"And why so soon? You've only just got here. You need feeding and fattening up. Just look at you. You look so thin and sad and tired. Let's get you sorted out with clothes and shoes. We can find work for you and we can all return to normality. Please John, don't be so impulsive."

Every mother in the land must have been as protective of their sons as she was, these days. Those men who had returned from the Front, they hoped were here to stay; to recover; to repair and to stay close to the family and their homes. She was one of those mothers.

"Mother, please understand. I am thirty years old now, and I haven't lived at home for eight years. During that time, I've seen things and done things that I would never want to share with you - nor with anyone else for that matter. Forgive me for being so blunt. Now, at last I can build a future for myself. And the person I do hope to share that future with, is waiting for me over there. She lives in Brussels which is nowhere near the place where there were battles. It is safe. You do not have to worry. I will not be pleased if you worry about me, because you have no reason to. She is living with her parents who are doctors. It is a professional household and they are good people. She and I met when she was working as a volunteer nurse on the Front, alongside her father working in the same field hospital. She is brave and beautiful and I think we fell in love."

His mother folded her hands and rested them on the table in front of her, admitting to herself that she would not actually stand in John's way. He had always been an ambitious and determined boy. There would be nothing she could say or do to stop him going away and leaving them again.

"And do you love her?" she enquired. She knew that it was inappropriate to ask such an intimate question, but after such recent emotional times, which every family had been through, it seemed an obvious and natural question.

"Yes, Mother I am very fond of her and I believe she has strong feelings for me."

She was immensely proud of him in her own quiet way, and she actually felt that without opposition from her and his father he would be more likely to return home with his new bride and settle somewhere near them, or at least in the same country. Times were changing so quickly, and since the end of the war there were new ways of seeing life, so she too must move forward accordingly.

John scraped his chair back as he moved away from the table.

"Excuse me everyone. I'm going into the parlour. I see there's a good fire going. I need to write some letters."

He wanted to write to Victoria, lovely Victoria, an only daughter from a family of comfortable means. The quality and breadth of her Belgian education before the war, fortunately, had taught her to speak English that was precise, clear and fluent.

He needed a job and there would be a possibility that he could work in Brussels for the time being, until after they were married. Yes, he was going to marry her if she was willing and he hoped she was. Then he could begin the process of bringing her to settle with him in England eventually. Manchester would be a fine choice. Close to family, it was the heart of the cotton industry providing so many opportunities for him to take a management position somewhere. He had his Maths & Physics degree plus the extra textile technical qualifications he had added. In fact, he had already had a note from her to say that there was a junior management position at a local turbine factory in Brussels which would give him an income to start with.

His mind was racing and he was bursting with impatience to travel back there to get to know her and her family and to start his life with her.

He sat down at the bureau in the parlour. It was cold at the back of the room where the heat from the fire did not reach on this late November afternoon, and he shivered as he lowered himself down on the leather chair. Removing the top of his age-old black fountain pen he began to write in his elegant and educated style.

"My dearest Victoria…."

Chapter 3

Brussels

"Thank you for providing such a marvellous lunch Madame Bratout. It was delicious. I can see you enjoy cooking!" John declared.

"And thank you for making me so welcome, both in your home and in this calm area of Brussels. I'm very grateful that you have accepted me and made me feel so comfortable in your company. Victoria and I are very happy, and now that you have given us your blessing to be married this morning Doctor Bratout, I could not be happier than at this moment."

He looked across the table into the brightly shining eyes of the doctor's daughter. Her dark eyes searched his own face with tenderness and excitement. They were to be married, and very soon too, in the Protestant church in the town. Her parents would arrange everything for them. Within six weeks they would be man and wife, having set up a home together in her parents' spacious town house and, for now he would be employed in the foundry as an under manager.

"If we may, we would like to take some fresh air in the garden. Would you excuse us?" John asked. "Go ahead, and have some time to yourselves. You will have a lot to talk about," replied the doctor. He leaned back in his chair enjoying the satisfaction that follows a good meal, glancing at his wife sitting opposite and they exchanged smiles, each recalling those times long ago when they too wanted privacy during early celebrations of love and friendship.

Victoria pulled John's hand, as she eagerly danced towards the door into a once elegant garden of roses and trees and shrubs now suffering from neglect during the harsh war years. The couple did not notice the brambles snagging their clothing as they headed for a rusty wrought iron gate at the bottom, which opened out onto a little meadow where once a few cows would have grazed. The grass was glistening with recent rain, dandelions and daisies were still showing their heads as they picked their way across the land.

"I want us to have a home with open space and to be able to see the sky, the sun and the stars, John," she chattered.

"You will, Victoria my love. The countryside where I grew up has been in my family for generations and one day, we will share it together."

"Tell me more about it. What did you do when you were growing up?"

And he started to describe the wildness and quietude of the fells around the village of Shap, and his long journeys to Clitheroe to his grammar school. He described how he would stride along the paths made by the sheep, with his head bent against the gusts of Westmorland wind and rain that peppered his young cheeks in autumn weathers. He recalled how when he opened the farm gate he would feel the dampness of the fell morning mists in the summer before the sun had burnt its way through, the light dampness resting on the shoulders of his worsted school blazer. Somewhere, unseen, he would be guided by the moaning of the sheep calling for their young ones or to each other. He would imagine they were keeping a distant eye on him, in case he lost his way.

He described his sense of urgency, sometimes panic, to get home before dark during the winter months, being so afraid to lose his way.

"How old were you?" she asked, curious to hear every detail, so that she could build a real picture of this young man she would be marrying, as he was as a youngster.

"Well, I was eleven when I gained a grammar school place, so I'd be twelve by the time I was attending every day. Father showed me the route and the speed I would have to walk to be arriving by 9 o'clock each morning. And then to be home by 5 o'clock in the evening! We reckoned it was about five miles each way. Then on to the school bus! It was good exercise and good thinking time I can tell you and I had to be punctual, otherwise I would not get to school!"

Her eyes widened, incredulous that to attend school had been such a daily arduous challenge. It was in sharp contrast to the comfortable and effortless routine she had experienced through home tuition and a private governess. Then she attended a private school close to her home in the city, but as she talked about that rather apologetically, he put his hand up to quieten her.

"My sisters, Anne and Emma didn't go out to school either until there was a bus to Penrith and then for a couple of years my parents sent them there. As for my brother William, well he worked on the farm from being fourteen. He was <u>not</u> interested in school work! All he wanted was to be a farmer like father. We had a governess too called Biddie and she taught us all until our teens. So we do have some similar experiences as children."

"We will have children won't we, John?" she asked. " I would like us to have a large and happy family, where there is laughter and freedom and fun in our cosy home."

He paused in the middle of the field and turning to face her, he took off his winter overcoat, laid it on the ground and lowered her gently onto a tussock of grass just to rest a while.

Laughing gently as he took out a pipe and tobacco pouch, he said, "We certainly will, my dear. We have all of our lives together to make our dreams and our ambitions come true."

Both fell into comfortable silence and she hugged her knees feeling the glow of excitement and anticipation. Then, picking up a dandelion head she said, "Pis-en-lit!"

He puffed at his pipe, "That's a dandelion," he said seriously.

She laughed, "It's French for wet the bed! If you pick one, that's what happens!" `

"Oh, yes we say that too, but we just give it a different name. I didn't know the French word," he said, rather defensively. He thought he would be learning a lot from this gentle, educated woman he had chosen to be his wife.

Suddenly, the wailing buzzards circling on the thermals above his head, threw him into momentary terror, and he found himself back in the fields in Normandy. He lunged forward as it took him back to that time, his pipe flying from his right hand. Lying prostrate on the ground with his arms over his head he lay silent, rigid in anticipation of danger.

"John, John what is it? Tell me! What is it? Are you hurt? I will fetch Papa! Speak to me! Please." Hearing her soft voice, he raised his head as if in a trance, and silently gesturing that he was fine he gulped and breathed deeply. He was embarrassed and felt weak and stupid.

Then looking at her said, "Oh it's nothing. Nothing at all really. Just the buzzards. I'm behaving like a weak and brainless fool. The noise they made just now reminds me of all of those attacks and the sound of soldiers screaming. Strange, nay stupid…. I really didn't mean to frighten you. This has never happened before."

Appearing to be reassured by him, she said calmly, "I believe this is a normal reaction to everyday events that men coming out of war are experiencing. I have been reading about it. I saw so many young men suffering, you know. There were so many with shell shock. It was much more severe than your experience just now, during the battles. It is important that we both understand that you will, from time to time, go through these flashbacks. Loud bangs, unusual noises, sometimes the way people react in ordinary situations can trigger a response. Flashbacks, yes - that's what we call them. It's nothing to be ashamed of, nor to be embarrassed about."

Slowly she stood up, smoothing the creases in her navy woollen frock as she said gently, "Come, let's return home for a cup of tea."

He scrambled to his feet, looking around anxiously for the pipe that had flown from his hands and having retrieved it, he took her hand and they made their way back through the gate, the wild garden and into the big house.

*　*　*

Immediate employment was John's priority. He needed to secure a salary and the means to provide a home for his new wife and, God willing, a family to follow. Through the contacts of the good Bratout family in post war Brussels, he was appointed the under manager of the foundry that had at first been suggested to him. It was not the position he was looking for, nor was it in the textile sector that he was most interested in which to build a career, but it was a promising start and would mean they had independent means from the beginning of their lives together.

Through detailed, often passionate exchanges of letters in the ensuing months they confirmed what each of them felt for the other and how they would share their hopes and dreams together. He had been able to return to his loyal family, and spent long evenings reassuring his own parents in that short time spent with them, that he was making sensible plans.

Now, it was so important that he introduced Victoria to his family, but the journey from Brussels to Penrith was long, arduous and expensive. For now, he would rely on writing letters and postcards, and taking photographs. He promised that he would send them regularly, so that his family and they as a couple, could remain in touch and connected. Eventually they would come over to England to live and to work and raise a family. They were both in agreement. Time was precious, and they were ready and eager to move forward in their lives together now. They were both thirty years old and had survived a world war, where they had seen those years through, suffering the outcomes of conflict, cruelty and loss. Mercifully, for each of them, they had survived. Both had faith and optimism for the future, believing in God and the power of prayer.

Victoria was tiny. She was thin and fragile looking, and her fine features with her porcelain complexion was in stark contrast to her short dark hair and eyes.

This appearance to the world hid a soft determination and ambition to be successful now. She was intelligent, well-educated and an avid reader. She had trained alongside her father during the early part of the war, and had nursed injured and mutilated bodies of soldiers brought to the hospital and those suffering mental torture and torment. She yearned for stability and security; was ready for affection and a sense of belonging. She felt that at last, she had found it in this serious and practical Englishman who loved the comfort of home and family, and who matched her own outlook on life.

Soon, wedding plans were in hand and the small family marriage ceremony would go ahead without any of his folks present and it would take place in the summer. The future lay ahead of them. There had been enough words; now it was time for action.

Nuptials throughout Europe during the post war period were typically simple and understated, focussing on the legal declaration of becoming man and wife. All wedded couples were eager to start a new future together.

John and Victoria were no exception, and so a quiet ceremony in the local catholic church that the Bratout family attended was arranged, and four or five family members were invited to attend.

The wedding breakfast took the form of a family meal, the only difference being the abundance of flowers around the front porch and down the centre of the meal table and the stray rice grains tangled in Victoria's dark hair.

The months passed uneventfully. They were busy, both building their lives together eagerly and with energy, knowing they were older than most newlyweds, and aware that the biological clock would be ticking away. So to receive exciting news that they had conceived a child was the happiest of moments.

In the month of May, almost two years since he had asked her to marry him, Victoria gave birth to a baby girl. They named her Victoria. It meant victory, and it had become a global fanfare for the significance of the name, after the world had come through conflict, loss and survival. It was equally poignant for the Belgian family, and for them she was 'Victoire. She was a hearty and healthy baby, and her loud cries and spontaneous giggles hinted from early days that she had a bold character and a strong spirit. No one would be controlling this little one!

John took her everywhere with him, and wherever they went he talked to her, showing her the birds, naming plants, flowers, shrubs and trees. He let her touch and feel them, learning their special names. He urged her to bring home leaves of every colour falling from autumn trees; and even a stray sparrow hawk feather found on the field side path back home to show Mama. Full of excitement and joy she would explain in her own way; the things she had seen with her beloved Papa.

At night before bed, sitting her on his knee, he would make up stories for her about shy hedgehogs and busy field mice, boxing hares and cheeky rabbits. He described the shoals of silvery minnows and frogs leaping in the nearby stream, that they had watched together. Her imagination blossomed and her vocabulary soon grew.

They were an inseparable pair and Victoria, her mother, was keen to conceive again without delay. She always seemed distracted and lacked confidence in her state of health and her fertility. She, unlike the child she had produced, was frail and lacked energy. Her body never seemed to operate as efficiently, certainly not as robustly as her mind, her intellect and her ambitions. She wanted to be the best for her new husband and for him to admire and respect her, as well as to love her.

There were pressures on them both to earn enough money on which to live and at the same time to save enough to move themselves to England. John she knew, would not settle now until they made that move but she could not get beyond the obsession to provide another child quickly. Besides little Vicky (such a sweet and gentle shortening of the little one's name, she thought) was ready for a sibling close to her own age.

One day, sitting beside the fire when Vicky was tucked up and asleep, she announced that she was pregnant again. John was elated and her parents were overjoyed. They themselves had only produced one child, so they were ecstatic that their daughter would be producing a second. As excited voices quietened, John held up his hand,

"This is the moment that I too, would like to make an announcement! I think that it is only right and fair to tell you that I have applied for a position in an English cotton mill. Please don't be surprised. Let me explain," he said, holding his hand up towards his parents-in-law, in anticipation of a possible protest. "We must continue to make our plans, and you know that my career can't be put on hold any longer. If I am invited to join this English company, my position will be as a General Manager. The foundry manager here, informed me this morning that he has received a request for a reference from him. The experience I have gained here has been invaluable, and I have you Doctor, to thank for the introduction to the business here in Brussels that has allowed me to gain so much experience. I believe they are disappointed that I am looking for another post, but they understand there is widespread and international progress in the textile industry and I want to be, well, not just a part of it but playing a leading role in pioneering techniques that have never been used before." Glancing at her parents and seeing crestfallen faces revealing every sign of the consequences of this change, Victoria supported his announcement using firm and reassuring tones.

"Dearest Papa and Mama, we have talked about this plan haven't we? Please support and bless our decision to form a new and good life for ourselves. We are not leaving you forever. We will arrange to see you regularly."

She wasn't sure of the last statement, but it was important to say it at this moment. She was painfully aware that they would be thinking they would have no daughter and no grand children to live close to providing purpose in their lives in times to come. No sounds of young voices, sharing conversations, laughter, family discussion and of babies crying at night. In short, the family life that everyone they knew had embraced. Well, all this seemed too much to deal with at the moment, and all that Victoria wanted was to create her own family life with her husband - in England.

The times of separation they had endured; casting doubt about their futures during war time, seemed to be at an end now. They had celebrated their reunion and the growth of their family in ways that so many people they knew, had not.

Chapter 4

May 1924

"*This is to certify that Mr.. John Bland has been employed by me as an under manager at the foundry for the last 9 months.*

He is painstaking, reliable and trustworthy and I can recommend his services most highly for any post of responsibility. I am exceedingly sorry that he is leaving me, and if at any time he should wish to return to Belgium I should always be pleased to give him employment."

A.J. van de Veld (Managing Director)

John arrived home with the copy of the reference, delighted with the positivity of the tone, and inwardly very sure that his application for General Manager at the Barnsley cotton mill would be secured. He was excited to show it to Victoria, to share the news and begin a frank discussion about the future. This would be a topic for them after dinner, as soon as their daughter had been read a story and tucked up in her little bed.

As he closed the front door, hanging his soft grey trilby on the oak hall stand just inside, he called out that he was home. It seemed very quiet. No maid arrived to take his jacket from him; no greeting from a now boisterous three old calling "Papa, Papa!" as she flung her chubby arms around his knees; no opening of the kitchen door where his wife had probably been baking, by now showing the signs of the later stages of her pregnancy.

He called out again, and as he did so, detected the muffled sounds of voices from upstairs. Slowly, wearily in fact, after a long and demanding day, he stepped towards the bottom step of the stairs. It was obvious that something was going on, and it was coming from the direction of their bedroom.

He took the stairs two at a time, and as he opened the door he saw his father in law, bending over the bed, a nurse holding towels and medical instruments which looked worryingly like forceps. Then, as she saw him, his lovely wife, ashen faced and faint, was lying there, propped up with pillows, surrounded by blood-soaked sheets.

"John, you're here at last!" she gasped. "Help me! I'm so sorry," her voice whispered, "The baby is coming too early. I fell……"

"Hush my dear, keep all your energy for saving this baby," urged her father, now adopting a professional tone whilst keeping his emotions at bay.

"You need to leave her to it, John," he said looking over his shoulder, focussing on the young man's baffled expression as he continued, "She fell down the back steps to the terrace, twisted her back and that has triggered labour pains."

His attention returned to his daughter, as she writhed in agony as the next surge of pain wrecked its way through her frail form and swollen abdomen.

"Yes, of course I will leave you and wait downstairs. Be strong Victoria. All is going to be fine," he said softly, reassuring her, worried that this accident had happened six weeks before she was due to give birth.

He turned towards the door and twisting the polished brass knob, he left the room. With heavy footsteps, he plodded down the stairs, in quite a reversal of spirit in which he had mounted them not five minutes earlier. How one has to adjust emotions in the space of a few minutes, he thought.

He recalled how such decision making in the trenches could be so similar, as situations changed just as rapidly.

He pushed the morning room door open, to find little Vicky sitting on her grandmother's knee engrossed in a picture book. At the sound of the door she looked up. The sadness in her expression revealed that she was aware of what was going on.

"Papa, Papa! Mama fell. She has pains in her tummy. She is having our baby now," she blurted out, repeating the facts clearly, as had been explained to her.

"I know and I have seen her. She is with Grandpapa and he will make sure everything will be fine," he answered. "Are we having some tea?"

He addressed the older lady, ensuring he showed no hint of anxiety in his voice. As she looked up, he could see she must have been weeping, obviously through fear and concern for her only daughter. Falling at this stage in a pregnancy rarely ended happily, everyone knew that, but without speaking she gently rang a small china bell at her side table, tinkling out the message that tea was needed. It was the hour for tea and they took it here every day. Shortly afterwards, the maid arrived bearing a tray of tea and cake. Changing this routine would not make matters any better, John thought.

*   *   *

Hours later, long after little Victoria had been settled to sleep, which tonight had been a challenge because she was aware that there was a lot going on in the household that didn't include her. It also meant that her dearest Mama was not around when she said her prayers, nor to kiss her and then tuck her cosily under the bedcovers.

The waiting. Listening to the cries of agony of his wife in pain, were difficult for John to bear. He stood outside on the back porch of the kitchen, drawing deeply on his pipe, staring into the distance, his mind totally blank in the middle of this sudden trauma. He had unbuttoned his collar and removed his tie and stood leaning against the doorway collarless and wild with worry. His mind began to race. It flew from one subject to another. Wife; child; work; England.

The collision of thoughts and images actually made no sense at present. He couldn't focus. Suddenly, he heard his name being called from indoors. Snuffing out the last of the tobacco in his pipe, he stepped back into the kitchen and through to the hallway, bracing himself for the news that would be awaiting.

The doctor moved towards him with arms outstretched, his palms to the ceiling, shaking his bowed head as he looked up to say, "It's over, dearest son. A baby boy was born but has not lived. My daughter has been the bravest woman I have ever attended. I am so proud of her. But she is very weak and her recovery is going to be slow and complicated. She has fought bravely and her back injury from the fall is causing excruciating pain. I need to find quiet time for myself now, to decide the best course of action for her if she is to come through this serious ordeal."

Perhaps the news did not surprise John. Perhaps he had been prepared for the worst. One thing was certain. His mission was to help his wife to recover; to boost her morale and to give her a determination to survive the ordeal. Her state of mind was his biggest worry.

"I would like to see her. May I?" John enquired, addressing his father in law, avoiding any sign of outward emotion.

Suddenly, her father looked old and frail, disheartened and disorientated, now that he was away from the bedroom. The events of today had sapped his energy, ripped at his heart and wrecked his emotions. He needed to sit down and pour a small cognac to steady himself, thinking that no father should ever have to witness the torturing pain of a dear daughter undergoing the premature birth of a second child, as a result of such a tragic accident, and less still to have to use personal medical expertise to supervise it.

"Yes, you can go up to see her, though I doubt she will have much energy to talk to you. She has lost a huge amount of blood and her back injury appears to be acute, more serious than we thought. She will find it hard to be talk for too long." Less still to walk, he thought to himself.

Pushing the bedroom door open, John was quite unprepared for the sight before him. Her tiny body was contorted against the pillows and her eyes were sunken in their sockets, blackened with exhaustion and grief. Her hair lay limp and damp behind her ears with the efforts of the last few hours. "Sorry," she whispered and held out her hand towards him.

He grasped it firmly and speaking tenderly he said, "Please don't say that. I am here and together we are going to make things better Victoria. Believe me everything is going to be fine. You have been so brave, and we will get over this and make you strong again. It's going to take some time, but we will make sure that we can get you back to normal."

As she tried to respond, he held his hand up, "No, don't try to speak. You should sleep now. You will feel better by morning and I will be by your side to help you build back your strength and courage."

"No, no John. I want to tell you something and it cannot wait a moment longer," she gasped in a weak voice and raising her head slightly she gasped, "You know our little Vicky is the light of your life. All I want for her is freedom and happiness and the love of family life. Take her with you. Find her all those things. Teach her the love of nature as you have done already. Find her a life in England. I'm…not well. I know that I am not. John, I may not make it."

She knew that the back injury was more than just a strain that had initiated the miscarriage. The height that she had fallen from; the impact of the solid concrete that smashed her stomach and breasts; the crack she heard coming from her lower back bones. She had cracked the back of her head against the kerb of the steps. And her legs felt numb.

No one could convince her differently either, because she knew how much blood she had lost as a result, both during the fall and in giving birth.

Her nursing training; her experience of battlefield injuries informed her all too clearly that her father had taken the right decision to keep her here at home. To move her to a hospital would have been too risky both for her and, at the time, the unborn baby. Her father had revealed his anguish towards her, in the way that he had feverishly attended her, spoke to her and fired out instructions to the nurse assisting him.

"Stop this! Whatever do you mean? You really are talking complete nonsense, my love," John protested.

"You are obviously in shock after this ordeal and in a lot of pain, but you will recover. Of course you will. You know I am always right. When have I ever given you anything other than the truth? Believe me, time will heal us all and we can continue making our hopes and dreams together, as before. Now try and sleep my love, and please, please don't worry."

He lightly caressed her damp forehead, smoothing her dishevelled hair. He noticed how pale her skin was, and gradually, her eyes began to close. After the rigours of the last hours, he backed out of the room quietly and reluctantly. He never wanted to leave her ever. She was such a treasured part of his life, and never more than at this moment, but he knew she needed to sleep, so that she would have renewed strength for the morning. As he clicked the door shut, resting his hand on the doorknob, he felt his whole body tremble. In his mind, pictures flashed in front of him, of writhing, screaming, contorted bodies peppered by the shrapnel shooting across from enemy lines. Across the battlefield lay bodies which were unable to find relief and where faces revealed the fear of pain and death approaching. He knew that he had seen such a face in that bedroom.

"Shock. Fear. Pull yourself together," he thought, but there was an irrational sense of foreboding. He turned towards the stairs on the dimly lit landing, and he straightened up, in military style, just as he would have done in the old days during such adversity. Coming towards him was the nurse on night duty to keep a watch on the resting patient in there.

It was his beloved wife.

Chapter 5

1924 Yorkshire

"Dot, where are you going?" called Sissie, as she pulled on an old coat before opening the back door of the farm cottage which led into a recently scrubbed yard.

"Look at you! exclaimed Doris. "It's time you bought yer sen some clothes, you're earnin' enough now aren't yer? Y'allus look so untidy. You can't always be relyin' on me you know, I'm courtin' now. I'll soon be married and gone."

Sissie looked at her sister and sighed. She felt underrated and immature, now that they were getting older. It was only because she liked the fresh outdoors and growing things, and just being at home. These days Doris preferred dressing up and going out with friends, to the dance hall in town.

As sisters go they were good friends, and they confided in each other when it suited them. The typical sisterly rivalry existed as it always had, being only two years between them. As the eldest, Doris had always had new clothes and Edith, or Sissie as she was known, wore all the 'hand me downs'. There weren't many of them and they were well worn but at least they were clean.

Now that they were grown up, Doris was preoccupied with her appearance, spending a lot of time browsing through women's magazines so that she could copy the latest fashion. Sissie was just not interested.

Money had always been tight, and their two younger brothers seemed to be given priority over the girls - at least when it came to food portions at meal times. Doris was allowed to stay up or stay out longest. Although Sissie admitted that she wasn't interested in going out and mixing with the lads who lived down the lane towards the town, which was a twenty-minute walk away from where the family lived. She thought these young men were loud and uncouth, bragging about what antics they could get up to both at work and at home. They drank beer until they were tipsy, and told jokes that she didn't understand, standing around with their jugs of beer in The Green Man, at the corner of the street. Those who were already married gave their wages to their wives, dutifully presenting the brown paper pay packet every Friday, before being offered a small proportion of the wages for beer. It gave the women control by restricting their husband's drinking habits, leaving enough money to feed the children. However, these young unattached men had much more freedom. For now, they lived hard and rough lives round there and they played hard too. Most were miners, employed since they were fourteen years of age, just like fathers and uncles before them, or they were labourers. Although the Horbury children lived on the edge of town, they had all grown up in the same neighbourhood and attended the local elementary school, where Sundays were always devoted to chapel and a day of rest at home.

After the war, Barugh had been selected for redevelopment from its former status as a village on the edge of Barnsley into an industrial centre, developing a couple of the older mills to boost employment alongside the colliery and to attract new people into the community.

Barugh was still rural when the children were born and they spent their childhood squeezed into a cottage that was tied to a local farm, where Father was a labourer and Mother did some housekeeping up at the farmhouse. They were good parents; teaching their children kindness to each other, forgiveness of others, how to look after themselves, and to exercise some self-discipline. They were a happy family which was a triumph during these hard and testing times of the post war years.

They grew a few vegetables in their small garden, as well as a few flowers for taking to the gravesides of the deceased members of the family. Two eggs laid every day from each of their three hens ensured that Mother could bake for the family. There had once been four brown hens but a weasel crept into the coop one night and bit the head off one of them which had caused some distress.

It was Sissie's job to collect eggs each morning and she was distraught to find a headless chicken lying in the grit, still warm after the massacre. She wept as she picked up its floppy body to bury it in the field at the end of the lane.

"Nay lass, you're too soft," sighed her father, watching his tearful daughter carry the poor creature away.

"This is animal life. It's natural. You can't get upset every time there's incidents." But his voice cracked a little with tender understanding and admiration for his sensitive daughter. He thought how different she was from his other children. She was the one who wanted to know the names of plants and how to sow seed for peas, potatoes and cabbages. She loved the fresh air, and she would sit on the west facing wall outside the house in the summer months to admire the beauty of a sunset at the end of a long and demanding day. She was thoughtful and kind and a bit of a daydreamer sometimes. He smiled to himself, and he hoped that one day she might find an equally sensitive young man.

They kept a pig of their own in the back yard after it had been weaned. The farmer was generous. It was his way of recognising and rewarding the hard labours and long hours the farm folks worked for pitifully low wages. Sissie could recall some childhood memories where she would hide under the kitchen table, frightened to come out as the pig, having matured enough by now, was ambushed in the yard ready for slaughter. Its panic stricken, wild and deafening squeals and screams would ring through the air as the taunting voices of the men chased it until it went quiet. Then there was a loud cheer from the little boys watching the barbaric event. They had enjoyed the excitement of it all.

Well, the whole event made her cry bitterly, and she would hide under the kitchen table shrouded by its green checked tablecloth, pressing her hands over her ears in an attempt to silence the noise. "Stop, stop!" she would cry out in anguish and terror, knowing the consequences of the bedlam out in the yard. Then crawling out, she would run through the open kitchen door, fleeing across the yard in a frenzy, away to the fields as far away as her panting breath would allow, to escape from the smell, the blood and the butchery that would follow.

Doris would be nowhere to be seen. She always did a disappearing act when there were jobs to do, and as a youngster she would be out playing with friends. Then as she grew older, chattering about fashion and hairstyles and about getting married. She liked to sew, although her patience was short and she was quite clumsy. They taught her in school but she never finished anything and often Sissie would quietly finish a bit of crochet for her.

"You never finish anything Doris," Mother would say wearily. Her two girls were so different in character and personality. It wouldn't do if they were both the same, she rationalised. She talked to herself quite a lot these days and wondered whether it was quite normal, but being a quiet and moderate sort of woman she accepted that it was just her way, and no more was said.

Sissie's brother Bill was a quiet boy. He was slow and ponderous. He loved his food and enjoyed being at home or working on the farm. He had never enjoyed school and he dawdled on the way there, and dashed his way back home every day. After elementary school and away from the strict and cruel ways of his teachers to force him to read and write, he left at the first opportunity. No one could blame him. In cold weather, all the boys and girls sat in rows of old pine desks in a bitterly cold, unheated classroom. Miss Oldroyd was the cruellest teacher in the world they said, and she demonstrated her dislike of children as she strode up and down the classroom in her fur coat, wielding a birch cane. She would fire questions at the children, who were always too frightened to give her an accurate answer. "Woe betide you, if you get this wrong. I have taught you this arithmetic for the last two weeks. I'm beginning to repeat myself now! Come along. This is an easy question," she would growl, turning towards Bill's desk. He would stutter out his answer.

"Wrong! Wrong! William Horbury," she boomed, as the cane struck his icy cold fingers that he had already proffered in front of her, knowing what the punishment would be if he didn't get the answer right.

He was ten years old, and he was used to his father's strap as punishment when he was in trouble, but a cane hitting cold fingers was not punishment. It was torture, and consequently they hated her for it. It was no wonder the least academic pupils left the school as soon as they could, and although the leaving age was now fourteen years old, many of them dwindled in their attendance during their final year, only attending those days when some practical education was on offer.

And Miss Oldroyd certainly did not teach that!

Thomas, their baby brother was very small at birth and was quite a a sickly child, so he was spoiled by everyone. He soaked up the special attention and indulgence bestowed upon him throughout his life. The older ones were too preoccupied with their own hopes and dreams and it was only Sissie who would put aside the time to play with him and to help him with his reading. She was not a confident reader herself, and her handwriting was simple and she was absolutely hopeless at spelling but she did persevere.

"The word never looks the same when I write it," she would sigh in frustration, chewing the end of her pencil.

Then there was Frank. He was the youngest of her father's brother's twelve children. They had little money to feed and clothe them all and to accommodate them all was quite impossible, so Mam said she'd take him in. He was a sweet boy and totally devoted to Sissie, following her everywhere. Every Sunday he helped her to give out the dog-eared copies of the hymn books at chapel, collecting them routinely at the end of the service. She would always take some time to read a line or two of a hymn that she would choose at random. It was usually one that they knew by heart anyway so it helped her to recognise the words. She felt a sense of achievement if she read with a little fluency, and it happened regularly as she got older. By the time she had closed the door of the Methodist Chapel behind her and scuttled home, Sunday dinner was coming out on the table.

"Get thy 'ands washed and quick, our Sis," called Mother sternly over her shoulder, from the coal fired range where the once-a-week hearty meal had been cooked.

The others were already seated and anticipating a tasty meal provided by their mother, who was a competent cook and could create something hearty for them all, from the scarcest of ingredients available.

First they collected her splendid Yorkshire Puddings which were the size of saucers, flooded in onion gravy, and scrambled back to the table. They were impatient to start, but they knew they must wait a moment longer.

Then Father would bow his head at last, and they all followed. "Let's say Grace, so now put your hands together," he announced as he always did. "Be present at our table, Lord. Bless this food and all who share it. Amen"

Then with a clatter of cutlery on crockery they would hungrily attack the glorious flavours of the eponymous and belly satisfying start to the meal.

After that, the small piece of roast pork mother would cut up to go to her husband and the five hungry children watching her serve from her place at table. What little was left, if anything, she would eat, but made it up with extra Yorkshire Pudding or mashed potato.

In quiet and appreciative silence, they ate, enjoying every mouthful and every moment, comfortable in their own thoughts. As everyone finished and sat very still, as was customary, their father would look at his wife, flushed from the heat of the oven and the pressure of serving everything hot at the same time and say,

"Thank you Mother, that were another good 'un. You can all get down now and clear up, and let your mother have a rest."

She nodded and smiled as always, appreciating the compliment and knowing it was the cue for the girls to clear away and wash up.

Chapter 6

A Job in England
July 1924

There was no time to lose, John must go to England to meet the managing director of the mill in Barugh. John knew that this position would be a step forward, and he was anxious to start the process of employment in England to gain experience and to advance his career. He was never more energised than when he was thinking, planning and actioning anything associated with work and the profession he had chosen - the textile industry. The position of General Manager at this mill would mean that he would be striking out in a new area for his family and its farming history.

Even as the eldest son, there had never been any assumption, nor expectation that he would continue the farming life, as his father and those of generations before had done. His parents were proud of his academic ability and achievements in everything he turned to. And they were encouraging and supportive of the life choices. But as they were getting older, he hoped that he would be able to live close enough to see them regularly. His siblings were different, and since the war seemed content to stay around the old family home.

"I can't wait any longer to leave here, if I am to carry out the plans we have made together for the future," he explained to Victoria's father.

It would be difficult to leave his wife in such a precarious state of health. She was making slow, minimal recovery from her ordeal. In her waking moments, she repeatedly urged him to start his journey, leaving her to get stronger.

Her father was gravely concerned about her prognosis and without putting additional pressure on the young and determined John, he directed his questions in such a way so that John was obliged to rationalise the situation to ensure that he was doing the best thing. At least for now. He made his departure simple and straightforward, showing little sentiment or emotion. It was an attempt to make things easier but it was gut wrenching and heart aching for all of them.

On the channel crossing from Ostend, John felt a glow of anticipation as if the weight of worry and anxiety he had been bearing in recent weeks had been lifted. His focus was on the future. If he couldn't provide stability and comfort for his family he knew they would all be unhappy, unfulfilled and directionless. He had always been someone with purpose, never one to talk about himself and his aspirations too much. It was only right that only his wife should know that. He gazed at the horizon for a few moments, offering a prayer under his breath. Suddenly he recalled a verse from Jeremiah that entered his head.

"…I will heal them and reveal to them an abundance of prosperity and security…."

Then he thought about the number of times over the last few years a prayer, psalm or story from the Bible would ground and calm him; give him some wisdom to see his way through a difficult situation or indeed a healthy challenge. He had usually been so reluctant to go to church every Sunday as a youngster, because it took him away from his books and schoolwork, but he thought how useful the wise words were from the Bible. The number of times on the battlefield he had reached for his pocket bible that dearest Biddie had given him on his sixteenth birthday. He would find something to read out to a dying soldier, or to calm the rantings and ravings of a fellow officer who was losing his mind, bearing such physical pain and agony.

His wandering mind stilled as the white cliffs of Dover came into sight and his thoughts turned to practical matters and the reasons for being here.

Arrangements had been made with the Mill management to discuss the parameters of his position, a contract and the salary. He would also need to find somewhere to live. It had been agreed that he would be there for a period of 7 to 10 days during which he could familiarise himself with the workings of the mill. He would observe and analyse the allocation of work among the women who worked there, and then he would work out some improvements in conditions, efficiency and management of time. Altogether fifty women, mostly young, unmarried and local came in to work as weavers, for between eight and ten hour shifts. He was eager to begin.

On arrival after an arduous and endless train journey, he was met and greeted warmly by the managing director, Harold Parkinson. He was a portly, jovial man in a smart grey wool worsted suit and matching trilby. He extended his hand, moving forwards as John walked into the factory offices.

"Welcome to Darton Mill," he beamed, gripping John's hand in greeting, his chubby face reddened by a sharp north wind blowing that day. "I'm glad you found us. How was the journey?"

He himself, had travelled from Huddersfield that day from the head office of the group of mills under his direction.

"Comfortable and without incident, I'm pleased to say," John replied formally.

Parkinson recognised the man standing in front of him whom he was sure, was going to be a valuable asset. He had scrutinised the precision and detail in the letter that John had written, and he was impressed by the reference provided by the Belgian company for whom John had been working.

Most significant was his intuition. He trusted his ability to form accurate first impressions and he liked what he had seen already, and as he took John's coat and small leather Gladstone bag, passing it to his waiting secretary behind, he offered a warm guiding hand on John's upper arm.

"Let's take you to the factory floor. We'll have a tour first and then we will return for a cup of tea and discussion. Betty will sort us out on that. If you like the sound of that let's get on with it. I'll lead the way."

John nodded amiably, as he followed the large frame of his prospective employer, who was still recalling the details he had received of John's education and previous employment. He had also noted his success as an army officer in more challenging times. When he wrote to John inviting him to visit, he knew he would be valuable to this small but significant mill in the north of England. Now he wanted to impress him, so that the young man would take the position on offer without hesitation. As they opened the heavy metal double doors onto the factory floor, the overwhelming noise of the machinery drowned any hope of talking to each other. No wonder he had been advised to look around, leaving any discussion for their return to the relatively calm office.

The rhythmic shuttling and clicking and clacking of the weaving machines was mesmerising and deafening. The women were working methodically and repetitively. Each one was clothed in the same uniform, of brown smock and hairnet which covered and protected their hair from becoming trapped in the vicious, unforgiving speed of the machines. Skilled lip readers for communicating in this noise, they signalled to each other that there were visitors on the factory floor. Eyes widened as they exchanged glances, seeing a new face amongst them. Every day was the same here, so any change to the daily monotonous routine, provided entertainment and opportunity for gossip.

And what a face! Who was this handsome, smartly dressed young man, walking beside the big boss? What could he be wanting in a place like Darton? They were used to seeing factory inspectors checking workforce rules and safety checks on the weaving machines, as well as measuring the quality of the air in there, which was suffocatingly thick with cotton dust. That was a regular occurrence. Most workers suffered regularly, from asthma, bronchitis or some type of chest infection at one time or another. Ghastly catarrh was a common ailment and most people complained of it. However, they knew when there were factory inspectors around, as they would be wearing brown coats and carrying paperwork. This person was very different. In fact, today seemed different.

The girls exchanged glances, with sly winks to one another and little elbow nudges, as the two men strolled past them, scrutinising machinery, intent on mentally noting every detail of the working routine, ready for discussion outside the noise on the factory floor. John nodded politely, pausing here and there, acknowledging one or two with a formal nod of the head as he walked past.

On return to the cool and calm atmosphere of the office area, Parkinson opened the half glazed door to an office.

"Take a seat Mr.. Bland. How about some tea?"

He gestured towards a leather chair by the desk as he lowered himself into the one behind it.

He tapped the top of a brass bell and within a few moments Betty arrived, with a tray of tea and a plate of shortbread.

"Give me your thoughts. Observations? Comments? Let's be frank and honest," he began.

John leaned forward in earnest, as he shared the sharp observations he had made on the working practice and efficiency that he had witnessed during his first visit.

"If you would like to hear my first impressions, Mr.. Parkinson I do believe that I'm the right person to manage this factory. My past experience focused on assessment of working practice. You will no doubt have some knowledge of it. It is called time and motion procedure, and I can see that I would be able to contribute a significant amount to improve efficiency and output here in Darton."

That was all Parkinson needed to hear. He knew nothing of this young man's domestic situation. This was not important right now. His priority was to appoint a general manager and to improve work output and achieve profitable outcomes.

So without hesitation, he offered the job to John, who smiled and, respectfully dipping his head forward, the new manager accepted.

As they shook hands firmly, Parkinson felt a sense of relief. Capable chap here, he thought. I can now return to Huddersfield without a worry.

Chapter 7

Unexpected News

There was always an air of warmth and friendliness when anyone stepped inside the mill. Perhaps it had grown through the camaraderie of the women who worked there because they felt valued by the management, who seemed to treat them fairly. There was a wide age range among them, but they all lived locally, had known each other since schooldays and many were related - sisters, cousins, aunts and family friends. They knew each other's family high times and low ones too, and they supported, celebrated, laughed and wept together during their tea breaks, while clocking in and out at the beginning and end of each daily shift as they exchanged their news.

Everybody seemed to make an effort to help John to become familiar with the layout of the factory, and the type and range of working practices and tasks for which each worker was responsible.

Smiles cost nothing they said, and every non-verbal gesture was important on the factory floor because the volume of noise from the machines made it impossible to talk. John took to it immediately and felt comfortable and welcome in those first few days and it was remarkable how it had been so pleasant, as he eased himself into the new job.

'Action not words' was as relevant here as back in the trenches when he had either barked out the phrase to bring a heated disagreement to a close or as a gentle reassurance for anyone thrown into indecision. He had lost count of the number of situations when the same old phrase had passed through his mind, and he smiled at how, the moment he had used it, it had proved to be the wisest and most appropriate motto that he felt anyone could follow throughout a lifetime.

As he walked smartly through the factory, smiling and nodding at the factory girls, who would scarcely dare to take their eyes off the looms in case the rhythm was lost. That would cause the threads to break and there would be trouble. His routine was to stand beside them, one here and another there, watching the working process; timing the efforts of each one and checking the condition of the looms. He timed the movements accurately on his pocket watch, then made notes meticulously, on his clipboard. It worked perfectly for the purpose of recording his observations.

Some blushed and lowered their eyes as this handsome young man stood beside the loom, concentrating on his work. Others brashly carried on, indicating their suspicion of the new manager writing everything down. They had all gone through so much change in their lives during the last ten years. They had lived through loss, poverty, hunger and pain. Now they had settled into a regular routine, which had established a daily atmosphere of security and reassurance in their lives, despite the low wages they earned for their unskilled work.

At the end of each day John returned to his office, which had been furnished especially for him. Now, bearing his name in bold print on the opaque glass of the door, there was confirmation that he was to be working here for some time.

It was late and workers were clocking off shift, but he had no sense of urgency to go back to his temporary lodging that Head Office had arranged for him. It was draughty and a bit small, but the simplicity of it really suited him. The landlady, Mrs. Williams was kind. She was a war widow and she let a room for a small charge, paid for by the mill company for John's convenience. She enjoyed his company, although he always seemed to be in a hurry. Living alone now, she was keen to chatter endlessly about local matters, who was who and their background stories. She would linger in the doorway watching him eat every evening, making conversation that he did not enjoy.

With that in mind he decided to complete the daily paperwork, so he sat at the desk gazing at the reverse of his name on the glass door. He wanted a simple 'John Bland' printed on there. That would be the most appropriate.

"Straight and to the point," he had emphasised to Betty.

"Are you sure sir?" she had asked. "You don't want Mister in front?

"No Betty."

"What about your letters after it?" she had checked again.

"No," he replied.

He had absolutely no wish to use the title that he had been awarded after army discharge in 1918. The discharge papers declared that he would have the rank and civilian title of Lieutenant for use on ceremonial occasions. The letters

MC and BSc he felt were unnecessary and seemed to him to be 'showy' and perhaps conveyed a message that he was a cut above others. It was not suited to the working world, and he neither needed nor wanted any outward declaration of academic success nor any acknowledgement of bravery in the battlefield, believing that those who knew and mattered were himself and his Maker.

"There's a lot of work here if I'm to make a difference," he puffed, feeling energetic and optimistic. Raising his eyebrows and widening his eyes, he swung round to look out of the little metal framed window that overlooked the back yard, confirming his determination to succeed with the job he'd been given.

He was confident that he had gained sufficient experience to make some significant changes, and he was motivated to get on with the job. He picked up his pipe that he'd left resting on his desk, tapped the old stuff from it, and began to refuel it.

"Now to sort these notes out. I need a plan of action," he sighed, holding the stem of the pipe in his teeth as he put pen to paper.

*　*　*

It was a nasty wet morning and for the end of June it was unseasonably chilly. Everyone clocking on was wet, cold and dispirited. Their saturated coats clung to their legs, headscarves were soaked and feet squelched inside their cheap leather lace ups worn daily for standing up during the long days. And for some of them, it would be a full twelve hours.

Low grey cloud hung over Darton, and on days like these, the acrid smell of the colliery was trapped beneath it. Out of town, visibility towards the fields and beyond was zero and everyone hoped for the sun to break through eventually to burn away the dampness and dry out the saturated ground.

As the workforce trudged in to take their places and resume the work of the previous day, there was always banter between them as they approached the factory gates. The younger women linked each other's arms as they held on to each other fondly, sometimes in a row of four of five joining up as they stepped together in time. They chattered constantly, laughing and teasing each other, often singing the latest popular lines of song heard on the wireless. Wearily, older women trudged the familiar lane towards the factory gates as they had done for years, only leaving their jobs to have their babies, then returning to earn 'a bob or two' to make ends meet.

This week the subject on everyone's mind was Wakes Week. The annual summer factory closure meant that everyone in town was on holiday for a whole week and so much had to be organised, planned for and outfits to be chosen. There would be outings and family get togethers and the chance to stay in bed longer for those who preferred.

"There'd better be a change in t' weather before we knock off for the week. We're off to Filey for some fun. Where are you going Jean?" shouted Maud.

She was the one who organised and planned weeks ahead for the next event that they would all celebrate. Month by month there would be something happening for her and the family (and anyone else who cared to join them) and birthdays were plentiful. There were parties for Easter, May Day, Wakes Week, Bonfire Night, Christmas. If there was a chance to celebrate, Maud would be organising it, but Wakes Week was the biggest event of the year and busloads of workers on holiday headed for the coast to escape the dreary routine, the industrial sounds and smells of town; They were looking forward to experiencing some freedom and frivolity away from the grimness of reality. Filey and Scarborough on the East coast were favourites, although Blackpool and Morecambe on the West coast were always good choices - a bit further but those resorts were bigger and seemed more exciting.

"I'm going to Filey an' all," replied Jean. "Me an' me sister are going together. Me Mam and Dad are staying at home. They can't afford it this year."

Groans of sympathy followed, before they all turned into the factory gate, breaking their linked arms, ready to clock in.

It was 7.00am.

John watched them from his office window, silently counting the numbers arriving, ready to record the figures for future reference.

The factory cat seemed to have checked him out. She was lean and ginger and such a good mouser. He thought she must approve of him, as she entwined herself around his legs when he left the office for his morning inspection in the factory. She seemed to be reluctant to let him go, as if to delay him a few extra moments to allow the workers to be ready at their stations. He was not fooled. He had decided he would make this his daily routine. It showed the women that he was already in the building, leading by example, and that once they were all in there he would be expecting them to be down to work, with no dawdling and idle gossip. They couldn't hear each other of course, but they tried to finish conversations when no one was looking. He walked towards the factory floor, making his route always in the same direction. This was only his fifth day, and he wanted to establish a clear routine straight away so that it would be noticed by everyone. He was not intending to play any tricks on any of them. He knew that he played a 'straight bat', as they say and as a cricketer himself, he felt it aptly described his management style here. John lived his life with no hidden messages, no inferences, just plain speaking or silence from him. Those starting to get to know him had worked that out and he wanted to gain a reputation and earn some respect for that.

He thought there were too many self-opinionated folks in the world, trying to fool folk into doing something for them, charging for the unnecessary and manipulating people's feelings and emotions.

By 8.30 he had finished his round on the factory floor and began to head in the direction of the office to be met by Betty. She was running down the metal steps from the offices, waving her arms about to attract his attention.

"Mr.. Bland! Mr.. Bland!" she yelled out beckoning him urgently, which made him increase his strides to reach her more quickly.

"As his foot touched the bottom step, she gasped out, "You have a telegram. I believe it's from Brussels."

Now Betty was the most discreet and sensitive young woman you could ever meet, and she had some knowledge of John's origins, from his letter of application, but she would never have shared that information with anyone. She knew that this telegram must be urgent news from his family over there. Telegrams, especially international ones were associated with bad or sad news, everybody knew that, and she was really worried for him. She did not show any sign of concern because that would be unprofessional, indiscreet and would risk triggering gossip; perhaps amongst others who were not so diplomatic. John admired her efficiency and her confidentiality. He had also noted that her secretarial work and service to the company demonstrated her loyalty and competence.

Betty was the backbone of this company in Darton. She had worked there now for twenty years and even had worked there when they converted it in 1915 so that they could manufacture parachute material. She had witnessed the bereavements of so many of the staff during the war years, and had always offered support and understanding in her usual quiet and gentle way when the girls had to come back into work after dealing with the news that their men would not be returning home.

Despite this, no one knew very much about her, because she was quiet and private and seemed always to put others' needs before her own. She had cared for her mother when her father had been killed during the war, and she had never married. Always neatly dressed and carefully groomed, her commitment to the Mill and Management was unquestionable and it was clear that because of that she had gained a lot of respect over the years.

Although he was outwardly calm, John could feel his heart racing as he met her and, seeing her anguished face, he felt a rush of foreboding making him feel slightly nauseous. Numerous thoughts raced through his mind. Had there been an accident? Was Victoria not improving? Had Vicky had a fall? And what about the doctor? He was getting older these days. And his biggest question of all was how quickly could he get in touch with them.

Then suddenly, he was reminded of what Victoria had talked about before he departed, when lying in her sick bed, so weak and pale and breathless after her ordeal. Barely audible, she told him in a confused and fragmented way of what she dreamed for him and their daughter. It was as if she did not expect to be with him. It had bothered him at the time. He had urged her to rest and he had tried so hard to silence her, to reassure and to placate her and had begged her to stop talking like that. He had been so preoccupied with his new job across the channel and away from home life it had slipped into a kind of obscurity.

Reflecting back on that now he felt weak and worried, and he dares not imagine what the news would be.

"Thank you Betty. I will read it in my office. Thank you for being so quick to contact me," he said calmly, as he cantered up the metal grid steps. The metallic sound of the soles of his strong polished shoes, seemed to intensify the foreboding news waiting for him as he made his way to the top.

He closed the office door and stared at the telegram. With trembling fingers, he slit it open using war office surplus letter opener, revealing its contents.

>*'Dear JohnSTOPOur Victoria has passed awaySTOPLast nightSTOPWe need you STOP Come homeSTOPLouis*

His fingers clenched around the flimsy paper, and he screwed it up in the palm of his hand. Racked and weakened in disbelief and shock on reading the stark cold message, he trembled uncontrollably, tortured in anguish and loss. He felt his heart was going to burst and his mind was going to buckle beneath those crushing words that he'd trapped in his right hand. He staggered forward, grabbing the desk in front of him to save himself from falling.

He sank to his knees and howled.

"Nooo. Don't leave me. It's not true. I've got to be dreaming!"

Crouched on all fours shaking with grief, he stayed there shuddering, trembling and making unintelligible noises. Eventually, gripping the edge of his chair, he slumped onto it, put his head in his hands and wailed.

He moaned for the loss of the love of his life and her abrupt end on this earth. He wept for the loss of all their future plans, and he sobbed for his motherless daughter. Overcome with sorrow, he realised the stricken situation he was in. Here he was, in England and there she was, in Belgium.

Then as buried memories and vivid recall of battle and of life losses surfaced in his mind, he sobbed again for all the tragic, painful and unexpected events that he had encountered throughout the war too. All those times as an officer and a soldier, he had needed to keep focused and dignified when tears were useless.

As his body rocked forward and back, in pain, loss and grief he fumbled in his pocket for today's yet unused cotton handkerchief, to dry his eyes and blow his nose. Exhausted, he stared into space unseeing, and disbelieving.

Betty could hear him and she choked back her own tears, so moved by the heart breaking sounds coming from the other side of John Bland's door. She could not possibly imagine what the news in the telegram could be to affect him so much. She had already observed him as a man who was steady, measured and so dependable. He was direct and uncomplicated, and in the short time he had been with the company he was becoming well regarded and respected for his calmness and sincerity.

It had to be the death of someone close, probably in his family, she guessed. So, with many questions in her head revealing around the circumstances he seemed to be facing, she wondered how best she should deal with this shocking situation. This would be a new experience for her to deal with and it was important she handled matters carefully.

"Tea," she gasped loudly. "I'll mash some tea."

She brewed the pot of tea and set a tray with a china cup and saucer on a clean white cloth. Deliberately, she chinked the teaspoon into the saucers so that he would hear and be warned she was within earshot which would give him a few moments to compose himself. She knew that he would not want to appear to be in a distressed state in front of anyone. Then, she tapped lightly on the door. She was right. She knew instinctively that this gentleman would not wish to be caught in floods of tears.

She need not have worried. There was no answer to her light tap, so she knocked again firmly. This time she did receive a response.

"Come in Betty."

"Here you are sir. I thought this might be welcome. What would you like me to arrange for you now?"

She made no reference to the telegram, nor of his distraught state. That would be inappropriate and insensitive, and he would not be pleased if she enquired. No, if he wanted to give her information, he would tell her in his own time.

"Thank you. The tea is very welcome Betty. Now then, I will need to be returning to Brussels immediately. Would you please make the arrangements for me to travel?"

And with that, he poured the strong steaming tea into his cup indicating that clearly there was a job for her, and she needed to get on with it. He was not going to share the reason for his emotional collapse, not today anyway, perhaps never.

*   *   *

No one ever knew what happened in Brussels after that. John kept it all to himself. He did not believe that telling the tragic story of the death of his young wife was necessary. He was unable to face the tragedy of the loss of a child in premature birth, caused by her accident. And he could not bear to recall the raw agony his wife had suffered and her inability to recover. He was sure that it would be of no relevance nor helpful for any of the new plans he must now make for the future.

His mission would be to raise his small daughter, now without her mother, so that she would become strong and confident and to grow up with a kind nature and goodness in her soul and with purpose and resilience in her core.

John did not need and nor did he want sympathy. He did not expect excuses to be made for him that would impede the progress he was after for success and his position within the family, and in his profession. He must step away from the memories and stride forward towards a new life, and closing the door on that time in his life he felt would be best for everyone.

Chapter 8

Wakes Week

Most people at the mill were aware that Mr. Bland had departed without warning, but there appeared to be no explanation. In general, it was understood that the initial time spent in Barnsley would be for him to set up and establish himself in the job, and possibly to find somewhere permanent to live. No information was forthcoming however, to explain this turn of events and it surprised them all at the mill because he had seemed to be a man of protocols and good manners and for no announcement nor explanation for his sudden departure prompted questions and some conjecture amongst several people.

Betty would never reveal the circumstances either. No one would dare to enquire anyway because they knew that she was the keeper of confidences and indeed anything discussed at the top of those clunky metal steps stayed up there. Still, this did not hide from them that she looked quite distressed by the end of that day. Some had noticed that she had been calling the general manager earlier on because a telegram had been delivered for him. Telegrams rarely bore news other than urgent and sad, everyone knew that. However, work must continue and so the days swiftly passed after his departure, as they counted down to the break for Wakes Week.

The women had their hair set in readiness for the holiday and they borrowed and swapped various items of their limited and meagre wardrobes, so they would look fashionable for their outings. Most would be as day trippers or, for some lucky ones, a few days staying in a boarding house on the front in Scarborough or in Blackpool.

It was summer time and the children were on school holidays. The atmosphere was vibrant with the buzz in the streets and an increase in activity with extra buses running and people browsing in the local shops. The local church and chapel each ran their annual Sunday School trips for the children so that parents might get a day of peace and quiet, whilst the brave volunteer teachers and other adults organised provision of buckets and spades and a few coins for ice creams for the children to enjoy at their chosen seaside town that year.

At last the time had arrived. It would be a few days out of the ordinary, that they had talked about constantly and had been looking forward to for weeks now. It was hard to believe that it was finally here. Excitement for a change in routine, lifted everyone's spirits and allowed them the freedom to forget the hardships and struggles that they had endured during the rest of the year.

Doris and Sissie sat on the bus together for their day trip to Filey. With neatly styled hair and pretty dresses made so skilfully by Mother, they wore matching duster coats over the top in case the breeze off the North Sea was chilly. They were ready for those photographers on the Promenade who darted in front of the trippers to record the day in black and white, placed in a souvenir card for a small charge. Everyone needed one to show others later when they were all back to work as the day became an ever fading memory. Shopping for souvenirs for Mam and Dad who had been left at home was part of the fun too. Postcards needed writing. Those saucy ones were a giggle.

This year the weather was beautiful, although a bit too hot for some folk. The sun had beaten down unforgivingly this year, so a deck chair on the sand seemed an ideal way of spending the afternoon, and who cared if their noses and shoulders got burnt. On the bus home a large pot of Nivea was passed round so they could ease the soreness, and no one refused.

This summer, someone came up with the idea of folding a large headscarf into a triangle and draping it around the shoulders. They had seen it in a magazine and it seemed to protect you effectively from sunburn.

Then of course everyone enjoyed a paddle. It wasn't a complete day at the seaside if you didn't, and lines of trippers could be seen standing at the water's edge gossiping to each other and enjoying the view, screening their heads with knotted handkerchieves.

"This is the life, luv," squawked Doreen blissfully. "Sort 'em out Mam!" Her five children were bickering and laughing at each other, looking so comical with their sandy ice cream faces, kicking sand at each other.

"Eh! Will yer stop that - now" called out her mother without much conviction. "Kids are kids aren't they? What harm? she muttered to herself.

"Yes grandma," they chorused whilst carrying on with their senseless game.

Children buried each other in golden gritty sand, chomped on gritty sandwiches and brought an annoying amount of the beach back home. When they arrived back with sand in the turn ups of shorts and the soles of this year's sandals, they were sent outside the back door to throw it out onto the yard.

"Don't you be bringin' that stuff in 'ere on me clean kitchen floor," shrieked Mam

Other days off during Wakes Week involved getting jobs done at home done and visiting relatives who lived further away. The time passed far too quickly and all too soon it was over.

So it was back to work and to wearing work clothes again. The holiday wardrobe was put away, in the hope that there would be a chance to wear things again before summer was over. Then it was back to the 'old routine' as they used to say. They exchanged stories - rushed at times, sometimes unfinished if interrupted, and others that were lengthy, especially if there had been some kind of incident. All sorts of tales were told and shared during that walk to work, usually setting everyone's minds up for day dreaming during their tedious, repetitive jobs. Never a moment of reminiscing would be wasted because the next break from work would be two days at Christmas. And that was months away.

They always asked themselves why that week flew by so fast when none of the others did! Back to work on Monday, they returned to their jobs, walking along together down the factory lane, exchanging stories about where they had been and who they had met, how much money they had spent and already where they might be going next year! Some had new hairstyles to be admired by the others and some were complaining that they had eaten so well they had gained weight. Planning for the holidays and telling stories about what had happened since they had all clocked off to enjoy them, was as much fun as the holidays themselves it seemed!

Sissie walked quietly with everyone, listening to the endless chatter. She laughed with them at all the right moments, because she had become well practised in looking interested and involved. However, today she was a little preoccupied, worrying about her father and whether he was going to get better. He had experienced a 'bit of a turn' last week and she was concerned, but didn't dare say anything. He was complaining of chest pain and that was a worry.

He was not one to make a fuss and so he would become exasperated with Mother. She was clucking round him like an old mother hen and he didn't like it. He himself was a worrier, and because they could not afford a doctor to come and check him out, they relied on old remedies. She made up hot poultices for his chest, suggesting he might be getting a chest infection. She draped a cloth over his head and forced him to inhale some eucalyptus oil in steam from a large bowl of boiling water. She knew how hard he worked in all weathers, all year round and for long hours too. He had the same routines all his life, and the farmer was dependant on his dedication and reliability… but he wasn't as strong these days as when he was younger. Sissie decided she would help him out when she got home from work.

As she filed through the factory gate along with the other girls, she looked skywards in thought, her face turning upwards towards the windows of the offices.

To her surprise, looking down at her was the general manager who was standing at the window watching them arriving. He was smiling faintly.

He was back!

Chapter 9

Return to Work

The journeys from Brussels back up to Barnsley, then Darton had been surprisingly simple. As he tapped on the door of his lodgings late on Sunday evening, he felt calm and in control again. There was a sense of optimism and purpose that had grown within him, as he had made his journey up north and it strengthened his spirit. Through the sooty film of the carriage windows, he stared at the passing English countryside that was so familiar to him, and as the train rattled rhythmically along the rails, he felt settled. He had left family matters straight, calm and in order for the time being. There had been an understanding between him and his parents-in-law that he would be returning to Brussels to collect his little girl to live and grow up with him. He told them how passionate he felt that from now onwards, he had to be the most important person in her life. Moreover, there was much work to be done to earn a decent living, to give her the best in life. They were desperately sad but understanding. With hearts filled with sorrow, they dutifully complied with his suggestions for the future, in the best interests of his daughter

As Monday morning dawned, he approached the paint-peeled iron gates at the mill entrance where the night watchman, after observing his arrival from his small wooden shelter, shuffled to open them. It was 6.30am. John had retired to bed last night after the demands of his journey, but his sleep had been fretful and fragmented. Unconnected thoughts flashed through his mind; a maelstrom of memories, future plans and emotions crowded his brain. So at first light, he was far from refreshed but he was keen to get into work and into a routine again. He rose early, deciding to take a brisk circuit of the factory before people began to arrive.

At least his time away from the place had been during Wakes Week when the factory gates were firmly locked and no one else had needed to replace him. Betty had been efficient as usual, arranging for Harold Parkinson to contact him so that he could take his leave respectfully, and without divulging details. He was thankful that she had made it so straightforward for him.

"Family matters" were offered as a reason for sudden departure, together with reassurances that this would only take the period of Wakes Week to resolve. It seemed to provide a satisfactory reason for the big man from Huddersfield. John had preferred it this way. He could not begin to provide any explanation. He neither needed nor wanted to describe the tragic detail of the circumstances, but then nobody would ask, respecting his privacy and status. He imagined the level of sympathy and sadness he would be inflicting on others. So he knew there would be no point.

He sighed. It was that old phrase again that stirred in him; all about taking action and less talking.

A full factory clean had taken place without the machines operating that week, and everywhere looked dust-free and ready for the next season up to Christmas. The windows had been cleaned and the early morning late August sunshine shone through the glass. He was under no illusion though. There would be a lot more ongoing regular cleaning and maintenance. Everyone would be aware of the dirt, dust and untidiness as it accumulated during the weeks until the next 'shutdown'. That was something else that he would like to see change - to improve factory conditions for every employee, but without being shackled always to legal guidelines and routine inspections. It was his ambition.

Today, he was glad it was a bright sunny day. People returning after the holiday would be slightly less dispirited after the excesses of the holidays and work output would begin well, he hoped. He exchanged greetings with a couple of supervisors as they clocked on ahead of the rest of the workforce.

"Grand morning sir, isn't it?" Fred said, as John smiled a good morning to him as he passed.

"It is that, young man. I hope you're refreshed after the break! And I hope you are ready for this lot after the holiday! They will still be in playtime mood eh?" John replied, without stopping to talk.

Nimbly mounting the stairs to his office and opening the door, he could smell the fresh polish coming from his desk and noticed the neatly stacked piles of paperwork and post laid out ready for his attention. He removed his trilby, hanging it on the clothes peg by the door, took off his suit jacket and rolled his shirt sleeves to the elbow. Then, suppressing a yawn, he turned towards the window to watch the factory girls walking into the yard, still busy exchanging their stories from the few days off that already felt like a distant memory.

His few days away were behind him, and he was ready to immerse himself into his work here. He was sure that if he could work relentlessly he would heal and repair his grief and sadness. He was doubtful that anyone would be interested in his personal circumstances. Too much had been happening in their own lives during the same period to be bothered. No one would dare to ask. There was nothing relevant to say to anyone over here, and in any case, the general manager role was a distant and pretty isolated position in the work place, and he preferred it that way.

Gossip was cheap and damaging and he would be at the centre of it, perhaps a victim of it. And the last thing he needed was sympathy.

"I'm anything but a victim. I have to be the victor," he said to himself, sternly.

No, he could not allow himself to dwell on tragedy and personal torment, on his grief and personal sorrow and perhaps, self-pity. Silence was everything he said, and he believed that talking just led to weakness and self-destruction if you repeatedly reflected on the past. It cracked you mentally and emotionally he believed. He was determined to remain positive, strong and forward looking for both himself and his dear little daughter. He wasn't thinking about those things now though.

"On, on," he thought, as he gazed idly down at fifty or so chattering women entering the gates.

His mind wandered as he imagined what their lives might be like, and how they would be managing on low wages, food shortage and cramped living conditions. They always looked and sounded so cheerful and full of hope and part of him envied that capacity. He envied the friendships and close connections that they enjoyed. He thought they were quite remarkable. He'd always been slightly aloof himself, and not a great socialiser. He had no friends, he realised. Perhaps all those growing up years, walking long distances alone to school and then immersed in his books at the end of the day shaped him into the man he had become. His own family relationships were warm and genuine it was true, but quite formal and one didn't talk unless there was something useful to say. That was his father's ruling as a strong yeoman farmer with generations of modest land owners before him, working the tough and challenging terrain of the northern moorland.

Seeing so many of them all wearing their loose brown smocks or aprons, arriving together ready for work was impressive. They looked purposeful and ready prepared with their hair tidy, perhaps tied back, or clipped and hair banded for safety from the speed of those machines. Stout and comfortable footwear was worn to minimise aches and pains whist standing all day. He noticed all these details. Callouses, bunions, corns and hard skin were hazards of the job and many a lass would be soaking her feet on the back doorstep at the end of the week. He wasn't aware of that, though. This work was not for the weak and faint hearted, and they each had a hard and no nonsense spirit that could not be matched. However, he did recognise these attributes. Today seemed different though. Refreshed, noisy and with renewed energy, the atmosphere was pleasant and happy.

"Long may it last," he murmured to himself.

Looking down on them, he noticed one pretty girl was walking quietly, slightly apart from the gaggle of other noisy ones with her hands clasped behind her back. She was detached from the others who walked together with linked arms. Pleasantly nodding along, acknowledging the banter, he could tell that her attention was wandering. Suddenly, she bent down to make a fuss of the factory cat, as it darted out from the shadows of the brick walling close to the factory building. The mill mouse catcher recognised her and mewed quietly, as she gave it a stroke. Then as she straightened her back she looked upwards and he knew she had seen him. For a moment their eyes met and he smiled at her. Shyly, she half smiled in return, lowered her eyes and in a split second, catching up with the others, she had entered the factory and was gone.

She wasn't the only one to notice him because other sharp eyes had seen him up there too. "Oh the Boss is back," murmured someone.

Another muttered, "Look out! Get yer 'eads down, he'll be round us wi' 'is clipboard checkin' up on us!"

The realisation that the working week had now begun, brought them all down to earth, as they filed inside

As quickly as the yard had been filled with the busy sounds of people meeting and greeting one another, it fell totally silent, and the night watchman bolted the gates, being his last duty before returning home for a breakfast tea and yesterday's bread. John returned to his desk to deal with letters, messages and memos awaiting his attention.

Betty brought in his tea, looking neat in her white broderie anglaise blouse and soft green skirt, wearing a welcoming smile and a notebook to hand.

"Good Morning sir. Welcome back. I hope you had a pleasant journey, "she said politely as she set the tray on the edge of the desk.

"Thank you Betty. I do hope your week's holiday was enjoyable. We have a lot to get through, and now I'm back I will be needing some clerical support from you straightaway," he replied as he passed her some papers with his notes carefully jotted in the margins.

Indicating for her to take a seat, he said, "Now then I'd like you to take some notes for me please."

Although his initial visit to the mill had been cut short, he had already identified and noted the changes that he wanted to make to increase efficiency and work output, without burdening this workforce with an extra workload. His lengthy journeys by train had allowed him the time to envisage the next direction for the company and to make some detailed notes.

It was not about working harder but working cleverly, he said to himself. 'Time and Motion' was the latest ground breaking innovation and he was in complete understanding of the concept. He had begun this work whilst in his previous post and had gained some approval for the methods he had used there. It worked on the principle that it would preserve the work force on current numbers, without overworking anyone. Productivity would be much better and people would feel less overworked. If people understood the principles and the reasons for some changes, they too would not feel doubtful or threatened.

He knew that people could feel nervous when they saw the management walking around bearing a clipboard, writing notes from observations. But this was the best way for him to begin the process, and to move on with the job that he had been employed to do. He was not deterred by appearances, nor what people might be thinking. He was keen to win trust and respect, and he was confident that, just as in previous situations, his personal style and confidence would gain that.

Keen to be on the factory floor during this first morning back, he left the office and Betty with instructions, notes and lists so that she could bring him up to date on the business that had fallen behind, and on preparations for what was to come. Taking off his jacket and pulling on a brown work coat, he stepped smartly down the steps, pausing halfway to get a bird's eye view of the factory floor. Everyone was on task, concentrating hard after the lack of routine during the holiday break. It was a gratifying sight he thought, and he breathing out relieved and encouraged by witnessing it. It meant that it was more likely that they would welcome improvements, and not be resentful of the changes he would soon be making to their current routines.

Walking purposely, he began his round, checking and noting places and positions of each work station and the repetitive activity that each worker made.

Watching each methodical routine before passing down the line to another he found himself gazing around the factory floor, idly wondering in which aisle the pretty girl whom he had seen in the yard worked.

It took him by surprise that he should be losing some concentration, as his mind lightly tricked him away from serious engagement towards a flight of fancy. To his surprise he felt quite liberated. Almost light headed.

Perhaps he shouldn't have been surprised. Life had thrown him some heavy and demanding emotions recently that had made him low and reflective. He hadn't really noticed how low spirited he had felt, until this moment. Throughout his body, his mind and his heart there was a tautness. He felt as if he was like a tightly pulled rope, that wouldn't allow him lightness of spirit or behaviour.

He moved up and down the lines and just as he spoke briefly to one of the supervisors, quizzing him on a technical detail with which he was unfamiliar, he saw her. There she stood, quietly and rhythmically operating the machine and totally unaware of his glances.

"Thanks for that information, Joe. That was very useful for this work study today," John said, nodding his thanks to the supervisor on the shop floor, as was customary.

He turned towards the aisle where this pretty young woman was working.

She looked up and smiled as he paused beside her. He pretended to jot down a note to maintain a formality befitting management, but his blue eyes did not hide a special sparkle when he smiled back his thanks to her. He found it difficult not to gaze too closely, but he tried to notice everything about her. She was small and neat with slim fingers which worked the loom. Her mid-brown curly hair was clipped in place and she wore a fine hairnet the same colour. Her eyes were grey-green and she had pink, plump cheeks that suggested she lived a country life. She captivated him in that single moment.

The deafening noise of machinery, and the echoing and reverberating sounds around the whole place prevented anything else but a smile and a nod and so he moved on.

John returned to his office his head spinning with the factory routines that he had observed, his ears ringing with the repetitive, deafening noises of machines. And that girl.

Removing his protective factory coat, he lowered himself into the office chair, and with a sigh he reached for his pipe. He lit it and stared into the space between his desk and the closed door leading into the factory.

"I must be mad! What's happening to me?" he chuckled under his breath.

Then he moved from the chair and turned to the window to look down on the yard where he had first seen her that morning. His mind was a void. He yielded, in disbelief at his own capacity for impulsiveness and yet, such vulnerability in being attracted to someone so soon after his bereavement.

Slowly adjusting to the events of the morning so far, he glowed with this new feeling. It made him feel curiously free and light and he shuddered in a thrill of excitement. He could not compare this sensation with anything he had experienced before. This felt different because it was different, and although he relished the moment, his instinct was to steadily calm himself and to return to his usual sensible and practical poise.

He noticed that his pipe had gone out, probably as he had neglected to relight it during his moment of reverie. A light tap on the door suggested that a light lunch had arrived for him, so he closed his mind on the matter, shook himself and turned his attention to food and then an afternoon's work.

Immersed in the tasks that he had set for himself, an hour or two passed and the day was nearing a close. Already he could hear people's voices and movements as they were leaving. There was still plenty of light at this early hour, as late afternoon merged into early evening. People would be joining their families for an evening meal and maybe a good catch up with neighbours on the street. Children would be home and would need organising. Some would be off to play in the street and some would be helping in the house. Then as darkness fell it would be bedtime for all.

Time flew by and as John reached for his trilby to leave the office he lifted his pocket watch from his herringbone waistcoat and to his surprise he realised that already it was already seven o' clock. "Not enough daylight left for a walk tonight," he mused. Then locking his door, he tapped swiftly down the steps and into the last of the evening sunshine, back to Mrs. Williams and her endless chatter. At least a ready prepared dinner was waiting for him.

Chapter 10

The Farm

The month of September opened all too soon, and the evening sun became mellow and low. It silhouetted the open cast mine heaps and pump frames against the pink and purple skies. Everyone had settled into their daily routines. There was a lot less to gossip about - not of all the fun and freedom now, with summer holidays a distant memory. It was more of concern because of the perpetual round of infections that children, now back at school brought home. Coughs, colds, sickness and diarrhoea invaded home life, infecting and incapacitating the overworked, over tired and the elderly. Exchanging remedies, offering advice for easing ailments, and helping each other with child minding or running simple errands was more the subject of conversation these days.

Annie was the mother of Sissie and Doris. She was from a line of country women who had worked the land and taken in washing to earn a basic living before she was married. She went on to have her four children. The younger ones needed her at home, so the family income was significantly less at the moment, as she cared for the toddler at home. However, she had significant practical knowledge for curing most disorders using her natural herbal remedies and at work, the girls were often approached by others, to ask their mother for advice.

Those men who worked down the mine were vulnerable to chest infections, working in wet and cold conditions for long hours and where the atmosphere was devoid of oxygen and sunlight. To have time off to look after a cough and cold was to lose money, and winter was coming, so they soldiered on, risking more serious chest complaints.

"Jack's really bad. He's coughed all last night and t' sheets were wet through wi' him sweating bad," complained one of them.

"Harry's same an' all," responded another, as she turned to Doris to ask if she could ask Annie for a helpful remedy.

Sissie was keeping an eye on her father and trying to ease his workload whenever she could, on return from her working day and at weekends. She loved being outdoors and never let the rain or high winds weaken her enthusiasm for helping him. There was always a job and she was so pleased that he let her do them, in spite of him calling out, "This is not a woman's work! Go in!" as she swilled out the milking parlour. But she never listened to him.

Then he would warn her, "Steady lass, they 're heavy," as she stacked fresh bales of straw for bedding for the expectant cows who would need it for giving birth later in the year, but she would pretend she hadn't heard him.

Her favourite job was bringing the cows in at the end of the day for milking. She had names for each of them, forty in total. Her father laughed at that.

"You get too involved with them, our Sis," he would say. "They're just animals!"

She didn't listen. To her they were like people, with feelings, each with their own particular character. Scrambling into her farm boots as soon as she returned from work and grabbing an old willow cane, she called them, tapping them gently on their haunches as they shambled slowly towards the farm gate, heavy with milk and following their daily routine.

One evening, as the September sun began to dip behind the trees, she noticed the figure of a man in the distance. She couldn't see who it was but thought it was an odd time of day to be walking down the footpath at the bottom of the field. No one walked around here at that late hour in the day, especially at this time of year. One of the joys of getting the cows in was the solitude and peace she enjoyed whilst doing something useful. She was a bit unsettled that she suddenly had company, albeit a long way off.

"Right lass, bring 'em in," called her father. "We're ready."

Then she turned and opened the gate to let all the cows file in through thick squelching mud, which never seemed to dry out now at this time of year.

As she guided each one into the stalls to be milked, she felt some slight discomfort in seeing the man walking alone near the land. She didn't feel it was anything sinister, of course, although she knew there were some odd folk around. But this did seem unusual. The way the man was walking didn't look suspicious. She thought it was rather mysterious. And she felt a flutter of intrigue. It was the sort of feeling that happens when something different alters the predictability and monotony of everyday routine.

"I saw a man walking on t'footpath at t'bottom of t'field tonight," she offered in conversation as she sipped her early bedtime milk and wheat cracker. "I wonder where he'd be going?"

No one seemed to hear her, as no one offered explanation nor even a humorous comment, except for mother.

"I don't know who that could be either, but remember what I've all'lus told you. Don't talk to anyone you don't know." And that was that. No discussion followed.

However, she couldn't let it go from her mind. She knew the footpath was not known to many people in town. No one ever walked for pleasure round here.

If people wanted to enjoy the country air they would probably go up to the Dales, and see some scenery and breathe in some clean air. But no, not here. Whoever that was must either have some knowledge of the area, or a map. Anyone who had a map must be have some knowledge and the money to buy one. Whoever it was must be living fairly locally as they would need to return home before the light faded. Then, enjoying this new detective style of thinking, she undressed carefully, laying her clothes out on a chair ready for the morning and climbed into bed. With these thoughts in mind, she lay on her back staring through the old net curtains at the still grey dusk of the sky, glimpsing Venus shining brightly through as she closed her eyes and slept soundly.

Chapter 11

Football

John was satisfied that his management approach was bringing results in modifying work practices, and he felt that he was winning the respect of the supervisors who were putting his methods into action. The changes were slight, almost imperceptible at first, as he believed that guiding people gently but firmly towards a change in practice was the best way forward. It was so important that he gained the confidence of his work force to improve productivity on which he wanted to establish his reputation.

A month later, Parkinson dropped by unannounced, to check that everything was in order. He stayed for a tea break and a walk around, John explaining this and that after which, satisfied that this new manager had everything under control, he left. He was reassured and complimentary after his observations, feeling the atmosphere of positivity that prevailed across the factory floor.

Shaking John's hand warmly, he said, "I will be very happy to be sharing my report with the Board when I return. Darton Mill is looking well, under your capable management. You deserve some recognition for your efforts, John. Now then have you found somewhere permanent to live? I am expecting you to stay with us for some time yet."

Smiling broadly, he added, "The lads will be asking you to apply some of the methods you're using in the factory on the Barugh football team! Your management style could help them I'm sure! At present, they're bottom of the South Yorkshire league. Did you know?! It would be good for the community to see them gain a bit of success. It'd be chuffed for them to win something on that football field. Have you thought about joining them? I'm sure they'd welcome you."

"No one has asked me! To be honest I wasn't even aware there was a team, Harold!" replied John tugging his pipe from his pocket, holding it casually, unlit, in the palm of his hand.

"But since you mention it, I would be very interested to get stuck in. I enjoyed both football and cricket when I was a lad at school and ever since. To be honest I do miss it."

In his head he was thinking how fortunate it would be to get involved, now that the football season had begun, and how all the practices and matches with other local teams would unite the working men with himself in such a constructive way.

He had been truly passionate about most sports as a boy and as a young man he was a popular team player, always playing a fair game, taking criticism without resistance and accepting praise graciously, and modestly. Because of that, and as a competent player, he was made captain of his teams repeatedly in each new setting - school, university and even a brief spell (very brief spell, he remembered!) during officer training. Getting involved here would offer a tremendous opportunity to become familiar within the community where he was living and working, as they were too.

Once Harold Parkinson had departed, he pushed the bell on his desk for Betty. In seconds she arrived at the door, as usual with pencil poised for instructions.

"Betty, I want to pick your brains. Do you know who is responsible for the Barugh football team?" She took a breath, and presented him with the facts in a form that she knew he would appreciate. She was getting to know his way of working by now. He was impressed that this remarkable woman held so much information and knowledge such a range of topics. There she stood, providing him with detail without being overwhelming. She gave him the names of organisers and players; the team colours and motto and mascot, the place where they played and the current fixtures on the calendar. Most important of all, she could tell him that today, after clocking off they would be going to the football ground to practise.

"That was very useful, Betty. Thank you. I think I shall stroll by and watch them play."

The ground was firm despite some light rainfall last night, and he could hear the roars and groans as he approached the football filed. Fifteen men had divided themselves into roughly two teams in order to practise before the Saturday match. In his gabardine belted coat and trilby pulled firmly on his head, he stood a little way back from one of the sidelines drawing on his pipe, studying the form and style of each of the players.

"Oh my, there are a number of things I can advise them on here, if they'll accept me," he thought. The players paused for a few minutes at half time and he wandered over to them.

"'Evening lads. I see some good stuff going on here."

"D'yer play Mr. Bland?" asked Bill, waving an arm to encourage the others to step forward a little to hear his response.

"Well, I have played over the years, but I'm a bit out of practice these days. Not as nimble as I was!" he smiled back.

"Oh you'd soon pick it up again. Why don't you have a go?" suggested someone else, trying to be pleasant in front of one or two who were already exchanging quizzical glances at the notion that the boss should be playing with them. They hesitated before making a comment. It proved not to be necessary.

"I might be able to use a bit of my own experience if you fancied a bit of management," he replied casually. He didn't want to push himself. It was important that they made their own decisions, especially out of the workplace where he wasn't their boss.

Amongst them there were murmurings and exchanges of nods. Some cast their eyes downwards kicking the turf beneath, contemplating and playing for time. There were no noises of dissent however. No-one dismissed the suggestion, which he felt that was a positive sign.

"Play the other half lads. Think on. I'm staying to watch anyway. There's no rush. I'm enjoying it." He spoke with reassurance in his voice, as he continued to stand on the sideline, and it drifted through the air to the centre of the pitch, as if to emphasise the importance of space and a little time between them to consider his proposal.

They returned to their positions and continued their game until the final whistle was blown. No goals had been scored by any of the players. Today's practice was over within twenty five minutes. That was normal because they all had other commitments every day, it seemed.

"Will you be available to support us at the game on Saturday?" Bill asked, stepping towards him as the others gathered their clothing from the goal end to trudge home.

"I'm speaking for the team Mr. Bland. Come with us and see what you think of us - we're all up for you managing us," he added, not wanting to sound too eager, but with a grin across his face, flushed from the efforts on the field.

"I would be glad to Bill- it is Bill, isn't it?"

The rest of the team were collecting their belongings watching the two men talking, looking for signs that they might be having a manager at last. Then, satisfied that it looked like there would be good news for the future of the team, they departed the football field, through the iron gate that secured it and went home; the studs on their boots echoing down the road as they disappeared out of sight.

John turned in the opposite direction to return to his lodging on the edge of town, feeling a new sense of purpose and energy. He hadn't realised how much he had missed involvement in team sport and the camaraderie it generated within a community. Many differences encountered in the workplace were forgotten on the sports field, and that was one of the many things he recognised you gained when you shared some good team challenges.

The events of the last few years had offered no opportunity to engage in leisure activities of any sort because he had been so busy with a new job and family life. Now there was a spring in his step as he turned down the street towards his home. It did feel like his home too, for now. Those lads played with heart, he could see that, as he stood at the edge of the pitch.

They had probably played against each other at school, he imagined, and here they were now as grown men with families most likely. They were working long shifts, to provide a home and to put food on the table. As he recalled the events of the evening he smiled quietly, as the prospect of settling here for a while suddenly seemed more appealing.

"Hello Mrs. Williams. I'm back," he called out, as he unlocked the front door to let himself in.

He always made sure she had heard him return. It could be unnerving for her if she was unaware he was back in the house. Her hearing was not too sharp and he was aware that an unexpected sound might confuse her. She had lived alone for many years and was used to her own quiet home, especially in the evenings, so to be taking in a lodger was a change in lifestyle for her. This evening as with most others, she would be at home. She loved to knit and always found yet another new baby in the village to knit for, either a matinee coat or bonnet and bootees. With no children of her own, she liked to indulge the little ones, if parents allowed. The village children knew that there would be the occasional pear drop or biscuit in her pocket if she saw them by the shops. Everyone knew her and looked out for her as she lived alone.

"That's fine, Mr. Bland. I've left you a tray in the back kitchen. Just take out that cooked meat and potato pie from the oven. It should still be hot as its not been in there long," she answered swiftly, concentrating on the play on her wireless in the back room. It was the final episode and she didn't want to miss anything.

He took the simple meal upstairs and sitting at a small table in the corner of his room he tucked in. She was a good cook who used plain ingredients, but it was well cooked and seasoned. She had taken the time to ask him about what he did and didn't like to eat when he first introduced himself. It suited him to dine in the privacy of his room on Saturdays. He didn't like to be too demanding of Mrs. W's weekend time and preferred some quiet time alone so that he could think, read and, as he would do this evening, write a letter to dearest Vicky. He felt that tonight he could at least give her some of his news about the football. He never had very much news for her usually, and he knew that this letter would be read out by her Belgian grandmother, hopefully showing her that he was settling into an English way of life again. He hoped the long separation from Vicky would soon be over. He knew that the current arrangement that separated him from his daughter was in no one's best interests, certainly not for a three-year-old. It was also challenging for him and for her elderly Belgian grandparents who, disappointingly, spoke little English in their home.

He didn't yet, have a clear idea of what would or could develop over here, nor how it would work if he brought her over to live with him. However, he didn't have the time to dwell on alternatives either, with the pressure of work at the moment.

"It will be what it will be."

He picked up his fountain pen and in his precise, rather formal writing style he wrote a letter.

My dearest little daughter,

I hope you are being a good girl for your grandmother, and that you are learning your numbers

*and letters so that you can show me and tell me when
I see you.*

*Your Daddie is very busy working in the big factory
in England and will be coming to get you very soon.*

*Today, I watched some young men playing football
and that was great fun. When you get bigger you will be
able to kick and throw a ball and we can play together.*

*I must close now because it is time for me to go to
bed. I hope you will have a good sleep my precious one.
I think about you every day*

Your loving father

He read it back to himself and thought he had written in rather grown up language, but trusted that her grandmother would explain it in simple words. He folded the letter carefully and placed it in a creased envelope that had been used before for factory business. He resealed it, and wrote the Brussels address on the front and then placed it in the pocket of his coat hanging on the door. He knew it would be reminding him to get it posted tomorrow.

He enjoyed writing. It allowed him peaceful and focused thought. He loved the personal space it provided and a chance for some deeper, more indulgent thinking. Nothing could disturb him when writing because he became so immersed, and it gave him so much satisfaction. He had always dealt with the paperwork when he lived at home, and as a young scholar his father would ask him to deal with all the accounts required for running the farm efficiently. Then they would be sent to the department of agriculture and for tax returns; copies also to the people who were buying and selling stock.

He read avidly, especially when he was at university. There were plenty of books at home, collected by family and past generations. They had all been encouraged to read each evening after dinner. There were so many exciting stories on the bookshelves, but he enjoyed the works of R.L. Stephenson and loved the easy style of the prolific writer Rudyard Kipling. Stories with action and suspense were a favourite and then by contrast, his reading of the natural world fascinated him too. These days though it was mostly work practice manuals and health and safety reports that he pored over, but his letter writing kept the creative side of his nature alive and he was content with that.

It was nearly lighting up time. He had a busy day ahead of him tomorrow, so it was important to get some sleep. Carefully folding his clothes on the chair by the little single wardrobe in the corner of the room, he prepared for bed. He didn't feel tired enough to sleep this particular night, and as he plumped up his feather pillow he knew it would take a while to settle with the events of the day still drifting through his mind. He was quite enthusiastic about getting involved with the football team. It would provide a useful diversion from the demands of his working week and establish himself into community life. It was important for him to feel a sense of belonging. He wanted to be seen around when he was off duty to allow himself to become a familiar face locally. How strange that these things just happen - unplanned and yet so meant to be. Time on that football pitch managing those young men would occupy him for some of his spare time and who knows what else was out there ready for his involvement? As his mind wandered aimlessly in the first wave of fatigue, he cleared his throat and relaxed his head down on the pillow. He turned over to face the window, his eyes prickling with the need for sleep, and as his eyelids drooped the Evening Star glinted back at him through the curtains.

"Ah, Venus! There you are tonight!" he murmured and with that he was sound asleep.

Chapter 12

Time to Play
September 1924

The following Saturday the team assembled at 9.30 for a pre-match discussion. More importantly, John was there as their new manager. He needed to learn a few names and the positions they played. He also wanted to observe their strengths, weaknesses and game tactics. The team they were playing this week came from Dodworth, a busy mining community a few miles away. These lads were known to them and mostly they worked at the colliery there. They were tough and played a ruthless game, but nevertheless, they were closely matched both in age and skill with the Barugh players. They all took the game seriously as an outlet for their energy and aggression, and each one gripped the will to win. They were all very determined to score and to leave with a sense of achievement and a sound reason to down a few pints of ale afterwards.

"Just play a fair and honest game and let me see your strengths, lads," said John, "then we'll analyse the game at half time and again at the end. No fancy stuff, just be yourselves."

Like so many local league games played on modest pitches in towns and villages across the country, it was a regular event which drew in the community, which comprised either of aspiring players, wives and girlfriends or just a pause on the sidelines by an interested dog walker.

There was the usual loyal crowd there, on time and ready to cheer them on always including the one who knew how to play better than the team, yelling advice, pointing and cursing them when they faltered until he was hoarse.

"Get down the field! Jack! Watch that one, Bill. Stupid, STUPID - you missed that beggar! You were a mile off." Then as his shouts faded, whoever it was, would turn his back on the players in exasperation.

John stood unobtrusively and composed, watching the game progress, concentrating on each player's moves and personality on the pitch. With pipe in his mouth and one hand stuck in his trouser pocket he took it all in.

"Mmm, they know what they're doing though," he murmured, tilting his head and nodding in approval at no one in particular. Not that anyone was looking at him, proving that they were focused on the game, determined to beat the opposition this morning.

At half time he strolled across the pitch to the team assembled in a huddled circle and they stepped back respectfully to include him.

"Well, how do you think it's going so far? What do we need to do second half?" he asked them.

This was a different style they thought - the boss asking them to analyse instead of barking out instructions at them and calling them idiots.

Several tried to talk at once, but John raised his hand calmly and said, "One at time, and keep your voices down. We don't want the opposition to hear us. For now, I'm thinking during that first half our defence looked weak, so let's make more effort round that goal mouth. Otherwise play on … and let's have a goal out of you."

His encouraging and faultless style inspired them, and they all regained their energy and felt a renewed vigour as they strode back onto the pitch.

"GOAL!"

The small crowd that had gathered on the sidelines jumped up and down in the air shouting in unison. The Barugh footballers hugged each other ecstatically, celebrating the only goal of the match. They had won!

John was so pleased for them. He really wanted them to have a taste of victory, understanding how important it would be for the players to show themselves at their best today. He smiled, raising his trilby in utter pride and pleasure for them, then waited patiently until they had shaken hands and saluted the opposition before they approached him for a post mortem.

"Well done! There was some nice method at work their team," John enthused, greeting each of them with a brisk, firm handshake.

"Now, what can we do differently to be even better next time? Anyone?"

Feeling quite empowered, listened to and valued, several had some practical comments. It felt a productive and satisfying conclusion to the morning. After twenty minutes, by which time John had learned a few more names and recognised some of them from the mill, they were ready for a pint or two of ale. They departed affably, with some going straight home to demanding families and weekend chores, others to the local pub.

John decided to stroll into Barnsley which would only take an hour. He was hoping to find a tea room there to enjoy some afternoon refreshment. So he set off down the road for a good Saturday morning walk with purpose and a firm step. He could have taken a bus but his love of walking allowed him time to himself and his thoughts, and to become familiar with the area around which he worked.

Alone now, recalling the ninety minutes of local sport, he felt optimistic about what lay ahead. Just for that brief time at the match this morning, he had let go of haunting memories from his past. Now he was in this no-nonsense Yorkshire area, living, working and playing with these people. It helped him relax. It surprised him that he felt at peace, for the time being anyway. He felt that he would like to find the local church now. He had always found comfort and inner strength inside church. He welcomed the opportunity it offered to collect his thoughts, preferably without a formal service, because, as he expressed it, he just needed 'to bow his head'.

He stuck to the main road into Barnsley as he hadn't looked at a map and so felt it wise to stick to a main route. It was quiet and the fields on each side of the road were ready for ploughing over. The cereal crops harvested by now had left behind short stalks which were standing stubbornly upright, creating a wasteland view around him. He realised he wasn't familiar with the work of an arable farmer, knowing only a sheep farming life, and he assumed that was probably out of date by now. He had read in the newspapers that there were now so many developments in farming methods, as the country built itself back into prosperity after the war. His sister Anne was working on a local dairy farm. She was keen to stay in agriculture but sheep farming was a hard life and as one of the first female apprentice agriculture students she was making a name for herself. He was so proud of her. He hoped she would meet someone soon because she was into her twenties already. His mother had once said "a man of the soil will be good for Anne" and he had agreed.

Occasionally a bus passed by on its regular route into town. Introduced soon after the war years, they had taken some getting used to as people tended to walk or cycle into town. The sounds on his route were of bicycle bells warning that they were approaching or of people hailing each other in recognition. It interrupted his rhythmic pace as he walked along, noticing and smiling at the high pitched trills and shrills of the wrens in the hawthorn hedging that flanked the route. It reminded him of the repetitive sounds of distant machine gun fire but he wasn't bothered by the similarity. Not today anyway.

He was absorbing the warmth of the September sun which dazzled him. It was low as it darted through the clouds and he pulled his trilby slightly to shield his eyes. The hedgerows were a tangle of wild hips, haws and the last few wild blackberries, missed by local foragers. He remembered that mother made hedgerow jelly from the fruit, and as children they would squabble over a crust of bread to spread the dark red sweetness over it.

Within the hour he strolled into the centre of Barnsley, drawn by the busy noise of the market traders calling out to sell up before the end of the afternoon. Most of their trade was done in the morning but there were still a few shoppers looking for a bargain. He scanned the main street for a sign of a tea shop, hoping for a place to read his Evening Post, purchased from the news stand. He had dropped his coins into the fingerless gloved hand of the young seller, who paused momentarily from yelling headlines to nod his thanks from his corner spot.

Opposite the market he noticed a pleasant looking tea shop which looked quite busy being market day. On a sunny September Saturday, people would be looking for refreshment and a place to rest from the weight of heavy shopping bags.

The shaky bell tinkled as he entered. He made his way to a table in the window and pulled out a dark brown bentwood chair to sit on.

"Blooming uncomfortable chairs," he grumbled.

It had always puzzled him that they were so popular, but he reckoned it was because they were so cheap. He knew what he wanted without looking at the menu, so he took out his newspaper and scanned the headlines until someone came to take his order.

A young woman, wearing a white frilled apron and hat stood beside him with her tiny notepad and pencil. "What would you like today sir?" she enquired politely.

"A pot of tea and a toasted teacake please," he replied with a perfunctory smile. "Right away sir, thank you."

As he watched her return to the counter, he noticed several other customers sitting at their tables. Older ladies chatting with their market purchases piled into baskets beside them; a young couple gazing at each other drinking tea going cold and forgetting about a piece of chocolate cake sitting untouched between them. They were totally oblivious of their surroundings. He smiled wistfully at them "Ha! They're in another world!" he smiled wistfully, reminiscing a little. In the far corner there were two young ladies, deep in discussion, their heads almost touching as they spoke in whispers. He wondered whether it was local gossip or exchanging confidences, that engaged them so intently.

He returned to his newspaper until his tea and toasted teacake arrived at the same time. He nodded his thanks and approval at the punctuality of the service, and sank his teeth into the warm and crisp top, the melted butter hitting his top lip which he relished with sheer contentment. He didn't realise how hungry he was. It had been a long time since Mrs. Williams had cooked him his Saturday eggs and bacon this morning. They had settled into a routine by now. She knew exactly what he liked and at what time he preferred to eat a meal. He was always precise and punctual and he hoped that she would be the same. So far it was working well.

He poured his tea, and as he turned the first page of the newspaper he glanced across the room at the young women. He swore he knew one of them. Her face seemed familiar. Shaking his head lightly to himself, he dismissed the thought, intent on reading the news and drinking this splendid cup of tea. He turned to the next page, and raising his eyes slightly, he looked across again.

"Surely that's the girl from the factory?" He couldn't be sure she was the one but on reflection he remembered seeing her in the yard. She was the one who had been stroking the factory cat before looking up and catching his eye. It was the same one he had seen again on the noisy factory floor. Well, well, he mused. She had enchanted him then and was doing something similar again in the teashop. He admired her pretty face and her reserved manner. She appeared to be quiet and quite shy, not like the other girls she worked with.

The other girl appeared to be doing most of the talking and she was listening carefully, so was unaware of his gaze. He thought how much he would like to know a little more about her, but this was neither the time nor the place and it would be inappropriate to approach her and strike up a conversation. So he sat behind his newspaper looking for the weekly bridge puzzle that he enjoyed solving, but today he couldn't concentrate, and he was finding it more difficult than usual.

It was Sissie and Norma sitting there. Norma was Sissie's closest friend. They had been best friends since they were at school and they shared all their secrets and worries and celebrated any happy time they could find. It didn't matter whether they were rambling over the fields, making cakes or altering dresses for each other to be in fashion as far as their budget would allow. Norma didn't work because she cared for her elderly, ailing mother and so she looked forward to Sissie's company and the chance to get out of the house. Although her mother realised her daughter needed some freedom and fun away from her, she tended to be on the possessive side and would often groan when Norma announced she would be going out for a couple of hours. Norma was desperate for a boyfriend, and she showed no shame in letting everyone know. She was actively on the lookout and Sissie was quite shocked and sometimes embarrassed, at how obvious Norma could be at times.

They had finished their tea ages ago and it was time to take a bus ride home. They paid the bill, put on their jackets and rose from the table. John was aware of them leaving so he flipped the top corner of the newspaper to catch another look, trying to be as discreet as he could.

As they moved towards the door Sissie recognised him instantly and lowering her eyes she looked across at him and smiled shyly. He smiled back, saying, "Ladies," as he nodded in their direction.

Norma giggled to draw attention to herself, but in a way that she hoped he would notice her, as she flicked her dark brown hair from under her hat.

"Good Bye!" she replied confidently, in her familiar flirty voice.

"Good Bye Sir," said Sissie politely, instantly realising that he had recognised her from work.

The women left the shop, the bell on the door tinkling as they left.

"Now WHO was that? He's a bit posh! You know him don't you?" Norma asked, excitedly.

"He's the manager at t' mill that's all," replied Sissie quietly. "And quick, stop talking, we need to get that bus home. I'm going to be late," she added.

She didn't want to hear Norma's silly flirty chatter all of a sudden. She wasn't sure why. It just didn't seem right, and Sissie was not the type to get involved in any pointless gossip about someone she really did not know.

"Do you see him every day? Does he talk to you? Don't you think he's handsome? Did you see his blue eyes? Oh Sissie he's wonderful!"

Sissie sighed. Dearest Norma, always looking for a drama, exaggerating every incident in her life. This would be the drama for her today! She would still be talking about it next week!

Sissie thought that it was probably because she was trapped at home every day, never seeing people regularly. She was somewhat embarrassed too, by the flurry of excitement Norma had shown over her boss, whom she herself didn't know, in any case.

The conversation was dropped, and twenty minutes later they got off the bus and hugged each other goodbye, arranging to see each other the following week. Norma lived close to the bus stop but Sissie had a ten-minute walk to the farm, so it gave her time to reflect on her seeing the boss in the tea shop and indeed to notice how handsome he was, as Norma had commented. He was dressed casually and looked very relaxed today, and that was different. He did seem nice. Norma had remarked that he looked posh, but she wasn't sure about that.

As she entered the back kitchen everyone was busy, each having their own Saturday chores to finish before nightfall and preoccupied with their own thoughts, so there was little in the way of conversation.

"Nice afternoon, our Sis?" asked Mam. "How's Norma's Mam?" "She's well, I think," said Sissie, removing her hatpin, then her hat. "What did you do?"

"Nothing much," replied Sissie. "Shall I peel some potatoes?"

Chapter 13

First Hello

On the last Saturday before Christmas the local tradition was for the village football team to play against the children. They set the rules to allow the boys who were aged between 10 and 14 to form a team. Every youngster talked about it for weeks, giving themselves an exciting topic for discussion, argument and teasing. But most important of all, an opportunity to practise their tactics and techniques for a real purpose.

The occasion offered an opportunity for families to turn out, and there was always the buzz of preparation beforehand to create a social event and enjoy the celebrations together. A few of the women set up a trestle table and brought large saucepans of steaming vegetable soup and plenty of homemade bread. Players were reminded to bring their own tin mug so that they would be sure to feast themselves at the end of the game. Some of the older women had made bread pudding which was such a favourite among them all. They cut thick wedges of it to feed all the hungry players at the end of the game as they rubbed their cold, chapped hands together, and felt the mud on their knees dry out and stiffen, as they stood together to queue for the food in the chill of the late afternoon.

Ben Brown, the publican, brought a few jugs of ale to share with the players as they reflected on the game. His main motive was to encourage the men to come back with him to the pub and down few more after the football had finished and enjoy some singsong as the evening unfolded.

It was a satisfying way to end the match for the winners and losers alike, and John was delighted to be amongst them all as he enjoyed observing them relax and play together.

He had seen her just before half time.

"Sissie! Sissie!" uttered Norma breathlessly, as she ran towards her, waving her arms and flinging herself at Sissie, who was standing with one or two others.

"I'm here! Me Mam was being awk'ard and she wouldn't let me come out!"

"Don't worry Norm', you're here now," Sissie calmly replied. "You've only missed t' first half." At long last! He knew her name!

He thought that Sissie was an unusual name. Maybe it was short for something else or her nickname. He tried hard not to stare, but he strolled around saying hello to one or two spectators whose faces he recognised from work or from around the village. He soon came close to the little group of women with whom Sissie was chatting. Then the whistle blew and the game resumed. This was a game of fun so he was not needed for team talk today. It was great entertainment for everyone and they all entered into the spirit of it, until the final whistle blew and surprise, surprise, the men had won! No concessions made here for the younger players although everybody clapped and cheered them as they left the pitch and each one was given a small paper cone of boiled sugar sweets.

Without warning, he was aware that the team had drifted towards him and Bill began to speak.

"Mr. Bland, I'm speaking for all the team here. We want to say a big thank you for what you've done for us this season, sir. We've played so much better, and scored a few more goals this year 'aven't we lads?"

They all murmured in agreement, and nodded their heads amiably. Each one of them looked directly at John until he felt a little self-conscious, but he smiled back at them all.

Bill continued, "We was 'oping you're going' to stay wi' us for a few more games like… anyway …. Eeh! Can us call you Jonny?!"

He blushed bright red as he blurted out the last bit in mild embarrassment, but he was determined to go through with it in spite of the others, who had taunted him, saying he wouldn't dare.

"It's been a great pleasure to work with you all," John replied, smiling at the mud splattered faces of the victorious team.

"It's been good for me too, you know. It's kept me busy on a Saturday afternoon for sure, Bill. And yes, do call me Johnny. I'm Johnny Bland to most people who know me!"

They knew that, word had got round, and they raised their arms in a cheer for him and Bill again came forward offering him a half bottle of whisky wrapped in tissue paper.

"This is from us all and big thanks sir, I mean Johnny! This is for all you've done for us lads this year." He corrected himself, his face pink and slightly flustered by the sudden informality of it.

The team drifted off laughing in good humour at the impromptu presentation, but they wanted to 'sup some ale' so Bill was left behind, shaking John's hand and enquiring if the manager liked whisky and hoping that he might enjoy a nip at the end of the day. And then explaining that they had had a 'whip round' to collect for him.

John was so touched by the gesture, that he was almost at a loss for words beyond expressing his thanks.

"So unexpected - you shouldn't have ..." he was adding, and then he faltered as suddenly he was aware of Sissie at Bill's side, smiling proudly as she placed her hand on his back in fond gesture. Her brother was talking confidently to the man she only knew as the boss of the Mill!

He stopped and smiled at her, and courteously lifted his trilby in the usual manner, and looking at her lovely flushed face he said, "You must be very proud of this young man. He is a decent player and also a brave public speaker!"

"I am that, sir! He is my brother and I watch him play at home games every week when I can."

Her voice was a light twinkle of sound and light, and it was lovely. Her grey-green eyes danced in the dusky air, hinting that it was the end of the afternoon as she spoke. She looked first at Bill and then at John, with warmth and pride shining on her face.

"Shall the three of us walk?" suggested John, aware that it would be dark soon and they would be stranded alone on the pitch, or the two of them would pair off without him. Most people had dispersed, even Norma was running, but this time to get home before her mother started complaining about her being late.

"Of course!" both of them responded in unison.

"Which way will you be going?" Bill enquired shyly. Off the pitch away from the others, he didn't dare call him 'Johnny'.

"I go left out of this gate, to my lodgings and then to pack, as I'll be going to visit my mother for Christmas," John replied promptly. "Which direction for you?"

"Yes, it's the same for us. Left at the gate too, and then to the edge of the village. We live at Low Fold Farm in one of the cottages. It's not far," replied Sissie, making a quiet contribution. She was inwardly surprised at her enthusiasm and eagerness to make conversation with him.

"My word, so you have a fair walk every morning to the Mill," remarked John.

"It's not far really, and sometimes I take my bicycle," she explained speaking deliberately and as correctly as she could in front of this gentleman, who after all, was her boss at the factory.

"Ahh very wise," he replied. "And Bill what about you?"

"Bike in every day, me. I'm a welder at t' mill," he reported stiffly in a simple no nonsense tone.

"I haven't seen you there, I will admit," replied John, his eyes shining brightly at Sissie as he spoke. "And so what will you do for Christmas this year?" he added, hoping to change the conversation away from work.

They chattered on in easy conversation, easier than any of them had expected. Walking and talking had always seemed a satisfactory way of spending time, and he was quite disappointed when he turned towards the gate to his lodgings.

"Well I'm here, folks. This is my humble abode," he announced cheerfully, "Let me say it has been a pleasure to get to know you and, well, haven't we had an enjoyable afternoon at the match?" "That we have," they both said together and giggled at the fact they had responded in chorus.

"Have a good Christmas you two and convey my compliments of the season to your family," he said with a broad smile, and he raised his hand in a friendly wave.

Then he was gone through the gate as sister and brother continued along the lane into the darkness. He turned the key in the front door, calling, "I'm back" to Mrs. W, and with a new lightness in his step, he mounted the stairs two at a time to pack a suitcase for his brief Christmas visit to be with his own family.

Chapter 14

Bowing His Head

ohn has always tried to be punctual, but he was always the last one to rush through the school gates, usually just as the bell was ringing to announce that the day was about to begin. He had earned a place at grammar school, but it was a long walk across the fell to be on time to catch the bus. As early as he could, he would start his journey but still he would arrive red faced and breathless as he took up speed on the last part of his trek. Sometimes his father would take him in the truck, but there were too many commitments in the early morning routine for that to happen often. It created pressures all round and as there was a small boarding facility, he was accepted as a weekly boarder a few months after he had settled at the school.

"Come on in, Bland!" instructed the senior master. He was quite a stern man but was not without some understanding of the demands that the small statured boy faced to get there on his long daily journey to school.

He was popular with other boys and a good scholar, being particularly gifted in mathematics and physics and he gave the school masters considerable pleasure and admiration for his diligence and academic achievements. He was an avid reader, encouraged from a young age at home, to find pleasure in the company of a book, so his success in English was evident. His fascination for languages motivated him to read further, especially into Roman history in Latin lessons and in classroom chanting and homework practising of modern French. As if that wasn't enough, he excelled on the football field too, and he was a competent bowler in cricket for the grammar school first X1. He enjoyed school. It was the place where he could satisfy his hunger for learning and pursue his own talents, learning more and more about himself along the way.

Morning prayers and hymns plus a reading from the Bible set the moral and spiritual tone for the day ahead. They all assembled in regimented rows, in the spacious oak panelled hall which smelled of old polish and damp woollen blazers. On Awards Boards mounted on the walls, were the gilded names of old boys who had left years before, with distinctions in Classics, English Literature and History. They were proud evidence that this school produced great opportunities for scholars who were facing a promising future. Within this awe inspiring space at the centre of the ancient building, John and his fellows were able to grasp a quiet moment after the rigour of their respective journeys, before they applied discipline and concentration, in the school room afterwards.

"Bow Your Heads, boys. Let us pray."

The Headmaster adjusted his gown as he solemnly instructed the group of 250 pupils to pray. Before him was a sea of identical grey woollen blazers, grey shirts with burgundy striped ties and a mixture of short or long trousers. In unison and in monotonous voice, they recited the Lord's Prayer "Our Father which art in heaven…."

After the last prayer, they were dismissed row by row, to attend to their studies.

Ever since those days, when John wanted to find some time for quiet reflection, to consolidate his thoughts or just to pray in the quietude of the church he would say to himself, "I need to go and bow my head."

He prayed at university and on the battlefield and he prayed in bereavement. After it, his heart would be eased, his mind energised and he felt that he gained strength and purpose. Finally, his spirit would feel at peace.

Now, as the beginning of this new life unrolled in front of him in Yorkshire, he was ready to find an appropriate moment for reflection and guidance. He would find this through prayer as he had always been taught, and he would continue to find strength and meaning for himself.

The day after the football match, a bright sunny morning, he went to church alone. Mrs. Williams had already told him that she was 'chapel' and he was relieved because it meant he wasn't obliged to accompany her on any Sunday routine. He was happy for privacy and non-involvement with anyone else when it came to his beliefs. He felt quite selfish because of that. The last thing he wanted was to appear aloof or stand offish, but he felt it was a private thing so he didn't let that inhibit his efforts to go alone into church for the early Sunday service. As the last peal of bells rang out, he slipped into the back row of the pews inside the local church and bowed his head.

At the end of the service it was obvious that the vicar would want to welcome him as he left the church door. After the last of the small congregation had dispersed, the old man, the stiffness of his white dog collar circling loosely away from his aging neck, extended his cold and bony hand, bearing a warm smile to welcome him. He had been in this parish for thirty-five years and he knew every member of his congregation. From baptisms to funerals and from Christmas through the ecclesiastical year to Harvest, his church was a significant contributor to local people's lives. He recognised, and was compassionate to, the needs of the wider community who mostly turned to him for such milestones and rituals throughout the year. They were comforted by his kind, calm manner and the peaceful and supportive understanding he had shown over the years, so he was well respected.

"It was very good to see you today, Sir. I hope you enjoyed the sermon. Are you new to Barugh?" "John Bland," John replied formally, "Yes I'm new here, Vicar, and thank you for a very pleasant service. My work at the Mill has brought me to this busy village, and so today I took the opportunity to come and say my prayers," he added with a smile, and turned imperceptibly on his heel, so as not to offend but to indicate that he did not want to be divulging any personal information. Not even to the vicar of the parish.

"Everyone is always welcome here. It was nice to see you, Mr. Bland. May you have a pleasant day."

"And I wish the same to you," replied John, impressed that the old chap was happy to let him go without further dialogue, thinking to himself, "He's probably ready for his Sunday dinner after early communion and morning prayers!".

He turned on his heel, thankful that he had made the effort to go to church today. Already, he was feeling calm and steady. It was a feeling he associated with Sunday.

Now he felt that he needed all his thoughts untangling and straightening out to feel in control of them. There was no doubt that 'bowing his head' helped.

After leaving the vicar, he strolled around the gravestones, hands pushed deep into his trouser pockets. They were lined up in random, but reverent rows throughout the churchyard, bearing the family names of people who had passed away over the past hundred years or so. He stepped gently down the narrow, mown paths between them towards the outer perimeter to reach more recent ones. There were no names of significance or bearing the names of anyone he recognised, and he felt a twinge of disappointment. After he'd read a few of the stones, he realised that in fact he was looking for a particular name. He was looking for the name Horbury. He knew that it was Bill's family name, and so clearly it would be the same for his sister. He felt like an amateur detective looking for clues. He wasn't just casually interested in the historical background to this village at all. It was becoming more personal than that.

He wasn't clear why he should be so intrigued to learn more about the community in which he was now living. He had never made such efforts before. Perhaps it was that it was a simple first step in learning more about people here and their heritage. And now he had the spare time to find out.

He was fortunate that through land registry and family documents, his own family ancestry was recorded, providing a comforting reassurance of continuity and stability with rooted, established evidence. But that would not be the case for many people.

However, he found nothing here. Not a single gravestone gave him the satisfaction of finding any clues that the family

Horbury had lived here. This had been an interesting way to pass the time he thought, but hadn't yielded any results to settle his mind. He was frustrated that he had drawn a negative return for his efforts.

Closing the ancient lych gate behind him, he turned into the lane in the direction away from the row of houses closest to the church, and headed towards the countryside. All was quiet. It was Sunday and within this hard working community it really was a day of rest. Even on a pleasant bright day like today people were indoors; in the public house, in their tiny gardens or working on their allotments at the far side of the village.

For now, John needed to find some freedom of space that walking out in the fresh air allowed. Here he could usually make his plans and dreams more workable and to make any relevant decisions.

As the lane became a public bridleway with rougher terrain underfoot, his stout brown leather shoes gripped the turf beneath.

He breathed deep and long. It took him in a circular route around the edges of the fields where he noticed some little farm cottages and the big farmhouse nearby. This must be Low Fold Farm!

The skylarks seemed to invite him to dream big, as they sang and soared into the Sunday skies. Relentless, their joyful, busy calls lifted his spirits and he wandered down the track feeling not quite so alone with his thoughts.

Sissie had occupied his thoughts since yesterday. Of one thing he was sure, he wanted to get to know her. He was so curious to know more about her and her family. He had to simply admit that he was intrigued, and he felt attracted to her.

He reflected on how much it had roused in him familiar feelings not experienced since…. Well, for a long time it seemed. Long before his time spent here.

This sensation was different. There was mystery surrounding her and her attachments. Her family, her friends and the workforce; he wanted to know more. He was aware of another thing too; how quickly he had felt an instinctive, irrational fondness for her, an urge to look after her and to protect her. But how could he feel such a nurturing instinct for someone he didn't really know? He didn't know much about her at all…yet.

"Now then, steady on lad," he cautioned himself, admitting quietly, he didn't want to cause any difficulties and possible complications, if he ventured towards her too clumsily.

He needed to be so sure that if he made any contact with her beyond the workplace context, he would have to be serious and sincere because inevitably it would draw attention to both himself and her. He would be horrified if he became the subject of local gossip, and above all else, he wanted to protect himself and Sissie from any tittle tattle from her work mates - and neighbours of course.

He began to imagine the relationship if it developed. He was guessing, and hoping that she may not have a young man in her life at present. Certainly, she was young and in her early twenties, he thought, but perhaps was still unattached. He wanted to know more and would have to find a way to be sure. He would like to make some contact with her, if that was possible. He thought it should be casual and by chance. And then he wondered how she would she react. She seemed a quiet and reserved sort of girl, which was part of her delightful character. This was surely the reason why he found her so appealing.

So many questions unanswered and plenty to wonder about. He wasn't clear of his next move, so he leaned on the five bar gate on his left, lit his pipe and imagined a chance meeting.

Church? Maybe not, she wasn't there today. The mill? No, too noisy.

Football match?

Yes, the Saturday football would be a strong possibility. Lots of family supporters in the village came to watch a game. He wondered if she went regularly to support her brother. He would look out for her because usually, he noticed Bill attended every match. If he saw her there, he might stand nearby her and strike up some conversation. He assumed there would be a few more matches after Christmas.

He was enjoying the idle thoughts that passed through his mind as he strolled along. He felt light headed and young again. As he drew on his pipe, he recognised those feelings associated with the recent past, and he didn't feel alone. Again he was reminded that this would be for the first time since....

"Well, a long time ago!" he answered himself again.

Chapter 15

Christmas At Barugh

Every Barugh farm labourer and his family celebrated Christmas together at Low Fold Farm, as they had done as far back as anyone could remember. It was a time for them all to get together; put their troubles away for the time being and to have some fun and frivolity. With good food on the table and cheerful company, they seated themselves around the huge table in the large farmhouse dining room.

Every year someone seemed to have produced another baby and so it was that the gathering crowd grew bigger and bigger. Everyone was expected to make a contribution, and so the table groaned under the weight of every offering of roast potatoes and Yorkshire Puddings, of Annie Horbury's braised red cabbage, Joe Grant's home grown Brussels sprouts, the chestnut stuffing and 'pigs in blankets' from the Harrisons. The turkey, nurtured and fattened since it had been selected just after Easter, held pride of place in the centre every year. It had been roasted and then presented at table by the farmer and his wife, and was greeted with loud applause and cries of appreciation and excitement. And as Farmer Neal and his wife entered the room, carrying the hefty load of food which was glowing golden and smelling delicious, it announced the beginnings of a hearty feast.

Every family was proud of their own recipe Christmas pudding. It had been the talk amongst the women for weeks, since the ingredients had all been mixed together. And as if a pudding wasn't enough, there were dozens of mincepies and apple and cinnamon tarts, served with gallons of custard to be consumed afterwards. The ale flowed from large earthenware jugs for those who wanted it and homemade apple juice was a favourite too.

Every child was asked to choose a simple toy from under the impressive tree which reached from floor to ceiling, its pine fragrance filling the room each time a door was opened letting the fresh air in on this happy crowd. Mothers could be heard insisting that thanks should be said to the farmer and his wife for their generosity whilst at the same time, echoing gasps of surprise that they had kindly provided just the right number of small gifts again this year.

Farmer Neal called for everyone to be quiet, and then he solemnly said grace. Afterwards, everyone shuffled into their places and pulled their chairs up to the table. Everyone plunged into excited chatter as they returned to the festivities, giggling at each other as they watched one after the other stick a paper hat on their heads, before settling down to eat. All worries and woes were put aside today, because they had looked forward to this for so many weeks now, and it was never a disappointment.

Traditionally, Sissie and Doris served the meal to the older members round the table. Then, when their duties were done, they settled down next to each other. Sissie loved to sing and so she would be encouraged to lead them into some carol singing at the end of the meal.

'The Holly and The Ivy' and 'Oh Little Town of Bethlehem' were firm favourites. The farmer's wife gently squeezed her arm as she passed her whilst serving, to ask her if she'd sing again this year.

"Of course Mrs. Neal! It'd be an honour!" beamed Sissie.

Most of the younger children had learned the words at Sunday school, so the sound of joyful and enthusiastic voices echoed through the farmhouse dining room and into the winter air as the meal drew to an end.

The sisters settled in their own chairs, ready to eat their own meals.

"I love Christmas," sighed Sissie. She raised her knife and fork and leaned towards Doris affectionately.

"I love Herbert,"' whispered Doris cheekily so that no one would hear her.

"You do make me laugh," giggled Sissie, slightly shocked at Doris's forwardness. "Do you really love him?" she continued.

"Yes, and he's going to ask me to marry him when he's been to ask our Dad for permission."

That was a sudden and unexpected announcement from her older sister, Sissie reflected. She gazed at her sister's face which had flushed with the confession. Of course, one day she herself would like to be married, she thought. She imagined herself settled with a husband and her own home. She realised that she wanted to become someone with responsibilities, instead of just enduring the daily monotony of factory work, and of living in the same tiny cottage with her parents and younger brothers.

She enjoyed the company of children, and she loved teaching them new things and listening to their playful chatter. Lately, she had volunteered to teach the little ones at Sunday School, and she felt that she was quite good at telling them bible stories, encouraging them to draw and crayon and to learn prayers and hymns. How satisfying to see them dancing home with their drawings and singing the chorus of a new song. She had taught them two hymns that they seemed to love: 'For the Beauty of the Earth' and 'What a Friend we have in Jesus.

And because she had loved these experiences so much, she dreamed that one day, she would like a family of her own and to become a good mother with her own little ones.

Doris was lucky to have met a young man at Barnsley fair back in October. He came from Blackpool. She wasn't sure why he was there at the fair in the first place, but they had been courting ever since, and consequently, the sisters didn't spend as much time together as they used to. Doris had changed anyway. She was too preoccupied with Herbert now, and could talk of nothing and no one else. Sissie regarded that as rather boring and lacked any ambition for the future. She wasn't attracted to anyone in the industrial area of Barugh and Darton and she was certainly not interested in anyone who was a miner. Everyone knew what a dirty and dangerous occupation it was. It claimed lives and caused pain and suffering, not to mention ill health in old age. No, she would like to get to know someone who had an interesting occupation, and might show her a world that was different from the only one she had ever known in Barugh.

Her daydreaming was interrupted, as she became aware that one by one they were all finishing the sumptuous meal. All that preparation, and it was gone in five minutes, they joked.

On the stroke of three o' clock Mr. Neal turned on his wireless, twisting the volume knob, checking that all could hear and then there was a hush in the room.

"This is an unbelievable moment in history," he announced as the first broadcast by the King was available here in this, his own dining room. Mothers glared at the younger children to be quiet and they all stood up to sing the National Anthem as it played over the air waves. Then they listened reverently to the King's Christmas Message that followed, gathering round to ensure that they heard his crackly voice as it was transmitted across the country. They murmured and nodded to each other, showing loyalty and respect as well as expressing incredulity and disbelief that such a thing was possible. At the end of the broadcast, there was a spontaneous round of applause and afterwards the room was filled with comment and discussion about how things were changing and who would know what would come next in their lifetime.

It was a long held custom that the younger women washed up and dried the many dishes that had all gone through that day. Then, as they found their seats at table again, Mrs. Neal gestured to Sissie to stand up, and, tapping her empty port glass with a teaspoon, she announced that the singing would begin. By now everyone was in hearty voice and the rousing and familiar sounds of Christmas songs filled the room and beyond into the yard, as they all sang their hearts out round the table.

Sissie sang clearly and sweetly, looking at all the flushed and festive faces who joined in with the singing of the familiar carols. She wondered what would be happening at Christmas next year and whether she would still be singing at the farm in a year's time?

As the light began to fail, the grown-ups were ready for some peace and quiet. Children, one by one, were becoming tetchy with tiredness, so people began to gather their belongings and drift homewards, extending grateful thanks to their hosts.

Sissie remained behind, loving the quiet time helping Mrs. Neal with tidying up and rearranging furniture and afterwards, to wander home with her own day dreams. She felt that this special time completed her own Christmas Day. Mrs. Neal enjoyed the gentle wind down at the end of a hectic day, with the bright and happy young woman, never having had a daughter of her own. They chattered on about new babies and new romantic relationships emerging in the village.

"And when will it be your turn Sissie?" enquired Mrs. Neal with a twinkle in her eye.

Sissie smiled but did not answer the question because it was time to go home and, although reluctant to leave, she hugged her coat around herself against the chilly air, and left the farmhouse, despite Mrs. Neal's persuasions to stay a little longer.

She wandered into the darkness of the evening, and now alone with the nostalgia of the day behind her, she recalled the kind handsome face of Johnny Bland and she could not put it out of her mind. On the Saturday that he had walked with Bill and herself after the match, they were able to share such easy casual conversation. She wanted a moment, the first since the run up to Christmas, to refresh her memory of it. They said that he was not married, and that he had no wife or young lady. She felt such an urgency to learn more about him. She wanted to ask questions to get to know more about him, and she wanted to tell him all about herself too, and describe her hopes and dreams. She wondered if he might be interested. She didn't want to appear too forward, but somehow she knew instinctively that he might be interested in her. Perhaps it had been the way his pale blue eyes held hers when they were talking, or the way the kindest of smiles spread across his face, when he looked at her. She had noticed that he had glanced in her direction when they were all watching the match and that, she was sure, she had not imagined.

She wondered where he had spent his Christmas Day. Was he having a day of feasting like she had just experienced? Did he listen to the same King's Christmas Message as they all did - wherever he was?

She was dying to know when exactly he might he be coming back to Barugh. And she would love to find out where he and his family came from.

She wondered whether he had brothers and sisters like she did. But most of all, why oh why had he found this job in Barugh of all places?

Reaching the back door, she peeled off her coat, kicked off her boots and shouted, "I'm back!"

No one replied. They were huddled around the wireless listening to the News Bulletin on the Home Service!

Chapter 16

Getting to know you

When the decorations had been packed away and Christmas card lists had been updated ready for the next year, John stepped into the new year with a clear, determined spirit. He had moved out of his lodgings, much to Mrs. Williams's disappointment. He had provided a great deal of comfort for her over the last few months, knowing that she had company in her home. She had been pleased with the modest efforts she had made to make John feel welcome, comfortable and well fed. However, he felt that it was high time to live on his own with more space and privacy. He thanked her profusely for her hospitality and generosity, promising her that he would not forget her kindnesses. Then he moved out and rented a small cottage on the edge of town which would now suit him better. He wanted space and a little more privacy, now that he had settled into the job at the factory. Something in the back of his mind prevented him from committing to purchasing a property just yet. He was looking for somewhere with a small parlour and a kitchen to himself and with just a modest bedroom and simple washroom facilities. He felt satisfied that this would meet his needs.

It was easy to find somewhere at this time of year and within a couple of weeks he had moved into his new home. It was sparsely furnished but immediately it felt welcoming, which suited him completely. This would provide the quiet uninterrupted time away from the workplace that he was seeking and he was pleased with what he had found. He had the resources to provide a deposit and the weekly rental was within his budget which would also allow him to save money for buying a house eventually. Perhaps, he hoped as a family home.

He was beginning to feel the burden of time passing by and his little girl was growing up so fast that he feared he would become a stranger to her if he didn't accelerate events for both his and her future.

Sitting in front of the fire in his new parlour one night, staring into the coals of a well-built fire, his thoughts turned to this lovely woman Sissie once again, and how he could get to know her better. A plan of action was called for.

"Action not words. Action….not….words," he repeated under his breath.

With this in mind he had an idea. He would take a walk in her direction at the weekend, now that he knew where she and her brother lived. He might come across her around the farm, perhaps near the tied cottage in which she and her family lived. It would be a nice coincidence if that happened. He doubted it! Then he wondered if he should actually knock on the door to ask her if she'd like to take a walk with him. He didn't feel there would be any harm in that. He assumed that she would be confident to accept his invitation, despite being surprised to see him on the doorstep. Surely, she would not refuse as that would seem unfriendly, and he imagined that it would not be her nature to respond in that way. It would be a pleasant experience for her and she could bring someone along such as a sister or brother to chaperone her, if that was what they still did in these parts nowadays.

The decision was made. Yes, he had made up his mind. He would head for Low Fold Farm on Saturday.

There had been a sharp frost overnight and the mid-morning air was crisp and cold but bright; the wintry January sun seeped through the clouds as if to encourage and motivate those who had planned any form of outdoor activity that day.

After finishing his breakfast of porridge and tea, John pulled on a second pair of woollen socks and laced up his walking boots. Over his woollen jersey and leather jerkin he buttoned himself into a tweed herringbone long coat and pressed his trilby on his head. He was ready for a walk, hoping to meet a certain young lady along the way. No need to use any fancy talk, just a walk across the fields with her to enjoy the countryside; take in some much needed fresh air and to learn a little about each other. Nothing could be simpler.

He could not believe his eyes as he drew nearer to the row of farm cottages. She was there talking so intently, that at first she did not see him approach.

"Good morning," he called out affably. "It's a fresh one today."

She turned towards him and he could see from the work clothes she was wearing, that she had been occupied already today with farm jobs.

"Good morning. er.. Johnny," she replied timidly. "We have a few ewes who are ready for lambing this weekend, so we have been checking that they are safe and well."

"Ah, yes, I've spotted a few up there on the hills. Have you brought them down to the farm?" "Oh yes, them's safe in t' barn now. Do you want to come and look at 'em?"

"May I?" he asked, as he followed her through the gate towards the barn.

As they walked together, he was aware that they were exactly in step with each other. He found it quietly amusing, almost as if this was a good sign.

Through the entrance to the wide open space of the barn, the ewes were fenced separately in freshly laid straw, and the sounds of them baying and baaing was deafening under the corrugated tin roof of the building. Some ewes had already birthed one and sometimes two lambs that had already been dyed with the farm identity.

"These two are dozy, so we need to keep an eye on 'em," said a rough voice from behind them. He was the young man that Sissie had been speaking to earlier.

"Can't afford 'ote happening that we lose 'em," he added.

"Sissie has a knack tho'," he continued. "She just has a way wit' animals."

John smiled at her with admiration

"Well done! It's important to have someone around who understands animals. Sheep are usually independent and like to be alone to birth but there's always one or two who need a helping hand!"

He leaned on the gate of one pen and surveyed the scene before him. There must have been fifty ewes he estimated, noting that it was a different scale to the ones he was used to - where some three hundred could be giving birth within a six-week period back at Whitemoor Farm.

"Thank you for showing me all this. I'm really impressed," he said.

"We are glad to but, what brought you up here?" enquired Sissie, curious to know why he should have appeared in the yard so unexpectedly.

"Well, I was passing as I often do, taking the bridleway for a brisk walk this morning and saw you here. The walk along there and to the footpath over the fields, forms a circular route of around three miles which I find so satisfactory," he replied, suddenly relieved that seeing her like this meant that he didn't have to go to the cottage door as he'd planned, in order to see her.

"Would like to join me. I'd love to have your company if you've finished your work here and you have nothing else to do."

"I'd like that very much. I think we're finished for today aren't we Harry?" she replied lightly, looking at Harry as she checked that the work was finished.

"We're done for today Sissie, ta. I'm knocking off now as well," said Harry digging his hands, red and chapped with the cold, into his pockets.

With that, she stepped towards the barn entrance saying, "Give me a few moments to put on walking shoes and coat please, and I'll join you."

She darted across the yard before he could respond further.

He strolled slowly across the yard from the barn noticing that in spite of the January weather it was neat and relatively clean underfoot and there was every sign that it was in good order and well maintained.

She appeared from the cottage flushed and with an excited expression on her face as she approached him, "Sorry I kept you. I'm ready now. I do love walking and I know this little route that we are taking today really well. It's a regular one for me, too."

It was as if they had known each other for much longer. The conversation seemed to flow so easily and naturally, as they walked side by side down the bridle path. Together, they listened and laughed light heartedly, as they exchanged anecdotes about the family, football and the factory. Three miles of public bridleway rolled away far too quickly, and both felt some regret that they were back at the farmyard gate so quickly.

"I enjoyed you company today, Sissie," John said looking into her pretty face. "I hope we can do this again. Perhaps we can choose another route, or we can do this one again. I really wouldn't mind."

"I have enjoyed it too and I would love to do it again. Next time maybe to the edge of the woods as there'll be the first snowdrops appearing - we didn't go that way today. They are so pretty," she replied. "But I don't mind where we go either because it just feels new and different when I'm walking with you."

He was charmed by her broad south Yorkshire accent that she spoke carefully and correctly, looking at him directly and confidently as she chattered away. Her conversation was easy and interesting and he could listen to her for longer, but the walk was over and although he didn't want it to end, it was only proper that they bid each other goodbye for now. It seemed so natural to be arranging another time to walk out together, weather permitting.

For each of the following three Saturdays they arranged to meet, taking different routes, not noticing the weather, too preoccupied with exchanging stories, hopes and dreams. They talked about when they were young and they described members of their respective families and the circumstances of each of them.

As the winter calendar flipped over to February, the snow fell and it was difficult to continue for the time being, and so one day they arranged to meet for an afternoon in the teashop in Barnsley. They walked into town together and took the bus back to Barugh as the light fell at the end of the day and over tea and buttered scones they talked about work and her frustrations and his ambitions.

One afternoon, again she asked tentatively, why he had come to this area in preference to anywhere else,

"It was the first job I applied for at the time because I was living over on the continent after the war was over," he replied simply. His reply caused Sissie to ask even more questions, one by one as they tumbled out.

"But why were you there? It was all over in 1918!"

"Didn't you want to stay over there?" "Whereabouts were you living?"

"Why did you want to leave? Or did you need to leave?" "What did your family say?"

It was then he realised just how much he trusted her and liked her and wanted her to be central in his life and in that incredible and inexplicable moment, the urgency to tell her in detail about his life in Belgium was profound.

However, he couldn't tell her here because this was a public place and even though they had discussed many things, this was very important, private and sensitive and he knew that in telling her he was committing himself to her exclusively.

Could he be absolutely sure that she was feeling the same intensity? Would she be loyal and in time be able to love him? He had imagined over and over, during these last few weeks, of a life spent with her. She had told him enough about herself that he could see that she could become the mother that Vicky so needed.

"There were many reasons why I came over here mostly connected to events that took place during a chapter in my life that I do want to share with you - I really do - but not here because it is too public. For now, I would like you to be patient and trust me when I say that I shall tell you when we can have some time alone."

Chapter 17

Growing up

Returning home during the following week, he found a letter waiting for him. He picked it up from the doormat on to which it had fallen, and turning it over he saw the Brussels post mark. He gasped at the unexpectedness of it. He went through to his tiny kitchen. It was cold and the smell of last night's roast potatoes and belly pork he had cooked for himself hung in the air. He shivered, boiled the kettle on the gas burner and brewed a pot of tea, set it down on the table with cup and saucer, milk jug and sugar bowl beside it. Mother had sent a tin trunk by road, and it was filled with crockery, cooking utensils and cutlery, bed linen and towels. She had put in cushions and curtains even though she didn't know the place nor what he would like, but she wanted him to have a cosy winter in his new home with minimum effort on his part.

He was grateful for the instant homeliness it had brought to the cottage.

Snow had fallen during the day and there was a definite chill through the house, as he swiftly put a match to a ready laid fire in the grate in the parlour. His homemade newspaper firelighters lit immediately, and flames licked around the short sticks under the carefully placed coals, crackling as the heat grew. He poured his tea and taking it to his armchair, he watched the fire take hold and burn strongly.

He picked up the letter, examined the address and turned it over slowly. He carefully slit the top of the envelope using a Sheffield steel letter opener, which had a silver and ivory handle bearing the chevrons of the Bland Crest on it. It had been given to him by his parents on his 21st birthday and he admired its fineness and skilful workmanship. It was ancient, and reminded him of his childhood home. He reckoned it had been in the family probably since the early 19th century, when sheep farming was very lucrative, bringing his ancestors greater wealth and status in those days.

Inside the envelope were a couple of studio photographs of Vicky. One of her sitting prettily in a large cream coloured armchair and another standing with a small doll in her arms. His eyes misted with tears as the composed, smiling face held his gaze. How he missed her! She was growing quickly, unlike me, he thought. There was also a picture she had drawn of herself holding his hand as a now four-year-old would do and a picture of a lady lying above them. Clearly this was of her dear Mama in heaven. The memories of his former life crashed over him and tears spilled over with sadness and grief. As the fire began to offer its warmth into the room, he broke down weeping uncontrollably, whilst at the same time struggling to locate a handkerchief from his trouser pocket. He held it up to his eyes and pressed it into his eye sockets to stem the tears. He hadn't realised just how much he had still been feeling the pain of his wife's passing, all this time, and of the tragic consequences that had been placed on his little girl's tender formative years. He reproached himself for leaving her and running away from the reality of the situation. He groaned with grief and guilt. Regret and remorse consumed him as he fell back against the cushions, helpless with the tumultuous emotions that he had buried deeply within, since he had left them to find a future that would benefit both of them. For some time he rocked backwards and forwards to calm himself.

He told himself that crying wouldn't help, so he tried to compose himself as he stared into the glowing coals of the fire. Then reaching for the tongs he placed another two pieces of coal on the fire. "It's time for action," he muttered to himself.

Several times in his life he had taken calculated risks in challenging circumstances, and had then to deal with the consequences. He recalled the numerous occasions on the battlefield when he had needed to make life changing decisions to direct and protect his men when they were either risking or facing danger. He was reminded of all those decisions he took on the front, to rescue severe numbers of casualties who could scarcely be counted after a charge had been made. The risk to stretcher bearers going out there, had to be carefully measured before commands were issued. He had always been in control of these situations and was able to keep his emotions tightly to himself, so why couldn't he keep them in check now?

Equally, his circumstances now demanded a calculated risk. He felt he was close to asking Sissie if she would marry him. He would seek out her father on Saturday at the farm and ask for her hand in marriage and then he would propose.

Going through things in his head, he realised that perhaps it was too soon. Before that he would need to tell her about his little girl and his plans to bring her to England.

He would have to invite Sissie to tea at the cottage, without delay, and he would tell her the story of his time in Brussels. Understandably, she would be shocked and quite unprepared for such a revelation, so he became agitated as he questioned whether she would accept his proposal after learning of his past and present circumstances. He would need to give her time to digest it all, and form her own opinions and also to clarify her own feelings after listening to his story. The biggest question of all, and one that he was most nervous about was, would she be willing to take on, not just him, but his child as well?

He had no appetite and therefore he didn't eat that night. He was too preoccupied with working out the trail of events that had to take place in the coming days. Sissie may ask him for time to think before making her decision, and he accepted that this was understandable. He must not appear too much in haste. It was imperative not to rush such important matters.

However, there was an urgency for him to take a few days to visit Vicky; to re-acquaint himself with her through play and by taking meals together. He had to find opportunities to put her to bed with a story and to share a quiet reflection of the day that they had just shared, in order to regain closeness, trust and warmth. He would need to tell her of his plans for her to come with him on his next trip to England, so that she would adjust gradually to the idea and the change that would be in store for her. It would not be long before she would accompany him. He hoped it would be in the spring.

So much to think about, to plan and so much to do!

Chapter 18

February 1925

"You remember last week, I mentioned that I wanted to tell you something important about myself and my life but I needed to find an opportunity when we were quiet and alone and private?"

John took her hand gently in his, as they walked away from the farm cottage gate and turned into the lane.

She looked forward eagerly to these Saturdays when they would walk out together, engaging with news and catching up on the events of their week as they stopped to gaze up at a buzzard searching patiently for something edible moving in the field below.

"Of course I remember, John! I've thought of nothing else since. And yes, I'm ready to listen whenever you choose to tell me," she replied looking at him in earnest.

"Now then my sweetest girl, there's no need to look so serious!" he replied, looking at her tenderly. They were exactly the same height so his eyes looked deeply into hers as she blinked back at him, wondering what on earth he was going to tell her.

For early February it was surprisingly mild and the sky was clear. He couldn't - he mustn't - wait another moment before telling her. Time was marching on and it would soon be her birthday. He wanted to give her time to absorb the news he was going to give her, then he could settle things before it, and he could celebrate with her. He wanted to give her just the facts so that there was nothing hidden both from her nor from him, for that matter. He expected her to ask questions and he wanted to allow time to answer them and to offer reassurance and guidance on the ensuing decisions they would have to make.

At the entrance to the bridleway was a five bar gate hanging open. As he drew her towards it, he said quietly, "Let's pause here for a moment, and I will tell you my story and then, when I'm finished, you can make a choice. You can choose either to return home, or to walk on with me for tea and cake in my cottage."

Her eyes widened further in wonderment, as she nodded silently and leaned on the gate.

"First of all and most important of all, I want to tell you, as I have told you before, that I love you and I know that you love me and…. if I wasn't sure of the love we both have for each other, I would not be sharing this story with you. My trust and respect for you is deep and unshakeable Sissie, and I believe we can have a life of contentment together and we can work together to be happy and successful."

Then, taking a deep breath he told her about his previous wife and child and the tragedy that had hit them. He was resolute in leaving detail of that period in his life and the relationship to a minimum. He had given this a lot of thought and had rehearsed the lines he would deliver over and over because he was determined not to explain any of those circumstances. It was history now, and had no relevance to his life with Sissie. In some inexplicable way he felt it would be a betrayal to Victoria and also to Vicky perhaps, as she grew from childhood into adulthood. He wasn't sure how Sissie would accept his account. He was worried that if he said too much it might affect their own emerging story. He felt that it would disturb the deepening attachment they now had for each other. In fact, in many ways he felt it could become a barrier to them, in their future lives as a couple. The focus for him was his daughter and her happiness. Sissie was a young, sensitive woman who could become a mother to his darling child, whilst at the same time, loving him as much as he loved her. This needed careful handling.

She listened, as he calmly related the events of his past, never taking her eyes off him, nodding to indicate she was taking it all in. It was true, she had spent several moments in her own time puzzling and pondering over what it could be that he needed to tell her. Knowing something of his courage in the war, she had expected a revelation that was more of a health nature. Perhaps he had a problem that was physical. Perhaps he was suffering from that awful 'flashback' that the men who had survived the front line experienced. She couldn't imagine a reason for such a private and serious discussion.

She was stunned and momentarily shocked as she listened to this disturbing and unexpected story. She felt an overwhelming sadness for him, that he had endured such a tragic period in his life, carrying the loss and grief all alone. The thought of the pain that he must have experienced…. she herself felt the same hurt now. An intense wave of sorrow for him enveloped her. She dropped her head shyly with pity, unable to look at him and she couldn't find the words to respond. Perhaps words were not appropriate.

A few seconds of silence fell between them. It seemed like an eternity, as John fumbled in his top pocket for his pipe, hoping for a response. How was she going to react to his story? Now that he had shared it, he was worried that it would be too much for a young country lass who, so far, had lived a straightforward and simple life. He knew that he wanted to protect her from any possible gossip because that had become the sole reason for telling her quietly and whilst they were alone. He was hoping that she would keep this basic account to herself now, because what was more important than that was creating their own story, a new and special story without any shadows from the past affecting it.

"How soon can we have our Vicky?" Sissie asked, as she stretched out her arms to draw closer to him. Kissing his cheek, she wrapped her arms around him and resting her forehead on his chest, she wept quietly with emotion. Her feelings for him tumbled out, as she realised that her tears were of love and devotion, and a matching passion for unity and strength that was already deepening. They were both growing to understand each other's feelings as each day passed and as they spent more time together. She had spoken to her mother, of their growing fondness for each other and how deeply they understood the depth of their relationship. Mam was cautious and warned her to be sure, that she might be out of her depth. Could this smart, older man be right for her, she asked. Sissie had reassured her, asking her to mention it to her father.

But she understood instinctively, that he was preparing her for their own destiny together. So she was utterly ecstatic and not at all surprised at what he said next.

"Let's be married first!"

He dropped down on one knee, took her hand firmly between the two of his and looked into her sweet face.

"Edith Ellen Horbury. Will you marry me?"

"Yes! Oh yes!" she breathed, closing her eyes momentarily as she savoured that blissful moment when all her dreams had come true.

Chapter 19

Betrothal

Although they knew Sissie had been behaving rather secretively lately, reluctant to reveal her movements, John's request to visit Sissie's house to meet her parents was made through her, and when she asked them if they could be available to meet him on this particular Sunday afternoon, they were suspicious and uncomfortable. What business could the factory manager want with them? They hoped their daughters were not in any trouble or about to lose their jobs. These days there was so much uncertainty in unskilled factory work. People were unemployed, being laid off all the time, all of it due to the shaky national economy.

The girls brought valuable extra income to the household, and it looked as if they would be losing Doris very soon anyway, as she was seriously involved with Herbert. She was spending more and more time with their family and it looked as if she might leave the village altogether, if he was not able to find employment here. They were hard working, simple folk who rarely left their home; working tirelessly at the farm and enjoying the quiet simplicity of their cottage when they had time off. Neither of them were in robust health though and during the winter months Mr. Horbury suffered numerous chest infections and arthritis in his knees and wrists. Working outdoors in all weathers with long hours was now taking its toll on him. If he was too ill to work, they would have no income at all and although Mam would take in washing to help out, and help clean at the farm, it wouldn't be enough to sustain them.

Mr. Bland's impending arrival prompted Annie to make a simple tea loaf and put butter on the table. A big pot of hot tea would be ready, as it always was when visitors were expected.

"If I can't offer a cup o' tea and piece of cake what are we 'ere for?" Mam always said.

On the dot of three o' clock, John arrived. Sissie had waited for him at the gate for some twenty minutes before he was due, and she linked arms with him as he stepped through it, and on to the yard in front of the row of cottages. Not a word was exchanged between them. They both knew the purpose of the visit today and were eager to seek the approval of her father. Both of them were nervous of the situation, but hopefully, after today, they would begin to make real plans.

A quiet confidence in herself was emerging after their shared soul searching after John had shared the details of his past. A new trust and a deeper understanding of each other was developing, as they talked about their love for each other and their hopes and dreams for a future together. She glowed in the knowledge of it, and from time to time when alone she found herself in a sweet daze, bewildered and softly incredulous at the reality of their romance and the attention of this wonderful man who had chosen her to share a life with him.

Awkwardness and formality hung in the air as soon as Sissie opened the door of the tiny cottage. Her father raised himself from a high backed wooden chair in the parlour, with her mother standing to one side of it, as John and Sissie, entered the room. The rest of the family had been warned away from their home this afternoon, since no one was going to know what news the factory manager would be bringing.

The family knew that Sissie was the quiet one. Not one for chattering nonsense, usually loving her own company or else the company of the animals, she never felt any urge to share her own news, local gossip or inner hopes and dreams. Doris always dominated anyway, and wouldn't be challenged on anything she had to say, but then no one had enough time, energy or interest to listen to Doris, and so from an early age she kept her thoughts and opinions to herself. She was happy for it to stay that way too.

"Mr. Bland, pleased to meet you. Welcome to our little house. It's not much but it's a happy one. I'd like to get to the point and ask you what brings you here. I hope it isn't bad news," greeted her father in clipped tones. He was wary of this rather handsome if mature gentleman whose overcoat and shoes were of quality and indicated without too much showiness, that he was a man of means, much greater than their own.

"Mr. and Mrs. Horbury, thank you for allowing me to come and see you. I know how precious Sunday afternoons must be for you and the family, but I'm visiting you with a very specific and sincere purpose"

Mrs. Horbury indicated for him to sit down and offered to make some tea, nodding to Sissie to follow her into the kitchen.

This, in her eyes seemed to look like men's talk, and therefore easier for her husband to handle without her being there.

The women removed themselves easily and discreetly to go and mash the tea and cut the simple cake.

"Do you know what all this is about our Sis?" enquired Mam abruptly.

"Well, yes I do Mam. John has come round to ask Dad for my hand in marriage."

"What the divil are you talking about? You 'ardly know 'im. 'E's your Boss. You're not good enough for 'im. We're not good enough for 'im neither. What would 'e be wanting to marry into this family for? How can 'e turn up 'ere just like that wanting to marry you of all people?"

Mam was perplexed, embarrassed and confused. This was a shock to her, and she knew that people would talk. They would regard it as a scandal and she had always said to keep your head down, do an honest day's work and the Lord would provide. But this….

"Mam, Mam, stop, please stop. This man is the man I have been seeing for a few weeks now. I have been wanting to tell you, but it's difficult to explain when I'm just a factory girl and he's the factory manager. We have been so careful that people don't see us, because they would say cruel things and we could not bear that. He is kind to me and tells me how much he loves me and I love him very much. I was very shy at first but he makes me feel useful and valuable if you can understand that. We have been out walking and we have taken tea together in town. In fact, we have been meeting each other quite regularly. I just want to tell you how much we just talk and laugh and share our dreams for sharing a future together."

Mam perched on the kitchen chair shaking her head in disbelief and then looking at Sissie squarely in the face she said, "Well lass, you're a dark horse I'll give you that. And I've never 'eard you talk so much in one go neither!"

"Oh Mam, I've wanted to say summat, but it was too soon and I was scared of what you would say," she gasped out, adding, "He has had a very interesting life and I just know in my heart that he will make me very happy. He is so clever, and he knows so much about nature, just like me, and he loves gardening and caring for animals as I do. He comes from a farming family too just like us. Can you believe it?" On and on she continued, "Oh Mam, I think he's wonderful. I know we can be so happy and that he will give me a good life. When you get to know him you will like him too. Please give us your blessing and let me marry him"

"Eeh lass, I'm thinking he's too good for simple folk like us. But a blessing? That'll be up to yer father," Mam sighed, unable to offer anything else that would indicate her own feelings on the matter. In fact, her real fear was for Sissie and how she would cope with the gossip and the possible scandal that would follow them, when folk learned of their connection, especially if they stayed here in these parts.

As the blackened and battered copper kettle began to whistle lazily, the two men entered the kitchen, and both women jumped up in expectation of favourable news.

"Well, our Annie," said Mr. H with a smile.

"John 'ere and I have had a little discussion. It seems he would like to marry our daughter and he came 'ere today to ask for our blessing."

Annie clapped her hands to her weathered cheeks, firstly, because he hardly ever called her by her Christian name. It was always 'Mam', and secondly, to hide the emotions that churned through her. She was in shock from what Sissie had told her. Finally, she was humbled by the fact that her daughter would indeed be marrying someone with social status far above their own.

"And what have you said, William?" she answered.

"Well, I 'ave given him my blessing and we 'ave shaken hands on the matter. Now he wants to propose a date for the wedding and make plans to find a home for themselves."

"Oh Mr. Bland, what happy and such unexpected news for us all to celebrate," said Mam through a curtain of tears. She tried to hide a choke, so she put one hand to her throat whilst at the same time offering her right hand to shake his warmly.

John was touched by their humility and simplicity that he would now be embracing as part of Sissie's family. It was obvious where she got her own humility and modesty from. He was relieved that the formalities had been easy and now, after sharing some refreshment with them, exchanging some details of their respective lifestyles and generally getting to know each other, he and his soon- to-be wife could make their plans for the future.

Sissie was as quiet and as contained as ever. She was content just to listen to the plain deferential tones of her parents as they asked John about himself. She wondered if he would he tell them about his first marriage and about his tiny daughter who would be nearly four years old, that he had asked her to be a mother to? Surely there would be an opportunity today?

She need not have worried. John had already told William his situation, before he had even asked for his permission to marry. John's honesty and no nonsense approach ensured that this would be a straightforward statement of fact, leaving no unanswered questions. There would be no need for further explanations either. He didn't want to make things complicated, so it was best to lay all the facts out at the beginning then there would be no secrets and no misunderstandings. Establishing themselves through their hard work, devotion and commitment to each other would be the living proof that they were well suited.

The tea pot had been refilled and was now empty, and the last slices of tea loaf remained on the plate when John stretched his arms out, palms down on top of the table and said, "That was a fine afternoon in your home Mr. and Mrs. Horbury and you have made Sissie and me very happy by giving us your blessing. Now, if you don't mind, we would like to take a short stroll before I go home, if you will permit us." Together, her parents nodded in approval, and as everyone rose from the table and took their leave formally, the betrothed couple stepped out onto the yard.

Chapter 20

Emma

"Well, I don't believe it!" Emma slammed the finely written letter down on the table. "John has asked this girl to marry him, and can you believe that she has accepted? So he is bringing her over here at the weekend to introduce her to us."

Her mother sat in her rocking chair, a soft home-spun woollen shawl over her legs. Her knees were painful these days, and her eyesight was fading with the cataracts that were now becoming a handicap for her fine needlework. She had always been rather pleased with her skills in crewel work, which so proudly distinguished family tablecloths and monogrammes on other linens.

Today however, she said nothing, typically, as she had become older. Emma could be so outspoken at times and there was no arguing with her.

Emma was disappointed in her brother, who in her opinion, had stooped so low in his choice of a second wife. How was it possible that he could be attracted to a factory worker who was fifteen years younger than himself? What was he thinking? She concluded that his mind must be deranged as a result of the traumas of battle and the horrors of witnessing the loss of lives during the war years. To be followed by the tragic and sudden loss of a first love who had become his wife had been incomprehensible. She had read about similar bizarre life decisions that war time heroes had made on their return; the consequences often blamed on the effects of shell shock and its legacy of mental infirmity.

In church the following Sunday, the one before the visit, she knelt on the cold stone flooring of the church, clasping her hands firmly together, grimacing as she shut her eyes tightly until they prickled. Then in passionate prayer, she appealed for guidance in how she might deal with the situation. She knew she needed to find fortitude and diplomacy from within, to enable her to accept the situation, otherwise she would be rejected by her brother, who was so dear to her. Without doubt, the rest of the family would just murmur their support, not revealing their feelings and with neither involvement nor judgement towards the betrothed couple. If they did have a point of view they would keep it to themselves. John was respected and admired by them all, with his kindness and honesty and his glowing achievements that he had always played down so modestly.

She herself was a kind and dutiful daughter who, because she had never married, still lived at home and now offered vital care and support for her mother and father, both of whom were getting older and weaker in health these days. She felt it was necessary for her to supplement their payments for the services of a lady's maid, housekeeper and general jobs man, so that they could live in comfort and with dignity. However, being well educated and independently minded, she could be forthright and opinionated. Speaking her mind from an early age had been admired by the family and had been encouraged in her teacher training. She found safety and comfort in her stoic Christian values but she was unfulfilled and unsettled with her life and was aware of time passing her by.

She began her teaching in the local Church of England primary school and within a couple of years she had been promoted to Headmistress. From a local established God-fearing family, the governing body saw her as a safe pair of hands for their rural school. The daily demand on her provided challenge and an outlet for her energy and intellect, and she enjoyed the children and liked working with her colleagues. She was well known and respected in the town and she thrived on that.

Young women who became teachers during the war and who received government training afterwards, were most likely to be spinsters, since they were not allowed to work by law once they were married. Usually these women were committed to their vocation and Emma was a typical example. She regretted that she had never found the right man when she was younger.

Well, perhaps there might have been one, but they had lost touch during the war and opportunities to meet anyone else just hadn't come along.

When she wasn't meeting the needs of her father and mother, she would enjoy sitting with them with her drawn thread linen work and perhaps a little embroidery. But her favourite way of passing the time was to ramble across the moorland, spending hours alone and free in the fresh air, noticing birdlife, plants and wildflowers. Often it encouraged her to draw, paint and pen some simple poetry during the evening.

Nothing was flowering at this time of year, but she still enjoyed the wildness, and the biting wind and misty sleet that stung her cheeks as she strode across dormant rush and grasses, noticing the last of the frost bitten flowers of the heathers.

With kestrels squealing overhead and the squawk of pheasants whom she often disturbed in the heather, she lost herself in dreams and schemes for the future.

It was no surprise then that her reaction to John's most recent announcement caused her such consternation. She was disturbed by the news that he was planning to marry this girl from a working class family. Farm labourers she supposed - simple folk without money or means. How had this girl trapped him? She was suspicious but worried for her brother's decision here. Well, they would meet her very soon, as the letter had indicated and they could make a judgement then. She needed to get Anne home for the impending visit, then they could meet her. Sissie, she was called! What sort of name was that?

She thought it was important to introduce this woman to a family of good stock! The biggest issue here though, was the question of the upbringing of this small child of John's. How would such a young woman, no more than a child herself, deal with a four-year-old when she had no experience of life herself, never mind raising someone else's? How could John be satisfied that his daughter would receive the correct guidance and an appropriate upbringing that matched his own and his family's expectations, if this new wife was involved? They would surely be having children of their own and how would that affect the little girl?

And through all this questioning, her thoughts began to shape her opinions and judgements. Of one thing she was sure, she wanted to become more involved in this new situation herself. And from the very beginning.

They didn't know precisely where Anne might be at that time. She had completed her agriculture training and was specialising in animal husbandry which took her round different farms and homesteads to observe and gain experience of current breeding methods and aftercare of the animals. When Emma returned however, there was a postcard from Anne. It was one of those posed, studio photographs that formed a postcard upon which one could write a short message, stick a stamp on and send to loved ones. She was in Preston at a duck farm.

"Oh, Anne! Whatever will you get up to next?" smiled Emma to herself, reaching for pen and paper as she sat down at the small lady's bureau in the hall. Quickly, without even removing her coat and hat, in her finely formed handwriting she composed a short note, placing it in a small matching envelope.

> *Dear Anne,*
>
> *John is visiting us next week on 10th until 13th February.*
>
> *Please try to take a train to come and meet him and his new lady friend at the farm. I want everyone to be here.*
>
> *Your ever loving sister Emma*

She addressed the envelope with the duck farm address. She knew Peter Burrows, as she and Anne had met him at the county show last year, so she was familiar with the place where her sister would be staying. The hinges of the parlour door whined as she pushed it open, "Mother, I am just going to the village to post a letter to Anne. I won't be long," she called out softly, as she reminded herself to get the hinges oiled.

"Yes, alright my dear," replied Mother, who had been roused from her afternoon nap. She closed her eyes again, returning to her snooze, and Emma shut the door quietly. Twenty minutes later her letter was in the post box on the corner of the village main street, to be collected at 9.30am for delivery the next day.

Chapter 21

Sissie meets the Blands

"Just be yourself my dearest, " John said in reassuring tones. She nodded to acknowledge him. "These are country folk like yourself, who have been working all their lives. We all share the same goals in life you know - to be successful in everything we do and not to be afraid of hard work. You will soon become part of this family when we are married, and we will work just the same when we are together. It is important that we all understand each other and that we arrange the time for them to show their approval of you - and they will - so we must give them this opportunity."

Sissie was very nervous and gripped John's arm tightly as they stepped off the train, looking for a farm truck that might be the one that Willie, John's brother, would be driving to take them to the farm.

She had chosen her clothes carefully, wearing a grey pleated skirt and a long sleeved cream embroidered blouse that Norma had lent her. She had tucked it in neatly under a knitted cardigan and over the top she wore the wool coat that she and Doris shared and wore for special occasions. She had had her hair done to look her best, and she had found a pretty burgundy coloured cloche to complete the ensemble. She had travelled in silence most of the way, taking care to sit straight and thereby avoid creasing her outfit. She watched the industrial townscape disappear as they travelled further north, where fields and woodland became more rugged, and the moors of the Pennines came in to view.

After John's proposal, a strange and unfamiliar time was emerging, and she was not entirely comfortable with the enormous and rapid changes that were taking place. She had spent several hours on her own, working out what her future might hold. Her parents had been sworn to secrecy and she had not confided in a single soul yet. She did not want folk gossiping and drawing the wrong conclusions about this new relationship. She wasn't ready yet to face the torrent of questions that inevitably would come her way when people learned of their plans. She had listened and taken heed of John's advice and experience. He was such a practical and honest man, and she utterly trusted him and had pledged her loyalty and faithfulness to him. If this was the next course of action, then she would follow.

"There he is!" John called out, with a salutary wave towards his brother. They had stepped out of the station building into the late afternoon light, grateful that it had been a dry day for this time of year. It made the first meeting with Willie a pleasant one.

"Hello there, young man! I'm over here!" Willie called out. "My word, you're on time. I've only just arrived!"

"Willie it's so good to see you! Before we do anything else I would like to introduce you to my Sissie."

Willie extended his hand towards her, and as she returned the gesture, he held it firmly and drew her a bit nearer in an awkward but warm embrace.

"Nay lass, you're going to be part of this family now, no need for such formalities eh?"

Well, that's broken the ice as they say, thought John, and he felt a brief delight and relief that things had begun well.

Sissie recovered her blushes after this unexpected amicable welcome, and Willie turned and briskly eased her into the truck saying,

"Let's get back for some tea and scones and meet the others."

She travelled on the back seat of the truck, quietly taking in the detail of the countryside and how unbelievably beautiful it appeared in its ruggedness; its bareness revealing the contours of the land on this February afternoon. The brothers exchanged news about the family and local people whom Willie knew well but whom John had forgotten, but was soon reminded of them from past times when they were all growing up.

"You remember Beattie who was Jimmy and Mary Carter's girl? She used to work in the dairy? Well, she's just had her fifth one. She married some chap from Penrith - railway driver. She's friends with my Magwen who likes a good gossip with all the kids around."

"No, I remember the name but can't place her. Five children eh? That's hard work - expensive too - plenty of train driving for him then, poor soul!" replied John amicably.

"And how is Magwen? Are you and she happy?" John enquired, by way of inviting news of a baby coming which, after three years of married life was still not evident.

"Oh, she's fine. Both of us are content with our dogs and cats. We are busy making a living," Willie answered lightly, clearly not intending to show any sadness that they were still childless, even to his older brother.

They travelled for a while without talking, allowing the loud engine noise of the truck to fill the silence. John peered over his shoulder at Sissie sitting in the back seat with her hands folded in front of her. She smiled at him. She looked worried, naturally feeling apprehensive at the prospect of meeting the parents and the sisters. He winked at her warmly to reassure her, and as an attempt to put her at ease.

"Not long now, my dear," he said. "There's not a lot to see at this time of year. Everywhere is rather bare and grey, but come the spring it is a beautiful place. Everything greens up and watching lambs frolicking is a pretty sight. We are a bit early for lambs at the moment though aren't we Willie? Are they all down at the barns ready for birthing?"

"Aye, the first ones will come next week I reckon," replied Willie. "We're keeping an eye on 'em." She listened and nodded in her own quiet way. She wasn't one for chatter until she felt comfortable. Only John knew how much she could talk and exchange her thoughts and observations, when they were on their own. It was a rather special and secret closeness that they shared and it had been like that since they first met.

Suddenly they turned onto the track towards the farm house. A large wooden sign beside the gate said Whitemoor Farm and confirmed that they had arrived. Sissie began to feel nauseous and her mouth was dry. She nervously adjusted her hair that had flicked up around her hat and then she pulled on her leather gloves that John had given her for Christmas, to try to steady her hands.

The truck pulled to a halt outside the front door and as they dismounted, the door opened, and old John Bland was standing on the threshold waiting to greet her.

"Welcome to Whitemoor," he said with a smile, as he stepped forward to shake her hand. "So this is Miss Horbury? Come in my dear. I hope you had an enjoyable journey."

"Yes, thank you," she replied politely, returning the hand shake, looking at him directly and noticing that he had a slight stoop and was leaning on a walking stick. He was a man of around the same age and stage in life as her own father, struggling with joints and tired muscles she imagined, after a lifetime of hard, physical work, but mentally sound and coherent and, more importantly, with a friendly manner.

As John was shaking his father's hand, squeezing the old man's forearm tenderly with the other hand, Willie guided her indoors and through the hall to the parlour. The flames rising from the heat of stout logs in the grate offered a welcome warmth, which calmed her. Emma, standing up with outstretched arms, stepped forward. Sissie was surprised at how small she was, almost bird-like with her nut brown hair tied in a neat bun at the nape of her neck. She was small, both in height and build and was dressed plainly.

Emma had decided to be open and honest from the first meeting with this young woman despite her doubts that they would have little in common.

"I'm Emma. Good journey? Would you like tea?"

It all tumbled out in false cordiality, as she looked past Sissie towards John for a sign that he was going to conduct the introductions instead of leaving it to her. He did not hesitate, and moving to the centre of the room, he kissed her lightly on one cheek and then presented himself to his mother, also named Emma, sitting in her fireside chair.

"Mother, you look really well!" he said smiling, "Let me introduce Sissie to you. We are here so that we can all get to know each other better and then I can tell you what our plans are for the future."

"Sissie?" responded Mother. "And with what name were you baptised child?"

"I was named Edith Ellen, but me older sister called me Sissie when she was but a wee lass 'cos she could no' say it properly," Sissie mumbled, slipping into her broadest Yorkshire, intimidated and feeling self-conscious by the sharp enquiry.

"Well, that is a fine name and one that I personally would prefer," replied the older woman, wincing at the broadness of the accent that came from the mouth of her son's new wife to be.

At that moment, Biddie, their now ageing governess from their childhood appeared and suddenly there was animated chatter and exchange of news filling the room. Sissie was bemused by the noisy chatter, but it made her feel less like a stranger since this was more like the kind of atmosphere she was used to. They were guided to the table to take late afternoon tea.

The white linen cloth bearing the monogram of the Bland family in each corner, was extravagantly laid with ham sandwiches, cheese scones, homemade bread and jam, Dundee Cake and Victoria Sponge. Sissie noticed that every piece of blue willow patterned china matched. That was something she had never seen before. Like the tablecloth, the silver cutlery bore the same monogram. It was that of the Bland family. She sat down and accepted the offer of tea, then carefully watched how each person began to eat and drink before attempting anything herself. John had briefed her on table manners and she had learned quickly. He had told her, without sparing detail, that his mother and sisters judged manners and people's behaviour unreasonably highly. I know that society is changing, he explained to her, but his family members were stuck in old ways that made them appear snobbish, formal and quite unfriendly.

He himself would not tolerate it. A book shouldn't be judged by its cover, and equally, he added with a rueful smile, no one should be judged by the way they held a knife and fork.

As the tea was poured out by Emma who was in charge as usual, the parlour door opened wide and in walked a small and dainty young woman, beaming broadly, her blue eyes twinkling.

"I'm here," she called out playfully. "You started without me, you greedy lot!"

"Anne!! You're here!! I didn't expect you," exclaimed John, as he jumped up and embraced his sister. Now things would liven up! Anne was the adventurous, relaxed and informal one, the type that he was sure Emma would like to be. She always filled the room with her stories of characters she had met during her training, and places she had been during her varied farming experiences. You counted on Anne being around to keep a buoyant and lively atmosphere on Sundays and celebration days and, what luck, now she was here!

She walked straight across to Sissie, who was sitting formally at the table but had twisted round to look in the direction of this voice that had suddenly filled the room. Anne placed her hands on Sissie's shoulders and said,

"So…. at last we meet you Sissie! Welcome to our family! They're all a bit stiff and starchy but you'll get to know them soon enough. Don't get upset by them - it's all bluster! Anyway, I hope we can all make you very happy."

Then she turned to John saying, "And John, do you really think I would I have missed this visit you were both making?"

She drew out a chair and sat down. "Tea and cake, and lots of it please," she chuckled at Emma who was still moving around stiffly.

In fact, one never knew when Anne would be here or away from home. She was a free spirit, loved life and unlike Emma, she just accepted everyone for their individuality, quirks and smirks and all.

Conversation was a little stilted throughout the meal and mainly existed between family members, so it was easy for Sissie to listen and smile and quietly observe each person carefully.

Magwen sat opposite her. She had sidled into the room just as Anne was taking everyone's attention, and she tapped Sissie lightly on the shoulder to introduce herself.

"Hello, you must be Sissie. I'm Magwen, Willie's wife. You look worried! Don't be! They're not as fierce as they seem so don't be nervous. I was just the same as you when Willie introduced me for the first time. But when they get to know you they are really fine."

Sissie was grateful for the simplicity and sincerity coming from this young woman, and it helped to have a friendly open face to look at across the table. As second helpings of cake were offered and refills of tea were poured, Emma tapped her teaspoon on her teacup to demand attention saying, "Quiet everyone, I believe Father would like to ask John an important question."

There was a murmur from the others and the old man stood up gripping the edge of the table to steady himself.

"Thank you Emma. Now what I want to say first of all, is welcome to the Bland family, Sissie. You must be a fine and honourable young woman for John to have chosen you, and be assured that all of us will be behind you both in the future. I do mean that. Your happiness is very important, and if you make each other as content as his mother and I have been over these past forty odd years, you will have chosen well. Now there's only one question to be asked, and if I'm not mistaken I think everyone around this table will be waiting for the answer. John, my son, when are you and Sissie to be married?"

John stood up, cleared his throat and looking down at her sitting beside him he placed his hand lightly on her shoulder.

"We have waited for this moment because we wanted to be sure that everyone in each family would give us their blessing. Thank you Father, for being so welcoming and openhearted.

We have discussed the future together as I'm sure you will have expected, and we agree that it will be important to move away from the Barnsley area. We do not want to present ourselves as the subject of gossip and judgement, given our unusual circumstances."

He paused to clear his throat again and to shift his eyes from his father to those of Sissie, to gain some hint of her feelings at this moment. She knew he was feeling awkward, so she looked down at her now empty plate, nodding in agreement as he spoke. He need not have doubted her composure and quiet support of his words, and so he continued.

"We would like to set a date in May to be married at Darton All Saints Church. I have attended several services since living over there and have made my acquaintance with the vicar. I shall be making some urgent plans to find work and a home for us and for Vicky, so that we can move in together as a family as soon as we are married."

Anne clapped her hands excitedly. Dear John had found happiness again and that was all that mattered to her.

"Congratulations to you both. No, really I do mean this," she said catching the expression of doubt and disapproval crossing Emma's face.

"You are going to have a wonderful life together I know it. And Vicky is a lucky little girl to have you to raise her."

Emma was obliged to murmur her approval but stayed quiet, feeling that Anne had said enough for them all.

"Thank you Anne. We do appreciate that. There are lots of things that are different between us but we want to work together to succeed, don't we my dear?" John replied and then turning to Sissie, he gazed at her fondly and lightly touched her shoulder.

"Thank you to everyone, from the bottom of my heart for making me feel welcome today," said Sissie in a soft voice, speaking as correctly as she could, and blushing slightly as everyone's eyes were drawn in her direction.

It was a fitting closure to the gathering and people began to rise from their chairs. Mother rose from hers saying, "Well Sissie, I hope you know what you are taking on. John is ambitious and strong - willed but he has a lot of love to give and if you can return it you will make him a very happy man. If my children are happy….. well let's say, that makes me happy too."

Willie opened the door for her, and she left the room so that the others could say their good byes for now, indicating that they would see each other in the morning. As the door closed behind the old lady, Anne sank into her mother's chair and kicked off her shoes.

"I'm having five minutes before I do anything else. It's been a long day."

Emma moved away from her place at the table, towards Sissie saying in her usual brusque manner, "Come on. I can show you where you are going to sleep tonight. Bring your overnight bag with you."

Sissie looked up at John, unsure of a fitting way to respond. She felt so out of place within these unfamiliar surroundings with people she did not know and with whom she felt she had been granted no time to connect. She just didn't know how best to behave. She wished she could run back home now! However, he smiled gently at her and nodded reassuringly, saying, "Off you go, my dearest. Emma will look after you and I will see you in the morning."

Then they were gone from the room. He could hear Emma talking pleasantly as they walked through the draughty hall up to the wide, polished oak staircase and he sighed, thinking that at least all the formalities were out of the way. Now, they could get on with planning and preparing for their future life together, no matter what the rest of the family thought about the union and of the woman he had chosen to marry.

*　　*　　*

The table had been cleared and the dark red chenille table cover thrown over it, to protect its ancient oak surface until it was laid for the next meal. Biddie and Anne had taken everything to the kitchen, where the house maid would be doing the washing up whilst they placed covers over left over cake, to be stored in the coolness of the cellar. Each had a job and the routine never faltered day after day, year after year. Mother took herself upstairs to bed, since she needed more sleep these days than in her younger days.

John and his father sat on opposite sides of the fireplace so that they could catch up on their own news, or perhaps to discuss recent national news. And there were always local matters that had surfaced since they had last talked. William and Magwen had left as soon as everyone had said their thanks, to return to their own cottage because by now, light had already fallen.

John took out his pipe and tobacco, and in no particular hurry to smoke it, he leaned forward to ask his father if he minded him lighting up.

"You know I'm not keen son, but you go ahead anyway. We don't see you often enough for it to bother me."

John smiled. His father was a strong man with principles to match, but his love and devotion to his children was unshakeable and he was becoming less of the disciplinarian and more of a sentimental soul in his old age. Certain habits that his children had slipped into he no longer questioned nor showed his disapproval these days.

"You're going soft," his wife remarked, but she did so with a smile and a certain understanding.

In fact, he was very proud of them all for what they had achieved, each in their own different ways. Each one had found their own purpose in life, not without experiencing setbacks along the way, but they had faced the challenges with their own determination and good sense. He liked to believe that he and his wife had been good parents and had done their best for their children, recognising and supporting their individual strengths, natural abilities and always encouraging them to follow their aspirations and ambitions.

Sending two sons to war had been a sorrowful and harrowing time, as it had been for every family left behind during those years. Mother had worked tirelessly for the war effort at home to fill the emptiness of their days, bereft of half of the family. Those days had gone now, and it wasn't in the Bland character to dwell on the past, nor of misfortune and disappointment they may have encountered. They firmly believed in their duty to carry on; to reach out through their prayers, for guidance and strength and to look forward to better times not back on things that were in the past and could not now be changed. This they had steadfastly instilled in their children as they were growing up. Father realised that John wanted to put his sad days in Brussels as well as the wartime experiences behind him, and he admired his resilience, but at the same time he was still concerned that John should not rush things in order to find peace, happiness and fulfilment. Perhaps this would now be possible as he committed himself to this new woman. She hadn't said much but she seemed pleasant enough and in time she would adapt to the ways of the Bland family, just as sweet Magwen had done a few years before, and she and Willie seemed content enough.

Relieved that permission had been granted, John lit his pipe and drew on it until the tobacco began to glow, exhaling silently into the glowing embers in the fire grate. Without the approval from his father he would be outside in the barn feeling the cold and damp of the February evening air, so he was thankful for the go ahead.

"You and Mother seem well," he began, hoping this would prompt some family updates.

"We are as well as anyone of our age would hope to be," replied his father plainly,

"This damp and cold weather is unkind to older folk like us but it's to be expected. We're just looking forward to spring and some lighter nights at least. But let's talk about you and your new soon to be wife, young man - or not so young eh? Have you thought about this difference in your ages that Emma has described?"

"I don't think age will be an obstacle for us, Father. I am going to marry a mature, sensible and practical woman. She has all the qualities that I am looking for in a wife and mother to my child. We are very fond of each other, and we are aiming for the same things in life so that we can build a secure and prosperous future together. I have seen her good work in the factory and I have met her own hard working farming family. I know that we can be successful and very happy."

His father gazed into the flames that had flickered upwards as a fresh log took hold, nodding his head thoughtfully saying, "Only you can make these decisions, son. Your mother and I know this and we know you will make the best decisions for yourself, as you always have done. You don't need to take notice of what Emma says. She has her way of seeing the world and wants everyone else to see it the same way. You must go your own way, and go with wisdom and your own experience. Your mother and I trust your judgement, son. On that you can rely."

"Thank you for saying that that, Father. I'll always remember those words as well. Thank you very much," he said gratefully, as he puffed at the pipe feeling relieved and relaxed.

The two men sat in comfortable silence, each digesting this short but meaningful exchange that had just taken place.

These people were doers, not fanciful dreamers who wasted time talking about what they were going to do next. They just did it!

Unusually, the old man continued to ask questions, something mother normally did.

"So you mentioned finding work away from Barnsley. Where would you consider settling down John, and what would you be looking for?" he enquired, "Will you stay in the textile industry?"

"I hope to move us out of Barnsley towards Doncaster, as there are some exciting developments up there in artificial silk production and with my experience, I could offer some expertise if there are opportunities available at management level. There are many new houses being built too. The town is growing and would offer some possibilities," John replied hesitantly.

Nothing had been confirmed yet and he was reluctant to give away too much information until he was sure of his plans.

"Well your mother will be disappointed that you will still be a long way from us, but you have your own life to build and you must do what you think is best for the future," the older man replied matter of factly.

"We won't be far away. The train and bus systems are improving fast so we will always be within easy reach. Don't worry on that front," John reassured him. He realised that future visits may be infrequent, given that they were becoming frail, therefore less likely to travel, and he would have full time commitments to his new family and to his work.

The old man pulled out his dented silver pocket watch from his waistcoat and, glancing at the time, he announced his decision to turn in for the night. Placing each hand on the arms of the chair, he raised himself up and reached for his walking stick.

"Time for me to call it a day, son. Things will be what they will be and with God's guidance we will all make the right decisions. It's been grand to see you looking well. Your mother and I are pleased to have met Sissie. We will see you in the morning."

Then reaching out his arm affectionately towards his son, they parted in comfortable silence. The conversation was over. The day was over.

Chapter 22

Sunday visiting

The next morning Sissie was woken by a persistent tapping on the bedroom door. She had shared the room with Emma, and it had taken ages for her to get to sleep that night. There had been very little conversation besides directions for washing and undressing. Emma seemed keen to go straight to sleep. It made Sissie feel uneasy and uncomfortable in Emma's company. She would have welcomed some contact before lights out, but Emma didn't seem to be interested. She was not at all like John with his easy banter and silly jokes that he cracked as he played around with words and phrases. She was more serious, more literal and restrained. She made Sissie feel awkward and self-conscious. There seemed to be little warmth and generosity in this sister.

She had tossed and turned all night listening to Emma's rhythmic breathing, and although her eyes were itching for sleep, her brain raced hither and thither with questions and doubts and fears and foreboding.

Would she fit in? Did they like her? How could she please them? How could she make herself more like them?

Another thing, her broad accent made her feel awkward and self-conscious in their company. It made her feel inferior and inadequate. She missed off her H's and G's at the beginning and end of words. She used local Yorkshire talk instead of the formality of the English style that was spoken. She wanted to learn the appropriate behaviour at the table, hers being very basic she realised. She was also keen to know the ways in which they ran their household, so that she could make John proud of her and be proud of her when they established their own home. It was true, she could cook and clean, and she had learned country ways of running a household thriftily but she didn't feel that this would be enough.

Then there was the big question in her mind, of little Vicky and if she would be good enough to raise this little girl, whom she had not yet met. She had no real experience of bringing a child up in the world. Sunday School teaching could hardly compare! She worried that the child may not like her, or if indeed, she herself would take to the child. She was realistic and sensed that these things did not happen by magic. There would have to be time and space and an understanding between John as the little girl's father, and herself as the stepmother. How she detested the word. It reminded her of all the fairy tales she knew from childhood; Cinderella and Sleeping Beauty - the step mothers were always wicked!

She wanted to encourage John to spend time discussing ways in which they would work together to make this little girl happy. These thoughts continued to revolve around her head until, exhausted she finally fell asleep.

A tap on the bedroom door preceded Emma as she entered the room, to find Sissie perched on the edge of the bed with her palms closed together in a quiet prayer. It was Sunday and her mother had taught them always to recite the Lord's Prayer before beginning the day.

"Oh Sissie, I am so sorry to interrupt," she gasped in surprise but at the same time, of approval at the scene in front of her. She had expected to find Sissie still sleeping, aware that she had experienced a disturbed night.

"I hope you slept well! We have to be ready for church in half an hour. We are all going today, if you would come too."

"Yes of course," Sissie replied, standing up in her cotton night shift, "I'm gettin' dressed now."

"See you downstairs then," and with that, Emma turned around and closed the latch door.

Everyone had assembled at the front door ready to walk together down the footpath, that formed the short cut to church in the village. When Sissie came down the stairs there was John's smiling face waiting to greet her and as she reached the bottom step he held out his hand to guide her and gave her an affectionate kiss on the cheek wishing her good morning and enquiring after her night's sleep.

"I slept fine, thanking you," she replied, feeling uncomfortable that everyone had turned towards them to witness the greeting, and then relieved that someone had opened the front door so that everyone could file out.

They dropped behind a little so that they could talk.

"I'd rather you didn't mention that you are Methodist this time, Sissie. They'll show their disapproval and I don't want anything to spoil the day," he began.

"But John, that's dishonest! I AM a Methodist. You know we do things different in t' chapel. They ought to know."

He squeezed her arm gently, "I know, I know, but just do this for me…. please ….there's a good girl. Just for today. Now let's not talk any more about it," he said, ending the conversation.

She walked quietly alongside him, into church and down the aisle to the pew designated for the Bland family worship. He stepped back to allow her to go in first to kneel and pray. She was hurt and rather bewildered. She believed that he was ashamed of her and that's why he wanted to hide her Methodist ways from the family. Why would he need to do that? It was so snobbish. What did he think they would do? Was he himself afraid of disapproval too? She bowed her head in silence.

The service proceeded and the small congregation seemed fully engaged. As the monotonous and uninspiring sermon was finished, she blinked back a tear or two, having spent the time dwelling on John's warning words. How she wished she wasn't there! She didn't know any of the hymns being sung today. She knew that people would hear that she was not singing. The hymns they sang were so different from those she knew in chapel; those that she loved singing so much that she knew the words and the music off by heart. Something else that was even more disturbing for her today, was the unfamiliarity of the Anglican order service and she felt bewildered and embarrassed that she could not understand the significance of each of the prayers nor the singing of psalms. She was lost in this ritual, which in contrast was so familiar to the rest of the congregation. Feeling relief that she could at least recite the Lord's Prayer however, but it came too late because by that stage of the service, people had noticed that she had not joined in.

They came out into the chilly February morning air and everyone exchanged greetings with neighbours and acquaintances from the village and other local farmers and their families. Then they walked slowly back to the house for Sunday lunch. Sissie was subdued, trying to put aside the recollection of her clumsy ignorance in church, but the family were light hearted, in good spirits and mercifully showed no memory of her difficulty.

No one mentioned the service around the dinner table. After Father Bland said grace, they devoured roast beef and Yorkshire puddings with gravy, china tureens of steaming green vegetables and Anne's famous golden, crisp roast potatoes. Emma excelled herself with her baked treacle sponge and custard and afterwards, everyone leaned back in their chairs with satisfaction that another Sunday was over, apart from a quiet nap in front of the fire or a brisk walk across the fell for those who still had some energy.

"Anyone want to walk with me?" asked Emma.

"Me," responded Anne, "But after we've cleared away."

"Well, of course! That's what I mean," retorted Emma.

John looked at Sissie. "Shall we join them, dear?" he enquired gently. He had not noticed how quiet and reserved she had seemed since he had spoken to her on the way into church. He didn't realise that he could be the cause of any uneasiness she might be feeling. Sissie on the other hand wanted him to know how much he had hurt her feelings, nay, he had insulted her. It wasn't right that he could say such a thing and expect her to accept and not react. She stayed quiet and shrugged her shoulders. "That's up to you," she said under her breath.

The response puzzled him and he felt uncomfortable. Oh dear, perhaps he had said something to hurt her and that had made her vexed. Feeling a twinge of remorse and concern he turned to the others, "I want to show Sissie more of the farm if you don't mind. I would like us to have some afternoon time to ourselves, but thank you for asking."

As the table was cleared and everyone drifted in different directions, he carefully pulled her chair away from the table saying, "Come on. Put your coat back on and let's get some fresh air." Obediently, she followed him out of the dining room into the back passageway out to the back door. John suggested she borrow Anne's wellington boots. It was wet and filthy in the farmyard today and he thought they would be a more practical alternative. So she pulled them on, buttoned her coat and tied a headscarf round her curls. He looked at her squarely and smiled tenderly, "Let's find some time to ourselves my little darling. Don't be cross with me!"

She dug her hands deep into her coat pockets and hunched her shoulders against the chill of the misty afternoon air, so that she did not have to rely on him for safety or comfort, nor any gesture of affection. So far today she had felt an overwhelming sense of being out of place and unable to get involved in conversation with the rest of the family at the table. Even Magwen, Willie's wife could not make her smile when she whispered a little joke about the mustard. She was uncomfortable and cross with him, and also with herself for not dealing with things.

She always tended to fall silent when faced with any situation she felt unable to cope with, mainly when she and Doris argued as sisters do and then Doris lashed out with her spiteful tongue. Maybe she was making too much of John's insensitive request to hide the fact that she was a Methodist. What did it matter to anyone else? However, she couldn't ignore her feelings and in her own mind she knew it felt wrong to have any secrets from the family into which she would be marrying.

She knew it would be Emma who would voice her opposition and disapproval when she got her brother on his own. Emma would be there to challenge his beliefs and feelings. She might suggest that she herself wasn't good enough for him.

She realised she had only just met Emma, but she had already identified a judgemental attitude in this woman and a 'holier than thou' attitude. To be honest, she did not mind admitting, it rather scared her.

He let her go a pace or two ahead, concentrating on lighting up his pipe. He always felt some sense of purpose and resolve when the pipe was lit. It gave him an opportunity to reflect, and to focus on the situation in hand. It was as if the world continued to spin around, whilst he could step back and get a measure of the things that were happening in that moment. He guessed that all this business this morning was just a misunderstanding and it would blow over. If this was the reason Sissie was disturbed and quiet, the best policy was to admit he was wrong, apologise and make up.

"Now then, now then my dearest. Please, do calm down. Let me hold your hand and tell you that you are my best girl and I am so very proud of you. My family are not the easiest, and I know who in particular can be a difficult one to cope with."

As she did not respond he continued, "I am sorry for my thoughtlessness this morning. I was in the wrong! I had no business preventing you from telling them you are a Methodist. I just didn't think that it was the right time to raise the subject. If I had known that it would hurt you so much, believe me, I would never have said a thing."

She stayed silent as she couldn't think of anything to say, and couldn't find the right words to respond. She slowed her pace, looking down at the farmyard cobbles that had trapped rainwater and farmyard slurry, thinking, "Well, there's muck and filth in this farmyard, same as in mine at 'ome. We're not that different," but she was still listening to his gentle reassuring voice.

She slowed her pace, looking down and took a breath, asking, "Why should it matter? Methodist? Church of England? Who cares that much John, and who do you think is going to judge us? I think you really are ashamed of me aren't you? I'm not good enough for you, am I? I don't think your family approve of me anyway. It's all very well when we are back in Barugh and you're living with my folks. P'raps you need to decide which side of t' fence you want to be on, before we go any further."

"Oh Sissie, Sissie don't say these things. It breaks my heart. It is you, and only you that I want to spend the rest of my life with. I've told you so many times. Believe me, I know just how well we go together and what a successful life we will share when we are married. Forget about the differences in our Sunday rituals. Whatever anyone else thinks about that is none of their business. That is between you and me."

"I want happiness too, John and I know in my heart that my happiness is with you, only you, but please let me be myself and make some decisions for us both as well. I think that there is only one God, and he doesn't mind whether we praise him in chapel or church. We both know our Lord's Prayer and we both learned the Catechism. We made our promises in different ways and at different times, that's all. Now we are going to be joined together, and I want us to put these differences aside. So I think we should say no more on the matter."

She spoke with as much courage in her voice as she could because she thought now would be the only chance to say these things. She hoped that he would understand her feelings, and after this they could stride forward together without any resentment.

"My goodness! You do have some common sense, Edith Ellen Horbury! I am humbled by what you've just said. More than ever, I am sure that we are a heaven-made match and no one will ever get in our path."

He moved in front of her and drew her shoulders squarely in front of him. They were exactly the same height and they looked into each other's eyes. For a few seconds there was no need for words, just mutual respect and trust in each other. Here lay a shared optimism and fondness for what existed now, with the promise of a future deeper understanding. They knew deep down, that they shared the same aspirations and desires.

She felt she was seeing into his mind and soul, too. She smiled shyly, to quietly confirm that she believed he now understood her.

"I want to be with you forever," she whispered. She didn't really have the right words and she was afraid of sounding foolish. But, it was at this moment that he knew that he wanted to be with her forever, to care for her and to show and to share his hopes and dreams with her.

"I know. And we are going to be fine," he replied softly.

Then the moment was over as they stood in the late afternoon air. They straightened themselves as he said brightly, "Come on, let's go and say goodbye to Willie and Magwen. They'll be going home soon."

Grasping her hand firmly, they strode together in step towards the farmhouse, where the lights were shining through the windows. Their hearts were in harmony and at peace, and they both felt that their little rift had been mended. Now there was so much to look forward to.

*　　*　　*

Every Sunday, after everyone had enjoyed a quiet afternoon nap, there was time for some quiet activity. However, it was largely dependent on the seasons and the weather. At this time of year when the days were shorter, it usually meant some solitary activity such as reading or sewing and mending. Sometimes Emma would play the piano softly to herself in the parlour, or she would jot down a few notes in preparation for her teaching the following week.

Today, Anne was scouring the shelves for jam and other preserves; wiping dust off the lids and checking the dates on the labels. She wanted to take something back with her to the working farm where she was billeted at present, as a contribution to her board. They could all hear her humming softly to herself.

Mother was dozing by the fireside, not feeling any inclination to move her increasingly arthritic knees to check up on what Anne was up to in her kitchen. Such a practical girl, she was sure that her daughter would be organising the cupboards.

Father had strolled out with William and Magwen. There was always something to discuss, as both father and son were committed to their farming heritage. They loved to share their well-matched ideals and aspirations for making a living, and their weekly discussions helped. Small successes and frequent problems that each might be encountering were exchanged. There was always something bothering either or both of them. They worked well together, understanding each other and chatting as they walked every Sunday kept them up to date. There was no doubt that it had bonded them, ever since the cruel war years had been put behind them.

The advice from the older farmer was always listened to, even if not always heeded by his younger son who had his own opinions, but they enjoyed a good argument and neither of them resented the other's hard line on certain matters. However, currently, there had been disturbing news that early signs of foot and mouth disease was on the increase. It concerned them, and so they set out across the farmyard to discuss the ways in which they could prevent it spreading to their flocks. In sheep farming though, where sheep could roam across the fell, it was an impossible task to control effectively. Today they were discussing intently ways in which they could spot the symptoms and diagnose the condition of each animal. Ways to manage disinfecting and then possibly the bleak prospect of destroying the animals to prevent it spreading, were priorities for them today.

John and Sissie opened the kitchen door to pull off their coats and kick off their boots. They rubbed their hands together, feeling some warmth and comfort out of the cold wind that was blowing today. Willie and Magwen followed them from the other direction. Father trailed some distance behind with Snip the sheepdog. As they arrived at the door at the same time, Willie turned to them and said, "Well, we best be on our way for today, so we'll say goodbye. John and Sissie, it's been good to see you both. I'll take you back to the train as soon as you are ready tomorrow. When do you think you'll be over to see us again?" He had enjoyed the short time spent with them and wished he could see his brother more often.

"Not sure Willie. We have lots of things to organise, what with a new job, I hope. And the wedding of course. We want to arrange for Vicky to come over here and move ourselves into a routine."

"Oh my word! You do have a lot on your plate there," exclaimed Magwen. "Let us know if you need any help, you know we would be only too happy."

"Thank you, that's very kind of you and we will," responded Sissie, hoping that by joining in, she might connect with these kind people at least. They seemed much more her type.

They left, and were gone into the twilight and home to their chickens and cats and an early night.

As the goodbyes were finished, John led Sissie by the hand into the parlour where Emma was still sitting at the piano, having called out her goodbyes from where she had been sitting now for the last hour.

"What are you going to play for us Emma? We'd like to hear something," asked John as they approached the piano.

"Oh, I'm just practising one or two chords for some nursery rhymes for the schoolchildren. Those children who were born at the end of the war have had such a mixed experience at home they don't know many little songs. The children I teach are seven years old and we have singing time every day and they love it!" she replied as she spread her fingers ready to play the opening chords to 'Polly Put the Kettle On'. With a lightness in her touch on the ivory keys, the sound brought the old oak piano to life and the flames in the fireside grate danced to the melody, flickering shadows across the wall. In the failing light of the day it brought lightness, tranquility and peace into the room. An air of calmness drifted around them. It created a sense of unity and contentment that was pleasant and reassuring to Sissie and John. It was in contrast to their experience over the last few days. Of that Sissie was certain.

As Emma played the last few notes of the song, she stopped and turning herself towards where they were standing, inclined her head appreciatively in response to their light round of applause.

"Let's sit down Emma and have a catch up shall we?" suggested John.

"Of course. I am sure there are lots of things we should talk about. We haven't had much of a chance this weekend really, and I do have things on my mind so it will be wise to spend a little time together before you go," she replied matter of factly.

They all sat down and once again, Sissie felt self-conscious and uncomfortable in Emma's company. She smoothed her burgundy woollen skirt over her knees and calmly rested her hands over them. John put another coal on the fire and eased himself into the fireside chair, normally occupied by his father.

"I gather you will be leaving us tomorrow morning and back to Barugh. I was wondering how you will manage yourselves, now that both families have been told that you will be marrying. Don't you think that will cause a stir in the community and at the mill? Surely you can't expect to keep going as you have been now."

Always direct, often insensitive to the situation, Emma spared no subtlety in her opening remarks, but she did have a pressing and relevant point.

"You are quite correct Emma and we are sensibly planning to move away as soon as practically possible. It is clear that Sissie will not be able to work in the factory, so she will be leaving. I am confident that I will find a position elsewhere, with a managerial role in line with my training and experience. As soon as we are married, we will move well away from Barugh. It's likely that I will look for work and find a home in Doncaster."

"That sounds promising. So the next thing on my mind is the situation regarding this small daughter of yours. Surely you must realise that she will need some considerable guidance and care in the early days of arriving here. How on earth are you going to manage that?"

She glanced briefly at Sissie as she spoke, conveying her doubt of the ability of the young woman to care for her brother's child. She herself was the blood connection to this little one, was she not? She had the appropriate training and expertise for handling young children. There was definitely a significant role for her here and they would be wise to recognise it.

"Steady on Emma. One step at a time. Sissie and I have already talked about the matter haven't we, Sis?"

He turned to her leaning forward in the hope she might say something.

"And we have some thoughts and plans for providing her with a family with love and affection as soon as we can. Perhaps we might have a child of our own in time."

"Hmm!" Emma raised her eyebrows in disbelief of the naivety of his response, as if to say you think it's as simple as that?

"I have a lot of love to give little Vicky, and I think I can be a good Mammie to her when John and I are settled. We want to make our own home together for her," said Sissie timidly.

John smiled at her reassuringly, but his sister interrupted, "All this romantic talk you've got now, but it won't work like that. Mark my words," Emma was using her characteristically overbearing tone.

"Anyway, let's see how you cope. She can always come here for holidays or weekends when it gets difficult. You do know that, don't you?"

And with that she stood up, tucking the piano stool away, "Well, it's an early start for me tomorrow. So I'm heading to bed. Coming Sissie?"

"I'll follow in a moment, Emma if you don't mind," Sissie replied courteously. She resented the atmosphere that was left in the room and it made her feel uncomfortable. As if Emma would know anything about anything to do with being romantic! All she needed now was to be with John - just for a few minutes so that the gentle closeness between them could be recaptured.

For a moment they looked at each other. Sissie sighed in exasperation. All her instincts were to run away from the tension that Emma always seemed to generate. She couldn't do that though. It was worse than that - she had to go and join this woman and sleep in the same room that night. Then, as if he knew her thoughts, John said quietly, "Let's say nothing until tomorrow, my dear. It's wiser that way. Today is over. Let's begin a new one when we leave here in the morning."

Sissie rose from the winged armchair that she had been directed to earlier, "That sounds like a fine idea, John. Now I must make tracks to bed, as I wouldn't wish to disturb Emma by coming into the bedroom too much later. I'll see you in the morning. What time do you think we will be leaving?" He jumped up immediately in response to her reluctant efforts to leave him, and holding her closely he whispered, "Six o' clock sharp but I know that I will be wishing the night away until I see you then."

"Goodnight then my dearest man," she whispered back. Then she was gone and he heard her tiptoeing up the stairs. Shortly after that, Emma's bedroom door could be heard creaking as she opened it cautiously.

The light in the bedroom was still on.

"I'm awake. You won't be disturbing me," declared Emma from her pillow.

"That's a mercy," thought Sissie because she wasn't sure she could deal with Emma's voice in the dark. She carefully folded her clothes and placed them on the chair at her side of the bed. Then she splashed water over her face and dried herself thoroughly with the rough, pure white linen towel laid out for her.

"So what do you make of us all then, Sissie?" asked Emma propping her head up to speak. "Do you think you will fit in with the family here?"

"You have all made me feel welcome and I am 'appy to be wi' John and among t' people he loves. We're leaving tomorrow but I am sure we'll be back again soon."

"Well, I do hope you will be, because I am keen for John to organise matters for his dear little Vicky without delay. These times may pass slowly for us, but time is racing by in this little girl's world and we need to be getting involved as soon as possible."

"I know and both John and I want to hurry along quickly too, but there are lots of things that we need to sort out."

"Exactly my point! You must realise that I too, have considered the present situation. You have both made things very complicated really. Don't you realise that the best thing is for me to have Vicky? I know far more about children than you do and I would be of a much better practical help than you can be. Where do you think she would live until you are married? Where do you imagine she would go to school? And just how can you make sure she sleeps in a bed of her own each night? If John had not met you, we would be discussing these matters because all we care about is the child."

She emphasised the last word and Sissie did not know how to answer without becoming tearful. She felt like a child herself because of the accusing manner in which Emma had spoken to her. She felt that her best course of action was to say nothing for now. She sank back onto the pillow recalling and repeating some of John's last words downstairs.

"Well I know there's a lot to discuss, Emma. We will all need a fresh mind for the morning, so maybe we should get some sleep now."

"Good night, Sissie." There was no more to say.

"Good night, Emma"

They turned their backs to each other, covering their shoulders with the blankets against the chill of the bedroom air, matching the silence that fell between them.

Chapter 23

Back to Barugh

They were on the bus to Penrith to the train station where the train would take them as far as Barnsley. Willie was busy with lambing and John, understanding what demanding work it was to ensure each ewe came through a successful labour, was insistent that he should stay at the farm and leave them to find their own transport home. John had already arranged that Sissie's brother Bill would pick them up. Bill would probably have received his letter earlier in the day detailing the arrival time. He would be there, being the reliable chap that was so characteristic of him.

"We must be sure that we have talked things through thoroughly, Sissie. By the time we have finished this journey today we will be back in Barugh. We should both be agreed on what our plans will be for the future. We are going to have to deal with people's questions and they'll have an opinion and plenty to say about it. Believe me!"

He held her arm gently as soon as they had settled themselves together on the green Penrith bus. It set off with an engine roar, a cloud of black exhaust and a determination to be on time as it left the farm far behind them.

"We have plenty of quiet time to ourselves whilst we are on the train to agree on things. What do you say?" John added. He wrapped her hand between the two of his own, for warmth and for her to feel his closeness.

He knew that she would be looking for guidance and reassurance from him. She would be relying on him being that much older and with experience and such a sense of direction and purpose.

"I'm a bit scared of what folk are goin' to say, John. There will be gossip, I know it."

"Yes, I've been thinking about this and that it is why I think the best thing now, is for you to give up your job at the mill. I mean - straightaway. Take the time that we still have, to be at home to help out your Mam and Dad. They would be so pleased that you can share some of the land work and dairying. That would suit you for now, wouldn't it?"

"Well, yes of course John but don't forget they do rely on me wages for board and food."

"Don't fret about that lass. I will make sure that they receive a little income. I can afford it. No one needs to know that I can help out like that, so there'll be no jealousies and no harsh talk."

"And will you still live in your little cottage?" she asked, although she wasn't sure if there was any alternative in the short term.

"That I will!" he exclaimed with a smile.

"We will both keep our own matters quiet and discreet in the coming months. Then no one will have anything to talk about. It's not going to be easy for us, but we know that eventually we are going to be very happy - oh so happy! We must keep looking ahead and not down at our feet."

They arrived at the train station and they got off the bus, hastily crossing the road in the driving rain and gusty wind of the morning. They went to the ticket office and once the tickets were paid for, and information given that it was on time, they hurried on to the platform for the ten-minute wait before the train arrived.

"There, that's the first part of the journey done!" exclaimed John as they stepped off the train. But Sissie could only smile at him feebly, expressing her self-doubt and nervousness for what was to happen back home.

"Yes I'm happy about that. I'm so glad to be 'ere with you John. We 'ave a long journey together - and it doesn't end at Barnsley railway station does it?" she sighed.

Things were happening very quickly and she felt almost as if she was trailing behind. It was a relief to be away from the tense atmosphere and the apparent unrealistic expectations the Bland women had of her. It was especially awkward with Emma last night in the bedroom. It had been clear that Emma needed to say that she wanted to be in charge of Vicky's upbringing, and she was quite blunt in the way that she had expressed it. Sissie could think of nothing to say, and certainly not without asking for John's approval. There were questions racing through her mind though. Why didn't Emma trust her with John's daughter? What must she do to gain the woman's confidence?

She was sure there must be some agreement between them in the best interests of what Emma called 'the child.' She felt that any connection and understanding between them was fragile now and likely to continue.

Yes, the distance between this future sister-in-law and herself was vast, and not just in terms of mileage.

She was in earnest to be accepted and to be on friendly and easy terms for John's sake as well as her own. She felt she could never feel any joy and peace in their marriage, if harmony was lacking within and between their families. She was thinking she would have to work on becoming a little bolder as she gained more of John's respect and trust. It would just take time. Perhaps then, Emma would not be so bossy and demanding.

And then privately and quite suddenly, almost in defiance, she thought that her accent had been wrongly interpreted as a lack of intelligence and common sense.

"I may be a mill girl but I 'ave a brain in me 'ead," she muttered crossly. "They'll 'ave to accept me accent because I'll not be changing it for no one - I'll be sure of that!"

"Here she comes!" John announced as the steam engine thundered past them, brakes hissing as it stopped alongside the platform, wheezing noisily. He loved train travel. It always felt like adventure with the noise and frenzied atmosphere, the smell of the coal smoke and the gassy fumes that spat out from the groin of the engine as it pulled into the station.

He broke into a trot with suitcase in one hand and Sissie in the other, looking for an empty First Class carriage. He was directed courteously by a guard who opened the nearest most convenient door and they stepped up.

Sissie was bewildered by the atmosphere. It was so deafening, with people shouting their hellos and goodbyes and then all this crashing noise of frenetic opening and slamming of doors with people scrambling out and bustling in. Finally, the station master blew his whistle to confirm that it was departing. They were on their way! They sank down side by side onto the prickly moquette of their allocated seats, sighing with relief that they had made it. Then as the guard lowered his flag, the creaks and groans of the carriage could be heard as the train began gliding solemnly out into the grey skies of Westmoreland, gathered speed to begin its journey.

"John, what are we doing? We are in First Class," whispered Sissie with some concern in her voice.

"Yes, we are, my dear," he replied quietly. "This may be something you will have to get used to! It's affordable, preferable and necessary when I have to travel distances with my work, when I visit far away family and when I go over to see Vicky. And I am fortunate to have the means to pay for it. So, relax."

This was sufficient for her to begin to realise that this was just the beginning of a life that neither she nor anyone she knew was used to. It appeared that she would have to accept and trust John's ideas, his decisions and his words because he was so much more worldly than she.

For twenty minutes or so they both watched the scenery passing by, as they enjoyed the warm proximity of their bodies wrapped in their overcoats. There was a comfort and a kind of intimacy that they felt only they could feel. Without a single other soul in the carriage, it was perfect for conversation, knowing no one else would be listening.

"Now then, my sweetheart. We have to think about dates and how we are going to work towards a proper life together. It is February and so, firstly, we must ensure that when we return you will work a week's wages, and then as we said earlier, it would be best to leave the mill.

I am going to continue my work there but I must go across to Brussels very soon to collect Vicky and to bring her back here for a little holiday. She has not seen me for a long time and soon she will not even recognise me! Now I am thinking that the best thing is for her to stay up at Whitemoor Farm for a little while. She will be happy there I'm sure. She can go to school with Emma and Mother will make sure she is clothed, fed and comfortable. We can make a visit or two. But all should go well and would suit the situation that we are all in at the moment."

"Does Emma know all this, John?" Sissie turned to look at him, remembering the exchange between Emma and herself in the bedroom. If Emma and John had discussed this, she was unaware. She wondered whether these decisions had already been taken, excluding her.

"Well, yes and no, as we have talked of this just as a 'possibility' until you and I are married. Before the child is much older we really must get her over here to become part of our family."

Sissie felt excluded. She was confused but then part of her felt a sense of relief since she knew that there were going to be so many adjustments to her lifestyle and her expectations for the future. Maybe for now it was best to let John organise things during these early stages of their relationship.

"And talking of marriage, let us think carefully about a date so that we can aim towards our future happiness. I suggest the end of the year. What do you think my dear?"

"I am happy with any date that you suggest, John. As long as my father is well enough to be able to give me away. That is my only wish," she replied with a steady voice.

She knew that they had so much to overcome before they could see themselves in their own home with a family that was truly theirs forever. Her abiding hope was that her own family would be there to witness the exchanges of vows between them, that would bring lifelong happiness and fulfilment. She also knew that they would need careful preparation so that they could accept the differences there would be to her lifestyle. She did not want to upset them or cause difficulties for them understanding these changes.

"There, that was easy wasn't it? We can make decisions together without too much difficulty can't we? It's the proof of a strong relationship and of a life ahead we are destined to share."

And he took off her hat and holding her flattened curls between his warm hands, he turned her flushed face towards him and touched her lips with his.

The next half hour passed in blissfully simple silence; each of them relaxing into a calm and comfortable reverie. Her's were of tangled thoughts and plans for handling the next few months of her new status in the wider community. The community in which she had been raised. Her humble but proud parents would be discreet and accept her future activities and events that would follow. Doris would have something to say, close as they were, to be sure. The younger brothers would not be affected. No problem there, although she did count on dearest Bill, so close as they were, to be a support and sounding board if necessary.

John drew on his pipe, gazing out of the window as he watched the fields pass by, occasionally fogged by the smoke blowing back from the steam engine. He was focused on practicalities for when they returned to Barugh. He was less concerned about his need to be doing things and much more of thinking about it at present. They both had to handle the next few months sensitively and sensibly. He was getting used to Sissie's placid temperament, her calm responses, her sensitivity and powers of observation. He felt this would complement his own tendency to restlessness and sense of urgency that had always been in his approach to things. Again, he reassured himself that this would be a good partnership and that love would grow deeply as they worked together.

"Mother packed us a flask of tea and some sandwiches. Do you fancy something to eat dear?" he asked her gently, squeezing her hand that was still resting in his.

"Yes, please. I was feeling peckish. It's a long time since we ate breakfast," she replied, smiling at him, her eyes sparkling slightly.

Never one to refuse a bite to eat, Sissie enjoyed her food and was particularly partial to homemade bread and cake. The plumpness in her face and body was testament to that. For him, it was appealing and the proof that she was a wholesome country girl who worked hard and ate well, which was unlike the current women's trend for boyishness and slenderness that appeared in magazines and posters across town. John reflected that Emma's appearance was slight and boyish like that. In contrast to Sissie, she didn't eat much. Being small and busy with her dedication to teaching and school life, she seemed to eat very little. Always "nibbling like a town mouse" his father once remarked, noticing the slight frame of his elder daughter even at the age of 33.

John was in charge and he untied the string of the sandwich parcel and carefully unwrapped the greaseproof paper protection.

"My word, these look tasty! Watch the crumbs!" John warned, as he passed her a hearty ham and chutney sandwich. She thanked him and bit into the fresh white bread and butter into which its generous filling was packed.

"Yummm.," was all she could say in appreciation with her mouth full, as they sat together feeling some strength and energy from their carriage picnic. They sipped the hot and somewhat stewed strong tea that scalded her tongue, which made her whimper momentarily with the shock, clutching her mouth.

"Are you alright, lass?" he asked her gently. He suddenly recalled the sickly sensation of weak, tepid tea served to the officers on the front. It would trickle down into empty stomachs which could never be satisfied on the meagre rations they were given. The pain of hunger lingered on and the dreams of home cooking tormented them all as they closed their eyes in fitful attempts to rest.

"Sissie, I'm going to say this just once. I want us to eat well like this always. I don't want there ever to be a shortage of food on our table when we have a home together. I want to enjoy your cooking and I always want to have a pantry with food for whenever anyone comes to call."

"Yes John, whatever you want. I can cook, and have learned the country ways of making food go a long way when hard times hit us. I want to have nice things to share in our family home too."

"Yes, I know and it is part of why I love and admire you. We won't have a rich man's table but it will be generous, plentiful and yes, for sharing. Let's agree on that, shall we?"

"Agreed!" she responded enthusiastically. Her love of growing food and then creating meals in the kitchen had always been her passion and something she had hoped she would be able to do one day. Once he had put away the remains of the picnic in the old canvas daypack he'd had since the war, they settled back on their seats and both closed their eyes and dozed for the rest of the journey. When housing and factories began to appear, indicating that they were drawing closer to Barnsley, the train started to slow down. The screeching of brakes pierced their ears and woke them with a jolt.

"We're nearly here," John announced, as he stood up and shook his legs. Then looking out of the window he said, "I hope Bill received my letter this morning. He should be there to meet us with a bit of luck."

"John!" she exclaimed, "you think of everything. I didn't know that you had written to Bill."

"Ah! You don't know what I get up to young lady! I wasn't going to have us get on yet another bus was I? I've got to look after my wonderful wife to be!"

She sighed, smiled and tilted her head to one side in tender acceptance of his funny ways of offering his compliment. At the same time, she hoped someone would read out the letter to Bill, otherwise they would indeed be catching the bus.

John eagerly unlatched the heavy leather strap of the sash window on the carriage door, moments before a guard ran towards it and opened it for them to alight. John jumped out and extended his hand to Sissie as she stepped down from the narrow step of the carriage.

"Careful! Watch your feet, dearest," he warned her. The train was stationary now, but she couldn't believe her eyes at the daredevil actions of some passengers jumping on to the platform before it had come to a halt.

Safely on Platform 4, they walked briskly to the barrier and into the grey, late afternoon light outside the station entrance. They stood side by side, looking for Bill to appear in the farm wagon. Up and down they paced together, looking left and right, peering at every vehicle waiting to pick up the arriving passengers. No sign of Bill!

"Don't worry. We are on time and we've only just arrived. He will come along shortly, you'll see," reassured John, adjusting the brim of his hat, then narrowing his eyes to look in the distance.

Sissie was praying that Bill would have received the letter because all through school he had never mastered his reading. She hoped he would have asked Doris to check it through for him.

The air was cold and damp and the light was fading in this gloomy wintry weather. The first class carriage had at least provided some form of heating and they had been sitting close together for the journey. The chill of the February air began to reach her under her coat and through the soles of her shoes. "Come on, Bill! Don't let me down!" she whispered under her breath.

The pavements outside the station began to clear and the buzz of people meeting their pick-ups and taxis began to subside. There was still no sign of Bill!

"Let's just stand still a minute and decide what is best to do. There's still plenty of time for him to turn up," said John trying to sound convincing.

John was confident. This young man was in the football team and he had seen him perform as a reliable and loyal team player. The last thing Bill would want was to let his manager down.

Sissie stamped her feet to encourage some blood flow around her numb toes, wishing with all her heart that he would appear soon. She then began to worry and she pulled at her ear lobe. It was red with the cold. She imagined he'd had an accident. Perhaps the tyre had burst. Things were always going wrong with that old wagon. She wondered if the letter hadn't arrived in time and that he hadn't seen it.

Her worries were soon over as suddenly the loud familiar horn of the wagon raided the air and from round the bend of the station approach appeared Bill, swinging the vehicle around for them to jump in easily.

He flung the door open whistling and shouting, "Sorry, sorry! I got the time wrong, didn't I? Doris sorted me out though! Have you been waiting a long time? Sorry again, sorry."

Sissie looked at him fondly, admitting quietly to herself that he was most certainly, her most scatterbrained brother; painfully realising how much she had missed him and her own family.

In her sensible way she said, "You're 'ere now, never mind. Worry not! We 'aven't been waiting too long, 'ave we John?"

She was back in a familiar world where everything was recognisable and she didn't feel the need to be on her best behaviour. She could just be herself, happy to be surrounded by her own folk. In that moment, she knew that she would always prefer it that way.

The men sat in the front seats, and she gazed out of the windows from the back during the short journey to Barugh.

She pulled off her hat, unbuttoned her coat and sat back to relax. Quietly reflective, she let them exchange the daily news and football. They compared the weather over the weekend which unsurprisingly, had been similar to that in Westmoreland.

"Are you coming to Low Fold for tea, Johnny?" enquired Bill as they turned into the village, "Me Mam's always got t' kettle on and there's plenty on t' table for a feast for yer if yer'd like to join us."

"That would be grand," John replied affably, turning round for approval from Sissie.

She nodded and smiled back, delighted that he was able to accept the invitation without feeling the need to ask for her approval. It helped her to understand that in fact they were stepping forward together positively and that from now on it would be with less formality.

They creaked to a steady stop at the farmyard gate. Little Frank, the youngest of her other brothers clumped towards the truck in boots that were several sizes too big. Keen to be regarded as more grown up, he pushed the gate open for them to drive through.

"Sissie, Sissie, I missed you! I'm so glad you're home!" he called out, red faced with his efforts to manage the heavy five barred gate. She stepped down from the back of the truck,

"And I missed you too, little man," she said with warmth in her voice, beaming down at him as she offered him her hand so he could help her down.

"Close yon gate lad will yer?" shouted Bill, keen to maintain security in the yard, always teaching the youngster to take some responsibility.

At nine years old, Frank was already behaving like a little man with his bold strides and his broad and confident voice. He had grown up so quickly, with his urgency to be like all his older siblings. Already he felt he was doing all the important things that grown-ups do. He didn't want to be treated like a child and he made it very clear as he demonstrated his independence and ability to help out around the farm. It deterred his older brothers and the farm workers from teasing him too. He idolised his sister Sissie, and thrived on her kindness and attention, always looking for a hug and her gentle words of praise for which she was so known and loved. They all called her Sissie even Mam and Dad. He had never heard anyone call her anything else. Doris was, well, just Doris, and you didn't play with her. You didn't dare ask! Oh no! She was the strict one and she never had time to talk to him. She was always thinking about herself and looking in magazines at the latest hairstyles and such like. She wouldn't run and play hide and seek or chase rabbits off the top field with him like Sissie would, so he kept his distance from Doris. There was certainly no love lost between the two of them.

Then there was Bill and Tom who stuck together. There were only two years between them and he'd heard his mother say they were as thick as thieves. He tried so hard to do all the things that they did. He cried when they called him a "babby" and then he would run indoors to Mam.

Tom strolled from behind the barn where he'd been having a crafty smoke, waving casually as he trudged towards them.

"Staying for a bit o' tea wi' us then, Jonny?" he asked cheekily, glad of a change of company round the table. He became bored very quickly having so much energy and so little work to do at this time of year. He was toying with the idea of going down the pit to earn some real money. It was filthy work he admitted but at least he'd have ready cash in his pocket.

"That I am young man. I'll be glad of a bite to eat. It's been a long day hasn't it, Sissie?" John replied jovially. He stepped forward, and extended his hand in a warm greeting, as he shook that of the young man.

They all trooped in and the heavy cottage door clicked shut as they all shed their outdoor clothes before washing their cold chapped hands. Proceeding to the kitchen, they felt the welcoming warmth provided by the stove which had been on all day. The familiar aroma of baking invited them in to sit at the scrubbed wooden table, laden with fresh baked bread, scones and butter for them all. Mam brought a large pot of tea, placing it by her side as she sat down.

"Grace," announced Dad and they all looked downwards. When 'Amen' was chorused, he looked across the table, "Now, go steady lads. Let the ladies in first," he cautioned.

"And don't forget when it's gone… its gone!" This was a favourite phrase he used in his attempt to slow down his hungry young lads who never seemed to satisfy their appetites.

There was silence as they all enjoyed Mam's best efforts to put the weekly food on the table, passing plates of cake and bread and jam back and forth. They argued, as they always did at every meal time, over who had the crust and comparing who had the most food on their plates. They emptied them quickly and sank back in their chairs when they had had their fill.

"How are your folks, John?" asked Mam. "I hope they are in good 'ealth and were pleased to see both of yer an' our Sissie didn't disgrace 'erself!"

"They are well and we had a pleasant weekend. It gave us the opportunity to share our plans for the future with them. Sissie and I would like to do the same thing with you later this week when we have recovered from our trip, if you have some spare time."

"Yes, whenever you wish, we are always 'ere," Annie replied. "That would be fine for you William too, wouldn't it?" as she glanced across at him.

"Aye, whatever you say lass is fine by me," he said gruffly, knowing that this would be about marriage and the prospect of losing another of his daughters.

It was only last week that Doris and her young man Herbert had announced their marriage plans for the summer. That would be one less income coming in, he had moaned quietly to himself when they had left the cottage. She was moving away to Blackpool to set up a life over there, where Herbert's family lived. She boasted that it would be more interesting than being around her own family in Barugh. She'll learn it'll be no different, he thought. Still, she was old enough to make her own mind up he reflected and he seemed a decent enough lad who would look after her.

"Well, if you don't mind, I need to be on my way home, Mrs. Horbury. I'll have to light the lamps before I turn in for the night. We're back to work in the morning," said John disturbing the ponderings of the older man.

"That you must, so we mustn't keep you," Mam agreed as she rose from the table, glaring at the boys to do likewise.

"And Bill will run you back."

That was a cue for everyone to move. As chairs scraped backwards on the quarried floor they all exchanged theirs thanks and said their goodbyes. John and Bill disappeared into the damp night air and Sissie followed them and from the doorway, she called out softly, "Goodnight John and I will see you tomorrow."

He tilted his hat, winked at her and then he was gone. With a spat of stuttering exhaust fumes and a clattering on the cobbles the old wagon crossed the yard and into the night air.

*   *   *

The little cottage was cold and dark. John placed his key in the lock and stepped inside breathing a sigh of sheer relief. He felt as if he had been holding his breath for the last few days because, apart from ensuring that Sissie was comfortable, he hadn't felt in control of events, of people or the new situation in which they had all found themselves. There had been so many different actions and emotions that had swirled around it all. Just as he remembered the tension inside himself when he was on the front line, he had been on full alert in the same way over the weekend with the family. He imagined that perhaps it was normal to be guarded and sensitive during such new and important stages of meeting and melding members of two families.

Sharing introductions and meeting one another's folks was new for him because in his previous experience he and Victoria had made their decision before meeting her parents. He had rehearsed the announcement to marry Victoria before reaching her parents' home at that time. In the early days after the war there had been much intensity of emotion between young couples. There was a sense of urgency to reach for peace and happiness, for calm and for routine so the traditional protocols had often been ignored. Consequently, she had never met his family and he only met hers when he arrived to outline their plans after a request, out of courtesy, had been made to her father for permission to marry.

It was not too late yet, so he felt it was worth making up a fire in the grate to sit and reflect on the experiences of the last few days, and most important of all, to finalise some plans for the next few months in his mind.

He'd left a few kindling sticks in the hearth and the coal scuttle was full, so he screwed up one to two sheets of newspaper to use as firelighters, and started the fire quite quickly. Then, as he realised he still hadn't removed his overcoat, he slipped his arms out of it, and reaching for a tumbler on the dresser he poured a small whisky. The wood crackled and the the coal smoke curled up the chimney as he settled in front of it. It would be comforting to end the day by himself with his own thoughts. He felt such pleasure sipping a tot of his favourite brand of whisky from the crystal glass that had come from his mother's collection, and he caressed it in the palms of his hands to impart some warmth, enhancing its flavour.

It seemed strange to be alone, and yet at the same time he relaxed in the seclusion and privacy which was so familiar to him and most welcome tonight. The sigh he breathed out now released the tension he realised he had been experiencing and he recognised a degree of weariness. It came from realising that they had achieved something important. Now they would be able to make progress as he and his wife-to-be moved forward together into the future.

Out came his pipe and with some consternation he noticed this was the last of the Christmas tobacco. He must send Betty out first thing in the morning to buy some more. Resting the pipe in his hand for a minute or two before lighting up, he began to visualise a way to overcome inevitable gossip that was about to follow as soon as people heard about their relationship. This he knew would clearly hurt Sissie and her family and both compromise and embarrass himself as manager at the mill. He could not risk harming the reputation both of them had through pointless gossip and spiteful words and prejudices of local folk who had nothing better to talk about!

As he lit his pipe he had an idea, so he reached for his fountain pen and some paper to write a short note to Sissie. He remembered that he had a stamp in his wallet so he could post it in the morning as he left the house.

Sunday Night 8pm

My Darling Sweetheart,

I have been thinking since we said goodnight and I have decided to go straight to Brussels in the morning to see Vicky. I have decided it is of some urgency that I bring her back to the family.

I also think it would be best to avoid any fear of gossip if you hand in your notice straightaway. Tomorrow. Just work the rest of the week. You know we agreed this would work best for us, just as we discussed on the train.

I will go into the office at 6.30am as normal and clear my desk and make arrangements to travel later in the morning.

We will not see each other because I will not be doing my usual factory round. (I will let Ned Armitage stand in for me this week.)

Do not worry and do not talk to anyone about anything between us- that is for us and only us. I know how sensible you are, and that you will trust me to find the best way to handle matters during these early days.

We know that these next few months are going to be difficult but we have made our choices and we must see them through knowing it will all be by far the best way to do things.

And my sweetheart don't we know how much we love each other and how we will work together to make the future good when we shall be on our own and we are working for each other?

I will write to you when I arrive in Brussels. I am your loving sweetheart. John

He read the letter back to himself, nodding in self-approval. He folded it neatly and before placing it in a small brown envelope, he held the letter to his lips momentarily, with flattened palms in a fond caress, then placed it inside and sealed it. Scribbling her name and address on the front he attached the stamp and placed it in his pocket.

His bag was still packed from the week away and so he replaced a few things, put in a couple of clean collars thinking he would be looked after by the Brussels housekeeper once he arrived. In a hurried script he wrote another note but this time to Vicky's grandparents to inform them of his imminent visit. It would be ill-mannered to arrive without warning them first. Betty would sort this postage out tomorrow, amongst the many other jobs and instructions she would have to work on, during his impending absence.

Now it was time to enjoy some tobacco, so he sat back in his armchair crossing his legs, swinging his foot in the characteristic pose of a man who is feeling at ease, and stared into the glowing coals.

He didn't sleep too well. He was becoming impatient with himself because this fractious sleeping habit was resulting in him becoming a little short tempered and he wondered whether he was as fulfilled as he thought he should be. He dismissed it, thinking it would be unusual if in these circumstances he would find restful nights until they were married and alone with each other. Surely he would feel restful and satisfied with Sissie lying in their bed by his side, he mused wistfully!

The day was still in darkness when he woke up but he was pleased to be up and ready to carry out his plans. He closed the cottage door at 6.15am and walked swiftly to the mill, slipping the letter to Sissie in the postbox on the way. The side gate of the mill was already open and he strode across the yard directly towards his office. It had been lit up by the night watchman already as he opened up after the night watch came to a close.

His in-tray was piled high so he quickly hung his hat and coat on the peg at the side of the door and settled quickly to work through it. At 7.00am on the dot Betty arrived and inclining her head round the open office door, she greeted him cheerily enquiring of his time off, not really expecting much of a response from him. By now she was familiar with his reticence for light conversation. She suggested the usual morning tea.

"That would be most welcome," said John, "but I'm out of tobacco. Can someone dash out to get some for me?" he added, offering a note to pay for it.

"Right away, Mr. Bland," she said as she took the crisp new ten-shilling note from him. "I've got that new lass learning in the office with me this week so I'll send her out now."

She was gone and he resisted the temptation to look out of the window as he heard the workforce arriving through the gates in the yard below. He thought it would be best not to be too obvious that he was back.

Within fifteen minutes there was a pot of tea and a new pouch of tobacco on his desk, and he proceeded to work his way through some paperwork before giving Betty full instructions of his plans and what was needed to be done in his absence. By midday he had left Darton Mill.

*　*　*

Once John had departed with Bill in the wagon that evening, they all resumed their duties. The women to clear the table and the men to sit in front of the fire to discuss the jobs for the week ahead. Except that today there was a different atmosphere. Mam was thoughtful as she put the bread and cake away. Sissie was suddenly feeling weary after the demands on her over the last few days. When she started stacking crockery ready to wash up, Frank blurted out, "Sissie. Are you going to marry Jonny? Are you going to live here or go away like our Doris will? Will he be...?" and he hesitated, nervous to say out loud, "like my brother then? Will you still visit us and come and play with me?"

His questions tumbled out, one after the other without waiting for any answers from her.

"Hey, hey one question at a time, lad," called out his father, "and anyway its rude to ask such personal questions."

He pointed his finger, crooked with arthritis these days, "You be seen and not heard d'ye 'ear me?" Frank reddened and hung his head.

"But I'm going to miss her when she gets married, Dad," he whined.

"Well, all of that has nothin' to do wi' you so you keep quiet and wait to be told," said his father in an uncompromising tone.

"Nay, it's alright for him to ask me. It's only natural Dad. I don't mind," said Sissie to lighten the situation and to reassure everyone that she did not want to keep secrets.

"But at the moment there's nothing to tell, so it will just be like we are normally, so don't fret Frank. Now then why not be a good lad and get ready for bed and I will see you tomorrow," she added in that sisterly voice that she always used with him.

Frank, who always listened to his dearest sister, turned reluctantly and in a subdued voice said good night feeling rather left out but knowing that it would be pointless to argue and Sissie seemed happy enough.

"I'll be turning in, too, 'night all. God Bless," said Tom who hated to hear disagreement of any sort. As he moved to the door, it suddenly burst open and Doris rushed in.

"Don't forget to say tha prayers," called Mam.

"G'night Tom. God Bless," the rest of them replied simultaneously, as they did with each other every night. Doris who had made such a noisy and dramatic entrance that they looked over towards her.

"Steady on love, who's chasing you?" enquired Mam, turning round at the sudden commotion.

"It's alright Mam, I'm just so eager to tell you that Herbert and I have found a house to rent an' it's just round the corner from his work! It's just right for us and we can just about afford the rent, if Herbert can get a rise in 'is wages," she babbled.

"And what about when you're in t' puddin' club? One wage coming' in and then what?"

"Well, I'm not that yet am I, Mam? So let's just bide us time and just be 'appy for us - we want to live on us own for now."

Doris and Sissie exchanged glances as Doris said, "We're to be wed in May, so don't you go fixing your dates yet, lady," said Doris in a rush.

"We haven't set a date yet Doris and we won't' be ready by May anyway," Sissie sighed.

Her sister could be so mean and unkind with her words. It was always best to agree with her or, better still, to say nothing. Doris seemed to have so much anger in her all the time. She wondered whether she was really happy and how Herbert coped with her temper. Perhaps he used the same tactics as she did. She had learned over the years that staying silent and not opposing or arguing with her sister had more effect. It prevented arguments and actually gave herself more control. She didn't want to share any of her stories with Doris anyway because she would usually be scoffed at, jeered at, or ignored. So she said nothing.

"Well, I'll be going up stairs first as I've had such a busy day and I'll see thee all in t' morning," turning to grasp the door knob and saying goodnight, Sissie left Doris telling her parents the fancy plans she had for a future with Herbert.

She undressed, laying her weekend clothes neatly on an old wooden chair in the corner of the bedroom she shared with Doris. Then she stepped into her nightdress swiftly so that the coldness of the room did not chill her as she got into bed, pulling the blankets round her shoulders.

Lying on her back, staring at the ceiling in the darkness save only for a small lamp in the corner, she reflected on the last few days and how the events had affected her. She felt special and wanted by John when he looked at her with fondness and admiration. When he held her close, like that time by the farm gate, passion and physical desire trembled through her as her body leaned into him. He whispered into her hair and told her how much he wanted her, telling her how beautiful she was, and how he couldn't wait to have her to himself.

"I want this," she thought, "I'm ready for this life with John. I know I can make him happy because he makes me feel special and safe. And I want to be a someone. I don't always want to struggle for money and food on the table like Mam and Dad. I'd like to be able to give them something back so they can have an easier time when they are too old and too weak to work for a living."

She knew that she would do everything in her power to make John happy and to secure a fine lifestyle for them both. She was not afraid of hard work and he was not afraid of facing the difficult time that they would be bound to encounter as they made their plans. No one round here had ever heard of a factory girl marrying the manager! This would certainly cause some gossip in the community. She didn't care though, because she knew how sure of each other they were. Patience, privacy and purpose would get them to the altar and then to life in the future together.

For the time being, her first efforts would be directed to two sisters…. Doris and Emma!

Then, as if on cue, Doris stepped quietly into the room, "Are you still awake, Sis?" she whispered, hoping that by adopting a softer tone she might gain some attention from her less talkative sister. "Aye, too many things ringing round me brain to sleep yet," Sissie replied.

"Let me tell you what me and Herbert are goin' t' do next," she whispered excitedly.

"Next Saturday, I'm getting me wedding dress wi' Mam comin' wi' us to choose it. Herbert 'as saved t' money to pay for it. Then after that, when we've been to chapel service on Sunday, we're asking t' vicar for appointment to get dates fixed and Banns read so we can be legal to get wed."

"Lovely," answered Sissie. It was so exciting and she was happy for Doris who so full of it all, but the next thing she said she was not ready for.

"Anyway, just to tell ye, I'm not having no bridesmaids. Not even you. I want to be down that aisle just wi' me dad and Herbert waiting for me. No one else to take any glory."

Sissie sat up sharply, not quite believing what she had just heard Doris say. She was shocked and disappointed. In a moment she had dropped out of her warm, romantic reverie and into the cold, harsh reality. What could Doris possibly mean? She had always assumed that they would be each other's bridesmaids because they used to dream and giggle secretively about it together when they were much younger. They would imagine which colours they would wear and what types of flowers to hold.

This announcement puzzled her. It seemed to reveal that Doris lacked confidence under her loud exterior, but underneath she seemed unsure of herself. She'd had her suspicions of that before. She wondered if this was the reason behind her behaviour towards her lately. Recently, she wasn't interested in listening to Sissie's stories about John. Perhaps this accounted for her brashness and pushiness; of 'showing off' really. They were attempts to seem better and more successful. If she could only realise that Sissie was not in the least bit bothered about competition. It would be obvious to Doris, that her sister would undoubtedly have the better prospects. Poor spiteful Doris, thought Sissie. How sad that they couldn't be happy for each other?

"Oh Doris, why not?" she cried, "We always said we'd be each other's bridesmaids. Don't you remember? We agreed 'n' we said we'd look after each other on t' wedding day! Oh my, I'll never be one now," and a tear rolled down her cheek in her sudden sadness and disappointment.

"Well, that was when we were little. It didn't mean anything. We were just romancin'. You're soft to think it were all for real," retorted the sister she had always regarded as a friend and confidante. Sissie couldn't think of anything else to say. What was there to say? She was on the verge of crying and the last thing she wanted was to cause a disturbance because she had just heard her parents coming up to bed in the next room. She cleared her throat and sniffled.

"You will make yer own mind up, Doris, I know you. You've decided you don't need me, so that's that. I'll say goodnight as 'tis late and I'm tired. I'll see thee in t' morning." Then she slid down under the covers turning her back away from her sister.

Some part of a sibling bond was lost between them that night. Perhaps it had been coming ever since Doris found out that Sissie was out courting with John and that Sissie hadn't confided in her first. Perhaps as the eldest, she expected to be the first to be married, and for everyone to be excited for her but Sissie meeting John had suddenly changed the sequence of things and she didn't like it. Perhaps, perhaps… there were endless possibilities for her change of attitude.

"Be like that then," Doris snapped back and throwing her clothes on the floor, she climbed into bed beside her sister, and she too turned her back.

Neither of them slept well. Much restlessness and sighing could be heard throughout the night until they were roused by their mother, rapping on the door to wake them up for work.

Monday morning - the toughest morning of the week, and especially as it was barely light and so cold at this time of year. They both washed and then dressed themselves in their work clothes in silence. They plodded heavily down the stairs and gulped a cup of tea and a bowl of porridge before leaving the farm cottage together.

They walked without speaking until Doris broke the silence. "I don't know why you're making a big fuss of this bridesmaid thing. It's not going to be a big weddin' like you'll have yer know. What's up wi' yer?"

"I'm 'urt our Doris. Really 'urt. You think that me - Sissie - is going to steal the limelight? At your weddin'? You must be mad! Yer know full well you'll be the most beautiful girl on that day. Every bride is on their weddin' day! How could you think anyone would want to spoil that? I'm your only sister and I am 'appy for you and I'm so proud of you. And - I always hoped to be yer bridesmaid - so there!"

"Well, that's as may be, but me mind's made up and I don't want to talk about it no more," she answered in a croaky voice.

With that she marched on in front leaving a heartbroken Sissie behind her, feeling wretched and bruised.

Back through the mill gates as usual, as the two sisters advanced towards the doors and collected their cards for clocking in. They found their own friends and chattered hurriedly, hanging their coats up along the row of once shiny brass pegs secured to the whitewashed walls. Then they filed in, feverishly exchanging news of their weekend activities, until their voices could not be heard as each machine was started up. They could not hear each other anymore as they approached their respective work positions.

Norma had been firing questions at Sissie. She wanted to know about the weekend and the reason for taking Friday off last week. It was easy for Sissie to dodge answering her because the air was buzzing with them all exchanging their stories. Doris was heard telling everyone about her wedding plans and the other girls expressed their excitement for her. She was loving all the attention.

Sissie hadn't noticed whether John was at his office window looking down as they all entered the yard. She didn't dare look up there for fear of letting on to the others that she was looking out for him. She must take care to be discreet from now on. Instead, she just laughed and giggled along with them and focussed on the work ahead of her today.

The familiar noise of the machines greeted them and the distinctive odour of grease and textile fibre filled the air as they all silenced themselves and the laughter stopped. No one could possibly communicate above the din on the factory floor.

Then everyone was into a ten hour shift with only a toilet break and half an hour for a pack up lunch to break up the monotony, not knowing what the weather was doing until twilight fell and it was time to go home.

Alone with her thoughts, Sissie could operate the machines with little or no effort because she'd been doing the same repetitive job for so long. Today at least, she felt she had something to think about. Firstly, she needed to adjust to Doris's unkind words and determination to exclude her from the wedding plans. She'd noticed that she hadn't been invited along for the wedding outfit shopping either. She was sure Mam would have had something to say about that. She had always encouraged her daughters to be good friends and to look out for each other as she had regretted never having a sister herself. However, Doris would not be listening to her mother on this subject now. She had made it clear, that she was going her own way with this wedding. Sissie told herself that she must try and resist becoming upset by the rejection.

Still nursing her wounded spirit, she decided that she must stop asking Doris questions and to appear disinterested. Doris would be unable to stop telling her about the wedding developments. It was in her nature to speak about them. Then she would listen kindly and patiently, avoid offering a point of view, but be available to assist if asked.

By lunch time she was sitting at her machine, just taking the first big bite from her sandwich, when there was a piercing scream from the across the gangway. It was Joyce Hill jumping wildly up and down on the spot and a few people were rushing towards her. She had trapped her fingers in the rolling machine and blood was pouring across the bench as the two severed fingers lay separated on the other side of the bench.

"Oh God!" Sissie yelled as she flung her sandwich down and flew across to Joyce. Everything seemed to happen in slow motion.

"Fetch First Aid. Get ambulance. Stay back!" she roared as she ran to comfort Joyce, ripping her apron off to wrap tightly round the girl's arm to act as a tourniquet. Everyone else stood by with their hands over their mouths. Someone fainted. In fact, Joyce was close to passing out but the adrenalin was racing through her so she just looked ashen. She began sobbing loudly now as the panic and the pain set in. The first aid kit arrived as Betty ran towards the little crowd shouting that the ambulance was outside and calling out to Sissie to guide the poor girl who was tortured with pain and confusion. Instinctively, she followed briskly, realising later that she herself was in shock. She reassured Joyce repeatedly that she would be fine until they reached Betty at the outside door. There stood the ambulance and driver waiting to take her straight to Barnsley hospital.

"We'll take it from 'ere lass," said one of the men. "Well done! She's in good 'ands now. You go get yer sen a cuppa - you look as if yer need it."

Sissie turned round to go inside when the driver shouted, "Eh up - did yer bring the fingers wi' yer?"

"Oh 'eck - yes I did!" she murmured, and trembling very noticeably, she passed him a soft and floppy cotton parcel soaked in blood, the evil metallic smell of it tainting the air between them.

She was visibly weakening with legs trembling as she dropped back when the ambulance doors were smartly shut.

"Come on, Mistress hero! Let's get you into the office and make you some strong tea," urged Betty, putting an arm around her waist and guiding her inside.

They entered Betty's little office and she gently eased Sissie to a chair.

"My word you soon snapped into action, my girl," she said with admiration in her voice. Betty put the kettle on to boil on the little gas ring in the corner.

"Wait 'til the Boss hears about it!" she exclaimed excitedly, "He'll be very impressed!"

Sissie said nothing. She felt she was trapped inside a tunnel where all the voices around her were muffled and unclear. Things had happened so quickly! She had never witnessed such a horrific accident like that before, although she had heard about other ones that had occurred in the past. It was the sight of the two fingers separated from Joyce's hand that now haunted her, together with those sickening screams from the poor girl. Everyone had crowded round but did nothing, just gawping because they were so horrified. She seemed to be the only one who had jumped into action. She kept reliving the scene until Betty passed her a white crockery cup and saucer with a little biscuit resting there.

"Let me put it down just here. Look at you trembling! You're going to spill it. Just take your time," soothed Betty as she bent over her gently.

"Is he about then?" enquired Sissie casually.

"No, not today. He's off on business," replied Betty, keeping confidences as she always did. She would not be divulging his precise whereabouts to anyone.

Sissie sipped her tea quietly. That was news to her. She had wondered why he had not appeared on the factory floor after the accident. He was not called out to the ambulance when it was waiting outside just below his office either. She wondered what Betty meant when she said he was away on business. Surely he would have mentioned that last night when they said goodbye.

Out of the blue she suddenly wondered if he had set off for Brussels. She felt momentary disappointment that he hadn't let her know in advance of his plans. Then it crossed her mind that he could have made a last minute decision, despite the fact that he rarely did things on impulse. Most of the time, all his actions were carefully thought through, down to the last detail. That would be his mathematical and ordered brain and his army officer training.

"Oh where is he? I'm missing him so much already and I want to tell him what happened today," she sighed, as she felt the tea warming through her.

Suddenly, she felt ready to get back to work so she eased herself from the chair speaking in a very croaky voice, "Thank you Betty. I needed that. You 'ave been so kind. I'll be getting back to work now."

She walked onto the factory floor and as she passed, several of the girls, one by one, as she passed them looked up, smiled and mouthed, "Well done," and, "Are you alright?"

Looking forward to the sandwich that she had barely started, she sat down at her place to find an empty wrapper and a few crumbs. She looked under the bench and around her. There was no sandwich to be seen!

"Hmm, where's that gone?" she wondered and looked around her in bewilderment. Her eyes lingered on the empty place across the gangway. Someone had very efficiently mopped up the mess from Joyce's accident, and now her place lay morbidly empty as a reminder of the tragic events that had taken place.

Reluctantly, she got back to work finding it difficult to concentrate, still feeling slightly nauseous and light headed, and just as she was thinking about asking if she could go home early, she saw Ned Armitage coming towards her. He gestured for her to switch off the machine.

"That were brave action, Sissie. Joyce Hill owes yer - that's for sure. Now then, I think best thing is for you to knock off early and get tha' sen 'ome. What d'yer say?" he suggested in a firm voice. "Betty is goin' to write a report that you can look at in t' mornin' to check if details are correct. I will be telling the boss what 'as happened today when he gets back. You lass - you need some time to rest up."

"If that's allowed, Ned. Yes, I think I need that. I feel none too good," she replied as her eyes filled with tears in reaction to someone else now showing some kindness and sympathy.

"Go on then and just take care. Si thee tomorrer." He smiled and with a pantomime style sweep of his hand, he indicated the way out.

No one noticed her as she quickened her pace to be out of sight, and on her way home where she could get it off her chest with Mam before the others came in for tea.

At six o' clock Doris swept in through the door.

"Well our Sis, I think that were incredible what you did today! Yer've got everyone talking about it, that's no lie," she said with a hint of resentment in her voice. That her sister's actions had become the topic of conversation at the end of the day did not sit comfortably with Doris.

Sissie ignored her, not unkindly, just creating a sense that no response was necessary. Instead she said, "Who's for tea? It's mashed and there's some bread and butter and cheese if you're hungry."

"I'm alright thanks. I ate your sandwich Sis when you'd gone t' ambulance. Seemed a shame to let it go to waste"

"YOU ate it?" Sissie cried, "What did you think I'd eat when I got back from t'ambulance?"

"I didn't think you'd be coming back," Doris replied sulkily.

"Doris, you are mean and selfish - and you are ALWAYS thinking about y'self," Sissie said quietly, glowering at her. She turned around and went through the kitchen door into the yard, needing to be alone in the fresh air, and in her own company.

"Nay, lass. That was uncalled for. You should apologise," said Mam who needed to show disapproval, but did not want to appear to be taking sides.

"Nah! She'll get over it," said Doris brusquely. "Let her be."

Sissie wandered down the farm lane in mild despair. She was assuming that John had set off on his journey to Brussels, so she wouldn't be able to unburden her feelings on him for the next few days. Being at home was becoming unbearable. She asked herself how she was going to cope without regular work. She knew she could be useful doing odd jobs around the farm, probably cleaning and cooking and hearing Doris bragging every day about her wedding plans. That would not be enough to occupy her though.

She stopped to watch the lambs gambolling and playing without a care in the world. Their only aim in life being to find the right mother who could provide milk for survival. At that moment, she wished she could be like one of them.

The strain on the friendship between herself and Doris, and the decision John must have made (after apparent discussions with Emma, not her) to bring Vicky back to England, made her feel powerless and at the mercy of other people's decisions. These were milestones, and she felt that she had little influence over these important moments in her life.

No one had asked her for an opinion.

No one cared that they were making decisions that affected her and none of them had the courtesy to ask her what she was thinking. She had been excluded from all these recent events because her natural quiet ways had been misinterpreted by them, as calm acceptance. They had misjudged her. She did have ideas and opinions and she wanted to have her say. She turned these thoughts over in her mind, becoming more and more upset. She was as entitled to have her say as well, as they obviously were. But at the moment she didn't know how.

Kicking the loose stones about in the lane, she trudged back home and joined them all briefly, but she had no appetite for food or conversation. She said goodnight to everyone and went up to her room. Alone, she was allowed some peace and tranquility which came to her in the quiet and the darkness of the night.

After the previous restless night and the emotional events of today, not surprisingly, she was sound asleep when Doris came to bed.

"You forgot to read this, Sis. It came in this afternoon's post," announced her sister as she entered the room, waving an envelope addressed to:

Miss EE Horbury, Low Fold Farm, Barugh.

There was no response, except for soft, rhythmical breathing from the other side of the bed.

*   *   *

She slept well for the first few hours that night. She was exhausted after the events of that day and because of the disappointment in Doris's mean and selfish behaviour. This was the sister she had always regarded as a friend and confidante, and today she had been especially disappointing and hurtful. After that first deep sleep she tossed and turned with disjointed thoughts and suppositions churning through her mind. She was beginning to think she wasn't much use in the lives of those near and dear to her and she was saddened and bewildered by her whole situation at present.

As the sky began to lighten and dawn began to break, she eased herself quietly from the crumpled flannelette sheet and blanket. The eiderdown seemed to have travelled to Doris's side of the bed. No wonder she had had to curl up so tightly to keep warm. She dressed herself and left the bedroom before Doris, who had not enjoyed a peaceful night either. Sissie left the house a good twenty minutes ahead of her sister, who preferred to grab more time in the bed she now had to herself.

She wanted to walk alone to work today and organise her thoughts. She really did not need Doris.

"Tha' doesna' look too 'appy this morning, love," Mam greeted her, using that typical invitational tone so that in response one could offer something of an explanation.

"No Mam," she mumbled as she pulled on her well-worn brown work coat. "I'll be alright though."

It was a brighter morning today, better than it had been lately. There was early birdsong and it sounded like spring could be on the way. "Am I 'appy?" she asked herself as she left the house.

She often talked to herself like this. It helped her to find a solution to the latest trouble she might be encountering, "Yes, because I've found a man who loves me and I love 'im," she answered with a smile, as his face appeared in her mind's eye.

"Ah, but is that enough to make me 'appy?" she asked herself. She knew that it wasn't that simple of course. "It should be, but it isn't so. So why's that?"

That she was admitting that she had some reservations startled her. This was no basis for married life! It was true that John was protective and wise and he seemed to have purpose and ambition, all of which she admired. She had so much to learn and she wanted to learn from him but there was definitely something else disturbing her. Why then did she feel, deep in her heart, that she was not completely fulfilled.

"I'm going to 'get to the bottom of things' as Dad says."

The day passed without reference to the accident yesterday although someone said Joyce had been sent home from hospital and was recovering at her mother's house.

Although the accident itself was not mentioned, Ned came across to see her. He enquired of her own health and asked her to call in to see him at the end of her shift. She agreed, and found herself knocking on the door of his little glass paned kiosk on the shop floor as everyone was leaving.

"Ah Sissie, come in. Yer know I'm in charge wi' t' boss being away an' all an' I 'ave instructions to make the day to day decisions. I 'ave an idea and I hope you'll 'ear me out while I explain. Did yer know we do not 'ave a first aid expert in t' factory?"

She shook her head without saying anything, wondering where this was going and why he should be asking her.

"You were that calm and so straight on 't accident yesterday. I were impressed I can tell yer. So was everyone else an' all! Yer'd make a good first aider. We used to 'ave ol' Taff but he's left now and its high time we got someone else trained up. What d'yer think? Would you do it if we got you trained?"

"Yes, I would like to do it," she replied without hesitation. "Does everyone feel ok about me doin' the job?"

"It doesn't matter what other folk say lass. I want you to take a course for it wi' St John Ambulance in town. End of story."

She coloured up slightly, with pleasure and pride that her actions had been recognised and appreciated. "Well yes, I'll gladly do t' training' and thanks for askin' me."

He passed her a couple of application forms to hand in next morning saying,

"It's 5 nights a week for basic training then after that it's up to you if yer'd like to take it further."

At last! People would have to ask for her opinion, her assistance and expertise and she would be listened to and respected for her knowledge. She expressed her thanks and said goodnight to Ned, and walked across the factory floor, appreciating the quiet atmosphere now that all the machines were still. She passed through the doors and stepped into the cold grey light of the early evening. She felt she had been recognised for her ability and competence. It put a spring in her step and because there was no one around to question it, she enjoyed the self-confidence it brought, and an excited anticipation of a new role in the mill. She clutched the papers carefully to her chest, so delighted to have been asked to do the training.

John had not appeared at work that day either, so when she returned home and found the letter lying there untouched, where Doris had left it, she sat on the edge of the bed to read it. Carefully she prised open the sealed envelope and read it slowly. She was relieved to receive some news but was quite surprised by directness of John's words. Then she kept re-reading the same part of his letter again and again:

> *I think it would be best to avoid any fear of gossip if you hand in your notice and just work the rest of the week, as we discussed on the train.*

She felt she was being instructed and again, she felt that no account had been taken of her point of view during these decisions. They had not discussed fully the plan to give in her notice and they didn't refer to 'gossip' when they talked together on the train did they? Now she was asking herself why they should be afraid of gossip. She was both irritated and saddened, and was desperate to talk to him. After her meeting with Ned Armitage, feeling recognised for her abilities, she realised that she didn't actually want to be discreet that she was marrying someone at management level. She was proud of herself and her family and the hard work and respect they held amongst Barugh folk. She didn't want to hide from the choices she had made for the future she was going to share with John. This part of the letter highlighted her uneasiness and made her feel restless and indignant.

She didn't want to oppose John's wishes but in a quiet and determined moment she decided she would continue to hold her position at the mill. Especially now that she had been offered the first aid training that would provide her with interest and incentive for the otherwise monotonous work that she normally did. It was possible that she might be on a higher wage with the responsibility too.

She did not want secrecy and silence about their love for each other. She would write back and explain her situation and hope he might understand. He would be in Brussels for a few days until he completed all the paperwork necessary for bringing Vicky back here. Then she could accept that the best way forward would be for Vicky to live with the Blands in the north until they were married and were more settled.

With three hungry brothers at the table already, and a self-absorbed sister who nibbled at the food laid out for their evening meal, it was easy to stay upstairs. In the privacy of the bedroom she could write a simple reply to John explaining herself and sharing her news. Then she would fill in the application forms ready to give to Ned in the morning.

By the time she had finished, she was hungry and went downstairs where she found a plate of food that Mam had left out for her. She ate alone quietly and washed up her plate and cutlery, before sitting quietly to hemstitch the boys' worn bedsheets that had been turned to give them a new lease of life.

She smiled inwardly, feeling confident and comforted, knowing that she had been recognised for her actions yesterday. She was taking responsibility for a decision, not only to stay working but to receive training to improve herself and, without anyone else telling her what to do!

Chapter 24

Sisters

"You mumble and mutter all the time, our Doris," complained Bill. "These days yer never seem to laugh at 'ote neither. What's up wi' yer?"

He was sitting in front of the fire, rubbing his feet to get the blood circulating. He had peeled off his thick wet woollen socks and they were steaming on top of the stove. He had been out since dawn, and he was shivering from the wet and bitingly cold weather out there. He was hungry too, having eaten only the briefest snatch of a sandwich and tea in the middle of the day. It was March, and the wind was harsh, cruelly cold and fierce on faces, hands and feet. He decided to challenge her as they were on their own, which was a rare occurrence in this family. Doris looked up from her knitting giving him a stony stare. "That's no business o' you'rn, our Bill," she retorted, continuing the row of stitches.

"Well, we've all of us noticed and folk don't want 'ote to do wi' yer as yer so nasty at times. Some o' time you are just sullen."

"Well, I 'ave nothing to smile about at t' minute 'ave I? What wi' t' weddin' an' all."

"I thought it were meant to be an 'appy event," he replied, rather pleased that he was getting a response.

"What I want, I can't 'ave, can I? It's too expensive. Herbert says no, no and no to everything and I'm getting fed up wi' it."

"Eee lass, don't be allus talking money, money, money. Yer forgettin' how to have some fun!" Bill advised in a soft and gentle tone, "Do things simple and enjoy it."

"I can't, "she answered miserably, "what wi' Sissie getting all the fuss. O' course she'll be 'avin' a grand 'do' wi' Johnny's family an' all. I want t' same sorta swanky do an' all."

"Eee lass, stop there and stop comparing! You are **you** an' she is **she.** Now, let that be an end to it," suddenly raising his voice this time.

She stared back at him at him, quite startled by his manner. This was Bill her young brother, and without her realising, he had matured into a sensible young and capable man on whom his father had increasingly begun to rely. She suddenly realised that he had developed common sense and practical application. Doris had never really connected with him. He always seemed such a silly boy, telling jokes and playing silly games. Looking back now, reflecting on them all growing up, she admitted that it was always Bill and Sissie who seemed close. She had detached herself from them all along.

"That's what our 'erbert tells me," she replied quietly.

"Like yer say, stop wantin' what yer can't have, love," he said, "and just get on. I mean to say - to get on wi' your own lives together. Make no mistake it'll be over before you've even begun."

She looked down as tears rolled down her cheeks.

Bill thought that she was indulging in self-pity and he knew that she would never change, but a good cry would make her feel better.

He put his woollen socks back on, and as he padded out of the room, he said, "If yer don't change yer ways yer'll 'ave no one - not even 'erbert - now get on wi' yer life an' stop watchin' t'others." He slipped the latch and departed leaving damp footprints on the hard floor behind him.

Doris sniffed and wiped away the tears, blew her nose and stared blankly into the flames. Bill had made her reflect. She asked herself if she was nasty. It was true that she didn't laugh much these days. She wondered why she had changed so much. Even Mam had told her she had a face like sour milk the other day. Herbert kept telling her to 'cheer up' and 'be grateful'. But she couldn't believe him with either of those comments just at the moment. She didn't want to be thought of as mean and miserable and she wanted to keep her few friends that she only saw at work these days.

She and Sissie had always been really good friends though, as long as Sissie did as she was told! She was the elder of the two, by just two years, but from the days when Sissie wore all the hand- me-downs to Sissie following her across the farm yard, copying the things she did, they laughed and played well together. Doris would tell her that she was the boss and the very best. And no one, not even Sissie would argue with that!

Growing up, they all got on well enough, even though the boys were much younger and more boisterous. Both parents had provided all that they could afford, in ensuring that they were well fed and clothed. They worked hard through the war years to keep the young family safe and unafraid of any danger.

They worked the land as their war effort, and they said the pit was very important for mining the coal to be used for industry and brought jobs for the area. She didn't pay much attention to all that though.

They were all adult now. Young Frank was the exception, although lately he acted like he was the same age as the rest. She also had Herbert's siblings to think of too because she desperately wanted to be accepted by them. He had a sister and a brother in Blackpool and she was making efforts to spend time with them. They were both married and all of them went out together to local dances and for picnics on the beach. She liked the idea of joining in with them. They didn't seem to have much money either, and they didn't seem to care. They just had a good time! She started to relax a little, imagining what a life like that could be, and she was surprised that it began to sound rather tempting and agreeable.

Slowly, she wound up the wool that had unravelled and fallen from her lap, placed the knitting needles and the unfinished sleeve of a sweater she was making for Herbert into a cloth bag.

"Doris, take yer self in hand and alter!" she muttered quietly.

She felt strangely light headed as she mounted the stairs to bed. She was the last one to turn in before her father checked that all the lights were out; that the fire was stoked for the morning and the doors were locked securely.

It would be Easter next week and then they would be on the way to her wedding day, and she wanted it to be a good day for everybody. Now she felt strangely excited, probably because Bill had told her earlier to have some fun.

She slept soundly and was woken by blackbirds bickering in the privet hedge alongside the bedroom wall. She looked across to Sissie's bed to find it empty and made up. She had gone to work already!

She scrambled out of bed quickly, and dressed for another working day. Then at the bottom of the stairs, she dived into the kitchen and grabbed a mug of tea and a piece of toast. Seeing Sissie at the gate already, she grabbed her coat and ran towards her, the coat flapping widely round her shoulders calling, "Sis! Wait, wait!"

Sissie turned round in surprise, "What's up wi' yer Dot?" she exclaimed.

She wondered what an earth would bring Doris running wildly at this time of the morning, shouting to her.

"Just thought we could walk down together that's all," said Doris breathlessly, her voice hoarse with the cold air.

"Fine by me," replied Sissie, wondering what was coming next. But there was nothing, except that Doris adjusted her step to fall in line with that of her sister.

"How's the first aid?" she enquired politely.

"Oh that? The training? It's the first night tonight, then after four more I receive the certificate," replied Sissie dismissively. She still expected a sardonic remark that had become so typical of Doris's communication these days.

"Yer did alright there our Sis! You were so good when Joyce cut her fingers off, weren't yer?" Sissie winced at both the rough and ready words that Doris used, together with her own still raw recollection of the incident.

"I'm pleased that yer've done the trainin' an' all, like, to be useful on t' factory floor. Do yer get extra pay for it?" Doris added.

Sissie knew that Doris would want to know if money was involved, so she hesitated before replying, "I wanted to train so's I can do better if there's another accident, God forbid! They asked me if I'd do it."

They carried on walking quietly.

"Can we be friends again, Sis? Doris blurted out suddenly. "I've been a bit busy lately and we seem t' be arguin' all the time don't we?"

Sissie remained silent. Then she said, "Doris, I think you have been very mean to me and I don't think it's anything I've done. Unless you can apologise for yer attitude these last few weeks, I'm leaving you to make your own way wi' no interference from me. There. It's up to you."

Sissie was trembling as she finished what she felt needed to be said. She didn't like upset, but at the same time she knew how important it was to tell Doris how her attitude had made her feel recently. She admitted that she felt rather sorry for Doris, who was not very worldly and not the most sociable person, despite being the eldest of five. She had probably always been like that even though she appeared to be the loud, bossy one.

"Well, I'm sorry if I said some 'orrible things but I didn't mean to. Gettin' married is a difficult time and I get vexed," she replied awkwardly. Doris was not the sort to apologise gracefully for wrongdoings because she never felt she did anything wrong!

Sissie smiled quietly to herself, knowing that this was a typical response she'd heard repeatedly over the years,

She knew that Doris would never change, but she wanted to end the conversation on a more positive note so all she said was, "That's alright Dot. Let's get on wi' the day."

Back in the cottage, the morning had begun much earlier. Annie Horbury began to clear away the remains of breakfast. The kitchen was quiet and empty now that everyone had started the working day. She would have to begin with her own daily chores. It was Monday, so washing needed to be organised. She had the same routines for each and every day. She was up and about at first light to warm the kitchen at this time of year and to ensure that bread and tea was on the table for the family. Today, she had lit the gas under the wash boiler to heat up the water, moving a small pile of clothing that was waiting for repair and alteration. She never seemed to have enough time to do it, and not being very skilful with needle and thread it was difficult to become motivated.

"Our Doris should be doing this lot," she muttered quietly, "instead of swannin' around dreamin' of her own future."

She was a slightly built woman but was strong and resilient. Her hands were red and chapped from the years of outdoor work in all weathers, and she was always to be seen in a clean wrap around apron that covered her serviceable skirt, blouse and cardigan underneath. By the evening she would remove it to relax for an hour in front the fire, listening to a bit of music on the wireless.

When Doris returned home that night Annie announced, "I've got a job for you duck." Doris looked worried. She didn't like surprises.

"There's a pile of mendin' in there," she indicated with her thumb. "Make yourself useful and do it for me. You can see better and you'll do it in quicker time than I can."

Doris sighed but daren't complain, knowing how hard her mother worked and how difficult she found the sewing.

"That's alright, Mam. I'll do it," she replied and went straight to the pile of clothing. As she picked it up, looking at a frayed collar and several socks that needed darning, an idea crossed her mind, "I'll advertise meself for mendin' clothes to t'girls in t' factory and they can pay me for doin' t' mendin'. Extra cash for t' future can't be bad," she muttered.

The more she thought about it, the more she realised it would be the easiest way to increase her income with no extra overheads. She could do it in her spare time of which she had plenty, since Herbert was still working in Blackpool.

Sissie returned later after the final training session was over, to find her sister quietly sewing and keen to tell her of her idea to earn some more money. Sissie was pleased for her and said with encouragement, "What a great idea Dot. So many people can't sew and don't even have a needle and thread to learn neither. It'll be a good little earner for thee."

Although she expected to receive some extra pay for her first aid responsibility in the mill, she had been careful not to let Doris know. So inclined to be jealous, Doris would have been unnecessarily spiteful. This seemed a perfect step forward for her sister and she was pleased for her. Perhaps this would stop her feeling so competitive and resentful of others' efforts to improve themselves.

Her own spare time was occupied with her gardening. She loved it. She liked sowing seed, planting out, weeding and harvesting. She gained a lot of satisfaction in growing the vegetables that would then go on to the table, but she enjoyed her small flower garden too. She knew she had a lot to learn but learning through doing was her way, and her successes balanced her failures and everyone acknowledged her pains to improve. She hoped for a garden when she and John were married. And so, both sisters worked towards their next stage in life, to be married and with homes of their own.

*   *   *

"Emma, you don't eat enough! Put some more food on your plate," reprimanded her father, John. She didn't like eating. She found it a nuisance in her busy routine, stopping to help prepare a meal and then to sit down and be sociable at table. She didn't care to eat most of what was put on her plate. The vegetables were just about recognisable, because Mother usually over-cooked them and so everything looked pale green, without texture and crunch. Eating lamb in particular, made her retch. To be eating the animals that they had reared and cared for disgusted her, but ever since she was a child she had been told to 'Get more meat on your plate. You'll never grow,' and so to avoid tension at the table she had struggled to at least take a small portion.

Regrettably, that warning had proved to be correct because at thirty-three years old she still measured only 4 feet and 10 inches and with the frame of a 12-year-old.

It was regrettable because Emma liked to be in control and always to be considered correct. She was uncompromising in discussion and debate. On the matter of food and nutrition, she was proved wrong but she didn't worry too much about her size and form. When she was teased the first time and the girls called her 'titch' she had retaliated scornfully. Consequently, at school and later at college, people stopped calling her names and referring to her size.

Her strong and determined spirit and her passion for reading had developed her imagination and her vocabulary and she was able to transport herself into different worlds to escape from the pressure of day to day irritations, challenges, frustration and sometimes sadness. She was very accomplished at stating her point of view, insisting that it was the right one and she criticised anyone who didn't happen to share the same outlook on life that she had. Indeed, she proved to be a difficult person to share time with.

Besides the extensive book collection of her father's, her own bookshelves in her bedroom were neatly organised in alphabetical order by author. There were those written by Jane Austen, the Brontes and Dickens. Of course she respected the books by Beatrix Potter, who lived and worked in the same county. Recently, she had discovered Kipling, but Stevenson and the works of Thomas Hardy were great favourites too. She would look for a new book every week in which to lose herself. She loved Longfellow's poems and she read them over and over until she could recall them from memory. She introduced 'The Song of Hiawatha' to her pupils and they each took a part in reading, using their best expressive voices under her guidance. To buy a book for herself was an indulgence, and the library in Preston had become special place in which to lose herself amongst its many collections. She looked forward to her Saturday bus ride every week into town and it was a highlight of the weekend for her.

When she was eighteen, she gained her scholarship to London's Whitelands College and she was beside herself with pride and sense of achievement. She had always excelled in her school studies and since being very young, her ambition had been to teach. The schoolboys she knew seemed to receive all the tutoring to help them succeed for university, which she felt was unfair. She wanted her teachers to believe in her ability and to offer her some extra academic support, just like her older brother John, who was two years ahead of her. She was eager to learn and never doubted herself, and so she won her place with ease, at the first women's teacher training college in the country.

Her parents were unsure about their daughter leaving the safety of home at this tender age, to go all the way to London. Emma was determined and persuasive. And so, for two years she studied in the rough and squalid conditions of the institution, exhilarated by the opportunities she gained for extra learning, that made it possible to meet the challenges of working in education. Her main ambition was to make a difference to children's lives. Expectations and standards of behaviour, discipline and adherence to traditional and ritual protocols shaped character and personality. She was so receptive to these ideals, alongside her contemporaries.

Her aspirations were lifted even further, living with, and becoming close to the other women with the same ideals, all of whom were living and learning in this environment.

Whitelands College had a long and inspiring history, specifically due to the influences that Ruskin, Morris and Burne Jones had made here. It confirmed that she herself would become strong and skilful enough to be able to broaden other people's outlook on life besides her own.

By contrast, and with her hearty appetite, Emma's older sister Anne was completely different.

"I'll have your potatoes, Emma," she would often declare at the table and, "Are you eating that last slice of bread?"

Her appetite extended beyond the meal table. People commented on her energy and enthusiasm for living life to the full. She had never been academic, although she'd always been quick to listen and to learn. She had an admirable memory and so she could be relied on to share a few anecdotes, whether from the past or about some recent remarkable event. It often provided entertainment when meal times were over and they were sitting quietly, relaxing in front of the fire. She would have a captive audience in those moments. Her personal joy and fulfilment lay outdoors when working on the farm, whether rearing ducks and hens or rabbits. Sheep farming was regarded as a tough life for a woman especially during the winter months, and was usually reserved for men only. She certainly did not agree with that assumption, and she made sure people knew her opinion on that matter.

Her sense of satisfaction lay in the predictability of daily routine, and she would wake up as the cockerels were crowing, to face the weather outside every day throughout each month of the year. Gulping her hot morning tea, she planned out and prioritised the list of jobs and chores assembled already in her mind for the day ahead. Her efforts were rewarded, and it was clear for everyone to see that she had an aptitude for farm work and husbandry. She had set up a small business selling eggs; rearing and slaughtering chickens for the local market. She also reared turkey chicks born during the Easter period. They would be raised, fattened and ready for the table at Christmas for those folks who could afford one.

When she said she was desperate to start some small scale dairy farming, her father was naturally cautious. He told her she needed get proper training and suggested the agricultural college at Holmes Chapel. It wasn't far away and it was a good place learn from people with plenty of experience, who would be able to guide her. "And I am sure, in time, you will be able to teach me a thing or two," he joked.

At first, she was reluctant to sign up for the study aspect of it, but when she heard that it was affiliated to Manchester University, she was more enthusiastic. That was the university that had set John on his way to the future. She danced around, delighted that she was going to make some progress and eventually, to realise her own ambitions. It certainly would be sensible to go and learn from other experienced dairy farmers.

"My word," said Mother, "we've three of them studying away from home now. I only hope William is up for keeping the farm going with you, John."

John said nothing, "It'll be what it'll be, Mother," he said calmly as Anne strode into the parlour to share the day's news from the farm with them.

Her cheerful and carefree personality lifted people's spirits and hopes for better times. No matter what scale of income people had, life was tough at the moment for everyone. Poverty and unemployment existed right across the country and within the family home they talked about 'the have's and the have not's'. They quietly agreed that they themselves were somewhere in between. Then father would say, "We must count our blessings. Bad luck can fall on any one at any time."

It was obvious that Emma was a scholarly sort, like John. By contrast, Anne would always be the practical one and could roll her sleeves back to make an active effort. It was in stark contrast to Emma's gravity, who analysed and made bold statements about what people should and should not do.

"You take yourself too seriously!" Anne teased her sister when something didn't go to plan or she didn't see the lighter side of anything that was unexpected.

"I don't! And don't you be so frivolous all the time," Emma quipped.

Anyone could see that in spite of their differences, they were good friends and supported each other in difficult moments, and there had been many of those over their growing up years.

Anne's reputation within the farming industry grew as her successes became evident, and her name became associated with reliability and a sense of fairness.

In this way, both sisters followed their ambitions in different directions. Both were independent and competent in their chosen professions and being busy people they worked their way through the first world war and afterwards with a single minded and courageous spirit, guided by their Christian principles to 'give unto others'.

In this way, they had both benefitted from the influence of their mother, also named Emma. She had been a teacher before she married John, teaching at the local elementary school, as several young women of her disposition did at the end of the nineteenth century. When she met John Thompson Bland she welcomed the role of farmer's wife. It was a good marriage and a splendid match for both of them. His family had owned sheep farms and land that was well established over centuries as established yeomen farmers. She was a practical woman with a kind and generous heart, but she didn't suffer fools and the people whom she respected were honest, God fearing and loyal. These were the qualities she instilled into her five children as she raised them. There were four of them now, as she still found it difficult to speak of the youngest born. This was James who, at seven years old did not survive the whooping cough. She would pause beside his simple gravestone every Sunday on her way into church, never saying anything but whispering a prayer before she stepped into the gloom of the nave for the regular Sunday service. Kneeling in the family pew, she put her hands together, dropping low on her knees as she thanked the Lord for the gift of her four other children in whom she was pleased and proud, as each one's steady nature and integrity grew.

The next thing to look forward to would be grandchildren and how happy and truly fulfilled that would make her. Her daughters would make fine wives and mothers, she was certain.

It was not to be. Neither of them had ambitions to be married. And they never did.

Chapter 25

Let Bygones
be Bygones

John banged his pipe on the heel of his left hand, clearing its spent contents ready to charge it again. Then he paused for a moment, staring reluctantly at the shoreline that was shrinking from view. This time it would be for the last time. There behind him lay a legacy of vivid memories that he would rather leave behind him; the many people he had lost and with whom he would never be reunited. He was leaving a country with different customs and traditions and language of which now, he had no desire to be a part.

The timing was right. Now he had laid his plans. He recognised that now in 1925, after the seven years since the end of the war, there were new horizons and he was focusing more clearly on the future.

He frowned and narrowed his eyes, as he imagined the prospect of the new and promising life that lay ahead for him, as he took on a new family. A family that he would create, nurture, support and treasure. The family would be waiting for him, trusting his decisions and his vision for a future in which he wanted all who joined him to become involved.

He promised that he would devote his time and effort to this innocent little girl by his side, who was so dependent on him now.

He looked down at her lovingly, and yet nervous of her, as he realised he didn't really know her too well. They had been apart for such a vast amount of time. He watched her, as wide eyed, she observed the activity surrounding them on the ship. It made her uncertain and confused. It was all so new to her, and she was unusually quiet.

Big changes were happening for her. The grown-ups spoke in hushed tones and there were occasional outbursts of raised voices before someone shushing to quieten conversations, and then there was the occasional sound of an older woman weeping.

"Grandmama is crying. Is she hurt?" she asked her nanny a few times.

Decisions had to be made and agreed, and it was time to take action. And that was the reason he was here.

She gripped his warm dry hand in total trust. This young, dark haired gentle man was called Papa. She looked up at him, appealing for an answer that perhaps she would not understand.

"Where are we going?" she asked quietly, and he noticed that she had a faint accent.

"We are going home, dear child. We are going to your new home, and you are going to live with me so that we can be together," he answered firmly and kindly, whilst stroking her straight dark hair. "Not long now."

Not long! It seemed to have been so long since he had travelled to collect her. He found her in the quiet, sorrowful household that housed the grieving parents of his deceased young wife. She had been their only daughter, and they were bereft and directionless now that she was no longer in their lives.

The cedar fragrance of the tobacco wafted from its pouch, and he carefully packed its short cut, wavy leaves into the shiny black bowl of his pipe. He paused for a moment to watch the undulating waves swishing past the ship, as the vessel carved its way through the murky grey water.

"Good to have a calm crossing," he murmured as he flicked his Tommy Trench Lighter and drew slowly to ignite the fragrant leaves. As the pipe began to glow, he began thinking about the lives of the people he had left and of the ones he was travelling towards. He was confident that with his life experiences so far, he was fully prepared both emotionally and pragmatically, to put the tragic past behind him. He was ready and determined to make the future a success for himself and his new family now. However, there was a lot to do and so much to think about.

It had been a long and tedious wait in Gembloux whilst all the little girl's paperwork was finalised. Now he was impatient to return to his own country. It was the one he could truly call home. Here lived the woman he loved now, and with whom he was so desperate to move forward. He was impatient to get on with it.

There would be some real work for them to do when he introduced Sissie to his daughter. She was so young and vulnerable and she was bewildered by all these changes. He would have to be more sensitive to her needs, and he and Sissie would have to work hard to settle her into their way of life. It was going to be a life which he himself admitted was unclear yet. Inwardly, he was a little nervous himself. He hoped he had made a full recovery from his war experiences, adapting to civilian life and working routines and then, falling in love. So much had happened so quickly. Keeping a grip on practical matters, he was aware that now he must also face some family and cultural differences.

He had written to dearest Sissie in his latest letter,

'Some day, I want to be somebody in this world.
I don't always want to stop as a small mill manager.'
'Won't we be so happy together my little sweetheart?'

He loved writing to her, to declare his feelings.

Lovely, loyal Sissie would be waiting quietly, so patient and so gentle. He knew how much she loved him, because she had already been good to him, showing her affections when they were alone. In the rare brief moments, they had spent together already, she had proved her love and loyalty and he could feel such tenderness and desire for her, too. She was sensible, thoughtful and kind and when he married her, she would be a wonderful mother. He knew she was not only right for him, but she was also the right choice for Vicky.

He hoped that the smoothness of the crossing would allow time for them to board the train from Dover so that he could be nearer to home sooner. The white cliffs of Dover loomed into view and the waves beneath the boat rolled along to match the wave of relief he was feeling as they approached the docks on dry land.

At the same time, he realised that there would be many twists and turns before he and Sissie achieved success in their new challenges together. No mathematical formula would solve this. This was not like the ones he had applied to gain First in Maths at University. He reflected on the precision and accuracy required and he recalled the thrill of achievement, and the recognition from mathematics professors at the time.

His head was clear and he was focused right now. He was keen to gain the feeling of success again.

He recalled how he had gained respect and success in battle, and he did not want that to be forgotten, but at the same time he wanted to be discreet. He had not expected to be awarded the Military Cross for leadership and bravery in the battle at Beaurain. Actually, he didn't feel worthy of it. He regarded it as one small achievement in action. His own recollection of that time was directed towards the many men he had known and fought with, in one of the last bloody battles of this war. They did not make it home alive.

He sighed, wishing for a little simplicity and straight forwardness for this next chapter in his life. He gazed at the wide eyed, angelic face of his four-year-old daughter, chattering away her first words in Belgian. He listened, and from time to time he gently corrected her in English. He was determined that the innocence of this lovely child would be nurtured and cared for, so that she could enjoy the freedom and happiness that he and his generation had fought to achieve.

He wanted to sweep away the haunting images of living a hard and raw existence, and of the endless cold, hunger and grief caused by the pain and loss of his battle field compatriots, which he had witnessed.

He was searching for hope and a belief in a better life. It promised to be in the form of his daughter. She was the future.

Then he realised that recalling the past should remain in the past. He was beginning to feel melancholy already. His thoughts recurred now as they so often had before, that 'the past should be left there'.

Suddenly, a chirpy little voice brought him back into the present. "Papa! Papa! Regard là!"

He looked in the direction of her tiny forefinger as she pointed, and tugged at his coat towards the commotion on the quayside as the ship approached its berth. They had arrived in Dover.

*   *   *

What a relief! It had been such a long journey from Ostend, and with having a small airless cabin, sleep had been fragmented and uncomfortable. He had heard her whimpering in her sleep. He decided to leave her, but her tousled damp hair tickled his face as she turned over and her arm fell over his own. He was overwhelmed with tenderness and devotion for her. Yet, he had certain doubts that he was not going to be able to help her face a new life nor show her how to deal with her fear and confusion in her new world. She was here with him, her father, and yes, he would be raising her now, but she needed a mother to whom she could find love and comfort, reassurance and confidence. He believed in Sissie, and her ability to take on the responsibility.

Leaving her grandparents behind after her mother's death was difficult and very sad, of course. It meant that she had experienced not one but two losses in her short life. The farewells were tearful and they all sensed the finality at their parting. He was anxious to depart quickly and they left the two bereft in-laws of his previous lifetime, sorrowful and alone.

He regretted the emotions at the quayside, but he couldn't have organised things differently because the elderly couple wished to close their chapter just as meaningfully as he wanted to open up his own. He breathed a silent prayer of gratitude that at least she was too young to fully understand her circumstances nor of bereavement, and that there were good times ahead. He would make sure of that.

Sissie would make a good mother to her now. He had chosen her carefully, not just following his emotions and his physical attraction to her when they had met. When she told him that her mother had raised Frank, the youngest of twelve, from her father's side of the family during the war he was humbled. Sissie's parents, like many others were raising fatherless children now. The war had taken so many young men away suddenly and cruelly, so this would not be an unusual situation for Sissie. New ideas were emerging now. Families were learning to cope in the home and in relationships, in the work place and in recovering from injury and loss caused by the war. Facing hardship, loss, poverty and poor health bonded society at every level in unique ways never experienced before. He himself felt blessed that he had a good job and was financially comfortable. There was a lovely woman waiting, whom he was to marry and a family too. Yes, this was a motherless child, but this was going to change for the better.

He did not doubt Sissie's ability, although she hadn't expressed her opinion on the situation that lay ahead of them.

He knew she was young and unworldly; most women of her age were the same. He had seen how honest and down to earth she was and he had noticed signs of selflessness. These were some of the qualities that he had been looking for in a second wife, matched only by his determination to find a mother for his daughter. He was confident that when they were married, she would develop the strength and energy to shape her role as a wife and as a mother. They had developed a trust and deep friendship already, and they would learn from each other.

Yesterday in one of the daily letters he had sent her, he wrote:

> *'I know I have my faults just as you know what your own are but we have to try and please each other. I just as much as you. It has to be give and take on each side, not one to do all the giving and the other all the taking…'*

He hoped she understood what he meant.

The rusty chains of the ship groaned as the men heaved them towards the capstan, shouting at each other so that they could be heard over the noise of the ship's engines which gradually slowed down to complete silence. His pipe had gone out. Not surprisingly, the early morning sea air had dampened and extinguished it. To empty it, he banged it on the ship's rail and threw the remains over the side. They blew back in his face which caused him to splutter. It made him realise that things you thought were over can always come back as solemn reminders.

He had all his papers with him to show officials on disembarking. More importantly, he would be able to show the little one's documents. It had taken such a long time to sort them out, back in Belgium. They both shivered simultaneously as they descended the shaky gang plank together, partly as a reaction to the brisk early morning breeze, and partly in anticipation for what was to follow on the next stage of their journey.

Crowds of travellers creating long queues at the border desk, reminded him of the lines of soldiers during the war, who queued to have their papers stamped and signed. A multitude of different languages and accents could be heard, and the confusion, together with the cacophony of noise was disturbing and so new for little Victoria. "Je veux partir Papa. Je veux rentrer," she shouted.

"We _are_ going Victoria, but we are here in England. We are going to find a train right now. There's no need to be afraid. You will always be safe with me. I'm your Daddie."

In that moment, he hoped that he would always be able to keep that promise. He wanted all the plans, the hopes and ambitions he was dreaming about, to materialise.

They quickly hurried onto the station platform. He was anxious to catch the next train. It was a long way up to London and then they needed to change and take the connection to Manchester. Such a big journey for a little girl in her new surroundings.

He knew that Emma would be waiting on the platform. She had been notified of the expected time of arrival and she would have blankets, food, a book or two and some treats with her. She was so eager to look after her niece. They had agreed before he had made the trip to collect her, that it would be most convenient and practical for Victoria to stay with her. John would then visit on his days off, or at the weekend and he had accepted that it was the most sensible thing to do.

"Just until you and Sissie are married," Emma had suggested.

It all made complete sense. He had to concentrate on succeeding in his new position at the mill. It was a management role that he had applied for and desperately wanted. Leaving the mill in Darton and transferring up to Doncaster for now would avoid unnecessary gossip until they were married. He was waiting for them to contact him. It would be any day now.

"Don't touch the windows little one. They are dirty! Sit still in your seat, there's a good girl," he said briskly. He pushed the bags on the top ledges above the seats. Then they settled in their places on the on the faded blue tweedy seating, threadbare with age and bearing the signs of use by so many travellers just like them.

The sooty smoke from the London-bound steam train had left a thin film across the window sills. The last thing he wanted was for Emma to see a tired, grubby child who lacked English, her only language being Flemish and French. She hugged her teddy bear close to her chest and her dark eyes filled with tears.

"Now then, don't cry little one. It's alright. We will soon be home," he said kindly, realising that he had been rather commanding. He tilted the corner of his newspaper, peering from behind it to check she wasn't still weeping. He smiled at her and he winked and it made her giggle.

The rhythm of the wheels on the track made them both doze off during the journey. Victoria's head rested in the crook of her father's arm, clutching her teddy, completely at peace against his sturdy firm body. She felt secure. Suddenly he woke up, disturbed by the newspaper as it collapsed, crumpled up and slid to the floor of the carriage. He took his pipe from his top pocket, glancing down at the sleeping child. In typical style, he tapped the pipe on the heel of his hand and blew through it before charging it with tobacco. Without lighting up straight away, he breathed in the sweet aromas from it, and reflected on the events of the week; his last one within the smart but subdued household of his former wife's parents.

He began to reflect on how he had met these gentle, kind people. They had welcomed him warmly into their family and their home; approving and supporting his relationship with their precious daughter, and the circumstances that had brought them together.

She had left the family home to join the war time medical aid, despite Belgium being uninvolved. As the daughter of a doctor, it was a natural calling for her when she responded to the national advertisement, and she went with all the spontaneity and enthusiasm that youth bestows. Eager to offer help, she was determined to nurse injured and dying soldiers on the front line. She was an only child and her life so far had been one of privilege, comfort and indulgence. She wanted to be independent and useful and so her parents eventually let her go with their blessings and pride in her courage.

He smiled at the memory of his meeting with her, as he admitted to himself that he was not usually a sentimentalist, despite quietly hiding a romantic core.

His upbringing in the harsh moorlands of Westmoreland and the experiences during the final years of the war, he thought, had probably closed the sentiment gate. By contrast, his growing up years had been far from indulgent! He had been taught to face hardship, challenge and sometimes, disappointment with courage, resilience and in a self-belief that you were doing the right thing. The young woman that he had met softened his tough approach and admired the resolve in someone so young. He taught her that to survive and succeed you just had to 'get on with it' and to use 'action not words'. How that had become indelibly marked within him, shaping his attitude and ability.

They met in the rough field hospital on the frontline near Lille and there was an instant rapport and their attraction to one another was shy and tentative. Her fluent English allowed for easy communication when they first met. Their first encounter had been amongst the many wounded young men who had survived those final and fierce battles towards the end of the war. Their tortured bodies moaned on flimsy canvas camp beds, as they fought against pain, loss of limb, eyesight, memory, sleep and reason.

He sighed sadly and lit the tobacco. The flicking sound of his lighter and the soft pop popping as he drew on the pipe, woke the little girl.

"Hello little one," he whispered gently. "That was a good sleep. You are a good girl. We are nearly there."

He carefully unwrapped the last portion of a now rather stale baguette, the cheese and tomato compressed tightly inside, and coaxed her to eat it. She nibbled it reluctantly. She was hungry but not for this offering.

"Drink," she whispered. "Need a drink."

Inside his worsted wool jacket, he pulled out a small stocky bottle of army issue, that he had used during his time at the Front.

"Water here. Drink some, my little lamb."

She took it carefully from his right hand and guzzled noisily from the cold metal top. "Merci, Papa," she said as she gave it back.

"Thank you Daddie," he corrected her gently.

He told her that they were 'nearly there'. The life he could offer her would not be at all like his own had been, nor hers before today.

Growing up on the moors had been tough and cruel at times, including the weather. It was assumed that everyone on the farm should be helping wherever and whenever they could. That was how successful farming worked, since his ancestors had farmed the land since the 1600's under King Charles 1.

As a boy he was secure, felt loved and listened to. Mother was an efficient, no nonsense housewife who raised her children with unshakeable devotion and tenderness. She could be firm and direct, because she liked routine, had high expectations and ambitious ideas for each of the children. She was an excellent and innovative cook and she made all the clothes for the girls. She turned the collars and cuffs on the boys' shirts and she darned their woollen socks once they had gone to bed. He hoped he would see the same qualities in Sissie.

And then there was Biddie. She was a spinster now, at forty-four years of age. Dear Biddie was a young woman who originally joined them many years ago, leaving her own family who lived at the top of the Fell. She had become part of their family, coming in every day to teach the children, then tutoring them to ensure they passed the entrance examinations for grammar school. By contrast, she let them have fun when the weather was harsh and treacherous, when she would stay the night and sleep in the girls' room on an old slatted bed. They would sing jolly songs in the evening and once she taught them all how to play cards. In the morning she would make the porridge with some of the sheep's milk instead of just the water mother used. Oh, those carefree days did seem so long ago now.

"My Vicky shall have that life," he murmured.

They sat comfortably in silence until at last, the train pulled into Manchester London Road station. The brakes squealed and the sooty smoke blew backwards, creeping under the sash windows of the carriage. A loud whistle echoed as the platforms began to come into view. People were waiting for their now weary passengers, eager to meet them. Their faces could be seen frantically scanning the windows to recognise those whom they had waited for, at the earliest possible moment. John watched, bemused by a young man in his urgency to get off the train and onwards with his journey, tugging at the broad leather strap to release the window. It slid downwards noisily and he stuck his head out as if this would make his departure quicker.

With a sudden jolt the train stopped. The engine snorted and hissed out its steam and the wheezing wheels ground to a halt. The screeching of metal on metal deafened everyone there, but no one seemed to notice. They were too keen to get off and get on with their onward plans, awaiting under white clouds; all that grey Manchester could offer this early spring day.

"Off we go! Take my hand, little Vicky. Let's find your Auntie Emma."

She was standing on the railway platform among crowds of others who anxiously and excitedly waited for the next arrival.

"Who are they all waiting for?" Emma asked herself, pulling nervously at her grey leather gloves in anticipation of the family arrival and gazing up and down the lines of strangers on the dusty platform.

Perhaps some were going to be reunited with old friends and family or with loved ones not seen in a long time, or maybe they were business connections. She, herself was anxiously waiting for a little girl, ably chaperoned by her father; her own brother who was now a father and of whom she was so fond. She imagined the little girl would be bewildered and frightened of the crowds, the noise and new smells and so overwhelmed by the unfamiliarity of the place.

She tapped impatiently with her slim, small stockinged foot within her lace-up leather brogues. Like her brother, she also had to have shoes made for her, being so small. Just like him, she had a huge spirit, a broad and thorough knowledge of today's world and a big voice to express it. She was decisive and single minded, and always looked for instant solutions to any challenge that she faced. Unlike her brother however, she was unshakeable in her belief that God would guide her in all her decisions, and as an active and committed church goer, she expected everyone else to make time and effort to pray just as she did. She could be scathing and judgmental of those who did not share her same dedication. At St Mary's, the church she had attended regularly as a child, up to the present day, she had made it her responsibility to line up the hymn books and arrange fresh flowers at the altar every week.

Her Sundays began with Holy Communion and closed with Evensong with the family, and with Sunday lunch between. Routine and godliness was her Sunday. So today represented a big change in her routine.

She was an avid reader which had given her imagination, a glimpse into worldwide history and geography. She read with enthusiasm, and she clutched a copy of Virginia Woolf's 'Mrs. Dalloway' that she hadn't had a chance to look at yet. The platform was far too hectic to have a quiet read today.

"Always with her nose in a book," her mother would say, shaking her head in bewilderment. She would never find herself a husband! Recently, it had been noticed that Emma had started collecting natural history studies currently being published. She was fascinated and the volumes satisfied her curiosity and thirst for living things. Not only that, they provided inspiration for some sketching and painting in water colour too. She enjoyed her own company as she walked; the solitude it provided as she identified birds and small mammals, with whom she shared her private thoughts and opinions of the moment. Finding and naming plants and wildflowers and rejoicing in the changing nature of the moorland from season to season was her passion. It was really a natural development of her fell walking days, long after the necessity of all year round walking to school. She had always had a busy mind, a vivid imagination and was at ease in her own company. Her eagerness and enthusiasm as she shared all her reading, discoveries, interests and hobbies were fulfilled through her teaching.

Her fine but wiry auburn hair was long, reaching the small of her back when she brushed it out at night before plaiting its length neatly for sleeping. An early riser, she would brush it through again, swiftly and accurately twisting it into a small, neat bun at the base of her neck. She was always neatly and simply dressed; her mother making all her clothes for her. A neat patterned, long sleeved cotton blouse covered her flat chest and today, she had chosen to pin her grandmother's Victorian silver and garnet brooch neatly positioned at the neck as usual. The gabardine skirt looked smart over her slender body and she carried a tartan shawl for extra warmth, over her arm. As she left the house, she checked herself in the hall mirror and smiled back at herself.

"Off we go," she whispered.

Being younger than John but equally educated and well read, they shared a lot in common, whether that was in politics or literature or in the natural world and definitely when it came to gardening. She had experienced more time at home in their own garden whilst he had been away at war. She liked to think that because she and John shared so many similarities, they were the closest. In her own private way, she admired his achievements, both before and during the war but now she was in no doubt that the choices that he had made since then had been questionable. However, one would not argue with her brother. He had logic in him and she admired him for that. He was focused and resolute and in any situation he seemed to be popular and well respected, and she knew that his calm and placid exterior hid his determination and drive towards personal aspiration and success.

"Praise be!" she sighed, as the smoke billowed from the funnel of the approaching engine pulling into the station. The noise was excruciating and the commotion on the platform perplexed her, as people ran recklessly alongside the carriages to catch the first glimpses of familiar faces.

Suddenly he was there, pipe in his mouth, lifting a small rosy cheeked child in a pale lemon dress and a mustard coat, buttons undone, off the high steps onto the ground.

He really is a handsome man, she thought looking at him as he walked towards her. Although of slight build and height he had stature and presence. The brim of his nut brown trilby shaded his eyes and his woollen tweed suit was cut well to suit his frame. Surprisingly, after the long journey the starched collar of his shirt looked clean and fresh. Perhaps he had refreshed it that morning, Emma guessed, always noticing every detail in any situation. Her heart was filled with pride and filial fondness.

Emma waved - one didn't shout - and as he looked to his left and then to his right, he spotted her and returned the wave as a kind of salute, bending as he did so, to point towards her to tell Vicky that her Auntie was here.

In a calm and measured way they walked towards each other and Emma stretched out her arms to welcome the child.

"Good journey, John?" she enquired perfunctorily, as she grasped the small hand that was clinging to the arm of a small teddy at John's side. And then, wishing to include the child straightaway whispered, "Hello Victoria. You are getting bigger aren't you? And how old are you now?"

Shy and not sure of the questions, she looked up at her Papa questioningly.

"You are getting big aren't you, Vicky because you are four years old now. And you have been a very good girl during this journey. Emma, I do hope we never have to make that journey ever again. It took such a long time, everywhere is so busy and its so FAR! Let's get her home, shall we?"

"Of course, of course. William is waiting in the truck. We will be home in no time!"

That was a slight exaggeration. It would take at least two hours to get to the old stone farmhouse but the house would be warm, with a fire going and the kitchen table bearing gifts of pork pie and fresh tomatoes, freshly baked bread and home churned butter. There would be a hardboiled egg or two from the farm hens that fussed around the stables at the edge of the yard. To be sure, taking pride of place in the middle, there would be the weekly cake. Perhaps a Dundee or a Madeira.

Emma slowly turned to Vicky. She wasn't sure the child would understand her, but she continued, "And then we can have something fine to eat before we give you bath time and bed my girl, after your very long journey."

Her instinct was to keep speaking English and repeating certain key words. This child was from educated parents on both sides of her family, and she hoped she would be bright and quick to learn. Under her guidance, she would be certain to achieve the best that the future would offer her now.

They stepped into the light of the Manchester afternoon and as Emma had said, waiting patiently in the farm truck was their brother William, tapping his fingers tunelessly on the steering wheel.

"Eeh! At long last," he called out, whistling through his teeth. "You've been in there for ages!"

"Nice to see you too, Willy," laughed John. "We're here and that's all that matters. Now, say hello to Vicky."

"Victoria," Emma corrected.

"No, it is to be Vicky. I've made my mind up. It's softer and friendlier and besides, I prefer it," he replied, unable to admit that her name was the same as her deceased mother.

He lifted Vicky up and swung her legs onto the backseat of the cab whilst William took their bags, placing them securely in the back. Through the open window to the back seat he offered a small package and said, "I brought some of Mother's fruit cake for the little lass to nibble on."

And then without any more delay, he called out "Everybody ready?" as he slid behind the steering wheel.

"Well, let's get going because I know someone who is going to be very excited to see you."

"How is Mother?" John enquired. He knew she had some firm opinions about the situation they were in. He was bringing a motherless child to join the family. He was fully aware of how his mother would be worrying about their future challenges. She would be anxious about the uncertainty of the future and Vicky's upbringing, whilst he himself was ambitiously following a career in the textile industry at the same time. Then there was Sissie. He knew Mother would be imagining how this young inexperienced woman would cope with a four-year-old, once they were married. There would be no doubt in her mind, that babies would arrive in their own relationship. He was certain that these would be the questions that kept his mother awake and troubled, at night.

The truck left the city of his university days, that seemed a lifetime ago. That was in 1911 and so much had happened since those days. His Mathematics degree, and his further studies that qualified him for work in the textile industry had been his only priorities. After his short spell as a teacher of

Mathematics at the old grammar school where he himself had been a pupil, he realised this was not his vocation. When war broke out he was obliged to join the cadet corps and would sign up, to be accepted as an officer with his university degree and formal training.

"But that's in the past, too," he murmured to himself as he gazed back at the little girl hugging her teddy. She was listening intently to her new auntie showing her cows and sheep grazing in the fields. The neat little farmhouses dotted across the hills would merge into the harsher terrain of the heather and ferns of the fells.

William concentrated on his driving. He didn't admit it but he had never needed to drive such a long distance. This was a return journey and all to be done in the same day! The driving required his full attention and he wanted to ask after Sissie and how they were both getting on but he was anxious that the truck engine may not handle this distance without breaking down. He had tools in the back, a spare tyre and a metal flagon of water to cope with anything unexpected, but the vehicle was so old and they had used it heavily for such a long time. He was glad to be doing something to help his brother though, and although his sister could be tiresome and pedantic at times, at least she had been company on the way here.

Emma sat upright in the back seat, her small hands folded on her lap, where her neatly clipped nails demonstrated an outward sign that she enjoyed precision and tidiness in her life. Quietly reflecting she realised that she did not feel comfortable in accepting this casual shortening of the little one's name. It irked her, as she preferred formality at the best of times before getting acquainted with people. Times were changing now she reluctantly admitted, and so she sat beside her niece in comfortable silence, and proceeded to ask her brother polite questions about the journey.

Perhaps the shortened version of the little girl's name would begin to grow on her. She herself, might take a little time to adjust to it but John was right, it did probably suit her. It occurred to her that Queen Victoria had been known affectionately within the royal family as young Vicky. Within their own family, William was 'Willy' and often they called Anne, her sister 'Annie'. Didn't John get 'Johnny' on the sports field and particularly when he was in the army?

So why did she not accept this name readily? Probably her own formal style, until she got to know a person prevailed. Even towards this little person. Times were changing now as the years rolled on since the Great War, and she was keen to contribute to progress. She was inspired that society was beginning to recognise the status of women beyond the kitchen and the nursery. Perhaps she should relax her rather rigid style and be more flexible now. Perhaps one could stick to convention but have a lighter touch of correctness and dignity.

Everyone was weary and heads were nodding as they dozed in the stuffiness of the cab. To lower the windows down was to invite draughty gusts of dusty air and no one wanted that. So for several miles, silence seemed a comfortable and simple way to travel the last part of this journey.

John was already thinking about the next part of his trip. He was eager to get himself to Barnsley and to see Sissie. Together again at last, she would be waiting patiently, at home with her mother and brothers, hopefully having stopped working at the mill every day.

"What a lovely girl she is," he thought as a picture of her drifted into his head. "Same height as me with the sweetest round face and kind but cheeky smile. Sixteen years' difference in our ages means nothing because we are well and truly matched in love."

He was honest and sincere when he wrote to her last week:

I have never been so comfortable in all my life as when I am with you. You know I love you. Won't we be happy together, my little sweetheart?

He smiled to himself, as he tugged at his top pocket to pull out his pipe.

"No, John. Please don't light that thing or you'll have us all coughing and spluttering!" Emma pleaded.

Chapter 26

Leaving Vicky
in Shap

John was very frustrated the next day as he could not return to Barugh, where his urgency to return to Sissie and to work beckoned. The train travel times were unworkable for him the as the timings and connections made it impossible to proceed with his plans. However, it did provide some unexpected extra time that he could spend with his little girl to ensure that she could settle, reducing any distress for her.

That day passed very quickly as he showed her the farm yard and they played with the dogs and sat on the farm gate watching the sheep on the hills closest to home. Emma gave her some paper and paints and she was able to express herself as she sat at the kitchen table, painting a brightly coloured sun, sky and green hills. Watching her drawing Papa made them smile and they praised her enthusiastic attempts, smiling as she concentrated on her creation, her tongue stuck on her upper lip in concentration.

She ate well and seemed extremely content. She was completely at ease with her new surroundings, until John told her gently that he would be leaving the next day and that she would be staying with her aunt and grandparents. Her face crumpled in confusion and disappointment and she clung to him crying, "No, don't go - don't leave me Papa. I want to come with you!" Her cries turned to uncontrollable sobs as her instinct took over to try and prevent him from upsetting this happy time she was enjoying with him.

"Now then, now then. What's all this fuss for?" he exclaimed, as he held her close to comfort her. "I'm not going away for long. Your Papa has to go to work and you have to go to school with your Auntie Emma. You'll have such fun together and then I will be back to look at some more of your pictures and to hear you reading. And you can tell me all the stories about what you've been doing on the farm."

He thought this was another difficult moment for her and a time for tough decisions to be taken. Her distress was heart wrenching as her small body shook as she gripped him tightly. It broke his heart to hear her pleading in between her sobbing. He let her have a few moments before he pulled out his unused handkerchief, and lifting her face upwards he dabbed away her tears, saying, "Blow!"

She blew her nose loudly into the crisp white cotton. He laughed and said, "What a noise from such a pretty little nose that was!"

She smiled faintly between her sobs and wiped a hand across her face, trying to feel calmer as she felt his reassuring voice.

He rocked her on his lap for the next ten minutes or so, not saying anything. It was much more important to calm her using his sheer presence and the quiet of the parlour to allow her to settle down.

Then the parlour door opened slowly with its familiar creak, and his mother peered in and with a bold but kind voice said, "I think I know someone who would like sausages for tea? Do you Papa?" "No, no grandma, I don't know anyone here," he replied, winking at Vicky.

"Me, me, ME! I like sausages!" she shouted out and scrambled down from his lap.

"Come along then, let's wash your hands and we will see what we can do," said his mother.

He was grateful for the interruption. The mood in the room had changed and Vicky was happier now.

He realised in that moment that if she was happy, he could be happy too.

He was glad to spend the rest of the day, eating with the family, getting Vicky ready for bed and ensuring that she fell fast asleep. She insisted that he read to her tonight and he was so pleased to do that small thing that he knew would be so important to her. Just like the times when she was a baby, when he read a story before she fell asleep.

Later, he sat in the parlour at the old mahogany bureau and wrote a note to Sissie updating her on events and informing her of his impending arrival later tomorrow:

"Vicky is settling nicely here. She told Auntie that she would have to sleep in another bed because she wanted her Papa to sleep with her. When I put her to bed tonight I had to tickle her back until she went to sleep. I only wish it might have been someone else's back I was tickling!

I have been thinking of you all day. The day seems so long without you, yet when we are together the time seems to pass before we know where we are. My darling, I shall be glad when we are together for always.

I am longing to get settled with a home of my own with you - my dear little sweetheart. Now, I think I will close with best love and kisses from,

Your loving sweetheart John

As he entered the bedroom he could hear the soft rhythm of Vicky's breathing. Very gently, he tucked her arms under the bed sheet, smoothed the eiderdown and gazed at her tenderly, promising himself that he would not let her feel as upset as she had been this afternoon, ever again.

Turning out the light, finding the house quiet and still, the reflections of the past few years that had dominated all day rumbled through his head as he got undressed for bed. With his mind still revolving and his head touching the pillow, he knew this would not be a peaceful sleep. Today had been emotionally demanding and energy draining and the turmoil in his mind didn't seem ready to go away.

*   *   *

After his restless night in the feather bed; a recent addition to the previously lumpy cotton stuffed one of earlier times, he was woken by the tugging of the eiderdown and a little voice calling, "Papa, wake up."

Opening his eyes slowly he looked down to see Vicky in her pin tucked nightdress. She was full of excitement, bearing a shy expression. She had hesitated, at first unsure whether to wake him, but she herself was awake now, and she wanted to play.

"Good morning, young lady. Now, if you please would you let me wake up and find out the time?" Any recollection of yesterday was far from the little girl's mind as she urged him to get up.

"Let's play, Papa. Let's go to the hens! Let's find eggs."

He groaned, the back of his hand shielding his eyes. He had only just fallen into a deep sleep and momentarily he was disorientated.

"Let's look at some picture books first," he mumbled,"and let your dear Papa wake up first."

She padded across the floor in her bare feet to find an illustrated Book of the Alphabet on a small bookshelf and wriggled into bed with it.

"Ouch! Your feet are cold," he complained in a half whisper. She giggled and deliberately touched his legs and he shuddered in a dramatic way to make her laugh some more.

"You're Miss Mischief," he teased.

She looked at the book of illustrated letters patiently, humming as she turned each page as her drowsy Papa slowly adjusted his eyes to the early morning light, glinting through the soft pink patterned curtains of his sister's room. His pocket watch on the bedside table had stopped, so he guessed the time as around 7.00am and so before she was about to jump out to find another book he said, "Let's get dressed and go downstairs for some breakfast. Quickly! Take your clothes off the chair and go and ask Auntie Emma if she will help you to dress."

She trotted over to the chair, grabbed a bundle of clothing and disappeared without a sound.

When she had gone, he slowly eased his sleep-weary body to the edge of the bed, the wooden slats groaning against its metal frame, as his weight shifted from the middle to the edge. Throughout the night he had relived as he did so often, sudden flashbacks of soldiers he had known who were blown to pieces. Images of the days when rain and freezing cold snatched at his wet toes in hard leather boots, and the burning sensation of chilblained fingertips haunted him. He felt the hunger pain that tore into the stomach and he could hear the relentless boom and crack of shelling and rifle fire. He woke up as always, shivering, rocking to and fro and moaning into the night time air in the bedroom, and all the bedclothes had been wrestled to the floor.

He wondered if there would ever be a morning when he could welcome a new day, refreshed and eager for it to unfold.

As he dressed himself, putting on a clean collar and then tying his tie, he could hear her chattering with Emma, followed by their footsteps as they went down the stairs.

"I am sure this time here will be well spent and so good for her," he reassured himself and with growing satisfaction and relief for the future that lay ahead for her and for him, he folded his jacket over his arm, picked up his pocket watch and descended the stairs himself.

He corrected the time on his watch from the grandfather clock in the hall. It was 7.30am. He recalled the days when at Vicky's age, they as children played hide and seek and someone would always climb inside the oak case of the majestic clock.

As he looked at it now, it was hard to imagine that they had all been so small, so young and so carefree.

Breakfast was well under way with porridge warming on the stove and mother pouring tea, one cup at a time, as people appeared and seated themselves. Today was no exception and his father was there first, as always, followed by Willie and Magwen, Anne and Emma and now, Vicky.

Everyone was up and whilst Father and Willie had been about the farm since dawn doing their routine jobs outside, they were ready for the tea, being poured just as John entered the kitchen.

In their usual way they exchanged a formal morning greeting, enquiring of each other's sleep. It was the customary introduction to the day, every day, and John sat down ready for the tea, and said that he would prefer some fresh bread and butter with jam.

"This one is bramble jelly. It's the end of the batch," Mother explained,

"We had a good crop of fruit with the rain we had last spring," she said watching Vicky wipe the back of her hand over her blackberry stained mouth. Clearly she had enjoyed her breakfast today, with porridge and jam.

"Use the napkin child. Show her, Emma," John said to divert attention away from the habits of a four-year-old whom he thought was behaving quite well, under the circumstances. "Anybody like to come and collect eggs with me?" asked

Anne in an inviting voice, looking at Vicky. "Me," responded Vicky immediately.

"Please," John and Emma chorused, looking towards the excited child. "Please," she repeated.

"Yes, indeed you certainly can love," Anne replied beaming at her, "but finish that breakfast before we leave the table."

Willie greeted John with questions about his return journey, enquiring of the time that he would need to be at the station. They agreed on timings and decided when they would need to leave for the stations.

As they were making their final arrangements, Emma interjected, "I don't want you worrying about little Miss Vicky Bland here, John. There will be no need. Leave her with us. She is ready for an education, and learning some good habits. We can provide all that here, both at home and when she comes to school with me. Sounds like you will have a lot of organising to do job-wise as well as with Sissie and there will be no place there for a four-year-old."

After they had met her, the Bland women had shared some concern about the choice John had made for a second marriage. Mother was especially reserved about his choice because everyone knew that she had firm opinions on social protocol and practice. She was proud of her son, who as a country boy had experienced a successful university education, had been decorated in the war, followed by good prospects in the developing textile industry. She was not sure whether Sissie had the maturity and family background to provide the support he was going to need.

Her reservations also lay in the age difference between John and this young woman. Sixteen years younger than him he was almost old enough to be her father. They had all remarked. She was working class and whilst there was nothing wrong with that, she reminded herself, this working class family from whence Sissie came were farm labourers and miners and did not have the same heritage that John had. She was sure that in time, it would become problematic because such cultural and social differences were seldom resolved. Sighing to herself that all the world was changing, she reluctantly admitted that perhaps she had old fashioned values and high expectations and because of that, she said nothing.

John smiled politely towards Emma and nodded in agreement, accepting that the circumstances for himself and his proposals for the immediate future would be difficult for his family to understand. Perhaps they did not sound ideal, but he was sure he loved Sissie and together they would work towards a successful life. So he replied, "Thank you Emma, nay all of you. It is wise for Vicky to stay here as you say. She is going to be very fortunate to have you all around her during the next few months. We will stay in touch."

There wasn't a lot more to say. It was settled, and he was eager to start his journey back to the woman he loved and his own plans for the future and his dear child.

After taking the last mouthful of tea, he rose from the table with Willie and said goodbye. Mother pushed a small pack of sandwiches in his hand as he was about to go.

"Bye, bye, Papa," shouted Vicky. "Me going with Auntie Anne and going to the chickens."

She pulled on some gumboots without a trace of sadness or tears and indeed, without any suggestion that she might be regretting all the decisions that had been taken for her for now.

John chuckled as he climbed into the truck. "She's busy," he observed half to himself, half to Willie. "I don't think I need to be worried, do you? Let's go."

As the truck reversed out of the yard, he could see her skipping beside Anne, dragging a wire egg basket behind her, excited to be involved in today's new adventure.

As the farm disappeared from view he settled quietly, pipe in hand, staring out of the window whilst Willie concentrated on the driving.

"Thanks again dear brother for your time. I really appreciate it."

"Think nothing of it. Pleased to help you… and Sissie," Willie replied. "Take no notice of the womenfolk. They think too much! Little 'un will be happy, make no mistake."

Willie's words offered some comfort and reassurance. On reflection, John had been aware of a sense of control in Emma's voice and he thought how this could be a positive trait in his absence, being in place of parents. However, he had some doubts, knowing how possessive Emma could be. Sometimes he thought it was because she lacked self-belief, and then lately he wondered, perhaps it was more likely that she had lost someone dear to her during the war after all, and there was now little chance of meeting anyone else and starting a family of her own. There had been whisperings among the family of such a possibility. Again, he turned over the questions in his mind. What had happened while he was away on the Front Line? There were murmurings that there had been a young man she had met, who was a Cambridge graduate in Theology. That would be entirely appropriate for Emma he thought. To be attracted to a gentle, educated man who would eventually become a country parson. To be married and to be the wife of a clergyman would fulfil her direction in life. Perhaps, like John, he underwent training to enter the Forces and so to war but had not returned, or had not returned her feelings. Who knows?

He could not bear to think that if she had been so hurt that it would mean she could never have an attachment to anyone else. She was thirty-three years old now and it would be unlikely that she would marry at this stage in her life. There were many young women these days who had suffered the same losses during that time and remained as spinsters forever. The papers were full of news about the national scarcity of young men who had returned, lost in the four-year bitter conflict. However, even if his mother knew of Emma's sadness and disappointment, neither she nor anyone else spoke of it. That was in the past and would remain in the past.

He reprimanded himself that he had dwelt on things for long enough. It was now important to face the challenges of today and the future.

"It's going to be a great help to me to know that she'll be safe and happy," he spoke aloud as he stared out of the window.

"Never fear, John. She'll be spoiled to bits," smiled Willie as he drove through the winding country lanes towards town.

Living in safe surroundings with the care the family would provide, reassured John. Fondness and affection bestowed upon his daughter and a sound education during these early years from his sister, was as much as he could have asked for, and he was grateful. Every day would bring routine and learning with new experiences to keep Vicky stimulated and content until he returned to collect her.

He was still not sure whether she understood that her birth mother was dead, and that she would never see her again, nor for that matter that it would be unlikely that she would see her maternal grandparents from whom he had taken her. However, in staying with his family for now, he knew that they would guide her, advise and inform her and best of all, she would grow to enjoy his beloved Shap countryside.

Here was the place where he had shaped his dreams and aspirations, where he learned about birth and death of sheep and rabbits and where he and his siblings in childhood had found butterflies and beetles and had drunk fresh water from rippling streams in the ever changing landscape.

Across the stony tracks that led them away from the farm, and onto the cross country road, the brothers travelled in comfortable silence, neither feeling the need to talk, and at 8.00am on this clear sky morning they didn't need to, but gazed out of the windows at the familiar scenery that they had lived with all their lives. That was what spoke to them both individually, contentedly and nostalgically.

"Penny for the thoughts, then!" Willie broke the quiet but comfortable atmosphere in the cab.

Only two years older, he loved to tease John, who had lived such a different life to himself. He had never had the brains and the love of learning like John, and usually skipped school because it was too hard for him to leave the freedom and satisfaction that physical work gave him working outdoors. He hadn't been bright enough nor keen enough to go to grammar school.

Biddie always said, "You are a practical person, Willie. You're gifted with your hands."

Biddie, the daughter of a neighbouring farmer had been employed by his parents so long ago, to teach them at home until they were eleven years old. She lived with them and was regarded fondly as one of the family. She helped Mother with small housekeeping tasks and she read to the children every evening from the classics off the shelves. They loved the way she read Rudyard Kipling and the adventures of Sir Walter Scott. She brought 'Little Women' to life with her many curious voices from the story and how she loved to make up her own tales to entertain them on long, dark winters' evenings. He felt secure, safe and contented at home and he never wanted to leave. So he was much more comfortable out on the farm, dealing with the flock and working alongside his father building up sheep stock, especially since the recent foot and mouth epidemic. He enjoyed the routine and predictability of day to day life. In 1917, he had met Magwen, a lovely, kind young woman from a Welsh family and they had married in a tiny chapel in the Welsh village where her family lived. They lived in a small cottage at the farm and, like his sisters, they had no children of their own either, probably as a result of the war experiences that Willie never spoke of. There were many barren couples at that time but no one talked about that either.

John puffed at his pipe. It was only a fifty-minute drive to the station and then he would feel that he was really on his way. "Oh, just thinking... you know... he tailed off then, "I hope Magwen is well." He had noticed that she was very quiet at teatime the day before.

"How are those hens of hers? Laying well?"

"She's very well, thank you. The hens? Do you know she treats them like children, clucking round them and talking to them as if they understand her, but they keep her busy and they are all good layers? We sell the eggs at market every week. Life is decent to us."

A modest man with modest aspirations, Willie's life changed dramatically after his discharge from action in France. With shrapnel in both of his legs, his time in the trenches had been traumatic. He never mentioned it. No one did. It was a solemn vow that every returning soldier had made.

He was invalided out, crippled with pain, after partial success in shrapnel removal but he was afflicted with debilitating shell shock. He had accepted work at home, hoping he could assist his elderly father, who had continued to work the land as his own war effort on the farm. As so many young men, injured in the war, William was struggling to deal with the horrific scenes he had witnessed in battle.

No one mentioned his howling in the dead of night; his cold sweats, as scenes from the bloody past crashed into his sub-conscious, at times during the day, as well as in the quietness of the night. His hearing wasn't as sharp as it used to be with constant ringing in his ears caused by the deafening noise of machine gun fire. He would often slip into quietude, seeming to be in a depth of reflection where no one could reach him. John knew and understood that Magwen would have a lot to deal with, but she was strong, proud and devoted to her husband. He admired her and was fond of her even though he felt he did not know her very well.

Willie pulled up in front of the railway station. "Here we are then, the train's already on the platform, John. Grab that bag and run. See you soon and look after yourself!" Willie called out.

"I will, and thanks again, Willie. Should be back very soon."

And John was gone without a backward glance. Striding smartly towards the train, trilby on his head, gabardine mackintosh buttoned and belted carefully around his neat and tidy frame.

Chapter 27

Back in Barugh

After a long and tiring journey, John was impatient to be back in his own home to regain the routine and order that so satisfied him. He stepped out of Barnsley railway station and alighted the bus waiting outside. With a sigh of relief, he eased himself on to the seat to complete the last stage of the journey.

He yearned to be in his own home, to eat something and to go straight to bed as soon as he arrived at the cottage, so that he would be refreshed for the following day at the mill. It had crossed his mind that he could pop in to see Sissie - just for ten minutes - to see her and to steal a kiss and a cuddle, but he quickly realised that it would not seem appropriate conduct in front of her parents and anyway, why the rush? They were going to share the rest of their lives with one another weren't they?

He pushed the key into the front door lock and stepped in. It was cool and smelled rather musty from being closed up during his time away. He opened the bedroom window and slowly breathed the cool evening air, before peeling off his jacket and unlacing his strong leather shoes. He wriggled his toes after pulling off his socks that had been confined for all that time that he'd been travelling. He had been one of the few lucky ones during the war, not to have suffered trench foot but he was still bothered by the constant itching and dry skin that were an obvious legacy from the dampness and cold that his feet had endured. He cursed as he recalled those rough woollen socks and trench boots that had to be worn day in, day out.

He was hungry. He was so pleased Mother had packed him a hearty food parcel of cheese and cold meat. He would devour it with that pickled red cabbage he'd been given by Sissie's mother. That would do for now. A whisky, and then to bed.

The sheets were cold but not damp and once he had arranged his pillow, he dropped off to sleep straightaway.

After a deep and peaceful sleep, probably a result of the demands of travel and the comfort of knowing Vicky would be safe and happy, he was woken by the early morning chattering of garden birds and the persistent 'chek-chek' sounds of squabbling blackbirds.

It was 5.45am. Fully awake, he pulled on his clean clothes for the day because he wanted to be down the road to the mill before the workforce arrived.

"Mornin' sir," called out the night security man, in the grey steely light of day break. He was a reliable and thorough worker and had been employed at the mill all his life, but in his later years had welcomed the opportunity to do a night shift watching the place. Home life had been quiet since his wife had died last year, and he liked to keep himself busy.

"And a good one its turning out to be, Jack," replied John striding through the gate, which was being held open ceremoniously for him. He paused for a moment to enquire of the state of the place overnight, "You've had a quiet night I hope Jack? Anything to report?"

"Nay sir. It's been a quiet 'un right enuf."

"That's grand. You'll be off to that allotment later; I expect? It's going to be a fine day." "Oh aye, I'll be busy. There's allus a job waiting,'" the old man replied.

John enjoyed engaging with the people who worked for him, getting to know a bit about them. He found time to initiate some small talk. Knowing something about their lives away from the factory was important. It allowed him to understand the pressures and the challenges they could be facing, all of which would affect their behaviour at work. There weren't many in his position who bothered with this side of managing people.

He walked on towards the office and up the metal grid steps thinking that he might be spending much longer here, before moving out of Barugh to new pastures with his dearest Sissie.

He glanced across at his polished desk with all the neat piles of paperwork. He wished he could take Betty with him to the next job, wherever that might be. She was such a good secretary, reliable and hard working. His eyes rested on a very full in tray.

Softly whistling through his teeth he said out loud, "Hm! That serves me right for being away." He removed his hat and coat and hung them on the pegs, and settled himself in his chair to tackle the morning's routine paperwork.

Before too long, he heard the welcome sound of a kettle whistling, and the familiar tap on his door. As he called out, "Good morning Betty," she appeared with tea and his morning newspaper.

"Good morning sir," she replied lightly. "We all hope your few days away were enjoyable."

She wasn't sure of the reasons he had taken leave this time but he seemed in good spirits when he left, and he appeared refreshed and in fine mood today.

"Very good, Betty. Very good," he replied simply, "and it's good to be back. Thank you for asking and thanks for the tea. Now would you send Ned up as soon as he arrives, so that we can catch up on events during the time I've been away?"

"Yes Mr. Bland, without delay," she replied and after enquiring if there was anything else he needed, she bustled out, clicking the door closed behind her.

The tea was hot and strong, just as he preferred it and as he took the first sip he glanced at the headlines and then turned to the back pages to look at the sports news. Turning the page towards the one or two before it, he scanned the print for any job advertisements but there appeared to be none of relevance for him so he turned back to look at football reports and results.

Feeling the pressure to begin to read through his in-tray correspondence, he folded the newspaper and put it to one side and made a start, selecting into piles of 'urgent' and 'important'. He trusted Betty to have sifted through the rest in his absence. He hadn't been reading through for very long when there was a knock on his door and the blurry figure of a man could be seen through the opaque glass.

"Come in, Ned," called John, expecting his assistant manager. Ned strode in. He was a big chap, slightly younger than John; a Barnsley boy who had worked hard and was ambitious for himself, his wife and three small children.

"Good morning, John," he greeted as he stepped in with a welcoming smile. He offered an amiable salute as a mark of respect.

"Hello there, Ned. Sit down here and give me a report on the week. What's been happening while I've been away?"

Ned related in detail, Joyce's accident and how Sissie Horbury had jumped to help and was remarkably calm and efficient in dealing with the hysterical young woman in excruciating pain. Then he reported that he had suggested she take some first aid training to become the named and qualified worker on the shop floor. Before he could proceed further, John interrupted him and raised his hand and as he did so.

"Stop there, Ned! There's a lot been going on whilst I've been away. Dreadful accident, first of all. I assume you've written an accident report. Is it in my in-tray?" He raised his eyebrows questioningly. "And how is Joyce?" he continued. "Can she do the work with two fingers less? Is she back yet? Is she looking for compensation? Have her union been informed? Come to think of it - does she even belong to a union?"

He fired out the questions in his concerned, anxious voice, because never fear, he knew there would be repercussions. There always were in such circumstances. He wondered if Ned had managed the situation as he would have done himself?

Ned looked at him steadily in the face and quietly reassured him. "The answers to all of those questions are in my report. There is no need for you to worry. I have followed the rule book to the letter so that we do not risk failure, neither to the person nor of the factory procedures. They call it 'duty of care' and I have assumed full responsibility in your absence. I hope that in so doing I will have proved to be a worthy Assistant Manager."

"Good, good. That's welcome reassurance. I don't doubt your competence and growing experience Ned, but I will need to read the full report as soon as possible."

"It is already in your tray, Sir. Betty typed it up in duplicate, a copy for the file and a copy for head office as soon as you approve it," Ned stated calmly.

John was quietly impressed and relieved to hear a confident younger man engage with him. He appeared unruffled by his officer-like tone that had emerged as his questions revealed his concerns. "That's splendid. Now then, you mentioned this first aid training for Miss Horbury. Continue."

In the same way, Ned related the sequence of events that had led to Sissie becoming the trained first aider for the company. It was a position that had not existed before, so he was pleased that he had been able to make a positive management decision as a result of the accident and he felt that it demonstrated his ability to be proactive and practical.

John was full of praise for what he had done and said so, standing up to shake his hand as the young man was finishing the report.

"Before you go Ned, I would like to thank you sincerely for the work you've done in my absence. Rest assured I will be notifying Head Office of your successful management style and practice." "Thank you, John. I'd appreciate that," replied Ned, colouring slightly with self-pride on receiving the compliments.

As he left the office, John sank into his chair and resting his elbows on the desk in front, his thoughts started racing through his head. Sissie! She had stepped up to take the initiative and to have used some courage, by the sounds of it. Why would she accept the offer of training though if she intended, or rather they intended, for her to leave the job and work at home? This must mean she had decided to stay on, and without even consulting him.

"My brave girl," he mused proudly. "You've got some backbone I'll give you that!" he smiled to himself as he pulled out his pipe, loaded it and began to draw deeply as he thought about a new strategy. This would need to be worked out between them if they were to avoid gossip and any awkwardness between themselves, the family and the workplace situation.

After twenty minutes, he pulled on a jacket and stepped out of the office and onto the factory floor. He left his clipboard behind as his purpose today was to stroll around to show everyone he was back.

He was pleased, but not surprised to see that everything was exactly as he had left it. It was so important to him to be amongst the women who worked so hard and with such commitment and as he strode up and down the aisles of machines he smiled and nodded greetings to people in appreciation. He knew that this was a routine that his predecessor had never done because Sissie had told him. It was she who had described the old manager as being 'invisible' and sent out his instructions without making any personal contact. Naturally that had made the workforce cynical of any change and resentful of the management who were making decisions, often not the right ones, in their opinion. He joined Ned at the back of the factory floor shouting above the noise, that everything looked shipshape and how good it was to see such productivity. He patted Ned's back, partly to convey his approval but also to signify that his assistant was doing all the things that he would be doing himself. He knew from his days as an officer that the more frequent encouragement was given to colleagues for good practice, the more they gained incentive to go another extra mile.

He continued onwards and as he approached Sissie, his eyes locked with hers as she looked up to return the steady gaze, under her brown unruly curls that seemingly had escaped from her safety hairnet. He made a 'thumbs up' sign as he passed; the noise in the place making any dialogue impossible, but it could be interpreted as a gesture of praise for her heroic episode and her subsequent training to anyone watching. And they were watching.

Returning to the office he called out to Betty, "Would you write a note to Sissie Horbury, please Betty. I'd like her to come and see me if she can spare the time at the end of the shift. I would like to compliment her on her brave actions and on her willingness to complete the first aid training. Perhaps you would deliver it to her as soon as you can today."

"Right away, Mr. Bland," she replied.

Ten minutes later, Betty was taking a welcome stroll across the factory floor to deliver the note to Sissie. She loved the noise that burst out as she opened her office door. It blasted out to broadcast toil and hard work and there was an industrial odour that hit her as she went down the steps. It was a mix of oil and textile fibre that was unmistakeable and unique. There was such an air of concentration and seriousness from all these women who, in half an hour as they clocked off, would be shouting and laughing, before bustling home to hungry children and demanding husbands. All of this she could only imagine but did not experience.

"Nor ever will now, at my age," she often thought.

Every night when Betty left the buzz of her working day, she stepped back into a quiet and tedious atmosphere at home, with only her mawkish mother and the wireless for company in their two up two down. It was no wonder she lived for her working life and any excitement it brought. She waved and blew a kiss or two at the ones whom she'd been at school with once, and with the others she wore a smile as she carefully walked, without rushing too much in Sissie Horbury's direction. "She's a nice girl," she thought. "Keeps herself to herself, not like her sister, Doris nor any of the others. Would be nice to get to know her better," and she promised herself she would try to make some contact somehow.

Running back up the steps, into her office she closed the door and leaned on it to think about how to make a few friends and get out a bit more. Then as the day grew to a close, she returned to her desk to clear up.

Chapter 28

United

At the end of the day, as with every day, the mad rush to get out of the building and to return home was frantic, especially now that the weather was improving and the days were getting longer. Sissie fiddled around, dropping behind the others who were leaving. Being the quieter type it was easy to dawdle without anyone urging her to join them; a situation with which she was happy. No one asked her about the note she had been given as they were too busy scrambling out of their positions to leave.

She took off her hairnet and ploughed her fingers through her curls before reaching for the rail on the steps up to John's office.

"Come in," shouted John as she knocked timidly on the glass.

Betty was putting the cover over her typewriter and as she reached for her coat she watched Sissie arrive upstairs with an air of nervousness and uncertainty. Her heart went out to her, as she looked so shy and uncomfortable.

"She looks so shy," she thought, "but she's no need to be. He is such a kind and gentle man." and she smiled at her, closed her door and went home.

John was aware Betty had left, having seen the office light turned off so he knew there would be just Sissie and himself now. Alone. Ahh, if only they could be sure!

She stood in front of him and as he rose to greet her, he invited her to sit down. Smoothing her skirt and apron she lowered herself awkwardly into an uncomfortable looking chair, to face him on the other side of his desk. Then he put a forefinger to his lips to say 'ssh' and in a formal manner he proceeded to tell her that he had heard from Ned about Joyce's accident and how impressed everyone was in how promptly and effectively she had reacted. He expressed his approval that she had agreed to take the training at Ned's suggestion and he was very grateful for her commitment and loyalty to the company.

A little caught out by this formal tone of voice, she blushed slightly but said nothing. She realised that it would be risky to be more familiar with each other here in the factory and anyway she was far too emotional to speak. She had missed him so much. The time away from each other had dragged and altogether had been unbearable. Thank goodness she had attended the first aid classes every night because it had occupied the time and made it easier to cope without him being there.

As he handed her an envelope, he announced that she would qualify for a slight increase in her wages. It would have to be confirmed at head office level but with the extra responsibility she had been given, he explained, would mean there would be some remuneration. She wasn't sure what 'remuneration' meant exactly but she was pleased she would have slightly more in her wage packet very soon.

She took the envelope from him, trembling slightly for reasons she knew were due to the feelings she was holding back in this strange atmosphere that they were both part of, at present. She was uneasy in his office too, because somehow it represented the 'boss' and she really hadn't known him as that for some time now.

"I'd best be goin' then," she whispered.

"Yes, do read my note, and then you will know what is in my mind," he said formally. There would be no chance that he could risk anyone overhearing their conversation beyond the topic of the accident and the aftermath, and he could not be sure that they were totally alone.

"Goodnight," she said as she turned towards the door. Leaving the desk, he moved towards her and with one hand on the door handle, he placed the same hush forefinger on the other to his lips and tenderly transferred it to hers. Without a sound, he mouthed, "I'll see you later."

She nodded and with a beaming smile, she left quickly and discreetly.

Hurrying home, her hand felt the envelope as it warmed in her pocket, as she walked along the lane. She relived that brief second when he had touched her and how ecstatic she felt, and again, she played it over in her mind. Again and again she went over it in her mind. Oh, how much she wanted to be with him. He leaned against the door after she had gone and shuddered with sheer emotion. He knew that he loved her and she was the only woman he wanted to be with. It was important to move their future forward as soon as possible. He hoped that she would visit him that night and they could start making their plans.

As soon as she returned home, she dashed upstairs to her room to read the note, which read:

Oh my little sweetheart. How much have I missed you. It has been such a long time since we had our own time together and you have been such a brave girl while I have been away. But you know I love you and when we are together we can show each other how much we care for one another.

Please come and see me at the cottage tonight. I cannot bear to be without you for another second.

We have to make our plans now.

I am yours, John

She sank back against the pillow and re-read his words. They were so simple and yet so beautiful that she almost needed to cry. But she didn't because 'only babies cry' and she was a Horbury and they did not show weaker emotions that easily. Instead, she splashed water on her face, combed her curls and pulled on a cardigan over her favourite, threadbare cotton blouse and headed downstairs to have tea.

"And where did you get to, our Sis?" demanded Doris, as she stepped into the kitchen

"Nowhere - just saw Johnny Bland. He wanted to say thank you for me training work and for 't accident that's all" Sissie replied quietly.

"Does 'e know yer stayin' on then?" she rudely enquired. "He doesn't know yet. I didn't let on," she replied quietly.

"Well, that's a fine way to carry on - if yer not tellin' 'im owt," retorted Doris

"I don't think it's any of your business," replied Sissie, as she buttered some bread and helped herself to a bit of cold mutton.

"Now then, you lasses. No fallin' out," said Mam trying to keep the peace whilst pouring the tea into each cup. The exchanges were clipped short as the boys tumbled through the door at the same time, demanding food, kicking off boots and slinging their school satchels into the corner of the room.

"Can yer 'elp me wi' me 'omework, our Sissie?" implored Frank, looking at her earnestly.

"Well be quick, our Frank. Got some jobs o' me own to do tonight," she replied as he scampered off to rummage through his bag for his arithmetic book.

She always had time for them, so he knew she could be relied upon to help. He was right. She was good at arithmetic and was only too happy to help the youngster as he struggled with his times tables and his long division. Together they opened up his book and as he chewed the end of his pencil she showed him how to do the calculations for the twenty questions the teacher had set for that night's homework.

"Get this done, then yer can 'ave yer tea," declared Mam. "I might find a bit o' tea bread for yer an' all!"

It didn't take long. He was quick to learn and he hung on every word Sissie had to say because she was always right in his eyes!

"There you are! Ye can do it!" she said, beaming at him. "You're a good 'un d'ye know that?" She squeezed him on the shoulders, and added, "Now finish the rest an' Mam'll give ye a treat!"

"I'm off then, Mam, I'll be back later," Sissie shouted out, and she left the room in a whirl, leaving ever such a slight fragrance of rose water in the air, as she closed the door behind her.

"Where are you off to, then?" Mam called back, but Sissie had gone. The older woman smiled to herself, knowing all, saying nowt.

*　　*　　*

John locked his office door and putting on his jacket and hat, he left the mill premises waving affably to one of the foreman across the yard, as he walked through the gates. It was only a ten-minute walk home at a brisk pace. There were early signs of spring and as the snowdrops faded and primroses were emerging on the grassy banks each side of the lane. Daffodils were blooming in people's gardens, dotted around the village and the trees were hazy green as their leaves unfolded across the whole countryside, anticipating the pleasures of warmer days to come.

He decided that he would make a fire for the evening because it was still chilly by the time he arrived home. He had asked Betty to order some bread and milk and other provisions to stock up after his absence, so he collected the box from the back door when he arrived home with everything in it, delivered by the grocer earlier in the day. His weekly grocery order was reliably delivered and saved him from going shopping, an activity he had always found tiresome.

Straight into the house; kettle filled and on to boil whilst breaking up a few kindling sticks and laying them over his newspaper firelighters, were his first chores of the evening. He took out his 'Tommy Trench' lighter and stared at it for a second as if really seeing it for the first time. My goodness, it had seen some action since he had first acquired it as a young cadet officer undergoing training. At the first strike it ignited, so he held it under the newspaper in a few places and watched the flames lick around the sticks. Jumping up at the sound of the kettle whistling he went into the kitchen to brew some tea.

Taking it through to his little parlour, the fire, thank goodness, had taken hold and he placed a few coals on, to establish it. It would soon throw out some welcome heat. He had teacakes and butter and jam, thinking that he could toast some in front of the fire when Sissie arrived. It would be cosy and intimate doing something like this together, so that she felt at ease in his home this evening, he thought.

He pulled on his Fair Isle cardigan that Anne had knitted so competently for him last Christmas. It was a fine example of the distinctive technique in shades of brown and maroon and orange and was not only attractive but was effective, against the chill air round his back, away from the heat of the fire.

People had noticed that it was obvious that John liked his clothes. He dressed smartly and in fashion as far as one knew it to be, living so far from the big towns and cities. He knew that being of small stature, he should make the most of himself and besides, he could afford quality materials and have things made so that they fit him perfectly. Having small feet, he preferred to have shoes made to fit him and he would commission every pair to have a slight stack inside to give him half an inch of extra height which he felt was important and also boosted his self-esteem.

Everything was ready. He glanced at the small table at the side of his fireside chair - cups, saucers, plates, milk, butter, jam, knives and teaspoons. Sugar? He'd forgotten sugar so he jumped up to fetch it from the kitchen cupboard and as he did so there was a knock on the door. He stopped dead in his tracks. She was here! She was exactly on time! As time went on, he noticed how punctual she always was and that was a delight for him, as he was a stickler for being on time himself.

He took bold strides towards the front door and opened it with a flourish and a broad smile over his face. "You came!" he exclaimed in delight.

"Of course I did," she replied with a self-conscious giggle.

Guiding her in with an extended left hand, he closed the door behind her. Then as she stood there, he pushed her tenderly so that her back was against the door and kissed her gently, then said,

"Here we are! Together at last my love. You are my one and only love."

She was trembling, visibly thrilled by the urgency yet sweetness of his kiss. She gazed adoringly at him, as she could find no words to respond, "Hullo," she whispered.

He eased her out of her brown tweed coat and placed it carefully on the hall stand, then he caught her hand to accompany him into the parlour.

"I've made us a cosy fire and we've got tea and we can toast some teacakes for each other, I thought," he said quite excitely, "Would that be alright for you?"

"Oh John! Anything! Nothing! I really don't care! I just want to spend time with you," she blurted out, putting her other hand over his, still clutching hers.

"Come on. Let's sit a while and talk and you can tell me everything that you've been doing while I've been away, and then I will let you have all my news. I don't know how we shall fit all of that in tonight, do you?!"

Her eyes were shining in the flickering light of the glowing coals and she was flushed with love and adoration for him. As she sank into the feather cushions of a fireside chair, opposite him, he looked at her with admiration and desire.

"Well," she began. And then didn't stop. She reported all the detail of the last week or so, of her actions after Joyce hurt herself, and the training she had accepted, which had led to her decision to continue working for a little longer. She chattered freely and without any of her innate shyness, relishing the intense concentration he was showing on her every word, spoken in her clumsy English and with her Barnsley accent. She felt free and frank and unrestrained, all because she could feel in every part of her, the depth of his feelings for her - because that's exactly what she was feeling herself.

He nodded quietly, listening carefully, allowing her to describe and explain everything and when she came to the end of her story he sat back in his chair saying,

"You have done so well and held on to your instincts, Sissie. My, oh my! You are really strong and straight to the point, aren't you? It makes me love you even more. Ha! I really didn't think you were like this! What a force you can show yourself to be!"

She laughed out loud, glowing with pride that he liked everything she had talked about, and didn't seem to be dissuading her from keeping the job and using her new training for a sound purpose. So many men would not have handled this turn of events very well at all.

"How am I to handle such a strong woman in my life, I wonder? I think you are going to have a certain determination for us both, don't you?" he declared, beaming at her.

"I want us always to be able to talk things through, John. And I hope that I will have some useful ideas and practical solutions that you'll agree with," she said, looking imploringly into his eyes. "Come here." John gestured for her sit on his lap and when she moved over, they held each other close so that they could hear each other's breathing and feel each other's softness and warmth. Their lips touched lightly, and as he pressed his mouth closer to hers, she yielded.

For several moments they explored each other until she pulled away slightly. He took the hint and suggested, "Let's toast these teacakes and have some tea," and she slid over his lap and said,

"I'll put the kettle on shall I?"

When she returned, they had both composed themselves. John looked at her and said, "Sissie, will you still marry me? Be my bride and let's start life together as soon as possible."

"Yes, yes John. I say this with all my heart. I want to be your wife, and I want to be a mother to your little girl and also to a child that I hope we can create in the future. This is the meaning of marriage."

She had rehearsed lines like this for such a precise moment as this one, and she said them with sincerity and without hesitation. John responded with a wide smile, "Whatever you want to do, we will do it. I would lay down my life for you if I knew that it would make you happy and fulfilled! You have to know that."

"Thank you, John." She said and prodded a teacake with the toasting fork and held it in front of the red embers, feeling the heat of the fire on her cheeks.

For a few moments they were both quiet, reflecting on the spontaneity of that romantic moment and the honesty of John's commitment to her. It was a timely activity to be distracted by the teacake toasting as they piled them onto their plates. As John poured the tea he said, "Look, I'm going to look for a job away from here, you know, away from the mill, Barugh and everything. I want more for us Sissie. I need to be a bit nearer Vicky and I think we should be making a home away from this place where we are not being looked at and judged for our decisions on things."

She knew he would be insisting on this direction because he'd hinted before when they had been talking about their plans for the future, during that weekend in Shap. She was falling in love with his 'big ideas' as she called them, but tonight he was reiterating and it sounded like he really meant what he'd said before.

Her mind was made up because she trusted him and the decisions that he would want to be making for them both. Whatever he proposed she would be with him, so strong was her belief and respect in him, and for him. It was unthinkable to challenge him. If he wanted to go that way, she would go with him. Leaving family might be difficult, but who could predict what the future would bring? It might even be possible to move her parents nearer to their own home and family.

The room had become dark by now and so John got up to put a couple of lamps on and returned to his chair to light his pipe, basking in the warmth of the room and in the woman he loved sitting by him. He lit the pipe and outstretching his hand and Sissie took it and kissed it tenderly. Looking at him lovingly, she whispered, "I want this moment to last forever, John. I don't care what folk say about us. We know what we have, and together we are strong."

"That's my lass talking! Can you hear her, you lot in Barugh?" he exclaimed proudly as he placed his pipe on the table. He pulled her closely and she knelt down so that he could cradle her head. "Always, we shall be together my little sweetheart."

"Always," he murmured into her curls.

Chapter 29

Vicky and Emma

"Never disturb a dog with a bone," warned Auntie Emma firmly as Vicky tried to pull the bone from the dog's bared teeth and grumbling growl.

"Why?" she enquired. "I want to play."

"Because he thinks you are going to steal it - or eat it" Emma replied shortly. "Why?" she repeated.

"Because that's how dogs behave when they have a bone," warned Emma. "Why?" the child enquired again in typical style of a four-year-old.

"Because.... Oh, just because that's what I say," Emma replied firmly, indicating closure of this particular conversation, and bracing herself for the next bombardment of questions.

No one had warned her that raising a four-year-old was round the clock care and commitment; working full time meant that she would have to bring the child into school or leave her for some of the time with grandma at the farm. Grandma was getting older and had a lot less energy nowadays and Emma did not want to burden her too often with the responsibility of a talkative, curious and energetic four-year-old.

She decided that teaching Vicky to read and to find enjoyment in stories would be the best way to occupy the little one. She was bright and learned quickly and it would be a sound discipline for her living in the company of busy adults. So every night, before being tucked into bed, they would sing the alphabet and together they would read some children's books, with Vicky being taught to recognise simple words as Auntie pointed them out with a poised first finger.

"Can we have 'Flower Fairies again?" she begged.

"Well there aren't too many words to read there, are there now? It's just pictures," replied Emma. "But let's find the book then we can talk about the pictures. How about that?"

"Yes, yes!" Vicky clapped her hands with delight and rushed to the bookcase where she knew exactly where the book was placed.

There were plenty of children's books around, but they were rather advanced just yet for a four-year-old, so it was frustrating to make progress without losing the child's enthusiasm for reading. Most children of the same age were not encouraged to read as books were not readily available to everyone. That was her task to teach them when they enrolled in school at five or six years old. Some of them had to be taught the correct way to turn pages, so unused to handling books at home.

"It's too hard Auntie," she complained one-night wriggling and fidgeting under the eider down when she was being encouraged to look at 'The Velveteen Rabbit' for the umpteenth time.

"You're tired dear. Let's say your prayers,'" replied Emma.

Vicky scrambled out of bed, kneeling beside it with her hands pressed together and her eyes tightly shut:

"Gentle Jesus, meek and mild.
Look upon this little child
Pity my simplicity.
Suffer thee to come to me.
Amen."

Emma recited the nightly verse as Vicky waited for the cue.

"God Bless.. Emma prompted.

"Daddie."

"God Bless..

"Auntie."

"God Bless.. she prompted again.

"All my family."

Then together, they recited, "Amen." and Vicky jumped into bed, nestling into the pillows.

"Time to sleep now, so settle down and close your eyes."

And as she did every night, she kissed her lightly on her forehead and tucked her hands inside the bedcovers.

"Leave the light on Auntie," called Vicky as she did every night when Emma left the room.

"Of course," reassured Emma.

Downstairs, she poured some tea and picked up the current novel she had started, to read quietly by the warmth of the kitchen range. She lived another way of life through her novels and she became immersed in a world away from her own reality. Reading provided a pleasurable escape from the sadnesses, the disappointments and the tragedies of the world around her during those confusing times during her teenage years, when she could not feel complete and could not find any inner peace. Then, life away from home during teacher training, had emphasised her uneasiness and impatience because she didn't relate to the frivolous behaviour of the other young women and the only way to find any fulfilment, was through books and through prayer.

Books and prayer had provided her with peace and escape after receiving the shocking news from the family of the only young man for whom she had felt any fondness. He had been lost in battle, presumed dead during his short time spent fighting in France as a young army officer. No words could describe her heartache and grief to hear about his death when they had known each other for such a short time. It was a time when she felt they shared the same beliefs and values and, as important, their feelings for one another. Would they have married if they had been given more time? Would she have become a mother herself, one day? There had been so many unanswered questions, and to dwell on a part of her life that she had been denied was pointless and quite frankly, stupid. Perhaps for her own peace of mind and sense of emotional survival, she found herself dreaming less and less about their brief relationship and to be honest, these days she struggled to even picture him in her mind any more.

The words of John Ruskin, whose influence in literature was universal and especially at Whitelands, the college where she was training, ultimately offered her inspiration and the impetus she was seeking when she read:

"Doing is the great thing. For if, resolutely, people do what is right, in time they come to like doing it."

She read more of Ruskin, admiring his works and essays and at the same time following the works of Virginia Woolf, which she read and re-read, whilst imagining the lifestyle of this popular author from the snippets of gossip she would read in the newspaper. How she would like to live and work in those circles! Then she found a new publication, 'A Passage to India" and was fascinated by the central character - a school teacher like herself. Anne had given her a copy for her birthday last year and she had not been able to put it down, being transported to a world beyond her dreams. Yes, she wanted Vicky to gain the same pleasure from reading, and she would be the one to guide her and encourage her.

One night, as she sat down after bed time reading, as she thought about the Flower Fairies publication, her imagination wandered. She knew that she could draw quite well, and felt she could easily make up some simple stories and illustrate them to help Vicky with her reading.

The idea struck her so suddenly and so clearly. Since becoming a teacher, she had realised that there was little choice available for younger children. She was frustrated at the dearth of publications available, because she had searched thoroughly for reading material for the classroom. Excited at the idea, she decided that it would be a pleasant way to spend time together with Vicky. She would encourage her niece to use her own imagination and together they would create some stories. The 'dog and the bone' incident earlier today or better still, 'life around the farm' came to mind, and she was filled with ideas for imaginary characters and animals in various settings. It would be a remarkable way to become close to the little girl, sharing some joint activity.

She decided to take the bus into Penrith on Saturday, taking Vicky along with her to buy pencils, paper and paints to begin her project. She thought it would be an easy way to spend the day together too.

Taking some writing paper from the dark red leather writing case that she had kept with her always, since her parents gave it to her when she had left home for her teacher training, she thought she should write to John to give him some news on Vicky's progress.

> *Dear John,*
>
> *Everything is going well here. Vicky is being a good girl. She is eating well and goes down to sleep without any bother. She is learning to read and has quickly learned the alphabet by heart.*
>
> *On Saturday we shall be taking the bus to Penrith to buy drawing materials. She will enjoy the bus ride I know.*
>
> *Weather is cold but bright. We hope all is well with you and we will see you soon. Your loving sister,*
>
> *Èmma*

Sealing the envelope into which she had carefully folded the little note, she wrote his most recent address on the front. She had always enjoyed corresponding because she felt that by writing regularly, she and John would remain close friends and this evening, feeling some sense of achievement after today's events, she turned off the lamp and went upstairs to bed.

Chapter 30

Looking Ahead

John slowly rose from the fireside chair.

"I'm going to walk you home, my dear, before it gets dark. I don't want you to be out too late - that wouldn't do would it? Let's get your coat and we can walk and talk our way back to Low Farm."

Sissie nodded in agreement, also keen to be doing things in a proper way, not because she wanted to leave just yet. She could have stayed there with him all night in front of the fire, in loving embrace, talking lightly and flirting gently with him, but this was a small community with eyes and ears and ways of jumping to conclusions. And she wanted to avoid that just as much as he did.

"Yes, I'd better go," she replied, momentarily flustered at the sudden interruption of the comfort of being with him, but knowing that it was the expected polite response.

He locked the door and they held hands as they walked up the narrow lane that led away from the cottage. It was a pretty place, part of the country house estate and once a woodcutter's cottage. It was rented out now to anyone who might afford it and sitting prettily surrounded by deciduous trees, it provided privacy and simple comfort for them when they were together and a separateness from the Barugh community for John. The farm lay in the direction out of the village so there was little chance of meeting anyone, especially at this time of the evening.

They dropped hold of their hands as they joined the main road and turned towards the farm.

Then, John said, "Tonight has been the most wonderful time with you, Sissie. I was pretending this was our own home already! Are you happy?"

He seemed to be asking for reassurance, and she felt an urge to hug him tightly and tell him over and over that everything for her was perfect and that she loved him deeply and wanted him to be with her forever. But she couldn't, not here while they were walking. It didn't seem right. She would find the right moment soon.

Instead, she said, "Don't be daft! I'm as happy as a lark and I can't wait to come to the cottage and see you again!"

"Tomorrow then," he urged. "You can come over again, can't you?"

"Yes, yes of course I can," she replied as a gust of wind blew her hat off and shrieking softly she ran down the road to catch it.

They were at the farm gate in minutes and as he opened the latch for her, he spun her round and kissed her cheek.

"Tomorrow," he whispered. And then she was gone, running to the farm cottage door. He watched her as she left him, turning to wave to him before disappearing through the door. He doffed his hat in response and made his way homewards.

"Is that you, our Sissie?" shouted Mam from upstairs. Always early to bed and early to rise, especially now the days were getting longer, Mam never rested until she knew her girls were home. She was used to shouting out to Doris, but this was a change shouting Sissie.

"Yes Mam, an' I'm fine," she replied, pulling off her coat and unlacing her shoes. She stood for a moment with eyes lightly closed, and hugging herself with utter joy and satisfaction as she recalled the nice things that had happened this evening. Then she slowly climbed the stairs to bed.

John marched swiftly back to the cottage whistling as he went. He didn't expect to have found love as intense as this again, in his lifetime. His main aim had been to find someone whom he liked and could care for, and who would be a mother for his child. But meeting Sissie had been beyond his hopes and dreams. She was sharp and quick witted and although she lacked much education, she made up for it with her practical approach to things. He loved her softness, sincerity and gentle spirit and how she responded so earnestly to his attention to her. They would make a good partnership, he was sure. He knew her well enough now. It was time to set a wedding date. Tomorrow, he would broach the subject.

Turning the key in the lock he stepped inside the cottage. Thinking that the fire had died in the grate since they had both left, he decided he would forego a bedtime whisky and he went straight to bed.

The prospect of a peaceful and contented sleep was denied him however, as he struggled to drop off initially and then restlessly. He rambled in and out of dreams. He saw Sissie injured on the front line; Vicky was stuck on the train and he couldn't reach her; Emma kept shouting and shouting again 'Stop! 'Stop!'

He woke himself up screaming hoarsely however, as enemy gunfire burst his ear drums and his eyes were stinging through lack of sleep, and he heard himself shout, 'Stop!'

He sat bolt upright, sweating with the effort and the activity of his dreams, and he was shaking with fear.... well, fear of what? What fears did he have? There should not be any more. Everything was fine wasn't it? Nothing was going to go wrong, he was going to make sure of that. No more sadness and disappointment and no more distress and heartache - he was determined to be in control. He fell back on his pillow weary and worn out. Eventually, when he relaxed, he breathed deeply, rubbed his eyes and drifted away peacefully at last.

The alarm was shrill and invasive. Startled by the sudden noise, he struggled straight out of the bed and dressed himself for the day, feeling sluggish after the rigours of the night still in his head, made him a little melancholy.

His walk along the lane to the mill brought him into the present and as he gazed upwards through the unfurling leaves of spring at the blue sky beyond, he told himself that everything was going to be fine.

It was the usual routine at the office, and he knew he wouldn't function until he had drunk that morning cup of tea. So when it arrived he was particularly grateful to Betty and her promptness. She was beginning to know his routine, as would any good secretary.

As he finished the first cup, his telephone rang, and Betty was putting a call through from head office. It was Harold Parkinson on the line.

"Good Morning John. I hope all is well down there in Darton," he began.

"I won't beat about the bush - straight to the reason for calling you. It's a request. Can you take yourself to Ripley? The management at that Derbyshire rolling mill there is struggling without sensible management. Needs a bit of sorting out. So I've recommended you. It'll be for a couple of months but you'll sort 'em out with your time and motion experience and we'll put Armitage in charge at Darton while you're gone. How does that sound?"

John wasn't prepared for such a conversation without advance warning but his mind snapped into action. This could be just the solution for Sissie and himself to make their plans and to avoid the inevitable local nosey parkers talking.

"It sounds very interesting. When do they want me to start, Harold?" he asked, playing for a few more moments to organise his thoughts.

"Well, it's the 31st March, next Wednesday, so I thought you could get yourself over there as soon as possible. That'd be a tidy start to your contract. I've organised some 'digs' for you with those dates in mind, and so you'd start on the Monday, that'd be the 5th. Obviously, I'll get this in writing to you, as soon as you say, yes. There'll be a salary increase of course, and your rent paid too, but it would be good experience for you and they would be pleased for a bit of advice and support."

John smiled and thought that this was an offer he couldn't refuse.

"Well, thank you for having the confidence in me, Harold. I'm willing to go over there but as long as it's only for two months. I have family commitments here but I'm confident that Ned will deputise well for me during that time."

"Jolly good show, John. I knew you'd be willing to support them!"

A few pleasantries followed and as they exchanged goodbyes he placed the receiver down on its cradle purposefully. Leaning back in his chair, feeling a sense of excitement and a degree of satisfaction, he called for Betty to fetch Ned to his office.

*   *   *

It was so mild for the time of year and Sissie was eager to get to John's to enjoy these spring evenings with him, especially when she arrived at the cottage the following day. It had been so hot inside the factory and it had drained all energy from the hard working girls making them feel tetchy and sluggish. They were all eager to get into the fresh air at the end of the shift.

She arrived at the cottage and as she tapped on the door it immediately opened and John stood there, beaming at her.

"Come in. I've been waiting for you, little lady!" he said as she stepped over the threshold.

She could hear the kettle begin to whistle cheerily so she followed him into the kitchen and John poured boiling water into a brown earthenware teapot, set on a tray with two cups and a milk jug.

It was such a glorious evening that they decided to sit on the backdoor step and hugging their cups of tea, they gazed down the garden that once, must have been carefully tended, but now was overgrown and looking neglected.

"We will have a house with a garden, Sissie," sighed John. "And I will plant vegetables for us and grow rambling roses that you can arrange in vases inside our cosy home."

"I'd like that, John. And I would like to plant pansies in the borders and grow mint and rosemary near the back door so that you can smell them as you walk into the kitchen."

"We will have plenty of work to do together but we will make a good team, won't we?"

He looked at her, tilting her chin towards him, looking deeply into her eyes, holding her gaze for a second until she lowered her eyelids feeling a little shy all of a sudden. Sensing her mild embarrassment, he turned the conversation towards more practical matters.

"Now then, I have some news! I won't be needing to look for another job away from here just yet, my dear, because I received a telephone call this morning from head office asking me to go over to Derbyshire for two months to sort out the management at the rolling mill over in Ripley, to be precise. It's not far."

"Oh my, John! 'Ow sudden is that? When will ye 'ave to go?" she blurted out, unable to adjust herself easily to this unexpected announcement.

"Well, I've to start on Monday 5th April so I need to get myself over there, put my bags down in the digs I've been given and get stuck in. So I'll leave a day or two before."

She groaned softly, "I'm going to miss you. What am I going to do? How am I to cope wi'out you?" she whimpered.

"Now, now - don't be soft! We said we would have to separate during this time before we're wed," he said reassuringly. John put his arm around her, hugging her tightly, to comfort her.

They rocked to and fro. After a few moments like this, he said, "We could set our wedding date for the first Saturday in July couldn't we? How would that be? There will be preparations to make. That'll keep you busy. And I will come home at the weekend. It won't be so bad after all," he added.

"No, I s'pose not," she answered unconvinced, but realising this decision had already been made and there would be no point in making a fuss; That would seem selfish and unhelpful.

"And 'ey up - look on the bright side. I'm going to be receiving more money doing it and my rent will be paid for me, so I can leave here and have saved plenty to help us to find a home to move into when we are married. That's a good thing, isn't it?"

She nodded with ideas and thoughts already running through her head.

"And yes, I can carry on working and sorting myself out for flitting from home," she said with optimism. She knew John would not tolerate weakness and whining, so she spoke clearly and with sincerity. "Shall we be wed at chapel or church?"

This was a sudden question aimed at him, out of the blue and one that he wasn't prepared for. Suddenly, he felt uncomfortable.

"I know we have our differences," he began, "but if you are marrying into my family I would like to marry you in church. I think that is only right. Many other families do it like this and so must we." As he spoke, his voice became more emphatic.

"That's alright," she uttered.

He kissed the top of her head and smiled at her with pride and overwhelming love and admiration for her sensible nature and her unruffled accepting manner. She wasn't showing weakness in her response to his proposals now, she was showing strength!

"I want you to have the finest wedding dress and I want you to carry a big bouquet of flowers and to wear flowers in your hair and a silken veil! You must have everything exactly as you want and I shall pay every penny for my sweetheart to feel the prettiest girl in the world because she will be the one that I shall marry!" he gushed and continued to stroke her hand and kiss it lightly as she blushed with pleasure and excitement.

"Oh John, you are so kind and I feel so thankful that you love me as much as I love you," she whispered, carefully articulating each word correctly to emphasise the depth of her feelings. They weren't used to expressing their feelings like this in her family. It was all taken for granted that they felt fondness and closeness without using fancy words. But this was different and she felt different when she was with John because each time they were together she learned something new from him.

"Now then, that's wonderful to hear, my darling. And now we are going to put all our words and feelings into action, aren't we? That's the way to be successful and happy" he replied. He pulled her gently to her feet and held her close whilst they twirled a funny waltz on the long grass that once was someone's lawn. She squealed with surprise and delight at his impulsiveness which seemed so unlike his usual deliberate, sensible ways.

It was soon time to go and so they put on their coats and stepped out into the lane and walked briskly towards the farm without talking. Both of them reflected on their conversation that night and already had begun to envisage the next couple of months. At the farm gate she dragged him playfully round the corner behind the hawthorn hedge waiting for the blossom to burst, and flung her arms round his neck.

"John! I'm the 'appiest girl alive!" she breathed and kissed him fully and firmly on the mouth as he placed his arms around her waist and responded eagerly.

"We shall have many more moments like this," he murmured and he leaned towards her again and they kissed each other a second time.

"Time I went," she said as she stepped away from him. She rubbed her face and turned towards the old wooden gate. He started to follow her, feeling weak with emotion and unfulfilled pleasure. But she ran towards the house, then turned and waved, and she was gone all too quickly.

*　　*　　*

The next day an official letter arrived at the office and John, knowing its contents, quickly scanned it. This was the letter confirming the temporary position being offered at the winding company in Ripley.

> *We are pleased to offer you the position of Foreman-Manager for an initial period of two months at the salary of £7.0s.0d per week, commencing on 6th April. We can confirm that a cottage will be available for you for a sum of 15 shillings per week.*

John was satisfied with the arrangements, pleased to have received such a prompt response. As he placed the letter down on the desk he blew through his teeth, and began to wonder from the phrasing of the letter, whether this could possibly become a permanent position. It would be the perfect move away from Darton mill and the village of Barugh, once he and Sissie were married. He was aching to tell her but immersed himself in his daily tasks, urging the time on until the end of the day when he could tell her everything.

Meanwhile, Sissie was working meticulously at her machine, impatient to reach the end of her shift so that she could walk up to Betty's office and complete the necessary daily log as Ned Armitage had instructed. Nothing had happened during the day and so this first entry, written by herself would be straightforward. She thought too soon. Suddenly there was a flash of sparks from Doris's machine and Sissie could see her, ashen faced, jumping up and down shrieking and holding her arm. The sparks had caught the textile fibre and flames were licking round the machine. She swiftly stopped her own machine, picked up her new first aid box mounted at the end of her bench, and made her way purposefully, without panicking towards her sister, who by now had attracted a couple of the other girls working near her to come across to help her. Gesturing to someone to dampen down the flames as she pushed through the little group surrounding Doris's workplace. "Let me see 'er. The qualified first aider is 'ere," announced Sissie in her best authoritative voice, and they let her through where she could see Doris was in considerable pain.

"Oh, Doris! What a mess we've got 'ere," she said sympathetically, looking at a rather large lozenge shaped blister beginning to form on Doris's forearm. "Let's get you t' cold water tap shall we? Then we can dress that nasty blister and keep them germs out," she soothed whilst grasping her firmly by the hand on her other side and leading her away from the other girls.

"Back to work, all," she called out. "She's going to be fine. Thanks to you all"

This was her first call out since becoming official, and it was to the rescue of her own sister! She was proud of her calm and business-like approach and she realised afterwards that despite her early self-doubt, she possessed a steady nature and sensibility in emergency situations - something for which she had not been tested before today.

Ned Armitage had been in the office with Mr. Bland discussing the handover that would take place during the next couple of months and both had been drawn to the top of the office steps by the commotion on the factory floor. The fire that had started, had been extinguished but Ned was worried that there was a serious injury to one of the workforce and this sad news for the injured party could be bad news for the company. However, he needn't have worried because it was clear that everything appeared to be under control and that it now needed some management presence down there for reassurance and recognition that prompt action had been taken. "There, there our Doris. Come on, it's a blister and it will 'eal nicely and ye'll never know y'd had such a burn in no time. I'll look after it. Don't you worry about a thing," Sissie reassured her. But Doris was angry now, and in accusatory tones was blaming the company on badly maintained machines and poor safety standards on the factory floor. Sissie realised that Doris was probably in shock, offering some explanation for her sister's outburst. She carefully bandaged the burn, and as she did so, Betty appeared with tea on a small tray and fussed round Doris, telling her what a brave girl she was and how everyone had admired her.

Sissie looked across at Betty and silently mouthed, "Thank you," whilst raising her eyebrows slightly to indicate that she felt Doris was being somewhat dramatic. Doris now began to enjoy the attention and sipped her hot tea appreciatively.

"Mr. Bland says you may sit down over there until home time and Sissie will walk you home. Won't you Sissie?"

"Of course I will, if ye'll wait for me Dot. I've a bit of paperwork to do but it won't take long," as she placed a reassuring hand on her sister's shoulder, hoping she would be able to fill the log book easily on the first day of her duties.

As she made her way towards the office to record everything whilst it was still fresh in her mind, she passed John and Ned striding towards Doris to ask after her and find out the details of what had happened. John's natural charm and confidence in the tone of his voice, reassured Doris and she enjoyed the attention that she was attracting, making her feel special.

"We will be making out an accident report, Miss Horbury," said Ned in an official voice. "Which will go straight to Head Office," finished John.

"A full investigation into the cause of the fire will be carried out and we will fix the damage as soon as we can," he continued.

"We hope you are now comfortable and will be able to return to work tomorrow to work at another machine."

They walked towards the now blackened machine to inspect the damage and to discuss the probable reasons for the fire. Factory accidents like this one were frequent in this industry and increasingly, companies were being held accountable by union members requiring them to complete full safety reports and even to offer compensation in serious cases. John was well aware of the possible consequences on a company name and its reputation - especially with an outspoken and discontented worker - like his soon to be sister in law.

Sissie was focussed on the clean page of the log book, nibbling at the end of her pen, before writing the date in the margin. She took a deep breath, and began to write her first entry of the day. The other girls were leaving by now and she could hear all their banter as they crowded out of the factory doors to clock off. Doris sat still waiting patiently, seemingly in no rush to join them because of the earlier arrangement to wait for Sissie.

She was just finishing the report when Ned entered the room, saying, "Well, Miss 'orbury. It's thanks to you that we didn't have a really serious injury and that your sister seems none the worse for wear. That burn should heal perfectly."

"I am sure Doris 'll be fine, sir. It's a good thing she's me sister so I can keep an eye on 'er! No trouble!" Sissie replied, as she tilted the log book to show him the entry. He nodded in approval. "Well done lass. now, get 'er 'ome. You're earning yer extra wage that's for sure!" he grinned.

As he turned to trot down the steps, John was coming up two at a time and squeezed past him as he entered the room. He wanted to look in on her and using a formal tone, he said,

"I would like to thank you, for your prompt and professional work, Miss Horbury. We have surveyed the machine, and there seems to be no serious damage, so it should be in working order again in no time at all." As he turned round to leave, he smiled at her and with the factory now being so quiet, he felt free to wink fondly at her.

She sat for a moment in the office in disbelief, that the two most important men at the mill had paid her a personal visit to thank her. She was glowing with pride as she picked up her pen again to finish the report and in no time at all she called down the steps, "Alright Doris. I'm ready. Let's go home!"

Chapter 31

Spring Days

The days of Spring rolled across the new green grass of the Cumbrian fells where columbines perked their pretty pink cheeks to the strengthening sun, then leaned their leafy shoulders against the sharp and sudden north winds that blew across an occasional blue sky.

So often, as the weather turned, the drifting clouds moved into a mean greyness that cast eerie shadows across the hillside.

"Take a coat!" Mother would cry as Emma and Vicky set off on their usual routine weekend rambles, to discover something new around the familiar contours of the land that had always belonged to the Bland farmers since olden times.

Emma was settled here now with few plans to change her circumstances. This was the place where she herself had grown up and learned about the environment and her place within it. She was known now as a formidable young woman with strong and committed views on education, family life and society, with a deep faith and a devotion to her local church, and as time moved on she had become dedicated to church business and to the thriving community that it served. She represented the parish within the diocese and reported back to the vicar and the other church members. She respected the ageing vicar for his experience, his approachability and genuine interest in his parishioners and his Sunday sermons had a sensitivity and vision that she approved of, and so she considered herself fortunate to be part of a meaningful Christian community.

Emma was well respected as a teacher. She had an unshakeable belief that every child had potential and that her vocation was to provide the building blocks for that to flourish. Children were a little in awe of her, and it seemed to be important to each child to earn her approval for things that they did well. Although she laid down strict rules and routines, she rewarded with pride and celebration. Always using their first names both in and out of her classroom, her kindness and confidence demonstrated an unshakeable fondness for each one of them.

Yes, Emma was a busy person!

Vicky was settling in happily to a way of life at the farm, having been taken under Emma's wing and becoming more and more dependent on her aunt as the weeks rolled by. Writing frequent letters to her father, had established a dialogue between father and daughter so that she was able to relate her activities, with help from auntie, in the form of simple notes and drawings. She was an imaginative child, with a busy mind and a cheerful temperament. Eager to please, her reading was progressing well for her age and Emma was a patient and persistent teacher, rewarding the little girl for her successes.

Her favourite way of spending time was playing in the woods, always accompanied by her aunt who gave her the freedom to explore, yet offering guidance, fond encouragement and friendship. One or other of the farm dogs would follow them up the grassy bank beyond the farm gate and trail behind as if to ensure that they were both safe. Then one day as they were walking, they found a lamb apparently lost, lying down in the bottom of the hawthorn hedging that divided the fields. It was cold and trembling with fear and it looked as if it had been rejected by the ewe who had given birth, perhaps a couple of days ago. It happened from time to time, but often the abandoned lamb was found too late.

"Auntie! Auntie! Look! Look!" cried Vicky, pointing as she ran towards the weak little thing. "Shall we take her back to her mother?"

"She will have to be bottle fed, child," replied Emma. "Her mother doesn't want her now. Perhaps her mother is poorly."

"You mean, like Mama?" answered Vicky as she knelt down beside the lamb, stroking it tenderly. This was unexpected, and it took Emma by surprise. She was unsure of how best to respond. Her life these days tended to be predictable and routine-like, and she was unable at first, to give Vicky a satisfactory response, as they stared down at the sickly animal. She decided to leave the little girl's question unanswered. She thought, rather uneasily, that it was best to leave that as a distant memory.

"I think the best thing for us to do is to take the lamb home and give it some milk from a baby's bottle so that it will have a chance of survival," she said quickly. Removing her headscarf, she continued, "Let's use this scarf to wrap up the little one and then we can carry her home."

Vicky danced up and down with excitement at the prospect of looking after a living creature - much more of an adventure than playing with her dolls.

"What shall we call her? Is it a 'she'? Where can we put her?" The questions tumbled out as she skipped alongside her auntie.

"You can choose a name if you like. Yes, it's a girl," replied her aunt. Emma thought that it would give her something to look after and help to develop a sense of responsibility. It would provide a good basis for conversation; for her reading and writing; drawing and painting.

They walked towards the farm in silence until Vicky burst out, "Star! I want to call her Star!" "And why do you want to call her that? That's a strange name for a lamb," replied Emma. "Because when I look at the stars at night, I think of my Mama," said Vicky, sadly.

There was no more to be said. The lamb would be named Star.

*　　*　　*

It was a sunny day towards the end of May when Doris and Herbert were to be married in the Methodist chapel in Darton. She had chosen a beige coloured tailored costume with a matching hat, a fine netted veil over her eyes, with the brim tilted coyly to one side. She looked very neat and delicately attractive, holding her small bouquet of lilies of the valley and white lilacs, chosen for the special day.

Herbert was proudly wearing a fashionable brown pin striped suit, with a white carnation in the jacket lapel, and wide legged trousers that were in vogue at the moment. Known for his cheeky sense of humour, he cracked his usual corny jokes with people as they arrived and everyone seemed pleased for the happy couple. The day was pleasant and there was a simple wedding breakfast laid on for them in the village hall before the couple departed for Blackpool to their new home. Herbert's brother-in-law Jimmy had hired a car to take them back to start their new life together and Doris was radiant as the centre of attention, looking so very happy to be friends with his wife Elsie, Herbert's sister and now, her new sister-in-law. Sissie felt a twinge of sadness that she had lost the closeness with Doris, but satisfied herself by thinking that it would be short lived and they would soon resume their close friendship one day.

"It will be us next, little sweetheart," said John quietly, as he squeezed her hand. She smiled back at him saying, "I'm counting the days John, but there's so much to do before we get to our happy day."

"Oh everything will be fine my dear," he reassured her, knowing that his mother had made a large fruit cake and would be icing it skilfully for them and that Emma had taken Vicky into Penrith to buy her a pretty dress and flowery headband so that his little girl would be prepared for their special day and a new way of life ahead.

The banns of their marriage would be read on Sunday and they had secured the vestry for a simple wedding breakfast as only close family members would be attending. After their discussion, both of them were resolute and in agreement that a big event would be inappropriate. It was more important to be married and to declare their devotion to each other in the eyes of the Lord, and in particular to show his daughter and both their parents that they were committed to sharing a future together.

Only here for the wedding, John needed to return to Derbyshire having worked there for two weeks and already showing his expertise as he modified the workforce and their working routines so that they became more efficient. He was confident that he could fulfil the obligation placed upon him in the time he'd been allocated, to shake up the present factory procedures and after that could move onwards towards a more permanent position elsewhere.

The two of them walked outside for a little distance, as the newly wedded couple drove away to the noisy rattle of tin cans and an old boot tied to the car's back bumper, with squealing children running alongside the vehicle as it gathered speed, away from the little crowd who had thrown all their rice over them. People were now slowly starting to return homewards.

"Well lass, that's first o' me lasses wed!" announced old William Horbury as he and his dear wife walked back along the lane to Barugh. "Another six weeks and t'other 'll be done too. I'm goin' to miss the next 'un though - she's always been so good to us all."

"They are both me girls and they'll both be sound, mark my words. But next 'un's marrying well," replied Annie. "I always knew she'd do well. She's a dark 'orse but determined and sensible. She's done well at t' mill, too. No one 'as questioned nor gossiped about her being betrothed t' boss neither. That 'as surprised me."

"She don't talk about no-one, that'll be why," he replied knowingly, nodding his head as if to emphasise his point.

On they walked in silence until they reached the back door of the cottage and into the kitchen for a welcome cup of tea.

John and Sissie strolled in the other direction, towards the railway station so that John could return, ready for the Monday workload. They talked of their wedding day and they discussed how they could ensure his parents could be made comfortable when they stayed here in Darton for the celebrations. They also talked about how Vicky could be brought over to live permanently in their own home. Suddenly, it all seemed so complicated and stressful. Sissie looked anxiously at John, but nodded in agreement as he described ways in which all of this organisation could work. She stopped abruptly, as she turned to John, looking directly at him. Speaking slowly and confidently, looking directly at him, "Today, Doris's wedding has made me think. I want us to ask ourselves what our wedding ceremony will mean to us, John. It'll be about you and me. It's not really about anyone else, is it? We won't have a home here so we have nowhere for anyone to stay. Why do we need to have them here? Neither of our parents are young and in the best of health, either for travelling or excitement. I am not sure whether Vicky is ready to see her father marry someone who, as yet is a total stranger to her. Let's get married and quietly exchange our vows - just you to me and me to you. This is all that matters. My father will give me away. You can ask Emma if she thinks your parents would like to attend, if you wish. But believe me, I don't need a big celebration with others, and if you agree, we could have a celebration another time, when we are in our own home."

She was desperately trying to help him to agree. She wanted to avoid the nervousness she knew she would feel in front of his family. She would be on show, and she would risk herself and her family being judged by them. She felt it now, and she knew she would feel like this forever, the social differences between his and her family. She took a breath and she walked on, with a little trepidation, awaiting his response to her suggestion.

Catching her up, John caught her arm, "Well, that is a surprise, Sissie. I am so glad that you can be so honest. That's one of the many things I love about you, you know. All I want is for you to be happy and I want to give you everything that you wish for. Like you, the most important thing for me is to be married to you and to begin this new life together. So if you are sure this is how you want our marriage to be, then so be it."

With outstretched arms and tears in her eyes, she hugged him tightly, murmuring into his ear her grateful thanks for listening to her and for understanding her so perfectly. "Thank you," she breathed. "Thank you. I know that it will be a perfect day."

The railway station appeared in sight at the end of the road so they quickened their pace to be on time for the train's arrival. They still had a few minutes to wait on the platform. It was quiet with a cool breeze that blew down the railway line. They both shivered, partly because of it, and partly because they hated being separated, even for a short time. It left them feeling a suppressed emotion as they struggled to find the right words to say, as they embraced each other goodbye.

"I'm going to stay on next weekend. Up there I mean, Sissie," whispered John with some hesitancy in his voice. "I've a lot of paperwork to do and I need to be finding a bigger place for us to live when we are married. I don't intend coming back to Darton Mill so I'll be applying for other jobs too. Now don't be worried and upset, you've got matters to attend to as well, haven't you? Tell me again."

She stayed in control, in order to hide her disappointment that it would be a full two weeks before they were together again. "Well, I'm going to sort me weddin' dress out wi' Mam and Norma so we we'll go into Barnsley on Saturday for sure. And then, I'm going to be busy at work aren't I? So I'll need to rest up at end of t' day an' all," she added.

She hoped the time would pass quickly - indeed these days it seemed to be racing by with little time to relax.

"Perhaps Doris and Herbert would like you to go up there for the weekend too, mightn't they?" he asked her, squeezing her arm under his as he suggested the idea

She sounded uncertain. "I don't see that 'appenin'. I don't know if our Doris is too keen. But we'll see."

There was still a lack of closeness and understanding between her and her sister. Perhaps it was too soon after the marriage, where Doris seemed on the crest of a wave, for them to reunite in the old way just yet.

Suddenly the piercing whistle of the approaching train drowned out any further discussion and they turned and faced each other to say goodbye. He held her face within his hands and gently kissed her mouth. "My good little girl, that's what you are. I am and l always will be proud of you and I know you will keep busy whilst I am away. Don't be sad. Never worry - all this will soon be over and we'll be together I promise. I will write every day."

As the train came to a standstill he stepped briskly away and onto the steps of the carriage that had 'First Class' inscribed in blue on the window.

Sissie stood for a few moments, until finally, she could see him finding a seat. As the train moved silently forwards, he waved and she waved back, smiling shyly before she swiftly turned and. left the platform. Watching him disappear from sight was too hard for her to bear.

*　　*　　*

"Why don't you come over to our 'ouse tonight after work Sissie?" asked Norma one morning the following week, as they were clocking on for their shift.

"Me Mam'll cook us summat nice and we can look at t' magazines for t' ideas for yer wedding dress, eh?"

Norma was very excited and so flattered that Sissie had asked her if she would like to go into town and help her choose a suitable 'wedding gown' as John called it. He had told her that she must choose the very best and not to worry about the price of everything because he would pay for it all. She had protested because she knew how proud her parents were and how they would react. They would feel that it was their duty to pay for their second daughter's wedding too, just as they had done for their eldest, but John would not hear of it and had spoken to father Horbury on the quiet. The two men agreed eventually, that John would foot the bill. Father felt awkward. He was a proud man and declared that he didn't owe anyone a farthing, but he knew a second wedding so soon after the first was going to be a stretch on his finances. So, in a gruff, embarrassed tone, he had accepted John's generous offer, suddenly realising that this daughter was walking into a lifestyle that was beyond him.

"That'd be grand, Norma. I'd like that. How about Thursday?" she replied thinking the designs she would be looking at in the magazines would be fresh in her mind for Saturday.

The days sped by and suddenly after a nice potato and leek pie that Norma's mother had prepared, they settled down at the kitchen table with a collection of magazines that Norma regularly purchased for her personal entertainment - and much of her day dreaming, for which she was so well known. Yes, she did prattle on a bit and she fancied herself to be so up to date with current fashion but she proved to others that she was quite an expert at spotting current trends and which celebrity would be seen wearing them, and the other lasses enjoyed her stories. This was how she spent her spare time whilst caring for her possessive mother, and Sissie rather admired her because of it.

There was so much to look at! The magazines showed photos and sketches of the latest fashion styles with details of cost and availability. It appeared that the current trend was for wedding dresses to be worn shorter to reveal the ankle and had dropped waistlines to reflect the recent trend set by the 'Flapper' girls. Fabrics were light and floaty, and fresh or silk flowers could be worn in the hair, as well as being carried in a bouquet.

"Ooh, there's too much choice," exclaimed Sissie. "I don't know how I will decide!"

"You will. I know you will when we go to Universal Stores in Barnsley. They'll 'ave a right good selection! Someone comes and 'elps you to decide an' you can try everythin' on an' all," enthused Norma, hardly able to hide her excitement. Anyone would have thought the wedding dress day trip was for her!

As arranged, Sissie and her Mam met Norma at the bus stop at nine o' clock on the following Saturday. All of them had dressed neatly, almost as if for chapel. This was an important occasion and they were out to make a good impression when they met those snooty shop assistants in the wedding gown department. They always looked as if they had a nasty smell under their noses!

When they arrived on the main shopping street, they walked towards the department store, and it was obvious that Norma knew it very well. She led the way up to the second floor where the soft lighting, the deep maroon carpeted flooring and the cherry red velour seating suggested this was a very special place.

"Good morning, Ladies. How may I help you, today?" asked a petite middle-aged woman, wearing a black sheath dress, and with her hair tightly fastened in a bun. She spoke in an even tone, as she approached them at the entrance to the wedding gown floor, and much to their relief, they noticed that there was no one else present.

Sissie could not take her eyes off the silver brooch pinned below the left shoulder on the woman's dress, glinting in the lights above them.

"I am getting married in four weeks and so I'm here to choose a dress," she replied with confidence.

"Of course, Madam. Let's sit down for a moment and you can tell me what ideas you might have."

Sissie glanced at Norma, saying "I know what I'm looking for. I'd like a dropped waistline, a shorter length and in an ivory colour."

"Oh. Right, you've thought about this haven't you dear?" replied the assistant smiling mildly. "Let's see what we can find for you and you can try on. Come with me."

Looking back anxiously at Mam and Norma, Sissie followed the assistant to another part of the shop and Mam looked at Norma and asked, "So what do we do now?"

"We just wait and see, Mrs. H - she'll come out to show us when she tries the dresses on. Oh yer going t' be so proud!"

"Oh right." replied Mam vaguely. These were fancy ways for her, and she wasn't sure how to behave in this situation. This was so unlike the way Doris had organised things. She had just asked Joyce Mills, the local dressmaker, to make her a wedding costume and had twirled confidently around the parlour when it was all finished. She didn't ask for advice or approval, just asked her Dad for the money to pay for it.

Just as she was making the comparison in her head, she was interrupted by a clearing of the throat coming from the smiling shop assistant entering the space in front of them, and with a sweep of the hand she eased Sissie into the centre of the room.

"Oh, Sissie! You look beautiful," gushed Norma. "It's perfect on you, just like the ones we saw in that April issue of 'Woman's Weekly!"

"Yes, it's nice. I like it," replied Sissie, feeling a little self-conscious, realising that everyone was looking at her.

Mam was beaming broadly, proudly. "Eeh! You look so lovely, lass" she whispered her voice cracking with emotion.

"Have a good look at yourself in that mirror," directed the shop assistant.

Sissie turned towards a floor length gilt Florentine mirror on the wall to her right side.

"It's very nice," she said quietly, feeling her face go pink with a mixture of pleasure and self-consciousness as she lingered for a moment, looking at herself. Tilting her head to one side, she splayed the pretty floaty dress in both hands to each side, admiring its ivory colour beauty and its silken splendour. She loved it!

"So, if you both think it's alright, I'd like to take this one," she announced suddenly, cheerfully swirling a little as she faced the assistant

"But this is the first one you've tried, Madam," protested the disappointed woman, who usually faced young soon-to-be brides who were unable to make any sort of decision or had any idea of what style they were looking for. She was used to this process taking at least a couple of hours, where her customers enjoyed the opportunity to try on and parade themselves in front of mother and sisters and girlfriends, who sipped cups of tea offered in china cups and saucers. This was part of the all-important pre-nuptial ritual, before making their final choice - and actually it was usually for the first one they tried on, come to think of it!

"Well, I 'ave made up me mind, so there's no need to waste time trying t'others on is there?" Sissie insisted, ever practical, with a smile. "But I do want to look at a veil though and a pretty headband or summat to 'old it on," she added.

This did take some time however, as they compared those at floor length with those that were shorter. But in the end they agreed that a double layered silk net with a delicate lace trim that draped nicely over the main part of the dress would suit her the best. After trying on several hair accessories, they chose a flowery headband made of silk orange blossom with leaves entwined. They all agreed that this was the prettiest style. They all agreed that the entire look was modern but classy. Norma was proudly describing it all using the language she had read in all the magazines. And indeed, it was exactly that. The new shorter length, drop waisted ivory ensemble was elegant and fashionable and she was sure that John would approve.

Sissie paid a deposit on her purchases, as agreed, knowing that John would be sorting out the balance. They left the shop, thanking the assistant profusely and confirming the date that it would be collected. She looked at them, fascinated that such a simple trio of women could be satisfied so swiftly when choosing 'the dress' for 'the day', spending so much money, too!

Leaving the revolving doors of the store and out onto the pavement, Sissie and Norma clung to each other, and danced up and down with glee.

"Thank you, SO much for coming with us," squealed Sissie. "I right enjoyed all that." Turning to her mother, she asked, "Did you enjoy it, Mam? Wasn't it grand?"

"Eeh, lass- it's a different world to me! But I 'ad a nice time watching you showin' off. Ye'll be a fine lookin' bride I'll say!"

"I want to do it all again," Sissie giggled. "It was like being a princess!"

"Well, you will be on 31st July, won't yer, when ye walk down that aisle?" said Norma. "I 'ope you 'ave a photographer booked!"

"I'm dyin' for a cuppa," interrupted Mam, unable to deal with all this dreamy talk.

"Well, let's have a cuppa in our usual teashop shall we?" suggested Norma. She led the way, confident and happy that she had been part of this important day. They turned the corner in the direction of the familiar teashop and once inside, found a round table bearing a pure white lace cloth just by the window, and ordered tea and a scone each. The young women chatted on excitedly whilst Mam listened quietly, raising an eyebrow now and then at their frivolity.

Then, as the tea was finished and only crumbs remained on their plates, Norma yelled out, "SHOES!!!"

Sissie and her mother looked puzzled. Norma exclaimed, "I suppose you will be wanting a pair of shoes to match won't you, you silly goose!"

Sissie snorted, "Whoops, forgot about them, didn't I?"

Pushing back their chairs on the old wooden floor they left the table, paid the bill and turned back into town to search for shoes.

Chapter 32

Wedding Day

A soft breeze wafted the muslin curtain, and the sun crept it's way into Sissie's bedroom window early on the morning of her wedding. She hadn't slept well, being too nervous and excited to settle to sleep during the night. Her sub conscious mind had been bursting with fleeting images of the day that lay ahead. Nay, of the life that lay ahead, with all of it's challenges and demands on her, and all of the highs of happy times and some of the lows of sadness, that she would be sharing with John. Leaving her parents pinched at her worries though, for their health and strength during these their later years still concerned her. However, her brothers would be at home for a while yet and it was time for her to find a future with the man whom she knew she loved so much.

She rubbed her eyes and sat up, gazing around the room that she had shared with Doris for as long as she could remember, but more recently alone since Doris had moved away. The pale pink flowers on the fading wallpaper would be indelibly marked on her memory. In fact, she had chosen the colours as the theme for her bridal bouquet - probably being made up for her this very moment, just as she was waking up.

"Sissie - it's 'alf past seven," called Mam from the bottom of the stairs. "Are yer up yet?"

"Yes, Mam - I'm on t' way down," she replied, hastily swinging her legs to the side of the bed.

She pulled on an old candlewick dressing gown that she'd had since Christmas five years ago. John had bought her a new one and two fresh cotton nightdresses, as well. She wouldn't be needing this one. Thinking she would be leaving it there when she moved out by the end of today, she hugged herself within it and sighed deeply, as the reality of the changes that were about to happen overwhelmed her. Standing very still for a moment, she pulled the curtain to one side to take a look at the view that was so familiar to her. Typically, at this time of year, stubble lay in the field opposite as the grass dried on top, ready for collection and baling. This morning, the persistent bickering of blackbirds could be heard down below, chasing each other and searching for a worm or two for breakfast.

She, herself could not face anything for breakfast, but she stepped dutifully towards the kitchen door to face the smell of bacon and eggs frying invitingly on the stove.

"No, Mam. No!" she protested as Mam turned to her with an expectant expression on her face and a wooden spatula in her hand.

"Come on, lass. Ye needs food in yer belly - for today of all days!" encouraged Mam, but at the same time understanding the nervousness her daughter would be feeling. She shook her head emphatically and pulled her chair out to sit down.

"I'll 'ave it," chorused the two younger boys jumping up and down in unison. "Oh shurrup, you two," called out Dad gruffly but not with much conviction.

His gentle natured daughter and farming companion was leaving home. He would miss her. That was certain, although he would never admit it. They had delivered lambs; surveyed and repaired fences; raised strong-breed hens and harvested apples and plums together over the years. Yes, he had his good lads and they each had their jobs. But it wouldn't feel the same as when Sissie was around, always with a story and an obvious enjoyment for the manual work that they would share.

All that he said then was, "Jack and Betty Neal are expectin' yer at nine o' clock, lass,".

The farmer and his wife were known for rewarding loyalty and hard work, and the Horburys in particular. They were also very fond of Sissie, and had offered a spare bedroom in their large farmhouse for her to dress for the wedding, and as if this wasn't enough, they had offered to host a wedding breakfast after the ceremony. This was a huge gesture of kindness and appreciation that they held for the family commitment on their farm and William and Annie were very grateful but had felt a little awkward in accepting their offer initially.

"Now c'mon, William - don't be so proud an' stubborn. I know what yer like. It's our chance to say a big thank you, both to you and t' family for everything you do on t' farm - always above and beyond," he said placing one brawny hand on William's shoulder. "And we do it for Sissie. That young lass is like one of our own as tha' knows, so it'd be our pleasure. So no more said, eh?"

Everything that she would need for the day ahead had been carefully transported, and every detail checked the day before. It was time for her to depart. So, after finishing a large mug of tea and nibbling at a piece of toast to keep her mother from insisting on the eggs and bacon option, Sissie left them all saying, "I'm off now. I'll see you in church. And - Dad - don't forget to come for me at 'alf past ten!"

She walked across the swilled and swept farmyard, smartened up especially for today by her brothers who had followed instructions exactly, under the watchful eye of Bill, who wanted the very best send-off for his favourite sister. He was going to miss her badly, and he couldn't imagine what home life would be without her. Even her absence at the mill was going to take some getting used to and not seeing her every day. He tried to push it from his mind today, as it was going to be a lovely day for her.

Already, Norma was waiting eagerly by the gate. Sissie had invited her over to help her with dressing and with her hair because she knew Norma would love to be involved and besides, she had all the best ideas in such situations. The two lasses embraced each other in silence.

"I can't believe it's 'appening Sissie!" shrieked Norma, excitedly. "Are ya nervous?"

"I can't believe it either! I feel like I'm in a dream," replied Sissie, shaking nervously as they began to walk on.

Then before they knew it, Betty the farmer's wife, had flung open the front door of the farmhouse, and she was calling out good morning, and a welcoming greeting with outstretched arms. So they quickened their pace towards her, to start getting ready.

Meanwhile, down the road, John was at Ned's house, carefully putting on his wedding outfit and being helped with putting a knot in his tie by Ned. He had arrived early that morning on the midnight mail train bound for Barnsley, and a knock on the Armitage front door at seven o'clock that morning announced his arrival, as expected. During his hearty breakfast of bacon and eggs - which he devoured with enthusiasm - he explained in simple terms that this wedding was to be small and simple, because both he and Sissie wanted little fuss and expense; a simple exchange of vows and a blessing before the Lord.

Ned and his wife listened intently, nodding together with understanding and politeness.

"It's your day, Johnny. That's all that matters," said Ned quietly. "And it's the future that is important now. Jess and I wish you every happiness, both in the new job and with your life together. We're all going to miss the pair of you at Darton, that's for sure. You've made a big difference in Darton. I am going to be stepping into big shoes."

John laughed as he said, "Well, in fact, my shoes are quite small - you may have noticed - but thank you for those kind words."

He finished dressing and as he checked his appearance in the mirror, he pulled on a pair of new handmade shoes, which were slightly stacked at the heel to give him more height. Smiling at Ned's earlier comments on size, he laced them, then standing up he tapped the floor with both feet to allow his trousers to rest perfectly on the black leather uppers. That was an old habit left over from his days, dressing as an officer on parade.

Jess had a pink rose for his lapel and as she pinned it to him, Ned appeared in the doorway in a soft grey suit and tie. John gasped in surprise at its significance. The memories of a pink rose he offered Victoria from all that time ago in Brussels.

"Got one for me, lass?" Ned asked. He looked across at John and continued, "Would you allow me to escort you to the church, Johnny? It'd be a great honour for me if you'd agree to accept me by your side."

"Well, yes if you like," replied John with a little uncertainty. "It would be comforting to have someone with me as we go down to church. I hadn't really thought about anyone accompanying me."

He felt his slight anxiety about the pending event disappear. He smiled to himself, unable to add anything useful, except to face the younger man. And with a slight croak in his voice, he added, "And I have to say, that's a very kind gesture Ned - far more than any words could say, my friend. Thank you."

The church was quiet as they entered. Floral arrangements decorated the inside of the church, that church ladies had arranged for Sunday worship. Everything looked so pretty, as the sun beamed through the stained glass windows, casting stripes of coloured light across the pews.

"We're first here - that's good," whispered Ned as they walked down the aisle to the altar. As if on cue, the old vicar appeared, with his arms hidden under the white, freshly pressed surplice.

"Not quite," responded the vicar. "Good morning, gentlemen. It's a beautiful day. And how are you feeling, John?" he enquired.

"Very well thank you, Vicar. And ready to meet my bride," John replied in a steady tone, hiding the inevitable nerves of anticipation, so typical at these events.

"Allow me to introduce a friend and colleague, Ned Armitage. He has kindly offered to accompany me today."

"Well, I'm very pleased to meet you, Ned," replied the vicar, extending his bony hand.

"Now, you must take possession of the wedding ring, and at the appropriate moment in the service, you will offer it to me for its blessing, before it is placed on Sissie's finger. Don't forget that I shall be calling her by her Christian name, today. That of Edith Ellen you understand?"

Both men nodded simultaneously, just as the introductory notes of the organ began warming the place with reverent sounds.

"I will see you later," indicated the vicar as he departed in the direction of the vestry.

John pulled Ned gently to a position on the front pew, before dropping on his knees to say a prayer for today. Ned likewise copied his actions, and on sensing that John had finished and was now moving to a sitting position on the pew, he followed. Then in comfortable silence, they gazed towards the altar where candles were burning brightly, in anticipation of the ceremony that was about to commence.

Outside, the farm's horse-drawn chaise drew up with Sissie and her father on board. He clambered down to help her from the other side hoping to minimise the bounce of the carriage as their body weight displaced it.

"Eeh lass, look at you!" he exclaimed with pride and joy at seeing his daughter looking so radiant. Her dress fit her perfectly and she felt very special with the veil surrounding her. Norma had styled her hair, controlling those curls around her flowery head dress and, daringly, had put a dab of lipstick on her. The large bouquet of pink roses, white irises, gypsophila and asparagus fern tumbling in front of her completed the bridal magic, and she glowed, feeling ready for anything now!

Suddenly, from the cool interior of the church the organist pressed the organ pipes to indicate that the bride had arrived. And as he played the familiar bridal march, a soft rustling sound could be heard as she walked slowly and deliberately towards the man she was going to marry, on the arm of her father.

John dared not look back at her. He was overwhelmed with emotion and excitement and he wanted to wait until she was by his side and then he would glimpse her behind the veil that screened her lovely face.

Mam and Sissie's brothers, together with Doris and Herbert were sitting at the front, ready to catch a glimpse of the bride as she passed them.

Slowly, the vicar emerged from the vestry and striding purposefully with outstretched arms in a gesture of welcome and inclusivity, he faced her, smiling kindly just as she reached the altar steps. John took a side step and slowly turned to look at her. He gasped in amazement at this picture of innocence on the face of this young virgin, who had just arrived at his side, and was looking into his eyes with such love and adoration.

"We are gathered here today," began the vicar. And so, the two of them were swept into a reverie of prayers, hymns and the exchanging of their vows, before sharing the vision and significance of the slim gold wedding band, as he placed it tenderly on her finger. Then, came the moment when he could lift her veil, as the voice of the vicar declared that they were now man and wife.

They turned to face each other, gazing into each other's eyes and smiling a little shyly, but feeling triumphant that this marked their first step into the future together.

The moment was interrupted by resounding cheering and clapping from a crowd at the back of the church. They both looked round in shock and surprise. They were expecting to be the only ones there with a few of her family and from the farm, but no! There, occupying three rows of pews at the back of the church were all the lasses and the lads from the Mill who had conspired to meet - each one being determined to show these two genuinely good people that they knew that it was their wedding day, and wanted to celebrate their happiness with them.

John and Sissie looked at each other, and laughing together at the unexpected warmth and fun coming from the back of the church, turned, and together outwardly applauded their unexpected guests in appreciation and fondness for their efforts. Then Sissie waved shyly, held John's hand and they moved together to the vestry to sign the register and to pose for a few photographs.

Half an hour later, they emerged into the church to an awaiting family and a few mill employees who had decided to stay until they reappeared, for a chance to wish them luck and throw handfuls of rice at them as they stepped out, into the sunshine.

But, just a moment, who was this sitting in the second row behind John's pew? A little girl and a sparrow-like young woman at her side wearing a prim hat to match a sage green linen suit. It was Emma with little Vicky, wearing a pretty dress and holding a posy of flowers!

"How?… What?… I don't believe it," cried John, confused but delighted at the unexpected sight of his little girl witnessing him marrying this woman - someone she had never met.

"Papa! It's me!" she shouted, as if he might not recognise her. She was about to run towards him instantly, but Emma held her back and said, "Wait child, until they leave church. Then, you can say hello."

"Let her be, Emma. Let's put you here between the two of us, my little lamb," said John, rather tactlessly but unable to contain his joy that his daughter was here.

Sissie was surprised at the suddenness and spontaneity of the moment, but she smiled gently at her, saying, "Come along, flower girl. You can hold my veil at the back and we will all leave the church together."

They blinked in the brightness and heat of the midday July sunshine and there was a sudden roar from the crowd and then three cheers. They were pelted with rice from well-wishers passing and others who had known them from the mill. The farm chaise was waiting with two dapple ponies kicking at the dust in the heat, as the newlyweds mounted in style to be driven away to the farm for a feast.

"Can I come with you?" shouted Vicky. But before anyone could answer, Emma quickly retorted, "No child! It's just for them only. You and I will take the car with the others." She could be so brusque sometimes. Vicky frowned, suppressing a groan of disappointment.

"See you back at the farm," John called out cheerily, as he and Sissie pulled away together, from the little crowd, rather dazed after all the unplanned but enjoyable action of the day, so far.

It was only a short distance from the church to Low Fold Farm, so there was little time for much conversation between the new bride and her groom. They shared their feelings and their delight that the ceremony had been as they both had hoped. They were delighted hearing and seeing the loyal crowd of well-wishers, who had given up part of their Saturday to witness their marriage. The new couple were touched to hear and feel the warmth and sincerity of everyone's support, as they called out "Congratulations!" and "Good Luck!"

Sissie was troubled by the unexpected attendance of John's sister, realising by now, that she was her sister-in-law. She was uncomfortable in Emma's company who still raised doubt in her mind that she would be accepted into John's family. Emma's distant, formal style lacked warmth, unable to offer companionship towards her on any occasion, less still an embrace, even on this special day.

However, she appreciated Emma's grounds for attending the wedding, presumably to allow the little girl to be present when her father remarried, yet she was not convinced this was the only reason for bringing her along.

Sissie had not met Vicky yet, and John had been clear that being married first and then introducing them would be a more satisfactory way towards getting to know her new step mother. But Emma always seemed to have a better idea and here again, she seemed to be controlling John. He would accept the decision without wanting to upset anyone. She was aware of that trait in him by now. She sighed, as she felt that this may become the pattern of things in future if she didn't take a more practical and pro-active stance.

"Here we are," exclaimed John. "Stay there and let me lift you down, dear," he continued, striding to her side of the chaise and lifting his arms upwards to ease her from it. Her veil fluttered in the summer breeze and despite the thoughts flitting around in her head, she felt special, because this was a special day.

"Oh Auntie!" a young voice called out. "Doesn't she look pretty?"

The car that had brought Emma and Vicky to the farm had arrived with other guests ahead of the bridal couple.

"All brides are pretty child," replied Emma drily. "Just especially for the day," as she gripped Vicky's hand, as if to leash her out of the way.

Everyone filed into the farmhouse through the front door which was so rarely used, only for special occasions. The new husband and wife moved across the threshold to be greeted by everyone.

"Are you going to be my new mother?" asked Vicky innocently, looking up at Sissie.

"Yes, if yer'd let me, Vicky. I think we are going to 'ave some 'appy times together. Well, I 'ope so!" she replied.

"All in good time, all in good time," Emma interrupted. "There's still a lot to organise and sort out yet."

Sissie, leaned towards the little girl extending her gloved hand, and said gently, "I think you've 'ad plenty of time wi'out yer Daddy 'aven't you, little lass? Let's find some cake for thee."

"May I have some, Auntie? Please?" the child looked at her aunt with pleading eyes.

"I suppose that will be in order," Emma replied reluctantly, as she watched the child skip alongside her stepmother, feeling unsettled by the new status of this rough woman her brother had just married.

Tea was being poured and people were helping themselves to dainty sandwiches and cheese scones. The Horbury boys were being restrained by their mother.

"Show some respect lads," she chided. "There's plenty more to eat at 'ome later."

As Vicky took her first bite of cake - not wedding cake just yet - there would be quietness in the room for the cutting of a three tiered iced fruit cake, later.

"Will I call you Mama?" asked Vicky with her mouth full of the delicious sponge.

"Mebbee call me Mammie," replied Sissie, knowing that John had approved when she first suggested it, some weeks ago.

"Oh ho! Are you getting to know each other at last?" enquired John, stepping closer to them holding Sissie at her elbow as if to give her support.

"I'm going to call her Mammie," blurted out Vicky, "Even if she isn't really my Mammie!"

The room went quiet and glances were exchanged as people had heard her but weren't quite sure what to think or say.

"That's right, my little lamb," said John calmly. "And she will love you and care for you as well, just like your mother did."

There was something in his decisive voice that closed the discussion and so she skipped off towards a cat. It was one of many that lived in comfort indoors, and it was sitting on the window sill, watching all these strangers making so much noise in his parlour.

Then there was the sound of a throat being cleared, and a glass being tapped to command some silence. Sissie's father stood up, hands in his pockets, to announce that the wedding cake would be cut.

"Thank ye for comin', folks. I'm very proud of me daughter. Me and our Annie wish 'er and 'er new 'usband, John as many years of 'appiness as we 'ave 'ad. Raise tha' glasses to the future."

"To the future!" they all chorused and everyone murmured their good wishes. This kind of formality was not customary. Plenty of ale and singing was more the style of celebration with which they were familiar, but Sissie and her husband seemed to want it this way and were happy enough, so that was an end to it.

One by one, they shook hands with the groom and offered an awkward hug for the pretty bride in lace and finery with flowers and a grain of rice or two caught in her hair, and admired the colour and style she had chosen.

With her cheeks pink with pride and her eyes sparkling with enjoyment and happiness of the day she did not notice that John had slipped out of sight. He had taken himself out to the back garden to light his pipe and to get away from the noisy crowd, the banter and party atmosphere. Now, he realised that he was married again and facing a future with a woman he was sure that he loved enough to be able to live with. And then together they would raise his daughter, suddenly hit him. This time, he found himself in nervous trepidation and understandable caution. He felt a deep sense of duty and responsibility for doing things 'properly' whatever it demanded of him, but he realised this was going to be challenging and would take a lot of effort to bring people together in harmony, and a common purpose. It seemed so complicated. This would almost have to be like charting a wartime strategy!

Suddenly, as he flicked the same wartime issue lighter to ignite the tobacco, he was overwhelmed by the vivid memories of his previous life before coming into these present circumstances, and as he drew in the fragrant smoke his eyes closed over to suppress a wave of tears. They were tears of sadness and nostalgia drawn from so many of the tragic experiences that he had encountered during that time. He leaned back against the rustic fencing, packed with the second flush of roses, their sympathy and sensitivity seeming to fragrance the air around him.

"Must stop this looking back," he sniffed quietly. "Must get on and make something of life anew. Want to be someone in this world."

He gazed upwards into the clear blue sky and the July sunshine that was reflecting on the glass of a greenhouse in the corner opposite. It dazzled him like a beacon of hope directing and focussing on him. So he resolved to put all his efforts into building his career and in establishing a secure and happy life for his new family.

For ten minutes he collected his thoughts whilst enjoying the comfort and solitude that his pipe always gave him. It allowed him private and personal time for reflection and prepared him for purpose and action.

"John! John!" called Sissie. "We 'ave to be goin' now! Its time!"

"Alright, my dearest. I am here and I'm coming in now."

He snuffed out the pipe, tucking it into his top pocket and made his way to the house where everyone was assembled for their big send off.

"Where are you going?" enquired a small voice. "I want to come with you. Let me come with you."

Emma quickly advanced to catch the child's arm in an attempt to hold her back as she wriggled her way through the adults. They were all waiting to give the bride and groom the traditional send off, as John and Sissie were about to leave in ceremonial style.

Now this might present potential change to their arrangements. They planned to go to John's small rented cottage for a few days to be alone together, before their big move to their new home in Doncaster. It would now be most difficult to leave without Vicky. Emma had meddled in the proceedings, and so now there were compromises to be made. John felt he must take the lead and decide a course of action that would avoid any extreme emotion and allow everyone to feel comfortable. It required some quick thinking and fortunately, this was his strength because Sissie looked confused and self-conscious and Emma was fiercely glaring at Vicky as if to prevent her from further pleading to be taken with them.

"Come along then little one, and you can see where we are going and then we can work out where you will sleep tonight."

Emma gasped and Sissie sighed and everyone breathed in relief that friction and tantrums all round had been side stepped for now.

"You can come and stay with us tonight if yer like our lass, though it's plain an' simple," announced Annie. "It makes sense as Sissie's bed 'll be empty," and everyone nudged each other, winking and grinning. Sissie would be in her marital bed tonight!

"Well, that's a fine idea isn't it? Many thanks for that offer! Come on! Hop up between us!" invited John, as he lifted the child into the chaise before climbing in himself.

Sissie's father hugged his own daughter warmly as he lifted her up on the other side of their 'chaise for a day' transport, and whispered, "Yer Mam and me's goin' to miss ye 'ere but, you listen t' yer Dad. I know ye'll take it all in yer stride lass. It'll all work out fine. An' don't worry about little 'un an' old sour puss missy they'll be fine wi' us."

She smiled. A man of few words, but when he did speak it was always using common sense and reassurance in his voice.

"Ta Dad," and she settled back to enjoy the closing moments of her special day.

"I'll walk and meet you at the cottage, that is, when someone tells me where it is!'" announced Emma irritably. Annie stepped forward to help her by repeating the invitation to stay with them that night.

"Them two'll be wanting their time alone tonight," she added quietly, as if Emma may need reminding that the day was not over yet for bride and groom.

Chapter 33

New Life

It was the morning after the wedding that they lay side by side in the bedroom of the tiny cottage, listening to birds singing and feeling the warmth of early morning sunlight promising them another beautiful day ahead.

Her nervous anticipation of their first night together had been soothed as soon as they arrived there. John was patient and experienced and had expressed such loving gentleness, showing her how to respond to him in the stillness of the bedroom. It allowed her to feel wanted and admired and it made her free to display her sensuality and eagerness to please him.

So many times they had come close to breaking the rules of any physical union before they were married, and perhaps the last few weeks with John working away, meant that there had been less and less opportunity to find moments alone, so their embraces and tender kisses had craved time to explore each other.

It had all been worth the wait! They were aroused and energetic in their emotion, and they were brimming with pent up desire. The night did not seem long enough for them to show and share the intensity of their love and passion for each other.

Then as dawn broke and their first shared night turned into day, they lay in dreamy silence, reflecting on the perfect connections they had made that would change them forever and they were reluctant to let the world in just yet.

However, the day ahead loomed and they had commitments to others. They discussed long ago that they must handle Vicky sensitively but firmly. They agreed it was important to leave Emma with some dignity and an understanding too. They would tell her that being left without her niece with whom she had become extremely fond, would not mean denying her time to spend together. There would be holidays, that sort of thing. They hadn't quite decided yet. What was certain was that Vicky would be living with them and on that there would be no negotiation.

"C'mon my angel- let's get dressed and go to Low Farm for some breakfast," suggested John, as Sissie nuzzled her face into his neck. She wanted to stay there a little longer in their own piece of paradise. She wasn't ready to face the outside world just yet. She groaned softly, understanding the pressure he would be feeling. So she smiled and raised herself up above the crumpled cotton sheets and said solemnly,

"I'm ready to go when you are John Bland. My dearest husband!"

Half an hour later they were tapping on the kitchen door before walking in to see the Horbury family, with Emma and Vicky, taking breakfast together. There was a cheer from the younger boys and Mam was pouring tea and offering bread and jam, as they seated themselves. Vicky jumped down to go and sit on her father's lap.

"Vicky leave your father alone. He's only just arrived," protested Emma.

"She's fine, Emma, just a little bit excited aren't you, child?" John replied adjusting the little girl on his knee so that she could face the table.

"Now then, what do you say to your Mammie?"

"Hello Mammie. How are you today?" she whispered, with lowered eyes.

"I'm very well, thank you and how are you?" replied Sissie in a formal tone, sensing this was a style of greeting the child was used to.

"I'm very well, too!" she responded. "And what are we going to do today?"

"We have to do lots of jobs, because we are moving into a new house and we have to pack our clothes and all our belongings," explained John.

During his temporary period of work in Derbyshire, he had been delighted and relieved to have been accepted as Manager of a new textile factory in Doncaster and had laid plans to buy a family house in the town. Sissie was pleasantly surprised with his news and was looking forward to running her own household, but he had given her so few details. There just had not been the time together to share the new plans.

"What are belongings?" Vicky enquired, as the adults smiled at her inquisitive little voice.

"Questions, questions," puffed Emma. "I can't keep up with her sometimes. She's going to be a bright one is this one. I hope you're ready," she added, as if warning John and Sissie of what was to come.

"Oh yes," they replied at the same time, looking at each other in surprise at their unified response - so simple and yet so effective!

As Mam started to clear away the breakfast pots and Dad put on his cap to depart for the next round of work, Emma leaned towards John. "Have you a moment? I need to talk to you outside, in private."

"Yes of course, but not without Sissie. If you are going to say something, say it to both of us, please. Now that we are married we don't intend to have any secrets," he added gently.

"Let's go outside," she repeated, appearing to have no objection to Sissie being there too. Wondering what she was going to say but trying to remain calm, they guessed that it would be something about Vicky and the future. They opened the door apprehensively and stepped into the morning air. By now, Vicky had moved away and was on the floor playing with the cats and seemed unaware that they were leaving the kitchen.

Into the bright light in the yard, they walked silently to the old five bar gate where Emma clasped her hands in front of her and took a deep breath.

"You may have wondered why I came to the wedding unannounced. It wasn't just to bring Vicky to see you get married, although I do admit I felt it was important for her to witness it. The fact is - I have some other news." She hesitated briefly and sighed, "I won't beat about the bush. Father has been hit by the deadly foot and mouth disease. He has to have the entire flock destroyed. Now, as you know although you were not involved, this is the second time he has been devastated by this wicked disease. This time though, there are serious financial implications. The first attack was ten years ago and as you know it was wartime and he, as well as other farmers took some heavy financial losses. Nothing came from the government and so he had to sell a substantial amount of land to cover that.

Now then, this time it seems, the consequences will almost certainly wipe him out. To cover costs, he will need to sell the rest of the land and the farmhouse. He is reluctant to tell me everything - I think it is all too painful for him and he doesn't want to upset me."

"Stop there! Stop there! Give me a moment to deal with this news, Emma! Surely we can find some way to save at least some of the land and the property. We must be able to help out in some way. This has been in the family for centuries. Isn't it possible to have a bank loan or to find some form of insurance cover?"

"No, John! Don't you think we have all been looking at the options? Anne, William and I have all tried to help him by contacting solicitors and bank officials so that he can keep his mind straight and to stay sane but he's sixty-five years old and we worry that this will seriously affect him. He sees the only way to solve the problem is to sell everything and to remain at the farm as a tenant farmer."

John whistled though his teeth and dragged his hand through his hair in shock and despair. Sissie was silently absorbing this devastating news and felt so tearful for the elderly gentleman. This was her husband's father who was such an honest man, with integrity. He was not only to lose his livelihood but he would be losing his self-respect and his legacy, too. John was disappointed that they had not contacted him for assistance. Being such a catastrophe for the family, he felt he should have been more involved. It sounded as if decisions had been made already, without any input from himself.

Out came his pipe. My word, how he needed this now. He would give himself a few moments to absorb the news and then be able to offer a sensible response.

"What happens now, then?" he asked. "You seem to have everything under control as usual, Emma."

He felt left out as an outsider would, with nothing of importance to contribute. It was true that once he had left home at eighteen he had sculptured his ambitions carefully and had become distanced from life on Shap. The first foot and mouth epidemic held little significance for him he had to admit as he was away on the Front line, but this time…

Emma ignored her older brother's remark, putting it down to distress and worry for their parents' well-being.

"John, you are a clever man who has a demanding job and you've experienced many past sadnesses and disappointments. I think we all felt that his would have been yet another burden on you. Believe me, our intention was to protect you from more anxiety and grief, not because we didn't care about the value of your involvement."

He drew on his pipe and turned to Sissie for a comforting smile and a reassuring look of love. He sighed softly, "And how can we help, now?"

"Just by taking Vicky under your wing to give her a stable and secure home life whilst we sort out the farm issues and get back on an even keel. First of all, I need to look after father and mother. I'm worried about their state of health and with no money now to pay for any medical care. They are going to occupy my time and I can't have Vicky around seeing and hearing things that little ones should not be experiencing at her age."

"Of course we will. That was always the plan, wasn't it? Will you leave her here with us now and return on your own?" asked John half knowing what the answer would be.

"Yes, that was in my mind, if you are ready to have her," replied Emma, glancing at Sissie as she spoke, trying to gauge her reaction.

"Of course we are," they both chimed together - this was becoming a pattern! It proved they were of the same mind and had the same sensible approach.

"Well, that's settled. I shall catch the afternoon train up to Preston. There's plenty of time and I can leave you to get yourselves organised."

Emma unclasped her hands and Sissie noticed that she was trembling - probably through telling them the news and the emotion she would be feeling in leaving the little girl behind. It was a very testing situation, and even a sharply spoken, no nonsense woman like Emma had clearly shown sensitivity and kindness in her heart. Sissie was hopeful that more of this side to her nature might surface in good time.

* * *

The next few weeks were very demanding. John's new position of General Manager at the newly created rayon plant in Doncaster held numerous responsibilities for him. He needed to recruit a workforce, train them in new ways to manage and operate the new technology, and calculate cost effective ways of paying wages and to profit from the changes to plant machinery.

There was little doubt that within a worldwide context, they were on the threshold of innovation and manufacture of a textile fibre that replicated silk. Silk was expensive and accessible only to those who could afford its luxurious properties. This new product would mean that such a luxury could be afforded by the many.

They were in competition with the Americans and other countries in Europe to develop a realistic and plausible product that could, and indeed would, change the characteristics and implementation of textile manufacture for the future. There was heavy investment in new methods and John wanted to become part of the development and marketing of these ambitious research projects.

The implications of this commitment took effect on the pressures that were felt by his new young wife, who was making and managing a new home for them, in a town with which she was unfamiliar, and at the same time trying her inexpert best to raise a bright and energetic little girl whose only wish was to be with her Daddie.

One Friday night after a long and challenging working week for them both, they sat in the new parlour, still surrounded by cardboard cartons and piles of unpacked clothing and bedroom linen. "Has she been a good girl this week?" John enquired, knowing that such an open question would prompt a torrent of stories and events that would cause argument. He would try to defend his daughter as stories were revealed of her truculence and inability to follow Sissie's reasonable demands. This was all according to Sissie.

"I'm sorry, John. She's not easy. She always 'as an answer for everything and she will do everything 'er way. She never does as I tell 'er."

"She's got a brain on her that's for sure and she's wilful I give you that, but do try and let her have her own way. No! No!" John responded as he held his hand up as if to silence Sissie's protests. "Just occasionally so that she can feel she has a voice, and so you can avoid all this argument, because that is not the way to build your relationship with her."

"She tells me I can't tell her what to do, John. It's hard to take."

"I know, I know," he said, trying to comfort her and sighing at the frustration that he could not be at home to support his new young wife.

"There's so much to do an' all. I want to get this house straight and tidy for you and I can't as she takes all my time."

"Well, let's try to be practical shall we? I will employ a maid for you who can live in and who can be available every day and help out with all the household tasks. We can afford it and we have the space. It's common practice these days among professional people. This will give you more time to spend with Vicky. It's a good solution."

Sissie gasped. A maid! What would the family say to that when they heard about it? She could hear Doris now, "Oh look at our Sis and 'er fancy ways - she'll not be speakin' to us now, so grand is she!'

"No, John. Not yet," she replied, a suggestion that would be a big help to her. He had bought a large four bedroomed house with an attic and with a scullery, main kitchen, morning room and sitting room. It had a big garden and faced the largest of the town parks. It was generally regarded as one of the more pleasant areas of town and their neighbours were doctors, solicitors and other businessmen, which made her feel completely out of her depth.

John loved a solution, and once he had found one to suit this particular problem he felt pleased with himself, and was reluctant to discuss it any further.

"No, my mind is made up, Sissie. I shall advertise tomorrow and by next week you will have some well-deserved assistance."

Nothing would dissuade him and she knew this, so that was the end to it.

They spent a comfortable weekend in the garden, sharing some time with Vicky, who behaved well enough, now that her beloved father was home. She was soon to change, when on Sunday evening after she had dried herself after her weekly bath, and Sissie had styled her freshly washed hair, she was asked to put on her nightdress and to choose a bedtime story.

Vicky was not ready to sleep! She really didn't want the weekend to end as she had spent such a wonderful time with her Daddie and Mammie and knowing that she would be left without her father for the majority of the week, there seemed little to be cheerful about.

Her protests began and she whined and pouted and presented some very convincing reasons for staying up longer, until Sissie stepped in to insist that it was time for bed.

Vicky swung round and snapped, "You're not my Mama! You can't tell me what to do!"

John jumped up from behind his newspaper having listened to the previous events but trying to judge at what point he should intervene. "Oh yes she can! How dare you say that to your Mammie!" he cried. And with one swift movement of his left hand, he slapped the back of her legs.

In shock and horror, she leapt back crying out, "That hurt me, Daddie."

"Yes, and it will hurt some more if you don't apologise NOW," he roared. "I will not have you speaking like this. Sometimes you must just do as you are TOLD."

"I don't think I like you, Pppapa," she sobbed, rubbing her legs dramatically. "You have hurt me."

"No, I haven't. I have just hurt your feelings my dear, but you have to learn that you must do as your Mammie says, like a good girl. You are not old enough to make decisions yet. One day when you are older and you have learned more about life, and how to speak with respect to those older than you, then you can decide things for yourself. Now say you are sorry."

"No!"

"Yes."

"Shall not!"

"Yes you shall, child."

"No."

"Come on, you are making matters worse. Just say you are sorry, otherwise there will be no book and no supper before bed"

"Don't want to."

"Alright then. Off you go to bed - without supper and perhaps in the morning we shall see a good girl."

She left the room silently and with chin firm and tears dried, she thumped up the stairs.

"Oh John, I feel terrible," began Sissie.

"Don't - it's not your fault and I will not have you apologising. She has to learn that she is not in charge. You are!"

After a few moments, he rose from the armchair after carefully folding his newspaper and placing it on the small table beside him.

"I will go up and tuck her in my dear. I can't bear to think of her going to sleep without trying to help her see that she must behave and that we still love her very much. She will be fine by morning."

Sissie sighed and reached out her hand towards him, as he crossed the room. He clasped it and holding it to his lips, kissed it lightly.

"I'll be back downstairs soon. This has to be done and I won't rest until I have dealt with it. Perhaps afterwards we can have the remainder of our evening in peace."

Slowly, with light steps he climbed the stairs, humming a little, hoping that she would hear him approaching. Muffled, gulping sounds of a small child crying bitterly came from under the blankets, as he opened her bedroom door. He felt overwhelming sadness and grief for all that had passed and suddenly an understanding of the emotional turmoil in which this child had found herself. At the same time, he felt guilty that he had spent so much time building a new existence since arriving back to England with her, that he had not allowed anyone, let alone this precious little one, to catch up with all the changes.

"Now then, now then, what's all this silly noise? I wonder where it can be coming from? Let me see…" He put on a playful voice, "I don't think there are any little girls in here… at least I can't see any!"

He walked around the end of the bed. "No. I can't see anyone at all," he added in theatrical voice. Suddenly the crying sound stopped and there was silence.

"Oh dear, I can't hear anyone, now. Perhaps there's no one here, after all."

"It's me," replied a little voice from under the heap of bedclothes.

"I don't think I know anyone called me," replied John, deciding to turn this into a light hearted game.

"You know me", urged Vicky, sensing the note of fatherly playfulness and wanting to join in.

"I only know little me's who can say sorry," continued John, reluctant to let the subject of this situation go.

"I'm looking for a sorry under the covers, Daddie," Vicky called out as the bedclothes contorted.

"And have you found one, child?" he asked patiently.

"Yes, I think so - here." And as she threw the covers back, she held her cupped hands towards him. "Have you found one in there? That's very clever of you! I think we could call Mammie and give that to her, don't you? Shall I call her and then we can turn off the light and think about what we can play tomorrow?"

Together, they called Sissie who responded to the call, and guessing there was some sort of charade going on, mounted the stairs apprehensively, not quite knowing what she was about to face. She had no need to worry. All seemed to have been resolved, and she joined in accepting the dramatically presented cup of sorry, whispering her thanks and smiling affectionately at the little girl.

"Now, that's enough for today young lady," said John gently. "Let's get you into this bed." Vicky dutifully said her prayers.

"God Bless Daddie, God Bless Mammie, God Bless Auntie Emma…."

The list of blessings seemed endless before they both tucked her in and left her to fall asleep, exhausted.

Later downstairs, as John took out his pipe to enjoy with his bedtime whisky he said,

"I think I will take tomorrow morning off, my dear, so that we can all have breakfast together. Then I can spend a little time with Vicky and that way we can get over this evening's episode. What do you think?"

Sissie took a deep breath before she spoke. "I have the doctor visiting tomorrow morning, John. I was going to tell you about it tomorrow evening."

"My dear - for what reason? Tell me - are you ill or in pain? What on earth is wrong?"

"Nothing to worry about, John. I just want the doctor to give me a check-up."

"But why? You have me worried."

"John - I wanted to see him before telling you because - I am sure I am pregnant!"

He paused with pipe held high in one hand and a whisky glass high in the other, and put both down firmly on the table beside him. He bolted from the chair to embrace her and he held her closely for several moments, until tears ran down both their cheeks with sheer joy and excitement.

"Oh my sweetheart, that is the most glorious news! I cannot believe this has happened so quickly for us - we are going to be the perfect family"

Chapter 34

Family Life

Dear John,

It is imperative that you return to the farm as soon as possible. Father had a heart attack on Saturday and he has been instructed by the doctor to take bed rest and to remain quiet and calm. I am concerned that he will not recover. He looks very poorly, and so I feel we all need to be around him, so that he can see how much we care.

Mother is distraught and I am not sure she will have strength to deal with any more upsetting news. Biddie is here. She has been a huge support and I don't know what we would all do without her.

I know you are busy, but there are many things that we need to sort out here. I hope you and Sissie and dearest Vicky are well.

Your devoted sister, Emma

Emma's letters were always direct and straight to the point and there was never a hint of sentiment in her writing. John folded the letter carefully, then unfolded it and read it again, before calling Sissie to share the news.

"When'll you go, John?" she asked in shock at how serious it sounded.

"Well, I have no choice, dear. Tomorrow, I must notify colleagues and make my way up north to be there. Father has become more and more frail over the last few years following all these setbacks. I worry this may be his last battle and he may not win it."

She clapped her hands to her mouth in horror and fear for the family and sorrow for John. "Should I come with you? It would be best if I came with Vicky to 'elp out, wouldn't it?"

"No, I think you should stay here. If this is so serious, I don't want Vicky there. It will be too frightening and confusing for her. No, she should stay with you and that baby that's growing in you. We don't want any worse news, do we?"

He had made his statement clear and when he spoke like this one accepted that he had made up his mind. She nodded her head meekly. After all it did seem reckless to travel all that way and risk feeling awkward, a spare part, and of little use.

"You've clean shirt collars, socks and underwear in your wardrobe. I'll pack for you straight after breakfast," Sissie answered calmly. It meant he could organise his work commitments and his travel without the added burden of packing. At least she felt of use here, and once he had left she would then be able to make further plans for finishing the unpacking of cardboard cartons and trunks full of their belongings.

"Thank you, my dear. You do look after me, but I sincerely hope you are going to look after yourself, too. Don't forget, this new maid is presenting herself for your approval on

Wednesday morning. You can offer her a month's trial period if you feel that she will do a good job for us. Remember what we discussed - her tasks, her role here with living in the top attic. Her wages are written down here."

He offered her the envelope containing the terms and conditions of the job and the salary, just as they had agreed over the weekend.

"Yes, John. I'm sure she'll be right for us. Her references are satisfactory and I think I can teach 'er us ways o' goin' on," commented Sissie as she coaxed him gently out of the morning room to prepare for his next few days away.

He checked the time on the grandfather clock in the hall, given to them by his father and mother when he and Sissie had married. It had been in the family for two generations and was a handsome time piece that he had been proud to accept. On accepting and appreciating the generous gift, it had overwhelmed Sissie with its grandeur and significance. John took great pride in ensuring it stayed accurate, and every Monday morning before leaving for work, he would carefully wind it up, synchronising his silver Hunter pocket watch against it, to verify its accuracy, appreciating the fine oak case as he stroked it, respectfully. Turning away after his routine, he always felt reassured of the reliability and unshakeable strength of the timepiece.

He twisted round to face the staircase with a dash of irritation, foreseeing the difficulties, both practical and emotional, that he would be encountering during the next few days. He detested sudden changes and there seemed so many of them these days. It appeared that nothing could become habitual anymore - a steady routine in which one would feel most comfortable and secure. Was he expecting too much? Was it an absurd hope - like a hangover of life's predictable and reliable course as he had experienced when growing up? Or was it because he had become accustomed to the ritual of taking and giving orders as an officer through his war experience, that had set such an expectation? Of one thing he was sure - life was full of surprises! That had become a recent cliché within his professional circle, and increasingly, he was finding it to be true.

However, the most important feature in his life at present, was indeed constant and reliable and comforting. It was being married to his darling Sissie! Here she was, plain and simple speaking, a sensible approach when facing daily problems; loving, unfussy devotion towards himself and his daughter, and above all, someone whom he could trust and talk to and who would listen intently, asking all the right questions at all the appropriate moments. He had much to be grateful for and so he reproached himself for doubting the real value of what he held so dear.

From his wardrobe, he gathered essential clothing and folded each item to fill a leather overnight bag that had travelled with him over the last few years, and toiletries to last him through the next few days, then buckling it closed, he left the bedroom and crossed the landing. Sissie and Vicky stood at the bottom of the stairs waiting to say goodbye.

"When are you coming back, Daddie?" Vicky asked, looking for reassurances that he would not be gone for long. She always seemed to be saying goodbye to him.

"Oh, I won't be long. Just a day or two. I want to hear that you have been a good girl and that you have been doing as

Mammie tells you. If you are good, I promise to bring back something special for you," he declared.

He looked at Sissie and winked. "This won't take long, dearest," he said optimistically, "Wish me luck and look after each other." He gave Sissie a kiss on her cheek and fondly patting the top of Vicky's head, he lifted the latch on the front door and hurried down the path on a brisk ten-minute walk to the railway station.

*   *   *

"I'm Evelyn, ma'am. I've come for the new position," stammered a slightly built young woman standing on the doorstep. Sissie opened the door in response to the timid tap that she had only just made out a few moments earlier, before checking if Vicky had heard anything.

"Yes, Mammie! Somebody at the door. I heard it." She jumped up and down with excitement that someone could be calling - perhaps someone new to play with. Peering from behind Sissie's skirt, she could see the outline of a slim young woman wearing a belted gabardine raincoat and cloche pulled down over her ears.

"G'd afternoon lass! Come in, come in," welcomed Sissie, stepping to one side to let her in out of the light rain, treading on Vicky's toes as she did so.

"Owww - owww that hurt me, "shrieked Vicky hopping up and down on one foot whilst holding the other.

"There, there don't make such a fuss. I'm sorry but you shouldn't 'ave been under me feet Vicky. Let's go in and get us a cup o' tea and get to know one another," she added, smiling at the nervous visitor.

She led the way into the morning room, indicating to the young woman to follow. Evelyn gave Vicky a broad encouraging smile and a little wink.

"You're just like me sister's eldest you are. 'Er name's Edna," she said in an attempt to smooth over the situation. She knew how such a scene could blow out of proportion when little ones wanted to be noticed!

Sissie glanced at her, approving of the way she had handled Vicky. This was the first promising sign that she would fit into family life here. There was much to discuss and just as she and John had planned, she had a few notes by her to remind herself of all the routines, expectations and daily chores that were required. Then finally, there would be the subject of salary....

Having poured the tea, they exchanged pleasantries and Evelyn was asked about her experience, of which she had none, and any school certificates she may have but again it was none! The lass was from a large Doncaster family, and several members had taken on work in service with modest households who required help in the home. Sissie described their situation, explaining that one day they hoped to have another child. She described Vicky as their only one, not mentioning that she was her stepmother. The girl did not need to know that - not yet anyway. She would be expected to live in and would have Wednesday afternoons and Sundays off duty, when it was expected that she would return to her own home, to come back refreshed for the next working week. All seemed acceptable on both sides and it was agreed that she would start on the following Monday.

"Will she be allowed to play with me sometimes Mammie?" enquired Vicky looking pleadingly at Sissie.

"We'll see. I'm sure we can find time for that - only if you're good, mind," replied Sissie, still not confident in ways to deal with this bright rising five-year-old.

After the business had been dealt with, Sissie led her upstairs to show her the room in the attic that had been especially prepared for a housemaid, and which Evelyn appeared to be pleased with, especially when she was told that she would be supplied with two uniforms. One of which would be black with an apron for mornings and the same but in brown for afternoons.

"Do you like it? Are you going to live with us?" Vicky asked excitedly. She liked to see new people and changes to her routines, unlike her father!

As she was escorted to the front door Sissie shook her hand. Using her best formal voice, she said, "I hope everything is satisfactory for you. My husband and me, well, we would like to offer a one-month trial period and then we can decide whether this position suits you and that you can get on wi' us too! I wish you goodbye for now." And she opened the front door, to let the new maid out.

"Thank you Mrs. Bland. I won't let you down. I think I'm going to be very 'appy 'ere!"

Evelyn smiled shyly, and as she took Sissie's hand she bobbed a little curtsey in respect and gratitude that she had been offered a position. She was eighteen years old, only five years younger than her mistress.

Sissie closed the door firmly, as Evelyn Loxley left the front porch and Vicky jumped up and down with excitement.

"She can play with me can't she, Mammie?" she insisted.

"Sometimes yes. But she is here to do some housework and help me with the cleaning and cooking so you will have to play by yourself sometimes. In September you will be going to school, so don't forget, you will not be at home as much as you are now."

Suddenly, Sissie felt overcome with tiredness and she realised that although this must be due to her condition at the moment, she would have many demands on her time with running a large house like this and bringing a baby into the world. She wanted everything to be organised and enjoyable for John when he returned home from his important management work and she didn't want to disappoint him. Vicky did not know yet, that a baby was coming. In fact, no one knew. She would prefer to wait until the doctor, having examined her a few days ago, would be able to confirm that she was most likely pregnant, after two months without a course. Within another week towards the third month it would be confirmed. Already, she was feeling the breast tenderness, fatigue and typical frequent lavatory visits that she'd heard other pregnant women mention. It was exciting and frightening at the same time, and it was such a new experience emotionally and physically. She couldn't believe that it had happened so quickly, and that she was capable of carrying a growing human being inside her, but best of all she was ecstatic that John had been so delighted with the news and so interested in, and caring for, her happiness and good health. She wished her Mam was nearer for advice though and that her family were closer for visits too.

Chapter 35

Death in the Family

John's arrival at the family home seemed to elevate everyone's spirits. He brought into their midst an atmosphere of hope, direction and new optimism for their father's improvement. From the doctor's notes, it appeared that the elderly gentleman had experienced a profound heart attack for which only bed rest could ease the discomfort and aid recovery.

John felt the enormity of his responsibility - first and foremost to his mother, with whom he realised he had had so little contact these past few years. He had spent minimal time with her, and had offered little support since his return to England, even choosing to settle many miles from home. However, she was a practical, strong woman and she had encouraged him to succeed in his ambitions, whilst keeping a little regret to herself, that he would be building his life a long way from her and the family, meaning she would not see much of him.

The recent shock to her husband John and herself in facing the foot and mouth epidemics had hit both of them hard. Her grief for him in facing the loss of his family heritage and in sustaining an honest living, was unbearable as she bore it silently whilst presenting a façade of strength, carrying the weight with him as impassively as she could. To show too much emotion would be ineffective and not particularly helpful. It wasn't in her character anyway. She had been raised to keep one's feelings private and focus on doing one's best in adversity.

John was surprised as he walked into the farm cottage - it was no bigger than the Horbury farm worker's cottage! He knew just how devastated they would have been to be living - nay - existing - so simply and humbly now, in contrast to the life they had been used to in that large rambling farm they had known before. There they had been in a place that they had inherited and therefore owned, but now they found themselves in a place that they had to rent and had to answer to someone else in their surroundings that they had to call home. No wonder the anxiety and feeling of loss and failure had affected his father so greatly which would have inevitably contributed to his heart attack.

Inside the dark little passage way into the cottage, Emma stood waiting. His sister looked tired and her boyish frame seemed to have diminished so much that she looked frail and vulnerable. He felt such sadness for her as clearly, she had been working tirelessly throughout the time since their father had become ill. Her eyes lacked their usual sparkle and the lines of worry and weariness across her forehead, were evident.

Her parents were her life, and she had never had any intention of living anywhere but with them both, to care for them, being so appreciative of their belief in her aptitude and ability, as she gained her teaching qualification during such difficult times. She looked relieved when he walked through the door, as William parked up the truck in which they had both returned from the station. She held her arms wide and he embraced her, noticing how bony her shoulder blades were and how angular her jaw appeared as he squeezed her firmly, holding her for a moment with fondness and reassurance.

Anne appeared from the kitchen, drying her hands on her apron as she stepped towards him, giving him a cheerful smile and kissing his cheek.

"Alright?" she greeted him, "Good journey?"

He didn't have time to answer as he turned towards Emma, upon hearing her whisper. There was not a moment to lose, now that he had arrived. "You should go straight up to see him."

Without hesitation he left them, to mount the creaking stairs. At the top, he tapped lightly on the bedroom door and walked straight in. Propped up on the pillows bearing the family monogrammed white pillowcases, lay his father with his grey tousled hair framing his thin, aged face, ashen and drawn in pain. He extended his veined hand tremblingly towards his eldest son.

"You came," he whispered hoarsely. "I thought you'd be too busy."

"Never too busy to come up and see how you're doing," replied John smiling. "We need to get you back to your old self, don't we?"

"No chance of that, son," his father spluttered with despair in his voice, and then with a deep breath he added, "Everything is gone, son - and now I'm ready to go with it."

John looked across at his mother, sitting quietly beside the bed who had only acknowledged him with a nod and a smile as he had entered the bedroom, knowing this moment was for father and son, that she would talk later.

"Now I don't want to hear that kind of talk, Father. That is not going to help you to get better is it?" John answered kindly, knowing that he was looking at his father, who had now lost hope and had given in to his situation.

"You know what Doctor says. You must rest and build your energy. Mother is with you here, and Emma is making sure you have the medicine and the right food for recovery. We all want you back as you always have been - at the head of this family."

The old man nodded wearily, having neither the energy nor the voice to continue conversation. He was exhausted, and was drifting in and out of consciousness but clearly feeling a great relief to see his son again. He thought everything would be fine and John would make sure Mother was comfortable. He patted the bedclothes and gently urged John to leave them both. And so John bent over to kiss his forehead, smiling at his mother as he turned away to leave them.

As he walked slowly down the stairs, he wiped his eyes with the back of his hand and went straight out into the yard to smoke his pipe.

Leaning against the privy wall in the cobbled yard at the back of the cottage, he recalled the days as a boy when he and his father would ramble over Shap spotting Marsh Harriers hovering overhead as they focussed on a small mammal in the grass, before plunging swiftly to the ground to catch it. On early morning jaunts, an odd barn owl would glide silently past them on its way home after a busy evening hunting. His father knew the names, habitat and behaviours of all the birds and mammals that they observed and together they would collect feathers and birds' eggs for their collections at home. He recalled the funny stories that his father would relate about the fishing trips he would share with his brother William and Isaac, the latter being very studious and who would eventually become a clerk in holy orders in Oxford. Oh, how they would tease him for his timidity and lack of courage outdoors and then he and William would hide so that the youngest brother panicked because he had no idea how to get home! Sadly, the gentle natured young man was lost in combat and never returned home.

Then he remembered the return to a warm and welcoming kitchen where the heavenly aroma of freshly baked bread would welcome them and Father would reach for his favourite blackcurrant jam that Mother made every year especially for him.

"Wash your hands, you filthy ruffians!" she would fondly cry.

He had a happy childhood he was proud to admit, and together with all his school success, he had experienced a full and joyful upbringing and that was more than so many young chaps he had met at university, and then in the army.

As he finished the last puff of the pipe, he sighed and turning towards the cottage to come back in, he looked up at the window of the bedroom where his father lay, probably feeling that he had let the family down. He had been struggling in a spirit of guilt and despair, for some time, and now everything that he had worked for was ending this way. In pain and discomfort, with his loyal wife by his side, as she always had been, John sensed that his father had finally given up the fight for survival this time.

John was certain that those special few minutes that he had just shared with his father today, would be the last time he would see him alive. And he was right. The old man passed away peacefully in his sleep that night.

Chapter 36

Doing what is best

My Darling Sweetheart,

I got here just in time to see Father and to pay my respects. He passed away peacefully the night before last and Mother was with him. We have been arranging matters today and the funeral will be on Friday.

It is very sad here and Mother and Emma are in a state. Anne and William are bearing up and I am doing all the paperwork.

I hope you and Vicky are getting along fine and she is being good. I know you will be tired but if this housemaid is starting to work soon this is going to help you, I know.

The family are not expecting you here so don't you worry about a thing. I will be home on Saturday.

You have had a rough time since you met me but when we are together and have our own little family we will be so happy and will love each other and give each other comfort, won't we?

Being here now, I know that love in a cottage is better than discord in a mansion and yes, I know I have

*my faults just as you know what your own are, but I
promise I will make you happy wherever and however
we live as long as we are together, forever.*
 I am

       Your loving husband and sweetheart,
           John

John wrote the letter as soon as he was woken up to be given the tragic, though not entirely unexpected news that his father had drifted into night time sleep, never to wake up again. He was relieved that it had not been necessary for the family to witness their dear father in prolonged and excruciating physical pain - and then he thought that the old man had suffered all of that, mentally and emotionally, over the last few years on his own.

Sealing the envelope and addressing it to Sissie, he stuck a stamp on it, always keeping one or two handy in his wallet for the purpose, and set off to post it. He felt he needed an escape from the oppressive and stifling atmosphere in the cottage that not just he, but everyone else had been feeling during the last day or two. As he clicked the kitchen door behind him to cross the yard he saw Emma leaning on the five barred gate at the entrance.

"Where are you off to?" she asked. She looked up at him accusingly, with eyes red rimmed from crying. She had always felt that John had dodged responsibility during the aftermath of the foot and mouth epidemic on both occasions - and had shown little commitment to their parents and the toll it had taken on their well-being.

"Just to the village to post a letter. I'm coming back."

"Hmm, perhaps I'll walk with you - I need the fresh air," she replied tonelessly.

"Of course," he responded. He couldn't refuse her. She obviously needed some company and a good walk was always beneficial, especially during difficult times. They strode out together along the farm track, feeling the crisp sweetness of the morning air. For several minutes they paced out in easy silence, neither one of them wishing to break the other's inner thoughts. Each of them reflecting in their own ways, through numbness in grief and sorrow, on the strangeness of living together as they did as children but now, within a household, without the presence of their father.

This was a time to lose oneself in unanswerable questions and randomly meandering memories. The 'what if?' and the 'if only' and the 'remember when' kind of phrases kept springing to the surface in odd unprepared, catching the breath moments.

Suddenly at the side of the track, Emma spotted a baby rabbit that looked injured as it sat motionless in the freshly cut grass. She bent down to look at it.

"Oh John! Look! The poor little thing has lost a foot - I wonder if one of the scythes has caught it - or maybe a buzzard has attempted to take it."

"No idea Emma, but that's nature's way of levelling us all. Leave it and either something will catch it or it will return to the rest of the family."

"No, no don't say that. I'm going to take it home and nurse it back to life and then let it free."

"You've got enough to think about at the moment, Emma. Don't be so soft," he pointed out stiffly. What was she thinking?

"I have no one to care for or to rely on me, John. I've so much that I want to give. I have no one - no one at all. Oh, I know what you're thinking. Mother needs me - well let me tell you, she doesn't really. She's strong and healthy and she has already been talking about moving into Biddie's place at Grange-Over-Sands to be away from the area that now holds so much sadness in her loss and many memories that are often fraught with anger and regret." There was a gulp in her voice as she bitterly raced out her words.

John was taken aback - he wasn't expecting all this to come tumbling out. Here was his sister whom he had always regarded as unemotional and rational, now allowing herself to show her vulnerability and sensitivity. The death of their father seemed to have unleashed a soft centre that she had never revealed before. Perhaps it had always been apparent, but he had spent so little time with her and the family in the last few years that perhaps he had not appreciated this mature Emma who had a softness and sentimentality for things she cared for. He was aware of her keenness for Vicky to stay and be looked after in the Bland family home but her manner appeared to be down to earth and of a practical nature rather than of nurturing and fondness towards the little girl.

They stood facing each other during this exchange until John broke the silence.

"Well, I think you should take the blinkin' bunny back to the cottage and I'll go and get rid of this letter before I miss the post, don't you?"

She smiled, knowing how John was all for the action, not usually taking time to explain or to express the circumstances in which he found himself.

"Alright then, I will see you later," she said as she picked up the tiny creature and wrapped it carefully in the scarf she'd taken from her head, one that she always wore to keep her fine hair in place when out walking.

"Take your time," he called as he turned on his heel to walk smartly away, towards the village where the post box awaited.

"She's a bag of unknowns, that one," he muttered fondly, as he breathed in deeply, appreciating the fresh air, as he continued the walk. He had been looking for some solitude when he first set off because he needed to gain some head space as well as escaping from the persistent demands of the rest of the family. They expected him to know exactly what to do, directing all their concerns and feelings at him. He endeavoured to bring them some leadership and guidance but it was demanding, especially when he too, was trying to deal with the loss of his father himself.

He popped into the little shop by the post box to buy a quarter of humbugs that he wanted to suck on his way home. He thought he should buy some tobacco too, if there was a brand that he liked. As he entered, he noted that it looked exactly as it done for years now.

"Good morning!" he said brightly as he lifted his hat in formal greeting.

"My word! I don't believe it - it's Jonny Bland!" exclaimed Mrs. Prewitt from behind the well-worn, oiled wooden counter.

"And what the divil brings you in here, after all these years? I don't think I've laid eyes on you since you were a spotty lad," she continued. "What can I be gettin' you?"

He placed his modest order after exchanging the usual formalities and picked up the local newspaper, as she weighed out his favourite brown and white striped sweets from the shelf of sweet jars on the wall behind. The tobacco was acceptable, so he pulled out a small leather wallet from his inside jacket pocket to pay for his purchases.

"And how might your father be now? Is he getting' over that heart attack? Is that why you're here-visiting?" she enquired pleasantly.

"Yes, Mrs. Prewitt I arrived a couple of days ago to see him and he was very poorly. However, I must tell you that he passed away peacefully that night. So, I'm out to post letters and to organise matters," he replied awkwardly.

"Oh dear Lord, please accept my condolences. He was a real gentleman, just like his father before him I'm told, and when I think how many years we have known him. His family have been in Shap for centuries and he will be sadly missed. Please give my respects to Mrs. Bland and if there's anything we can possibly do ...."

She tailed off as John picked up his change, tipped the brim of his hat and bid her good day.

"I most certainly will. Thank you very much. Much obliged. Good bye." He left the shop hearing the familiar tinkle of the little brass bell, as the door opened then closed. How many doors had opened and closed in his life since his last ha'penny was spent as a boy in that little shop?

Outside in the road he carefully opened the paper bag containing the sweets, and placing one carefully in his mouth he could feel the comforting warmth and sweetness as it sat on his tongue to spread slowly through to the back of his throat, evoking a sense of home and safety and happiness that he had felt as a boy.

He slowly walked on, feeling the trickle of hot tears spill from his eyes in a torrent of emotion. Images of past times flickered through his mind's eye; of all the days when father would give him a ha'penny for humbugs to suck on the way home from school.

"Bless you Father, for all that you gave me. I'm going to do my best to be as just and as fair with my own, as you were with us," he whispered looking upwards at the bright sky.

The mid-September sun was still warm on his back, as John strolled back to the cottage. As he approached it, a shroud of gloom and sadness veiled over him as he opened the heavy gate and crossed the yard. Those few moments of nostalgia, as he had walked back from the village had lifted his spirit momentarily, away from the grim reality and reason for him being here in the first place.

As he opened the door into the kitchen, the cool dimness made him blink a little, coming in suddenly from the bright sunshine and this atmosphere emphasised the solemnity of the household. No one smiled a greeting; no one looked up to connect and offer reassurance. Each person was steeped in their own private sorrow. They were coping with the immediate pain and recognised that they had another day of this before the internment would take place. The ritual and the detail of the service had been discussed and agreed, reminding them of the lifelong Christian commitment of the head of their family and they did not want to let him down as he was passed over to the Lord.

John muttered a greeting nevertheless, and took himself into the tiny parlour so sparsely furnished, containing several recognisable family furniture pieces and a selection of books from the extensive library they had once possessed. John had been able to take a number of pieces after he and Sissie were married and he had taken all the gilt and leather bound books that had been awarded to him, for all his successes during his school and university days.

He lowered himself into a threadbare tapestry fireside chair and pulled out his pipe and a piece of paper on which he had jotted a few notes to himself for guidance during the funeral service. Now, as head of the household he wanted to be sure that everything would run smoothly. There was no room for awkward unplanned silence. This solemn occasion had to be dignified but simple, as his father would have wished and he would make sure that it was.

Mother called that lunch was ready so he made his way reluctantly to the kitchen and to a table laden as it always had been, with cold meat, cheese and a huge bowl of home grown buttered potatoes, steaming invitingly in the centre.

"John to say grace, please," announced his mother.

They bowed their heads to pray as he recited the family prayer mechanically but meaningfully.

"Say it as if as if you mean it, son," his father had once told him when he rushed through it as a youngster.

After a soft 'Amen' in unison, they each served themselves but without enthusiasm; no one seemed to have any appetite

"How is the rabbit?" John enquired in his attempt to lighten the atmosphere.

"It was dead by the time I got it home," Emma replied wearing a blank expression. "I think it was probably in shock as I picked it up," she added

"Oh, I'm sorry about that Emma. You had such good intentions. Still at least you gave it a chance. I hope its death didn't upset you too much," he added rather lamely.

She didn't answer. Suddenly the small talk seemed pathetic and so inconsequential.

Anne had spent last night resting and before that, sleeping with her mother who, being so overcome with grief, asked for company through a sleepless night. As usual, Anne's homely nature prevailed and her mother was rather pleased that she volunteered to be there. Emma had her strengths but she could not provide the comfort and understanding that her mother needed at such a sad time.

She spoke up to tell them that the women would be going into Penrith to collect their mourning clothing and that William would be taking them. They had ordered food for refreshments for the funeral guests after the service but had decided to use the church room at the side of the church in preference to the cottage with its limited space. Anne ran through the details perfectly and mother nodded in approval.

There was little else to say and so they finished the simple meal and each got up to head in various directions, trying to keep their emotions in check. No one wanted to get involved in small talk as had been the case all of their lives.

The time could not pass quickly enough for him and he felt like a caged bird. The following day he wrote to Sissie.

My Darling Sweetheart,
    Just a few lines to tell you that I haven't forgotten you although I shall probably see you before you receive this letter. At night we are in bed by nine o' clock and last

night it was half past eight so you can see what a fast life we are living. No one wants to walk with me so I ramble on my own. Emma reads all day and Anne clucks like a kind mother hen making sure Mother is comfortable and not left alone. William goes home every evening so Magwen is not on her own.

The funeral is tomorrow and then I can leave here on Saturday so hoping to be with you by eight o' clock in the evening. This has been a very testing time on all of us.

My darling, I wish I were with you now.

I am your loving husband, John.

Chapter 37

Changes

John's key turned in the lock of the heavy dark green front door with the stained glass window bearing the name of the house 'Gable End' above. Inside, a dog barked and he could hear the sound of a very excited little girl shrieking, "My Daddie is home! Mammie - he's here, he's here!"

As he walked through the door into the hall she ran to him, grabbing him, with arms stretching upwards, so that she reached his waist, and almost knocking him over with the full force of the bombardment.

"Woah, little one! Let me take off my coat, then we can have a big hug!"

From the kitchen stepped Sissie smiling broadly at him, wiping her hands over her rounded abdomen, as she smoothed her apron tidily. He noticed that she looked tired and weary.

"How was tha journey, Luv?" she asked. "You must be deadbeat. I've made tea and there's fruit cake if y'd like. It's laid out in t' front room"

"I'll have a kiss first, if I may - I've missed you," he laughed and drew her towards him leaving Vicky hanging on his jacket sleeve.

"Hey, it's me first!" she exclaimed.

"No one is 'first' - or 'second', for that matter. We're not going to play that silly game," he said with kindness, ruffling her shiny brown hair, cut neatly into a bob - just like her mother used to wear hers, he reflected momentarily.

He kissed Sissie lightly on the cheek, winking at her fondly. Then he bent down towards his daughter to embrace her too.

"And have you been a good girl and helped Mammie whist I've been away?" he enquired, looking at her first and then at his wife. He felt there would be a complex answer coming! The two were not, and perhaps would never be natural company for each other. He had realised that before he left them alone. They had managed well enough during the early days when his work took him away from home, but the new job allowed him to travel daily now and he was full of optimism that they would all be able to establish a steady routine in the remaining months up to the baby arriving.

He noticed that Sissie was noticeably larger and there could be no doubting now that she was pregnant. People would be starting to ask her if there was a baby due, and he was unable to contain his excitement at the prospect of a second child coming. Although, he was aware that he was pushing into the back of his mind any negative thoughts and anxieties on the safety and survival of mother and child during and after the birth.

"Some of the time she's been good but then she 'as been rude at times wi' me. I'm not going to stand for it an' I 'ave told her - 'aven't I, child?"

She looked across at Vicky who had clambered onto John's lap as soon as he sat down in his armchair. Sitting astride his knees, she faced him and cupped his face in her hands, forcing him to look at her.

"I've missed you Daddie. That's why I was naughty." She nodded gravely as she gazed into his face and then, laughing, she added, "I didn't mean it really, though. I said sorry didn't I Mammie?"

She twisted her head around as she tried a brief explanation because she wanted to talk about other things of course.

Sissie spoke slowly and deliberately, before John could intervene.

"Well, we'll leave it for today. Your Daddie doesn't want to hear about it for now."

"Perhaps not," said John. Taking the hint, he pulled out of the top pocket of his waistcoat a little chalk mouse that he cleverly manoeuvred across his chest so that it looked as if it was alive. He had it tied on a piece of fine catgut that was almost invisible especially to the eyes of an inquisitive nearly five-year-old, who was convinced that it was real.

Vicky was mesmerised. "Is it a real mouse Daddie? Where did it come from?"

"Ssh! You have to be very quiet or you'll frighten him away," he replied, delighted that she had believed it was so real. Sissie grinned, appreciating the lightness of the moment that had distracted them all from tales of the tension and friction that had existed during his absence.

"Again! Again! Let me see him again!" she whispered hoarsely obeying his instructions for quietness.

"Let me see if I can get him out again - oh here he is, but you have to be careful. He's so fragile and shy - no, no don't touch him! You'll frighten him!"'" As he spoke, he pulled the waistcoat button around which the catgut was tied allowing the chalk mouse to move from the pocket. Vicky was beside herself, incredulous at this little creature that seemingly lived in her Daddie's pocket, and she kept looking first at the mouse and then at her father wondering whether to believe it was real or not! Questions followed, one after another, about where he came from, how he had found it, where it would live. And just before she could hold her patience no longer, John manoeuvred the little toy mouse back into his pocket.

"Oh look! He's tired. The poor thing. He's been travelling on a train all day. Just like your Daddie has. He needs to rest so let's leave him to sleep for now. Say, 'See you tomorrow.' Realising the game over, she whispered, "Good night little one," copying the same tone of voice and inclination of her head that her father used when he whispered a good night to her.

"Let's have tea and a bit of cake, and then it will be time for us all to go to bed. It's been a long day and we've had some excitement too, haven't we? We are going to need our beauty sleep aren't we Mammie?" He addressed his wife, turning towards her. He looked at her longingly, because he could not wait to be alone with her tonight at last. But the first important thing he must do was to make sure his little girl had her bed time story and then to have her back tickled until she fell asleep, content now that her Daddie was home.

*　　*　　*

The big change that the Bland family had experienced when they moved from their large farmhouse involved parting with generations of papers and books that had laid neatly in trunks and reinforced boxes, always there for referral and referencing. Furniture and furnishings that had occupied the same rooms since the last century at least, (no one could say specifically) so they were given away, or just left behind.

However, the move from this small rented cottage was substantially simpler than that had been, easily managed with the help of a small local removals company.

The difference this time was that there was less nostalgia and more urgency to make some changes. Father was gone, God rest his soul, and now, Mother was wandering in a wilderness of confusion and grief. Her life had been stripped of all purpose and direction and she was uncharacteristically acquiescent. It was difficult to accept this new disposition because she had always been so resourceful, purposeful and decisive.

So Emma was in charge and now she was the one to be giving all the instructions, putting on her brave face so that the others would follow and be strong for each other. She was beginning to realise that it was one thing to present an opinion and judge others' actions and quite another when one was actually doing!

As usual, Anne had commitments elsewhere in her farming work - and it was groundbreaking because, as a woman in the male dominated world of livestock breeding she was determined to become recognised and respected. She was single and comfortable with that, unlike many other women of her age whose only ambition was to marry and bear children.

Emma knew that William was under pressure to make a living alone without the family business of sheep farming to support him now, and therefore had become more reliant on farm labouring, which meant working long hours as laid down by the farm manager he now worked for. She worried about him and Magwen coping in their changed circumstances, but they were proud and private, so any possibility of discussing their struggles was unthinkable.

Biddie had offered her home in Grange-Over Sands which was small but could accommodate herself and Mrs. Bland in comfort whilst providing privacy for both ladies. She had always said that her time spent as a governess to the four Bland children had been her happiest. Never marrying, she stayed on in their home as a companion and lady's maid, until the farm and the land had to be sold. She would feel lost without the company and comfort of the family around her.

Emma worked efficiently, packing belongings into trunks, each one of which, she felt, would be going in different directions, and the sadness consumed her. Here before her eyes, she was seeing the family breaking apart. Fragmented. Scattered.

She didn't cry. That would be a wasted expression of emotion! "Get on with it, lass," she chided herself. "There's so much to do."

There was indeed, because she had secured a loan from the bank based on her teacher's salary in order to buy a little house. So, after settling her mother into her new abode she would set about arranging her belongings in her own home, a prospect that filled her with a degree of excitement and optimism.

The next academic year, she was to take on the Headmistress position in the school that she had worked in since she gained her teaching qualification. She was thrilled and proud to have received the recognition for her service and dedication to the education of the eighty-eight under eleven year olds in the village school. Together with her involvement in the church, she was looking forward to a new direction and more independence. With every promise to visit her mother and also, now her mother's companion at weekends, she had reached a satisfactory point in her life. Almost.

It was demanding work, lifting boxes for the removal men to put on the lorry and constantly keeping a watchful eye on how they handled the furniture and other personal belongings. At the end of a long day the vehicle was fully packed and laboured its way out of the yard onto the road to Grange. Mother was silent and looked first at Emma and then towards Biddie before she spoke, "Where are we going now?"

"Mr. Greenwood is going to drive us to Grange to be at Biddie's, ready to meet the removal van in the morning," replied Emma steadily.

"Oh," replied her mother with another confirmation that she was aging quickly. Emma thought it was quite sad that her mother was so accepting, which made her realise how much she had aged since her husband of almost fifty years had died. Both had never recovered from the shock that their change of fortune and lifestyle had brought to them, leading up to old John Bland's death.

Within the hour, after they had checked that nothing had been left behind and that the cottage was clean and ready for the next tenants, they heard the sound of a car. It was Mr. Greenwood, the farm manager, as punctual as they expected him to be.

"Cleanliness is next to Godliness," Emma murmured to herself wryly as she scrubbed the kitchen floor. It was the last job on her 'To Do' list. Now, she leaned back in the front seat of Mr. Greenwood's car and closed her eyes momentarily with relief. She eased her shoulders back and breathing outwards. It was all over.

It was a long drive, and they were all very weary after the last few hours of physical work, before closing the door that housed such sad and unfulfilling memories. No one was inclined to engage in conversation. Mr. Greenwood was a man of few words and concentrated on completing the route as quickly as possible in order to get home before darkness fell.

Biddie's house was the last one of a row of four older styled terraced cottages along a small lane that led to woodland, and its secluded setting delighted the women as they approached.

"Mother, this is going to suit you so well. You will be able to take walks in the woods and look out over the bay where I believe you will enjoy some lovely sunsets. Am I correct, Biddie? You face west here, don't you?"

"That's quite right, Emma. And it is so blissfully peaceful here at any time of day and throughout all the seasons of the year. It's going to be a very pleasant place for your mother to live with me. I know that I will so enjoy her company," Biddie replied as she assisted Mr. Greenwood with the small Gladstone bags that Emma and her mother had brought with them for their comfort that night. Mother looked around saying nothing but it was clear that she appreciated the environment and nodded gently as she listened to the two women.

"Let's go inside, shall we?" Biddie suggested as she brought out the door key from her well-polished handbag.

"Will you stay for a cup of tea with us, Mr. Greenwood before you face the return journey?" "Thank you, Ma'am, but I'm going to turn round directly and head back. If I stop to relax, I'll not feel like getting back in that car," he answered jovially.

"As you prefer," Biddie replied as Emma stepped towards him extending her hand to shake his, saying, "Thank you very much for your kindness, Mr. Greenwood - and indeed in giving up your precious time to bring us here. It has helped us all to get through to the end of a very demanding few days!"

"My pleasure, Ladies. And so farewell, and may I convey the many good wishes that come from us all in this new venture for you." He closed the boot of the car and swung himself into the driver's seat. Leaving them with a formal wave, he was gone down the pebbled track.

"Let's go inside, shall we?" invited Biddie, and they entered the cool and sweet smelling hallway of the house, as Emma placed a guiding hand on her mother's back, partly to support her across the worn and wooden threshold and partly to reassure her that this was going to be fine.

Later, as she brushed, then plaited her hair ready for bed she decided to write a short note to John to update him on the removal and resettling of their mother.

> *Dear John,*
>
> *We have arrived safely at Biddie's after a very busy few days packing and leaving that awful place. William was close to tears throughout. He can be so emotional at times. However, the jobs are done and we shall meet the removal men tomorrow with a few of mother's things.*

I shall then travel with them so that I can furnish my own little place with a few basics.

She is bearing up. A little confused, but Biddie will be good company and they will share their embroidery and reading and Biddie will encourage her to take walks. The little house is in a delightful position. I am sure Mother will be really content here. I shall spend weekends here as frequently as I am able. I shall enjoy that. I would like Vicky to come here sometime too. The beach is a short walk away and the woods close by will provide us with some nature spotting. Mother will want to see her grand-daughter as she grows, and it will give you and Sissie time before the new baby comes and in the early days after it is born.

I hope you are all well.

Mother and Biddie send their love.

Yours fondly
Emma.

Chapter 38

A Baby is Born

"It looks like my promotion will take effect from January 1st," announced John over dinner one night in November, as Sissie was wiping her mouth on the corner of her apron, which she had forgotten to remove. John resented her coming to the table still wearing it but being only a couple of weeks away from the birth of the baby, she was tired and forgetful. It was not easy keeping on top of the household, even with the help of her maid, and Vicky was becoming increasingly resistant towards her over such silly things. There had been several scenes where the five-year-old was argumentative and disrespectful. It was testing her patience but she couldn't be relating every incident to him when he came home from work. He expected peace and calm and a good meal on the table, and she wanted to make sure he came into a home that was warm and calm and welcoming.

"That sounds very good, John. I expect you're pleased, aren't you?" she replied dutifully.

She didn't fully understand what the job entailed but he had sounded enthusiastic about it when he applied for the position of General Manager at the new 'artificial silk' mill that had recently been built on the edge of Doncaster. If he was positive, then so was she.

He had explained carefully one evening last week, after Vicky had been tucked up in her bed, that this was an exciting development in textile manufacture. A new fibre that was manufactured from chemicals would create a product that would look and feel like real silk but at a fraction of the cost. It sounded unbelievable. The factory would have German ownership and he would be under their management. He had told her that he may even have to go to Germany to the factory over there to gain understanding of the principles of manufacture. That part of which, however, she was not so enthusiastic.

"Oh yes, I will be able to wind down from this job and then with the Christmas break it will be ideal for starting afresh in the new year." He was already planning ahead.

"Don't forget we will be having a baby in between will you?" She laughed, trying again, to hide her disappointment that he so rarely mentioned the upcoming event. He seemed detached from her at the moment. She was big and clumsy and she was always so tired that she resisted his loving embraces and attempts to charm and seduce her. Consequently, he had become distant and more solemn. She reassured herself that all would be well after the birth. They would become the close and loving couple that they had been before the pregnancy.

"Good God! No, of course I haven't. But there's little use I can be at this stage, is there? Be realistic, my love. When it is here I shall be as excited as any father can be with a new son or daughter."

She smiled at the rhetoric hoping that he truly meant it. Soon, they were going to face a lot and if he was now saying he may have to go away…

"I know that Emma would like to take Vicky for a week or so. She keeps asking. Why don't we let her go and stay until after the baby is born?"

Sissie had worked hard on her grammar and the way that she formed her sentences, as she was conscious that Vicky was copying her, sometimes mimicking her rough way of speaking. She still retained her accent but in speaking more slowly and clearly she was steadily improving. John was pleased and often remarked on her progress, even though it had been one of her endearing features when they had first met, and he loved that the way she spoke made her sound innocent and unworldly.

She thought that this evening was the right time to suggest Vicky going away, thereby relieving her of the constant drain on her energy levels in the final days before the birth.

"If you feel that would help you, I don't see any reason why she shouldn't go," he agreed. "As long as we get her back for Christmas here with us. It will be our first Christmas all together, after all."

"Of course. It will be a lovely time for her to get to know the new baby, won't it?" and she clasped her hands in delight.

"I will write to Emma tonight and suggest a date when she can be taken over there. Mother will be very surprised to see how she has grown. It will be a happy time for everyone, I'm sure." He liked the idea of decisive action that would suit everyone involved.

Evelyn came through to clear away the dishes and offered tea by the fire, glowing invitingly at the other side of the morning room so they both moved away from the table.

"Take that apron off, for goodness sake," he snapped, then hearing himself, adding quickly,

"Sorry! Do come and sit down, dearest. It's been a long and tiring day for us both, so let's sit together, think about Christmas whilst we enjoy a cup of tea."

She settled herself into the armchair opposite his and wedged a cushion in the small of her back. Oh how tired her body was - no one had ever mentioned that pregnancy was so hard! As she leaned back she felt the unmistakeable movements of the baby rearranging itself inside her and she giggled to herself. It was nearly time to come out!

As soon as the tea was finished Sissie went upstairs to prepare for bed, while John enjoyed a final pipe smoke and a drop of whisky in his favourite crystal tumbler that had been used habitually by his father. His earliest memories were of his father pouring a drop before bed, claiming it helped him to sleep. Cradling the glass in his hand he stared into the fading embers in the fire, casting his mind back to those days when as a child he had taken for granted the solid security of family life. It had routine and there were certain ways of doing things that no one ever questioned. The family rituals and protocols had embedded peacefulness, confidence and satisfaction in one's abilities, and each of his siblings held a self-belief, trust and firm friendship with one another.

He had experienced so much since those times, that he sensed that without that sound upbringing he could well have crumbled under the danger and despair he had been exposed to, as a young man striking out on his own. He was determined to provide the same stability for his own family, that he had experienced. Then, they too would be prepared to face any challenge in the future. Sighing, he knocked out his pipe on the hearth, put the fireguard up and switched off the lights. It was time for bed.

The day however, was not over, because as the moon appeared from behind the midnight clouds Sissie felt a sharp pain followed by another and another. She sat bolt upright in bed.

"John, John!" she whispered. "I think the baby's coming."

"Nay lass, not yet surely? Go back to sleep. The little one will be moving around that's all," he replied in the hoarse voice of his first deep sleep of the night.

She raised herself to the edge of the bed to wriggle her toes into her slippers and felt warm liquid trickling down her legs.

"Oh no! Me waters 'ave broke," she cried out. "Quick! I need t' midwife."

The panic in her Barnsley dialect was enough to have John leaping from his side of the bed. Pulling on trousers over his long johns, he galloped down the stairs to make a phone call to the midwife.

How fortunate to have a telephone. It was a rare sight in the home these days, but it was a necessary feature for him so that if there were difficulties at the mill, he could be contacted out of working hours if necessary.

Iris McAllen was born in Doncaster. She had lost her husband and both of her sons in the Great War. She lived for her work. It was her 'calling' as she described it. She had learned her skills from her own mother who had been an experienced midwife and naturally, in this small town, everyone knew them both. Iris liked to be busy and in demand because it drew the focus away from her own sadness and nothing could be more rewarding for her than to bring new life into the world. It was not without its tragedies and disappointments, but the successes brought joy and hope for the future and frankly, she had never been so busy. Everyone was having babies in the aftermath of the war years, and she was proud to be instrumental in supporting both new and experienced expectant mothers. She loved entering the family home and she usually allowed herself some time to evaluate the surroundings. Sometimes the simplicity, and often the poverty that she stepped into horrified her but it served to give her even more determination to help those in such circumstances start with a positive purpose and a will to provide the best that they could for this new life, born into a world of uncertainty, and to learn and understand how to provide love, security and happiness.

When her telephone bell rang she had only just arrived home from delivering twins across town. That birth had been interesting as the expectant mother had no idea she was having two babies.

"Oh my dear! Look, you have a little boy," she exclaimed as she grasped the bright red little thing as it slithered out into her hands.

"Not another one," grumbled the woman breathlessly. "That's three lads I've got now!"

"Oh! OH! My word - NO - I don't believe it - wait a minute, Mabel, I don't think you've finished yet lass! There's another one here." And out rushed another bright red creature exercising it's lungs already.

"Looks like you've got a little girl here an' all" she cried out "Now then, that was a surprise wasn't it?" she added excitedly.

Mabel was elated. She couldn't believe it! She had a daughter at last! Never mind that there were now two to feed and clothe at the same time.

"Me 'usband 'll be in shock now!" she shrieked and she smiled broadly with tears of pride in her eyes as she cuddled both babies, Iris then explained how the twins must have been lying one behind the other, synchronised in heart beats and in the same position.

Exhausted after that birth, Iris returned home hoping for a few hours' sleep and as she took off her uniform gabardine raincoat there was the familiar ringing tone in her hallway. Sighing, she picked up to hear John Bland on the smart side of town, calling for her assistance. It seemed his wife was in labour a couple of weeks earlier than expected.

"Get the hot water and towels ready for me, and I'll be with you in twenty minutes. And if you could arrange some tea an' all for me if you please, Mr. Bland as I've not stopped since four o' clock this afternoon," she added.

She placed the receiver down, belted her raincoat and went back out of her front door to her bicycle which was waiting in the shed at the side of the house.

Evelyn opened the door as soon as she knocked and beckoned her inside where the sounds of a woman in labour could be heard and John was standing nervously in the hall holding his daughter's hand, as she had been woken up by the commotion.

"Oh hello. And what are you doing awake, young lady?" asked Iris with a beaming smile and a wagging finger. It was often the case that the older children would be roused by the noises in the home, that the arrival of a new baby makes. It was a familiar sight for her.

"Is my baby coming?" enquired Vicky in a sleepy voice, bewildered and suddenly shy at witnessing such change in this normally very orderly household.

"We hope so my pet," replied Iris. "Now then let me go and see your Mammie, please," she added, looking at John for directions.

"Oh yes, of course Mrs. McAllen. I'm so relieved to see you, I forgot my manners. Sissie is up the stairs. Turn right at the top. Evelyn will take you in and then bring you some tea." The gratitude was evident in his voice

Evelyn led the way and Iris thanked her saying that would be all, and tapping lightly on the bedroom door she stepped inside. Sissie was propped up on several pillows and as directed there were towels and hot water on hand at the side of the bed.

"Well Mrs. Bland, let's take a look at you. Now then, this is your second isn't it so you'll know what to do."

"No!" Sissie exclaimed. "This is my first"

"Oh beg pardon - then who have I just met at the bottom of the stairs?"

"My husband's daughter, Vicky, from his first marriage," she panted. "Her mother died while she was a toddler. I am the stepmother"

"Oh, that explains things. Well she is very excited, I can tell you that! Right then, let's get cracking. You're dilated so it's not going to be long."

She examined Sissie, finally placing her hand on Sissie's mountainous belly and pressing gently. "Now then, Sissie - I may call you that, may I? I want you to listen to me and do exactly as I instruct you. Then we will have no nasty surprise injuries and baby will come easily."

Sissie nodded dutifully, before letting out another roar....

An hour later the baby was delivered safely and there were whoops of delight from the bottom of the stairs as John heard the first gutsy cries from the new born and the midwife yelled out "It's a BOY!"

*   *   *

John knew that Emma would arrive as soon as she could, for all sorts of reasons. The birth of a baby in the family excites everyone - that was a well-known fact, and Emma was no exception. She was keen to support her brother and eager to develop the fond connection she had made with his daughter, whom she felt privately, rather presumptuously, would be receiving less attention and would be at risk of feeling left out of things once the baby was born, if she herself did not become involved.

Emma never wasted time. Perhaps if she had been less hasty and allowed people time to balance their lives naturally, without her intervening, there would have been less pressure on everyone concerned and more of a possibility for things to settle down on their own.

But that was not Emma's way.

Her need for order and control had always been extreme and she became even more so as she aged. Ever the one to leap into action, often impulsively without discussion, she could not see that this was an occasion when a natural course of events was called for, by the couple with their new family unit, and that it did not require her presence which could only lead to interference.

Before going to bed on the night of the birth, John had written a short note to his mother informing her of the arrival of her second grandchild.

He knew she would be delighted at the news but perhaps not so happy that they had decided on naming him Ronald. Naming the child had caused lengthy discussion between the new parents. His preference was for keeping the family traditional names of John or William, to be continued through this child who would be heading the next generation, but Sissie was looking for a more unusual name for her precious son.

Mother was pleased that mother and child were doing well and passed the letter to her daughter to read aloud to her several times. Emma was aghast at the modern name that had been bestowed on the heir to the Bland family and soon after as she had read the news, she packed a bag and made her plans to travel to their house to "be there to help" as she explained.

"Don't interfere dear," were Mother's parting words, as she held the door open for her daughter to depart. As the door closed, she turned to face Biddie, sighed and shrugged her shoulders.

"What can you do?" she asked in mild despair.

Two days later, a knock on the door announced Emma's arrival. John opened the door - just reaching it before Vicky - to see her slight form silhouetted in the porch, clutching an overnight bag in one hand and a satchel of books in the other.

"Tea please, and plenty of cake. I'm exhausted. And how are you all?" she declared with a sigh.

"Hello, dear sister and how was your journey?" enquired John, ignoring her abrupt and demanding tone as he eased the luggage from her as she stepped inside. He thought she was even more like a tiny house sparrow, with her brown hat and her grey wool coat, but with the bearing of a hawk in combat!

"Long, cold and rather boring. Fortunately, I had plenty to read," she replied shortly as she wiped her feet meticulously on the doormat before stepping inside.

"But I've come to see my big girl and my new nephew, haven't I?" she added, looking past her brother, smiling and softening slightly as she stroked Vicky's cheek gently.

"And, so that we can do some rambling and some reading and drawing and painting together and to leave Mammie alone with her new baby." She removed the pin from her brown felt bucket hat and placed it on the peg on the oak hall stand. She unbuttoned her coat and carefully placed it under the hat, and smoothed her skirt and cardigan indicating that she was ready. Looking around, she noticed the grandfather clock and John's Military Cross citation which was framed and mounted on the wall beside it. She made no comment on that nor the hand woven Indian rug lying on the polished wooden block floor, but she had noted it and wondered how they could afford such a luxury.

As soon as Emma stepped into their home she seemed to demand correct etiquette and order, and if there was uncertainty on anyone else's part, it faded because, as always, she led any proceedings with her forthright and decisive style. Again, as on so many occasions, it affected everyone, making them reticent and unsure of themselves, and so it was much easier to accept her ways, just making sure that everything was correct and as organised as it could be, so fearful of her disapproval.

No one ever imagined that her manner hid her own personal inadequacy in handling new situations and social practice. She was actually quite unsure of herself, and so she used firmness and high expectations of people and their habits to cover up her own awkwardness and limited self-assurance.

Action right now came as a pot of strong tea. It was served in the morning room when Evelyn called them that all was ready.

Sissie was already seated on the edge of her chair and the baby was sleeping peacefully in his day crib in the far corner of the room. Sissie rose to embrace her sister-in-law and Emma returned the welcome asking her how she felt and enquiring as to whether the baby was 'being good'. The usual pleasantries were exchanged - weather, journey, Mother's wellbeing and after a little awkward sigh, they all sat down.

As Sissie poured the tea and John offered a plate of small cakes, Emma patted her lap and Vicky who was watching her aunt the whole time, slid shyly onto it.

"Well now, my big girl," she began, "and how does it feel to have a little brother?"

"He cries a lot," replied Vicky. "And he is not old enough to play with me just yet because he is a baby."

Her language was advancing rapidly for her tender five years and Emma remarked on it. It showed that she was used to being spoken to as an adult rather than using baby talk as was customary with children of this age. John read to her constantly, and he loved showing her the shapes and sounds of letters and reminding her of familiar words as they enjoyed the vast number of books in their home. Sissie was apologetic. "I'm not too good at reading things, am I Vicky?" she said in an embarrassed tone, and Vicky was prompted to respond, saying that she would help her one day, when she became a 'big girl.

They all laughed at her kindness and honesty and there followed a brief silence whilst they drank some tea and nibbled at the buns that Evelyn had made.

Emma didn't seem to interested in the new baby beyond peering at him sleeping peacefully in the crib.

"And why have you not called him John, or even William to carry on the family names?" she demanded accusingly, "Ronald sounds American. Why ever did you settle on that name?"

"It's the name we agreed, Emma. We like it and we will be shortening it to Ronnie won't we, Sissie?" John replied looking at her fondly. "We like the sound of Vicky and Ronnie together too."

Emma returned to the crib peering down towards the baby again.

"He's like you Sissie," she sniffed, before turning to face Vicky. "And you are like your father and me."

No one responded, although both John and Sissie were to discuss later that she seemed far too possessive and she was making every effort to stake her influence in the development of their older child. Neither of them were particularly concerned at the moment, and John shrugged his shoulders and sighed acceptingly, "Emma always was the one in charge of everyone."

An hour later Vicky was in bed and sound asleep after listening to a story read animatedly by Auntie Emma and afterwards, the adults sat round the table to Toad in the Hole and Apple Crumble, prepared earlier by the most reliable Evelyn, who had by now, agreed a mutually beneficial partnership with the 'lady of the household', and was proving to be a godsend to Sissie as she was now, in these early days, so preoccupied in learning how to become a good mother.

John pulled out the ladies' chairs for sitting down one after the other, before saying grace. Emma adjusted the cutlery in front of her, examining the clean white napkins. That's not a three screen fold she thought - I must show her how to do them some day, she promised herself but she said,

"My first thoughts were to come over and be of use to you both. I imagine it's quite a change in routine for you and I am happy to entertain Vicky and let you get on minding the baby while John returns to work," she explained.

"That's very thoughtful, Emma," said John, "but we do need to be working out our own routines so don't spoil us!"

His voice sounded like a caution, as if to warn her not to overstay her welcome, and he knew that Emma would detect it. She was well meaning but he didn't want her taking over and he didn't want to risk hurting Sissie's feelings and diminishing her role within this household. He was already concerned that her comment on the name they had chosen might upset her.

"Of course, of course. I would like to occupy Vicky and give her the attention she will need in these early days that's all. It would seem your maid is accomplished and organised so you don't need me for washing and drying dishes, do you?" she quipped.

"Certainly not!" replied John smiling, as Sissie moved over to the crib where the baby was beginning to stir.

"It's time for the four hourly feed so you'll 'ave to excuse me," said Sissie as she picked up the baby to leave the room for upstairs. It would be unlikely to come down again, so she turned to face Emma, "I'm going to say goodnight, 'cause this will take time. So I'll see thee in the morning Emma. John will show you the spare room. The bed is turned down for you." As John jumped up to open the door for her, he smiled reassuringly, "I won't be long dear."

*　*　*

After a few days, Emma needed to return home to her teaching, leaving these people to get on with their lives. She had read all her books and had spent each day with Vicky engaged in play and in the garden teaching her the names of all the plants, insects and birds. Vicky was enthralled and like a sponge she soaked up all the interesting facts and snippets of stories that Emma would make up to encourage the little girl's imagination and grasp of language. You could take the school mistress out of school but you couldn't take the school out of this mistress, there was no mistaking that.

Sissie was preoccupied as she attended to the needs of the new baby who was a hungry and fractious little thing and seemed not to want to sleep for more than a couple of hours at a time, day or night, and so she was exhausted and hardly saw anyone. In any case, she felt uncomfortable around Emma whom she guessed did not approve of her. She did not approve of breast feeding which was not 'done' in professional circles, but Sissie was determined to feed her child herself. She had plenty of milk and it had been the accepted and natural practice in her own family circles. Neither of the women discussed the matter.

Emma did not have much patience nor understanding of the situation either, and so whilst John was at work there was little contact between the two women save for meal times and the contact with Vicky. Emma could be so merciless when she expressed her opinion on any subject, so she would correct Sissie in the way that she laid the table and the clumsiness of her ironing. After several mealtimes of feeling irritated by the shortcomings of the younger woman, she decided to teach her the three screen fold for napkins. Sissie privately thought it was very small minded and questioned why it seemed to be such an important feature at table.

When Emma suggested that Vicky should travel with her to stay at her house for the next week, Sissie was in full support of the idea because she was gradually losing her patience with the woman's constant interfering. John was not so sure at first, but gave in to the two women eventually, rationalising that perhaps he didn't fully appreciate the additional demands of motherhood that were now being placed on his young wife.

Both of them had experienced a mixture of delight and shock when the pregnancy had been confirmed. They hadn't felt ready for a baby as they wanted to set up home and enjoy being there together. Above all, John wished for them to connect securely with Vicky, who had experienced so much change already during these early years of her life. Their announcement surprised everyone else too. It was commonly described as a 'honeymoon' baby as people discreetly counted up to nine on their fingers, thereby reassuring themselves that the child would most likely have been conceived in wedlock.

The day to day reality of home and family life had been far from idyllic for any of them. Sissie was suffering from the post-natal pain and discomfort, and being so tired caused by the demands of the baby boy, made her recovery slow and patience in short supply. John would retreat to the office and immerse himself in his new management role. He was able to escape the atmosphere and so he felt some relief when Emma's proposal surfaced. Reluctant to lose his little girl again, he could also see the benefits all round. Once her little bag was packed, she expressed such excitement to be travelling on a train with Auntie that he felt it had been a wise choice of action, after all.

Suddenly they were gone, after sharing hugs and promising to write to each other. John and Sissie returned to the morning room, and Sissie rang for some tea so that they could share a moment's peace together.

"I hope she will settle with Emma who can be so strict at times with her," said John, half aloud, half to himself.

"She's going to be fine, John. She will be busy and your mother will give her things to do as well. Leave her to get on. Then you and me can get on."

"You and I," he corrected her. Her way of speaking had improved, it was true, but again, there were certain things she said that irritated him, and he did not want his children influenced by her way of speaking.

Sissie ignored the comment, seeing it as the best way of dealing with him. She knew she could not possibly change everything about herself. She was learning fairly quickly but part of her resisted because she didn't want to become so different - then she wouldn't even recognise herself, she reflected. Besides Doris had already remarked that she was putting on 'airs and graces' and 'who did she think she was' and that had hurt her feelings on more than one occasion. Doris was also rather put out that Sissie had become pregnant before her. She had been married longer and as the eldest. Yet again as with the wedding, she insisted that she should be the first across the line in all these events.

Evelyn brought in the tea and a plate of scones sitting on a cotton doily, already split and buttered "Thank you Evelyn. So good of you, looking after us today." John said warmly. She nodded in appreciation of his kind remark and closed the door quietly as she left the room.

"Are you happy with her dear?" he enquired. "Is she doing things well for you?"

"Oh John, she is more than I ever dreamed of!! I don't know what I'd do without her. She seems to know what I need and when I want her help. She's a good worker and I know she's happy here. She's told me"

"Well that's a big relief to me I can tell you," he replied. "Because, if I do need to go away on work matters I shall feel content that you have the necessary help."

There, he said it again! When he had first mentioned the possibility of going to Germany to learn more of the textile processes, she guessed that it would be more of a certainty, less of a 'possibility' and that was because she knew how energetic he was; always seeking new ways of doing things and hungry to be involved in progressive techniques - 'ways of going on' as she would put it. She had no choice but to stay strong and support his ambitions. She was reminded of those words he wrote in one of his earlier letters: 'You know that someday I want to be someone in this world…' He wasn't just dreaming. He really meant it.

"Of course!" she replied simply.

"Now then, I wonder what I shall be having for my dinner, today?" he enquired, adding cheekily "And what you might be offering for 'after's?

Chapter 39

Town Life

John was satisfied that Vicky was settled and happy, just as Emma had described in her letters but after a week away from home, she was expressing a reluctance to return, preferring her time with Auntie and with Grandma Bland. He was saddened, unable to reconcile the convenience of her being entertained away from him with the urge to be raising her himself alongside his new child who had joined the family.

She had learnt to recognise some simple words and could recite her alphabet and sing some popular nursery rhymes. She would count easily to fifty and she loved her drawing and painting. She had been to Sunday School over two Sundays now and loved the bible stories being told alongside other village children, providing her with essential contact with little ones of her own age. There was no doubt she was receiving a rich and varied diet of experience during her time with Emma.

However, John was insistent that she returned home and so he travelled up to Grange-Over-Sands to collect her and bring her back. Sissie had enjoyed some brief respite during her absence and felt more in control and organised as the baby Ronnie began to settle into a routine. She was besotted with the dainty little thing with blonde wisps on the top of his head and bright blue eyes, clearly taking after his father. She was a little apprehensive on the subject of how to best handle a bright and busy five-year-old, who was learning her three 'Rs' rather quickly. She privately felt that she wouldn't be able to maintain the progress, feeling inadequate and suddenly uneducated. John was dismissive of her worries, telling her that to provide a secure and loving family, where routine and shared activity were the most important things at this stage for his small daughter. There would be no competition between them in who was doing a better job.

They burst through the front door together laughing, with Vicky holding her father's hand tightly. "Mammie I brought you a gift," she called out, unable to restrain herself.

"That's nice, love. Let's get tha coat off and we'll have a look," responded Sissie, holding out her arms in greeting and the child rushed towards her, in excitement.

"It's here in my bag! I made it myself!" she exclaimed and pulling out a small paper parcel with a white ribbon fastening, she pushed it into Sissie's hands.

"Let's go into the morning room and Mammie will open it," John suggested, eager to close the door as the cold wind blew in to the hall.

Sissie sat down with the parcel on her lap and Vicky stood in front of her waiting impatiently for her to unwrap it. Sissie carefully removed the ribbon and then the paper to reveal inside a linen tray cloth with a simple embroidered flower in the corner and a drawing of the same flower on a card which read,

'To Mammie and Daddie
With love from Vicky xx'

Someone, probably Emma had written it and Vicky had traced over the letters. John thought it was a good idea, and very considerate.

"It's lovely and it's very clever of you to do this. Did you do it on your own?" whispered Sissie, a little overwhelmed by the thought behind the gift and the help she'd had to create it.

"Well, Auntie helped me a bit," replied Vicky modestly. "Because I'm a bit young yet for sewing," she added matter of factly, clearly repeating what Emma had said.

"Well, thank you and we shall use it when we put the tea on a tray every day," said Sissie reassuringly, smiling kindly at the little girl's animated face at giving a present to someone.

"Have you got one for me?" she enquired.

"Hmm, I don't think we ask for presents, do we? It's a little bit rude. You will have to wait and see," said John in immediate response.

"Oh, that's alright, Daddie. I don't mind if she asks," replied Sissie. "In fact I have a little present for you too," she added. Pointing at the dresser in the room she said, "Vicky, look in the left hand drawer. There's something in there for you."

Vicky skipped towards the dresser in excitement and, only just tall enough to pull it open she peered inside to find a small packet sitting on the surface.

She picked it up, turning round to wave it in front of Sissie. "This?" she enquired.

"Yes, that's it. Bring it here and open it."

She tore open the paper to find a neatly folded pile of ribbons of different colours and widths.

She squealed with delight, "Oh, thank you. I can wear a different one in my hair every day." She shook them out and swirled around with them flying in the air.

"We make this material in the factory" explained John matter of factly, knowing that it would not mean much to her but it might explain the reason for such a gift.

"You will look very pretty when you wear them," added Sissie, pleased that such a small thing had brought some lightness and joy into the room.

There was significant movement coming from the crib in the corner of the room, as the cot covers were kicked aside. Ronnie was growing fast and it was almost too small for him but it was convenient to have him downstairs in the house as the four hourly feeds were still in action. Then there was a whimper so Sissie jumped up before it developed into a roar to tell her that his little belly was empty - again!

"Ahh, it's baby Ronnie. I haven't seen him yet, have I? Can I hold him?" exclaimed Vicky

"No, he's very small and he's hungry. Maybe you can hold him later," replied John. "This is the time for Mammie to take him upstairs to feed him now.

"Why?" she asked

"Because it's nice and quiet up there and not for little girls," he answered, adopting the formal style of parenting that was already beginning to appear out of date these days.

"No, you stay here with me." "But why? I can help."

"No!" said John firmly. "This is special time for Mammie and the baby while he feeds."

Vicky was confused. This baby had just spoilt things. They were having a lovely time and now it was a horrible time. She didn't think she liked him. She remembered that Auntie had told her that Mammie would be very busy with the baby and probably would not have time for her. She said that she could go back to stay with Auntie whenever she wanted to. She thought she would like to go back there now. She pouted and hung her head and stayed silent and Mammie left the room and Daddie lit his pipe and picked up the Yorkshire Post to solve the daily bridge problem on the back page.

"Be a good girl. Look at your book," he instructed her. And Vicky felt all alone.

John paused on the scrubbed stone porch step and drew breath, before turning the front door knob. This evening, he planned to break the news to Sissie that he was going on the business trip that he had hinted at some time ago. He knew it would not be received well because Sissie would not understand how much it would advance his career, which was so important to him.

The wireless was on in the kitchen and he could hear the familiar voice of the six o' clock news reader, behind the sounds of saucepans being put on the stove and Evelyn moving about preparing the evening meal.

Entering the morning room, his eyes found Sissie as she sat with baby Ronnie on her lap and Vicky on a footstool at her feet, in her nightdress, ready for bed, being read a story. It felt like a scene from a novel - such homely contentment and tranquility to walk into. This truly was family life. This was his family, and he felt a flush of pride and yet humility, realising that such simplicity could feel so satisfying to him. However, his job was important too.

It took a moment for them to look up, as they were so engrossed in the story of the flower fairies, carefully studying the detail on each page.

"Daddie, Daddie!" Vicky called out. "Look what we are reading!"

He walked nearer, kissing first the top of Sissie's head. Her curls still gave him pleasure and pride - then the baby, and then his daughter.

"Hello everyone, and what are you reading child?" he replied, whilst settling into the armchair facing them.

"It's a book all about fairies, named after different flowers. And I'm the Bluebell Fairy because that's my favourite colour and Mammie says it's a very pretty flower and we are going to find some soon aren't we Mammie?"

She gazed at him with her wide brown eyes, before adding, "And can I sit on your knee now please?"

"Let your Father relax, Vicky. He's been at work all day," chided Sissie knowing that he would of course allow her to sit on his lap, whilst brushing her hair as he did most evenings when he was home at a reasonable time.

"C'mon - bring your brush." He smiled at her as she rushed towards him. The baby gave a sigh and Sissie hurriedly rocked him gently so that he would not wake just yet to give them all a few moments peace.

"How was work today?" Sissie enquired politely without really understanding what went on at the factory, but she had learned that it was polite to ask after one's husband at the end of the working day. She was reading women's magazines and she had heard on the wireless about how to be a good wife and mother and she wanted to be just like that.

"Let's get these children into bed before we talk about the day, my dear. There's something I want to show you and something I want to tell you later," he answered with some mystery in his voice. She raised her eyebrows questioningly. "Well now, let's go up the 'wooden hill,' young lady and I will put Ronnie into his crib so that your father and I can have some time together this evening."

Twenty minutes later, she came downstairs and opened the morning room door to find a brown paper parcel sitting on her chair.

"What's this?" she asked, picking it up unsure of what the occasion might be for such a present - mid week too.

"Open it and I will explain," he said drawing his ready lit pipe and watching her pull out the strings that were securing the parcel.

Inside was a carefully folded amount of the most beautiful silver grey silky fabric with a darker grey paisley repeat motif running through it.

"It's beautiful," she breathed in a whisper. "But…. this can't be for me, John."

"This fabric, my dearest is the fabric we are making at the factory. It is Bemberg silk and yes, this is for you to have made into a dress and coat outfit- whatever its called these days - by a dressmaker whom I have contacted, especially for you. This is just the first run of many yards of similar material and when we start a new design pattern, I can bring home the first run off for you so that you can have it made up for yourself. Do you like it? You will be the best dressed lady in town. How about that?"

"Oh, John! It's too good for me! I can't possibly wear this in Doncaster. Everyone will look at me and think I'm swanky. I can't have that."

He looked disappointed. He should have known she would react like this,

"Now don't be silly. You can wear whatever you like. This is classic and not at all showy. I want people to see that you are smartly dressed and besides it advertises this new material being used in fashion."

She didn't reply. She knew there was no point in further protest so she rested both hands on top of the fabric, feeling its fine, silky surface as it lay on her lap. It did feel lovely but she knew that she would put it in a drawer and pretend she had forgotten about it for now.

"Now then, there's something else, and I don't want you to be upset or sad or worried when I tell you, d'you hear?" He began crossing and then uncrossing his legs so that he could face her squarely.

She knew what he was going to say and she held his gaze steadily. She refused to make it easy for him because she knew she would be upset and worried. She had been anticipating this news from him for a week or two now.

He loftily explained that he needed to gain knowledge of the techniques currently being used, and to observe how the deployment of skills necessary for manufacture could be brought back to the England factory. They had to guarantee greater efficiency and quality now. The pressure was on. She didn't understand all the technical jargon, so she sat still, staring into his face in bewilderment.

He was a little nervous telling her and he couldn't predict her reaction. However, he was prepared for her opposition to his news. The timing wasn't ideal he admitted. But if the English partners of the Bemberg Silk Company were to succeed, it would require this level of commitment from the management team. He knew that visiting the factory in Germany would improve business and productivity. The result would mean that it would be used from everything from parachutes to high fashion clothing, and at a fraction of the cost of the natural fibre that it was imitating.

The pressure to make rapid progress was intense. The Americans were developing a similar product at the same time, calling it 'cupromonium rayon' and they knew how effective at commercialising their efforts the Americans could be. They had to move fast. The company could lose a lot of revenue and investment, if they did not act quickly and efficiently.

He rambled through his detailed, fully rehearsed announcement and then, realising she hadn't understood a word, he softened his tone and continued, "You won't be surprised, I know, but Bill Townsend and I are going to take a short trip to Dusseldorf to learn more about the way this 'silk' is being made by the Germans. It won't be for long and I shall be able to write every day and send you postcards of the area and news of what we are doing. It's strictly business, and will provide the opportunity we need to bring important information home. It will be good for the company and it will be good for my career."

Oh how John had long rehearsed all of this before saying anything to her. He had sat on the arrangements, already made for a few days now and he felt awkward telling her, knowing what her reaction would be.

She said nothing.

After a few seconds passed, which seemed like an eternity, "I need to check Ronnie," she whispered, rising from the chair and leaving the room.

"Oh Lord," he thought. "She doesn't understand and she's going to go silent on me as she does when she is annoyed or upset."

He was right. Sissie was upset, and she didn't utter a single word to him for all of the next two days, even when he asked her a direct question. He felt as if he didn't exist and so he busied himself in the garden and hid behind his newspaper. The atmosphere was tense and strained. She had done this before when he had chastised her for telling Vicky that she was rude when she took a spoonful of sugar straight into her mouth at the table. He had stuck up for his daughter instead of supporting her, his wife. This had been her strategy then, and continued to be the same now, being her only form of protest and defence without shouting and letting her rough grammar surface. She would be distressed and in fear of spending time on her own while he was in Germany. Germany of all countries she would be thinking! The one they had been at war with - through the most awful and bitter conflict anyone had ever known. Yes, Sissie was fearful, distressed and angry!

Eventually, he decided to give her the dates of departure and the first address where he would be staying because Townsend, the production manager, was urging him to commit himself to the dates and the rest of the arrangements. He had experienced a lot less opposition from his wife. She enjoyed a lively social life with or without him, and he was as glad to be away as she was to see him go!

John was keen to get out there, not only for the important business aspect, but out of sheer curiosity to visit the country with whom they had been at war. He wanted to see historical buildings in interesting cities, and to walk in the countryside.

He wanted to try the food they ate and experience the family life of the past enemies of his own countrymen.

Sissie's silence did not deter him. It was decided that he would travel the following week, marking the beginning of a new month and he would be away for four weeks. He knew she would be unhappy but he was committed now, and he would not be allowing her change his mind.

In reality, Sissie had adjusted to his news and although disappointed, she realised that she had married a man who was not like the men her sister nor those others in her closest family and friends had married. John was intelligent, practical, ambitious and loyal. She did not want to change him really, but it made her feel different to everyone else. She had expected him to help her to adapt to this different way of life. This lifestyle had set her apart from family and the people she grew up with. They had been together for such a short time and the changes were sudden and strange to her. She would have liked some guidance from him in dealing with these new ways of doing things. Now it seemed he was running away from her and from his responsibilities. She wondered if he had behaved like this when he left Brussels a few years ago. She didn't dare to dwell on that, when her brother Bill had made the observation on Sunday, at teatime at his house. She had taken Vicky and baby Ronnie on the bus to see him and his new lady friend, and had left John behind, planting potatoes in the garden. It was another way that she could take a little control in dealing with these differences from him. Part of her wanted to hurt him in the same way that he had hurt her, with the news that he would be going away. But she wasn't too sure how to resume speaking terms, after punishing him with this wall of silence.

She needn't have worried. He was at the bus station waiting for her to alight from the bus with the baby and Vicky. He gathered her close and whispered, "I missed you."

"I'm going to miss you," she replied with tears in her eyes.

They walked home in comfortable quietness, to the warmth of their home and an early night for them all.

Chapter 40

Germany

"Well, here we go!" Bill Townsend was in a cheerful mood. He was looking forward to time away from his home that always seemed to be in utter chaos with four children between the ages of six and six months. What could he and Sylvia have been thinking to make the decision to have their children in rapid succession. It was true that they had domestic help and his parents were living in the next street, but it was still hectic, demanding on their marriage and truly exhausting for them both. He was the first one to admit it.

An ambitious man, like John he worked in earnest to gain experience in management and in developments in the textile industry at this time and just as John aspired, Bill also wanted to prove himself in the front line of innovation. Countries across Europe were moving forward in the discovery of textile fibre that imitated, so convincingly, the natural fibres that were becoming so costly because they were in such high demand.

"We are on the brink of something big in artificial fibre manufacture, and we need to be at the forefront of it. It's time to use the experience we have gained in old methods and apply them to future developments," he had explained during his address to the team in the Doncaster factory.

John was equally passionate about growth in the industry, and he could bring his mathematical mind and experience in workforce investment, efficiency and profitability. They were a good team and they respected each other, enjoying each other's company. This was an opportunity to share their time researching and bringing back their findings to English manufacture and it could prove to be groundbreaking. He did feel it was ironic that the advancement in textile manufacture was out of Germany, though. True, they had put the Great War behind them. It was over now, and almost a decade since peace was declared. But he was inspired by the new opportunities the industry was offering him in his particular chosen career path.

Sitting opposite each other in window seats on the London King's Cross express they were comfortable watching the grey starkness of mining country, giving way to the agricultural scenes of the Lincolnshire countryside. Fields were freshly ploughed, the soil ready for spring plantings in varying shades of chestnut and chocolate brown. They were framed by the skeleton of trees and sparse winter hawthorn begging for the next few weeks to transform them into springtime hope and green growth. There would be two days' travel before arriving in Cologne where they would meet their host, who would be their guide and would provide entertainment until they arrived in Dusseldorf to the factory. And so, they were granted the luxury of time, appreciating and comparing the changing scenes of rural England, France and then Germany. They were looking forward to the whole experience. John had warned Sissie that he would not be able to write until he had arrived. He didn't want her worrying or suspecting he was doing anything unseemly!

Gradually, he felt a sense of escape from reality and a glimpse of freedom and it was allowing him to relax a little, and so for much of the journey he dozed and read the newspaper and enjoyed the peace that smoking his pipe brought to him. He was reminded a time or two of the frequent trips he had made from Brussels to his home country and how much he had looked forward to some private time away from the pressure and expectation from others. Only travelling could offer him that.

The train through France and into Germany provided an opportunity for the men to talk about themselves and family life, although John was not keen to divulge too many of his personal details. They were colleagues after all, not best friends. However, Townsend liked to talk. They called him 'Talker Townsend' in the factory, so it was easy to listen to him sharing stories about his childhood, war experience and busy family life.

"So, who is the gentleman we are meeting in Cologne?" enquired John, changing the subject, as they crossed the German border. "What do we know about him?"

"Not much, John. Just that he is our opposite number in the German parent company and he has offered to chaperone us while we are over here. I believe he has found some good city accommodation for us during our time in Cologne. This part of the trip is for us to explore the city and the surrounding countryside and to recover from our travels. Then, I imagine that he will escort us to the factory where we will do some business."

"Very good," replied John. With his love of historical buildings and walking great distances in the countryside, the suggestion appealed to him immediately. He was looking forward to the whole adventure.

* * *

As the train puffed and sighed its heavy weight into the railway station in the heart of Cologne, John began to see the signs in German and observed the differences in familiar characteristics of an English railway station. He felt a wave of apprehension, which he put down to recollection of a time that he had buried since returning from the Front. It took him by surprise. He didn't expect to feel like it.

So much had happened since then and yet, suddenly it all seemed so recent. He shrugged off his invading thoughts, rationalising this momentary disturbance in his brain by reassuring himself that of course he was going to feel something. It was the first time he had visited Germany since those dark days.

"Pull y'self together man," he reprimanded himself under his breath.

As the never ending screeching of brakes silenced, they lifted their luggage from above their heads, adjusted their hats and made their way through the corridor to the nearest carriage door.

Waiting for them on the platform was a smart looking gentleman in a suit, holding up a large card which read 'Bland/ Townsend'.

"That must be Kohler," shouted Townsend over his shoulder as he turned the door handle, and stepped lightly off the train, followed by John in a more measured manner.

Calling out a greeting to them, the German, of the same age and build as the two Englishmen, stepped forward stiffly, extending his arm to shake hands. John thought that perhaps he too, might be feeling a degree of apprehension, meeting the Englishmen for the first time on his home territory.

"Willkommen in Deutschland, meine Herren. Wie war Ihre Reise?"

"Sehr gut," spoke John carefully. His command of German was limited to basic pleasantries and no more.

Townsend looked at him aghast. "I didn't know you spoke German Johnnie," he said.

"I don't really - that's my limit, I'm afraid!" replied John with a grin. "I think we should try to use the basics to show willing though, don't you?"

"Do not worry, my friends," spoke out the German, still shaking their hands enthusiastically. "I speak English, all part of my school education!"

"Oh well, that is a relief," sighed Townsend. "It could have been quite tricky otherwise. I'm Bill Townsend."

"I'm John Bland, Herr Kohler," John added politely.

"Please to call me Karl, and now we have a short walk to our small hotel here in the city," he replied formally but with a smile.

The three men walked quietly through the turnstile at the station exit and into the street where Kohler led the way. Within five minutes, they arrived at a timber clad hotel building facing the square in the centre of the city.

"I suggest some refreshment after your journey. We can meet in the bar for a drink and dinner and then I expect you will be looking for a comfortable bed to sleep in tonight after your long journey." This sounded like a simple and sensible plan for John. He was craving some quiet time without Townsend droning on and on and he nodded appreciatively, saying, "Excellent idea, Danke."

*   *   *

The evening had been a pleasant one, formal and short. Neither of the travellers had energy for more than a small beer and a simple meal from the chef's menu suggestion, so they proffered polite apologies before retiring to their rooms.

There was wisdom in their decision, and the next morning John woke up and peered out of the prettily embroidered curtains to focus on a frosty morning and clear blue skies out there which promised sunshine later. He had slept soundly through a peaceful, uninterrupted night in a very comfortable bed whose headboard was heavily carved in dark oak. It was unmistakeably Germanic and of late nineteenth century design, he assumed, with its characteristic oak leaves and acorns adorning the top ridge.

He stretched his arms over his head, eager to meet the day as he pulled on suitable casual woollen trousers, cotton shirt and V-necked Lancashire woollen jumper. He checked the time on his pocket watch, and pushed it into the trousers with today's clean cotton handkerchief. Sissie always took great pride in ironing it carefully, so that he would think about her the first time he pulled it out, shaking it open to use it for the day.

Breakfast was very traditional, with crusty bread, ham and cheese on the table, with a pot steaming with hot coffee. Not his preferred morning beverage, it was true. Tea was his first drink of the day but he accepted it graciously. The others were down there before him and had begun to discuss plans for the day ahead.

"Good morning, John. I would like to suggest the cathedral this morning and the cathedral quarter. Bill is keen. Are you?"

"Most certainly I am, Karl," John replied as his coffee was poured out for him. "It looked magnificent from the outside as we walked by yesterday."

"Make the most of its glamour and glory. It's a bit disappointing on the inside," laughed Bill. "I've seen a few postcards of it before."

"Now don't spoil it for me, Bill," replied John. "Let me judge for myself!"

They continued conversations, getting to know each other better and then they eventually agreed that a brisk walk outside the city would do them all a power of good. A short ride later on the train, out of the city limits, would provide some agreeable walking for them all, so firm decisions had been agreed.

Bill was right. The exterior stonework and carvings were beautiful, detailed and undamaged by wartime assaults, but the interior was plain and austere. John bought a few postcards to send to Sissie. He was eager to post something to her. She would be expecting a few words from him after today. The sepia photos on the postcards did not do justice to the elaborate workmanship of the cathedral but they offered a glimpse of his activities for her at least.

After some coffee and 'kuchen' in the square opposite the cathedral, they walked briskly to the train. A short ride later they arrived, stepping out into hillside forest area and winter sunlight falling around them. With map in hand Karl led the way. All three men were used to walking big distances and so a smart ten mile walk followed by the short train journey back provided a most satisfying first day for them all.

The plan for the next day was to visit Dusseldorf but on their return journey from a ramble up country, they were informed that the mainline trains had been held up. The explanation was vague and frankly incomprehensible, so it would be necessary to stay another night. They all agreed that it would be the best option.

John was inwardly pleased because it now offered an opportunity to learn more about the country. He was keen to explore and to fix in his mind the features of the landscape, the lifestyle and language of the people whom he had faced as the enemy during the last decade. None had much knowledge of each other, except that he, with his army were defending freedom and searching for peaceful solutions. By contrast, the enemy were defending the ideals and ambitions of their power seeking rulers.

"I would welcome another opportunity to walk," he said, initiating a discussion about the choice of activities to fill this gained time. The other two men were in agreement, as both enjoying rambling and were interested to learn more about this country. Neither of the Englishmen had much knowledge of life here in rural Germany, so it provided a perfect opportunity for them.

The next morning his first priority was to write and then send off a couple of postcards home. So he left the men with a map and excused himself momentarily, explaining that he had some correspondence to complete.

When he returned they had plotted a couple of routes, one of seven miles and a lunch stop followed by a another of just five miles for the afternoon. The weather was favourable that day, and although cloudy, was mild for the time of year and they set off after a short car ride out of the city limits.

Once John had given his postcards to helpful hotel staff for posting, he joined the other two to share their plans.

Yesterday, he had been impressed and somewhat surprised at the similarities in the countryside here with those in England. The scale was different though. Everywhere seemed less developed, less industrial. They encountered deep forests, high mountains and many small, remote villages during the day.

So, after a detailed discussion about the route plan for today, he found himself expressing a preference for a solitary walk and a chance to distil his thoughts. He had suddenly realised that walking alone, as he had as a schoolboy, had embedded a love of nature, and a chance to consolidate his inner thoughts, learning more about himself. Yesterday, he realised he had not had any opportunity in recent years to indulge like that and he yearned for it. Here was that opportunity. He wasn't in the least bit interested in small talk. One could never get a word in when Townsend was talking anyway. And so, once he had quietly but firmly, let the other two know his wishes, he felt a curious excitement.

"Look, gentlemen. I'm just thinking that I would welcome a little time alone today – just to collect my thoughts and plan for tomorrow's factory visit. Would you mind if I took the day to myself and let you do a ramble without me?"

They stared at him not knowing what to say at first.

"I think we respect your wishes Johnny, don't we Karl?" responded Bill quietly. "However, it might be wise to let us know where you're going in case of emergency though, don't you think?"

"Of course," replied John showing them his map, tracing his route with his forefinger, whilst the other two looked on.

He felt strangely liberated even though they seemed puzzled by his request at first, but he was pleased that they respectfully agreed and that they themselves would walk as a pair, to leave him to make his own way.

So, synchronising their watches they all agreed to meet in the bar at six thirty for a refreshing beer and to compare stories.

Chapter 41

Changes at home

"We're flittin!'" announced Doris, pushing an iced bun into her mouth as she and Herbert sat in Sissie and John's front parlour, taking afternoon tea.

"Oh? Where are you moving to?" enquired Sissie. "I thought you said you'd never leave Blackpool."

"Well, we've changed us minds 'aven't we 'erbert?" She turned to her husband who was helping himself so quietly to buns and scones from plates that had been laid, each with a starched white cotton doily. He self-consciously put a spoonful of sugar back into the sugar bowl, hoping she would not have noticed that this was his fourth one.

"And d'yer know why we've changed us minds, our Sissie?" she continued. "Because WE are 'avin' a baby!"

Sissie jumped up with delight at the sudden news, and hugged her sister tightly. "That is wonderful, Doris and when is it due?"

"End of t' year," she beamed proudly as Herbert blushed.

"We're coming' to live in Donny," he said. "I've found one o' them new 'ouses down town."

Sissie was delighted. To have her sister close by, especially at times when John was away sounded perfect. She would no longer feel alone and detached from her family.

"Well, I'll be needin' some 'elp and so we're 'avin' Mam and Dad to live wi' us an' they can 'elp wi' t' rent an' all," she continued.

Even more elated, Sissie clapped her hands at the news. Baby Ronnie stirred, disturbed by the excited raised voices, almost indicating his disapproval of such news. This would change his routines; of that he was certain!

"Oh, it will be such good timing, and our little ones will be able to play together as they grow older," she said enthusiastically.

There followed half-finished excited sentences from each of the sisters as they discussed preparations for moving; the changes for their parents and the arrangements, and plans for their first baby. When they left to go home, Sissie was eager to share the news with John - but how could she tell him when she had no idea of his location in Germany? She didn't even know how long he would be staying in one place before moving on to another. She checked the calendar that he had left for her, so that she could cross the days off. My goodness he had only been gone a week!

There were three more to get through before he came home. The way Doris and Herbert were talking they would be moved into their new home by then. What a shock for John! He had never been very comfortable in their company. He had been Doris's boss at the Mill although he would never remind of her of that, but he didn't approve of her clumsy manners, her pushy behaviour and outspokenness, which was rarely diplomatic and usually judgemental.

She sighed as she put baby Ronnie to sleep and turned to Vicky to read another story to her. She would just have to wait to tell him all the news when he eventually arrived home.

*   *   *

The next morning, she received two interesting letters addressed to her. One was from John bearing his characteristic elegant spidery handwriting but the other was less recognisable. It had a small, neat, rounded style suggesting the sender was precise and paid attention to detail.

Eagerly, and feeling rather important, she opened the one from John using his ex-Army letter opener with a fine ivory handle, set in a decorative brass holder. This was the second letter she had received since he had left having received the first one only yesterday.

"He can't be that busy," she thought, as she pulled out three sepia postcards, each of views of Cologne and crammed with news of things he had seen and done.

"Sounds like a holiday to me," she reflected, as she read the report-like account of his activities, together with a reminder to keep all the correspondence safe so that he could read and keep on his return home.

"Not very exciting really. Not for me anyway." She smiled, feeling relieved she wasn't there with him.

The second letter was more intriguing but before she opened it, she rang the bell for Evelyn to bring her some tea.

When the tea arrived, she carefully slipped the letter opener along the sealed edge of the pale blue envelope to find a neatly folded piece of matching blue paper inside. Turning it over she read from whom it had been written.

Emma!

She wondered why a wave of unease shuddered through her. It felt as if a lead weight had dropped inside her stomach. She knew she hadn't done anything wrong. Or had she? She had remembered birthdays and she had asked John to write to his sister and his parents to explain the reasons for travelling to Germany. There could be no reason for Emma to be writing to her, unless....

She started to read the letter:

Dear Sissie,

I know that you will be finding things difficult at the moment with John being away on his business, as he calls it.

I expect with having Vicky and the baby Ronnie will be a lot of extra for you on your own so I propose that I come across at the weekend and collect Vicky so she can come and stay with Mother and me for a few days.

This will help you out and I am sure that you will be grateful for me stepping in.

I will find my own way to your house from the train on Saturday morning and I will leave with Vicky on the Sunday.

Please pack a few things for her.

Emma

Sissie put the letter down on her knee, resisting the temptation to crush it in her hand. This again, was mighty, interfering Emma who had been so quiet recently. How dare she assume that she would be finding things difficult and to jump in when John was away. Sissie realised that she had no grounds for objecting to the offer of help which she knew was based on Emma's belief that Vicky would be falling into the rough and ready habits of the Horburys! There would be no arguing with her. She had announced her imminent arrival and her intentions, and it would be pointless to resist or show any resentment for her proposition.

It was Wednesday, so there wasn't much time to prepare Vicky for another change, too many changes, it seemed to Sissie - for packing things and for travelling.

Oh, why couldn't John be here to sort this out? If he hadn't been away Emma would never have made the suggestion in the first place. She was saddened and disappointed and felt a sense of inadequacy and weakness and she still needed to share the plans with Vicky.

Vicky bounced into the morning room. "Are we playing in the garden today, Mammie," she asked as she hopped on first one foot then the other, practising her balancing skills.

"Yes, love! I think that would be a nice thing to do. It's bright and sunny and I can tell you what's happening on Saturday. Let's put some boots on because it's very wet and muddy down there," replied Sissie in sombre tones.

They walked into the bleakness of the garden. It was one of those dull, wet days where rain had just fallen and more was about to, and the only hope was for a fall of snow that at least created prettiness and playtime for the youngsters. Evelyn pushed the black coach-built pram underneath the washing line and put the brake on, so that baby Ronnie could be entertained watching the clothes flapping feebly in the damp January breeze. Today was not a good day for drying the many towelling nappies that hung there.

"Let's go and look for the daffodils at the bottom," suggested Sissie, as she held the little girl's hand. "Then we can pick a few and count them together."

It was true, she had to spend a lot of time entertaining Vicky now that she was getting older and was developing so quickly. She was a bright child, a quick learner, bursting with questions. So, teaching her numbers and the alphabet was becoming quite a challenge. Maybe Emma would do a better job whilst she got on with weaning this growing baby boy, Sissie thought.

Saturday morning rolled through into afternoon as they waited anxiously for Auntie Emma to arrive and then, as dusk fell, there was a sharp rap on the front door and Evelyn answered it, politely inviting Emma inside. Emma shed her coat and hat, parked her overnight bag beside the grandfather clock in the hall.

"Where are they?" she asked.

"This way, Miss Bland," invited Evelyn opening the front parlour door, indicating for her to go through. A comforting waft of warm air emitting from a glowing fire in the fireplace met Emma, as she entered the room.

Sissie rose from her fireside armchair to greet her sister-in-law, and without embracing, Emma sat down opposite her, rubbing her tiny hands together, always red and chapped with cold, before holding them up to the fire to warm through.

"Leather gloves look smart but they don't keep the hands warm," she remarked. "The train was draughty and I'm thoroughly chilled," she added

"It's very nice to see that you have arrived safely, though. Have some tea, Emma and enjoy the fire, while we talk," replied Sissie, carefully reverent.

Emma surveyed the room, noting the chenille cloth that her mother had given the couple when they were married, after Sissie had admired it one day. Today, it was overlaid with a cotton tea cloth bearing some new looking china cups and saucers for tea.

"Did you do the drawn thread work on that cloth?" asked Emma, noticing how accurate it was.

"No, it was a wedding present from Magwen. I think she did it - special," Sissie replied, colouring in slight embarrassment that she had never learnt to do such fine linen work, preferring to knit jumpers and cardigans for the family in her spare time.

"Good cup of tea, Sissie," continued Emma approvingly, as she took a sip, examining the detail of the china underneath the saucer at the same time. "Whose is it?"

"It's Rington's Tea. John suggested we have it delivered now that they have come into Doncaster. We like it"

It was true. The company was growing in popularity and those households on this side of town patronised them. It was a completely new experience for Sissie and she enjoyed the weekly visit. The doorstep delivery allowed her to exchange small talk and updates of town events, that was so new to her. Her family would have regarded this habit as completely above their status so she felt indulged and rather special.

The evening progressed tediously, even though Vicky was allowed to eat with her aunt and step mother. She was subdued, sensing she must remember her manners and it inhibited her so she didn't seem her usual free and fun loving self. Sissie noticed it and felt sad, especially knowing there was little she could do now to change the arrangements. In that moment, she realised how afraid of Emma she herself was, and she despised herself for it.

"Now then, dear child. How would you like to come with me on the train in the morning and stay with me and your grandmother for a few days?" Emma asked Vicky in a kind voice, which she reserved for talking to children.

"Yes please, Auntie. Can we go to your school?" Vicky replied politely.

"Of course you can and you will meet the other little boys and girls to learn and play with," she answered reassuringly.

"Well then, up to bed for you little one, for a good night's sleep. It's going to be a big day for you tomorrow. And when you wake up in the morning you may go with Auntie," added Sissie.

The next morning, as soon as breakfast was over, the slightly-built bird-like figure left the Bland household, her hand grasping the dark haired little girl, who skipped excitedly down the garden path beside her. Sissie stood there at the gate, holding her baby on her hip, waving and smiling at them, saying, "Have a good time."

Neither of them looked back.

Chapter 42

Sisters becoming Mothers

*J*ohn had his own map. He wasn't too concerned about where he walked, he was just looking for space to himself and a peaceful, yet demanding ramble so that he could liberate his thoughts and analyse himself and the life that seemed to be emerging for him.

Since he had graduated from university, life had been like one of those roller coasters - that phrase that was becoming all the rage these days! So many things had happened to him and for him since he had left university and those early days of employment. He had found it so difficult to disengage from one situation before the next one seemed to jump on his back. Many of his decisions during that time had tended to be reactive, but now he was ready to ease the pace and take time to appreciate what he had now and aim for what may lie ahead. He was sensing that there was a degree of control and direction required, but he still held high hopes for lasting success, not only in his work but for his family too.

Fresh air and solitude today was a gift. He thought it would be a chance to consolidate and plan and take stock. These useful phrases were so often used in the work setting but now, so relevant.

The day was grey and cold and cloudy but he didn't notice, as he set off with water and a chunk of rye bread and hard cheese in his haversack and with a purposeful spring in his step.

'How old am I?' He asked himself. 'What have I achieved so far with my life?' He continued. 'Am I happy at home?' 'Am I satisfied at work?' Questions like these tumbled around in his mind. All of his answers were positive except when it came to the 'at home' question. So, he spent a long time deliberating and discussing inwardly his present situation and how he could influence how it was going to develop.

There was no doubt, Sissie needed more support and guidance from him, he admitted. He had overestimated her capacity to run a large household and to elevate to the social level that he himself took for granted. She would get there in time, he was sure, but not on her own. He had vaguely hoped that Emma would become a reliable source of support and example but she was too harsh with criticism and lacked empathy and understanding - all of which were based on her disapproval of Sissie and her family and therefore for the choice he had made, to marry her. She was jealous too. There! He had finally admitted it. All Emma wanted was for Vicky to be hers, and to raise her as if she was her own child. It was a completely selfish point of view and it exasperated him. She had no understanding that the child should be with her father and she was giving Sissie neither the time nor understanding to build a warm and loving relationship in her role as a mother to the child.

"I've got to get home to sort my family out. I'm not having disharmony and unhappiness in my house. And I don't want anyone interfering in the ways I'm going to do things, either," he growled into the damp cold air.

He marched on, gazing at wild gorse-clad hillsides and the distant granite peaks that were top hatted in snow in front of him, feeling focussed and resolute and strong. And yet, he knew he wouldn't be as determined and decisive when he faced the realities back at home.

For the next hour or so he climbed up rocky mountain slopes beside rushing cold streams swishing then trickling towards the river bank at the bottom. It reminded him of the days when walking to school across the Cumberland fells around Shap, except today, there were no comforting sounds of sheep accompanying the squelching noises as his leather boots navigated the wintry conditions of the land around him. It didn't feel strange – in fact it was remarkably similar terrain to his own, back home. He had always enjoyed the keen chill at this time of year, when the prospect of spring was beginning to wipe away the dismal reality of winter cold and dampness.

It was after midday when he found a place to have some lunch. As he settled down to eat his modest snack, he could hear the sound of cow bells somewhere - out of sight - but it broke the peace that he was looking forward to and it disappointed him. Why was the world becoming such a noisy place when quietness and solitude should be embraced, he asked himself. After the noise of war with its deafening sounds of shell fire and gunshot and soldiers' moaning, screaming, teasing, swearing, snoring and farting, to have no sound at all, was paradise for him. Factory noise was relentless too, and its volume was at dangerous levels almost to a point where hands covering ears was the only bearable way to pass though the factory. Perhaps constant disturbance to the quietness of the natural world had become the norm and the only way to find such noiselessness was on a mountain slope - and even then.... The cow bells clonked as if to agree with him.

Taking a swig of water from the greasy canvas coated flask that he had carried throughout the war reminded him of the men he had been in battle with - whether his own boys or whether the enemy - and it seemed such a long time ago.

There was no place right now for reflection, for recollection or for remorse and regret for all those atrocities. It was over and it was time to face a future that would prepare and provide for the next generation and their prosperity. He felt a keen sense of duty to work with his German contemporaries to fulfil that.

"I'm becoming morose," he thought as he stood up lifting his haversack onto his shoulders. "Time to move on."

*   *   *

During the evening that John was rambling with his daytime thoughts, Sissie was knitting and thinking too. She was finishing a grey woollen jumper for Vicky. It had a green stripe running through it and her eyes ached because the colours were difficult to distinguish easily in the morning room lighting. Her efforts would not be recognised really because it was a serviceable and practical piece of clothing for the little girl to wear during her first year at school. It just did not compare with the dainty pale blue matinée jacket and leggings that she had just finished for baby Ronnie. Someone was bound to comment on the differences, and it would dampen Vicky's expression of gratitude that she was expected to offer. The next thing she would make would be pretty and more appealing, she promised herself.

The grandfather clock struck eight o'clock. She yawned wearily, and got up to make a cup of tea for herself. There might be a slice of fruit loaf in the tin that she would enjoy as she listened to the Home Service on the wireless before going to bed. She was missing John. It gave her too much time to dwell on things. Vicky was still at Emma's and it left her with her head full of suspicion and doubt about Emma's real motives for having Vicky over to stay with her. She felt such a burden of inadequacy and inability that had been thrust upon her by Emma. It made her submissive and nervous in her company, and at five years old Vicky would detect it. No matter how many times she went over in her mind that Vicky's rightful home was with her father and herself, that the two of them could best provide for the lass, the more she felt uncertain and anxious. She was convinced that no matter what she did for Vicky, it would not be enough, and with John so steeped in his work he could not possibly understand the difficulty she was facing daily.

"Emma wants the child to herself," she murmured. "There! I've said it out loud now," she sighed.

The kettle whistled for attention so she lifted it from the stove and quickly warmed the pot before dropping two spoonsful of tea from its caddy, bearing the stern faces of King George V and Queen Mary.

Taking the tray through to her armchair by the fire, she glanced at her reflection in the mirror hanging from its sturdy chain on the picture rail over the fireplace, noticing the first frown lines appearing between her eyebrows.

"Hmm, time to sort yer sen out, lass," she whispered "Or he'll not be fancyin' yer in this state when he gets back." She shuddered, hearing her own rough accent before sinking into the chair with a rather flattened scatter cushion in the small of her back. "Right, I'm going to take 'em on - that I will - and I'm goin' to be the one who'll win 'ere,'" she declared. And with that, she took a large bite of the dark fruit slice.

She let the fire burn slowly and after finishing her second cup of tea, she rose from the chair to prepare for bed. Ronnie had been peacefully asleep until now but had chosen this moment to wail for his nightly feed.

"No peace for the wicked," she said out loud. She turned off the light on the landing, and entered the bedroom, where the drop sided cot was positioned at her side of the feather bed.

"I'm here little lad. Your Mammie is here - with all the love and all the milk in the world. Just for you."

His chubby arms and legs kicked in anticipation of a good feed and a cuddle and as she lifted him from the covers the back of his blond curls were damp with the warmth she felt from his little swaddled body.

"Who's Mammie's best boy then?" she whispered, as she adjusted him in her arms to put him to her breast. It was something that embarrassed John and he preferred to leave them to it. He believed that babies should feed from a bottle, and indeed his son did so during the day, now that he was growing. But at night, this was a time for comfort and closeness between mother and son and she would not change that for anyone. She stroked his plump pink cheek, gazing in adoration and incredulity that here in her arms lay this beautiful little boy that they had created, whom they had talked of endlessly, as they shared those first nine months of married life. How unexpected it had been! She never thought that she could fall pregnant so quickly, and it certainly got people talking - and counting!

How she wished John was here to share this moment with her; for him to wrap his arms around them both; to hold her tightly and to rock her and their child in one precious moment of safety and blissful fulfilment.

The little one closed his blue eyes, completely satisfied, so Sissie laid him back down gently, kissing the top of his head tenderly murmuring "God Bless!"

She climbed back into bed. It was cold and empty and it didn't feel like it was hers, somehow. They had been married and living together for such a short time. He should never have agreed to go abroad and leave her because family comes first and he didn't seem to believe in that. Expecting a baby so quickly was a shock as well as a delight, she admitted but she nursed a theory that now that John had found a mother for his daughter he felt able to return to his career. Where did she fit in? That self-doubt crept in and she felt she might be left behind somehow, disconnected from him - and then she wondered if they were ever connected? Her worries and fears, suspicions and anxieties floated endlessly around in her weary head without conclusion and sleep did not come for some time.

At six o' clock sharp Ronnie was awake. His day had begun and so she dragged herself from a deep sleep to settle him with an early morning feed. It was time to get organised. Doris was coming round to see her this morning so she needed to be up and dressed to provide tea and a chat.

She wondered what Doris would be wanting. Her sister never visited without a reason and that usually meant borrowing something, which was rarely returned. Sometimes she would just call in unexpectedly to check out anything new in the house, that she had not seen before.

Evelyn was downstairs, the kitchen floor was still wet from its morning mopping and the kettle began whistling at the exact time that Sissie opened the kitchen door to offer her morning greetings. "Just toast and tea for me today, Evelyn please. And would you make a batch of currant biscuits for later. Our Doris is coming at about eleven," she added.

"Right away, Mrs. Bland and I'll sort the bedroom afterwards" she replied in her usual bright enthusiastic voice.

The front door opened and a voice called out, "'ullo? I'm 'ere!" And Doris stepped inside, dripping from head to foot. Evelyn came into the hallway to meet her as Doris stripped off her soaked raincoat and pulled the cloche from her head.

"The 'eavens opened as got off 't bus!" she exclaimed. "And I can't run can I? Not in my condition!"

She patted her swollen belly as if to prove that she was expecting a baby.

"Oh Mrs. Winwood! I 'ope you're alright," enquired Evelyn politely. "Come in to the warm - and I'll get the tea."

Doris followed her through the morning room door where Sissie was sitting with Ronnie across her lap. She had just changed his nappy and he was bouncing up and down on her ample skirt across her knees.

"Well Sis, don't get up will yer?" announced Doris in greeting.

"Sorry Doris, his nappy was soaking wet. I had to change him," Sissie smiled. That was so typical of 'no nonsense' Doris she thought. She would soon find out how demanding a baby could be.

"An' I'm soakin' wet an' all - it just chucked it down as I got of t' bus," Doris repeated just in case Sissie had not heard her exchange with Evelyn.

"Well you're here now, so that's the main thing. How are you feeling luv? You've only got one more month to go haven't you?" replied Sissie.

"Oh, it can't come quick enough. I'm fed up now. I just want it over," she sighed as she sat back in the armchair.

"Anyhow, I won't beat about the bush. I'll tell you why I'm 'ere. I'm thinking there might be some bits and bobs that Ronnie's grown out of that I can 'ave - save buying stuff. What 'have yer got?" Sissie was rather taken aback by the abrupt and sudden way Doris had leaped into the reason for her visit. She thought they might at least have had some tea and a catch up on news. Doris was so tactless. She lacked grace and any sensitivity towards other people's feelings. She would never change!

"Yes, I've plenty of things you can have. I don't need 'em any more. Some little matinée jackets people 'ave knitted for Ronnie and he has never worn, an' he's too big for 'em now," she replied. She gave him half a biscuit, calling Evelyn as she did so.

"I wonder whether you'll have a boy or a girl?" she pondered. "Are you excited?"

"Yea - I suppose so. I don't care what it is as long as it's 'ealthy," Doris replied matter of factly.

"Ah Evelyn, there you are. On the top of the chest of drawers in my bedroom there's a pile of first size clothes - they're too small for Ronnie now. Can you bring them downstairs please as soon as you get a moment? Doris will take them."

Evelyn dutifully brought the pile of clean baby clothes down and offered them to Doris who placed them on her lap, lifting first one garment and then another.

"Them'll be fine Sis," she sniffed. "They're all white so it won't matter if its a boy or a girl will it?"

They paused to drink some tea and for Sissie to ask after their parents and if Herbert was ready for his new role as a father. Doris was swift and to the point with her answers but Sissie could sense there was something else she wanted to ask.

A little silence fell between them as Doris watched the pretty baby gnaw at his biscuit, "He'll be too big for 'is crib by now won't he?"

Sissie raised her eyebrows, "Yesss?"

She knew what Doris's next question would be! To save her asking for it with her usual abrasive manner she leaned forward to speak. "Do you want it for the new baby?"

"Well, you're not needin' it, are you?" she retorted. "It'll be put it to good use, for sure."

Sissie nodded affably and said nothing. "Oh Doris," she thought, "what happened to manners?"

The sisters went silent again before, both awkwardly blurting something at the same time: "When's John back….?"

"When's Herbert home…?

They giggled self-consciously before Sissie said, "Not for another week or so. I'm really missing him."

"Well at least yer've got Evelyn to bring in yer coal," replied Doris accusingly with envy in her voice.

Sissie sighed. What was the point in trying to have any reasonable conversation with this woman? She was so twisted with jealousy and self-pity. She hoped that there might be a change in her attitude once the baby was born, but she spoke carefully.

"Well, that's not the only reason I'm missing him but yes, Evelyn is a good girl and helps out. How about Herbert? Is he well and is he enjoying his job?"

"There's talk of laying off the new lads" said Doris quietly "if that 'appens I don't know what we'll do. He'll 'ave to go on t' Dole I suppose."

"Well, let's see. Maybe John could find him a position," Sissie replied. She couldn't bear the thought of Doris's state of mind if her husband wasn't working. She would be consumed with jealousy, yet again comparing herself with her younger sister living so comfortably.

"Anyway, there's a bus due in ten minutes so I'll just make it if I go now," replied Doris, easing herself out of the deep armchair. I'll send 'erbert round with a 'barra' for the crib at t' weekend." Sissie made her way to the door. Evelyn was upstairs, still tidying the bedroom, Doris had stayed such a short space of time.

"Well, take care of y'self," said Sissie, as she helped Doris with her still wet coat. "And let me know if anything happens wi' baby coming,'" she added quickly.

Doris turned to the door. "Thanks for 't tea," she responded. Then she was gone.

"So much for the company today," thought Sissie as she closed the door behind her sister, who was scurrying up the path, even though it had stopped raining.

"She's a funny one," she reflected, always loyal to her family.

Chapter 43

Perspective

John was pleased he had brought his field glasses with him on this trip. He tended to carry them whenever he was out hiking because there was usually something to focus on; too far away for the naked eye. It could be a bird soaring up above him, enjoying warm air currents, or perhaps a deer in the distance, sensing potential danger approaching. The fact was that he hadn't done much of that in the last twelve months.

The glasses were heavy and of army issue - for officers only - and he had looked after them carefully, their sentimental value being important to him. Civilian models manufactured in recent times were lighter in weight and had more efficient lenses but he didn't mind. His own army issue did the job well. He liked to document the things he had seen and today was no exception. He was sure the raptor soaring and gliding overhead was just a common buzzard - its head shape and it's white under-wing span suggested it was so, and he perched on a rocky outcrop to get a clearer view.

Eager to take a closer look at the bird of prey's performance, he stepped forward to find his notebook and pencil in the outside pocket of the rucksack. Where the devil had he put that pencil? He rummaged through the outer pockets when suddenly he lost his footing and his left foot slipped heavily forwards on the wet, mossy surface of the rock. He tumbled to the ground, feeling an excruciating pain rip at his ankle. He cried out in agony, clutching it, and rocking to and fro hoping desperately that it was just a sprain.

"No, no, please don't say I've broken it," he moaned. The ankle throbbed more and more noticeably, and the foot felt increasingly hot beneath his woollen socks within the tough leather of his hiking boot. Afraid to take the boot off, he hugged himself as he continued rocking back and forth to ease the agony, hoping that in time he would recover. But he felt the searing pain getting worse, as he reached forward to grab his water bottle. Taking a large gulp first, he then dribbled the cold water down the inside of the boot to offer the ankle a chance to cool down. This might control the swelling, which was becoming more apparent with every minute that passed. His boot began to feel uncomfortably tight.

He glanced at the pocket watch inside his jacket. It was only two o' clock. There was plenty of time to rest before making an attempt to move onwards.

"Damn, damn, damn!" he shouted. "So stupid."

He leaned back on his elbows suddenly feeling exhausted. The effort he had exerted; the pain that had ensued from the tumble and now the significant anxiety that was setting in, made him realise that he was in trouble. He was a long way from civilisation and if he couldn't walk..... what would happen then?

He continued to watch the graceful silhouette of the bird of prey circling ahead before it dived smartly into the long grass, clearly spotting a tasty morsel in the form of a rodent or a rabbit for his meal tonight.

"Freedom," John thought. Such freedom could only be appreciated when you watched the movements of a majestic predator like that one.

We all fought for freedom and thank the Lord we achieved it, he reflected, but not without pain and loss. So many poor souls fought for that freedom but were never to be blessed by their efforts to enjoy it. He sighed heavily, a despondency taking hold as he recalled the memories. Then with a choke of sorrow from his chest, he felt he was slipping deeper within himself.

"Doesn't do to dwell on things. Promised I wouldn't go down that path," he muttered. He clutched at his booted ankle and tried to raise himself up to try to ease his weight on it. He cried out in pain. It was worse. How on earth would he get back? He scanned the horizon and looked through the field glasses in an effort to focus on a small farm or building where he thought there might be people and that he might be able to make some contact.

Nothing.

Now he was concerned - what next? A rocky hillside, alone, in February, was not a place one would wish to be with an injury. He searched through his rucksack, and at the bottom he found his officer's whistle. It was a battered specimen these days, but he blew it, and it worked. So he blew it again harder and longer. There appeared to be no one out there responding. In growing despair, he slowly realised that he was in a dangerous situation and he would very likely be stranded on this hillside tonight.

Three short bursts - he blew again - an emergency call - a signal to anyone hearing it, that there was someone in trouble. Then he waited awhile before blowing again.

"Patience John. You've been through worse than this. You can survive this," he told himself. Without warning, his eyes filled with hot tears and he suppressed a sob that caught in his throat. He was realising the danger he was facing alone.

The gloomy nature of his memories a moment ago, were now being replaced with the images of his dearest wife and his two children. He clapped his hand to his clammy forehead, overwhelmed with the realisation that they were the most important and the most precious thing in the world to him.

More than anything else in the world, he wanted to protect and provide for them; to give and guide them and to love and look after them forever. What would they do without him if he was unable to survive this incident? He blew the whistle again. He was angry with himself. How selfish and pig headed of him to come out here on his own. He had ignored the golden rule always to walk with someone in case of such an accident.

And he could not be anything or anyone else if he couldn't get out of this situation safely.

Nay he did not want to be anything or anyone else when he succeeded in getting out of this situation, he told himself.

He stood up, placing his body weight on the good leg and blew the whistle again and at two or three minute intervals.

"I'm going to get out of here, and I'm going straight home. That's where I should be," he said out loud to sound more confident than he felt. The afternoon wore on and as the light began to fade, he became more and more worried that no one would find him.

Suddenly the cow bells that he'd cursed earlier sounded closer and closer, until down below him he could see them plodding towards even lower ground, clearly on their journey for milking. He blew the whistle again then shouting through cupped hands to increase the volume, 'Help!… Help!' His plaintive cries sounded feeble in the damp air.

Around the back of the herd of thirty or so cows came two feather capped young men in brown smocks and leather waistcoats keeping the damp air off them. John waved frantically, shouting in German, "Hilf, es ist mein Knöchel." Pointing at his ankle to explain himself further, as he was not absolutely sure of his abilities in the German language. He watched as the two young men exchanged words and one of them ran nimbly towards him to tell him to stay there, gesticulating, first to stay and then pointing in the direction of the distance he needed to go, and that he would return. John was not totally reassured. He didn't understand the words fully, but the gestures helped and he just hoped that they wouldn't leave him alone.

He watched them disappear as they escorted the cows to safety. After what seemed like a lifetime, they returned with another man who was dragging a stout wooden barrow behind him. They parked it a little distance away before striding towards John. At first, he wasn't sure what they were going to do next. He was helpless, and if they decided to be mean with him he wouldn't have a hope in hell's chance of surviving any sort of assault or abuse. As they drew nearer the big guy was grinning and he could hear them speaking roughly to each other. They squared up to him, and made gestures that they were to carry him. Then, without wasting any time, they lifted him up bodily under his knees to carry him down the slope; one of them heaving the rucksack on his own back as they manoeuvred themselves down the hill.

John's relief that they had returned was overwhelming. How easy it would have been to leave him there to perish, with some misguided notion that they could avenge the conflict of the past. They might have regarded the time and effort that it would take to lift him to safety to be not worth it. They could have left him and turned back from whence they came, if he had frightened them.

They looked at him with curiosity and amusement, but not without some concern, as they gathered him up and slowly moved down the wet, grassy slope.

He caught some of their exchanges in the native language, not really understanding them, but he had picked up a satisfactory amount of German when in the war, and had remembered it.

In laughter, they remarked on the 'little Englishman' - so light and so small. He didn't care what they said as long as he got to safety and obtain some transport back to his hotel in the city. He had money on him, and that might encourage them to make the necessary arrangements.

"Please God, they can take me back," he thought.

Again, the actions of these country folk back at the farmstead far exceeded any words - in either of their languages - and he tried to extend his thanks whilst explaining the pain he was in from the ankle injury. This now seemed relatively insignificant now, and he was embarrassed that he had caused so much inconvenience to them when their farm work was particularly challenging at this time of year. But, before he knew it, he was back in the hotel foyer, paying the driver who had volunteered to take him back into the city. He extended his gratitude profusely, shaking his hand demonstrating the relief he was feeling.

Bill and Karl were just heading for the hotel bar.

"What the....? John? Hell, man! What happened?" called out Bill, who had seen him arrive through the large oak, gilded glass doors.

"A slight accident old boy. Nothing serious. Get me a crepe bandage would you?" asked John calmly.

Although the ankle was throbbing, he was relieved to be back in civilised and familiar surroundings. The kindly farmer's wife had given him hot tea and cake, in front of a roaring fire and then the men had brought him straight here.

"Didn't we say 6 o' clock in the bar?" asked John rhetorically with a grin.

*　　*　　*

John had spent an uncomfortable night's rest. It couldn't be described as sleep because it had been impossible to find a comfortable position that eased the persistent throbbing in his ankle. An examination had been carried out the night before by his unqualified but well meaning, not to say anxious colleagues, to ensure nothing was broken. It was reassuring that he could wiggle his toes and incline his foot to the left and the right satisfactorily. All three men had experienced war time injuries during the fighting, and it reassured John that thankfully, nothing was broken. The hotel had plentiful first aid supplies and his foot was expertly bandaged to support the extreme sprain that could sometimes be more painful than a break, they had all remarked.

The plan was to breakfast early and catch the first train out of Cologne to Dusseldorf which was just a short, half hour distance away. A car would be waiting to take them to the factory and it would be a smooth and efficient day visit, before the return to England. John's sole focus was to leave for England as soon as possible and to omit the factory visit which had now become something of an inconvenience. All he wished for was to be back to family and his home comforts. He craved his own bed and the love and attention that only Sissie could provide. His suggestion to miss out Dusseldorf and return home on his own fell on deaf ears, however. Both men were astounded at the idea. How would he manage without a travelling companion to help him get there they asked. It would be impossible to negotiate the journey alone - he may even make the injury worse they pointed out. They had discussed his suggestion for a long time over a beer the night before, and then dinner, but he was overruled. And so he submitted reluctantly, to their persuasive reasons for remaining another day before returning home.

A soft tap on the door at daybreak woke him from a snatched doze after such a troubled night. He groaned, as he eased himself to the edge of the bed looking down at the plump bandaged foot. It wasn't throbbing as much this morning. The real test would be when he tried to put weight on it. He dressed himself, after hobbling to wash and shave using the vanity unit in the corner of the room. At least he wasn't sharing a bathroom in this hotel - he would have foregone the ablutions if that had been the case!

Down at breakfast, he found Bill and Karl sitting at a round table in the corner of the hotel restaurant. They had started without him, and after morning greetings and enquiries after his injury, he drew up his chair cautiously, to avoid wincing with pain from his foot.

"Everything is as good as can be expected, gentlemen. I'm pleased to say that perhaps there is marginal improvement. So I'm keen that it should not get in the way of business. Now, what time is our train due?"

This curtailed their sympathies immediately, and it seemed as one, they pulled on the mantle of 'business as usual' and after a second coffee they departed for Dusseldorf. There was work to be done.

Lots of questions; copious note taking; acknowledgement of the ground breaking methods being used, all contributed to a sense that the visit had been worthwhile and without doubt of value for setting up and maintaining production back in Doncaster. John did not regret this final day of the trip but he wanted to get back home, although he knew that Bill would be enthusiastically suggesting another extra day, were it not for John's incapacity.

After all the farewells and thanks had been extended, they headed to the train for the return journey. John was relieved and ready to find a comfortable position to rest and to catch up on his lost night's sleep and he mentioned it as he settled into his window seat on the Dusseldorf express train. Bill left him alone, suppressing his urges to chatter, and the next thing they both knew, they were heading for the ferry across to London dockland. After an overnight in a small city hotel, they caught the train home.

Their conversations along the way were focussed on strategy and management practice and on workplace efficiency based on what they had observed in the German factory. Both agreed they could improve on current methods and exceed the efficiency of the Germans at the same time. Both men acknowledged that they had enjoyed their visit and how worthwhile it had been. John could not wait to get home.

It was a nuisance that he had sprained the ankle but in many ways he was thankful that the incident had created an opportunity to reflect and for him to take a grip of himself. It had provided him with space to examine what he was doing with his life. The time he had spent alone, wet and cold and in pain on that German hillside, served to show him how frail and vulnerable each of us, is, and how little it takes to change our personal hopes and ambitions and the way we look at the world. He hoped it was not too late to refine and improve his outlook on life and to direct his priorities towards his most special people who were all dependent on him, to be in good health and in sound mind and with an income to support them comfortably as well.

He thought that he would like to write all about this one day.

Chapter 44

Road to Damascus

$\mathcal{E}$mma was neatly hemming a set of pure white damask linen napkins, brought with her so that she could advise Sissie on how they should be used at meal times.

"I've also brought a few silver plated napkin rings as well, so that each person can call one their own, and then they can be set out with each person's knife and fork," she explained carefully, looking Sissie squarely in the face to ensure she was concentrating.

"I see," replied Sissie, uncertain of this new way of going on.

"This is the correct way. It's the way we've always done it and John is used to it. I noticed you hadn't put any on the table when I was here last so I thought this would help. Obviously, you'll need to show Vicky and then Ronnie, eventually of course. It's so important that they know their etiquette," she continued. Sissie nodded but inside she doubted that it was necessary.

Emma had arrived with Vicky the day before and was making herself useful. Never without a job, Emma liked to be occupied even if it could feel rather like interfering at times, and she always managed to find something useful to do, either indoors or outside in the garden. She was full of ideas and hints and tips on the most efficient way of doing things, partly because she made it her business to know best, and partly from the traditional country housewife ways she had learned from her mother. Sissie always felt put down with her brusque, sensible manner because this sister-in- law was so practical. She admitted that Emma was a help, and she quietly admired her efficiency and common sense. She just wished that Emma would show her how to do things without making her feel ignorant and inadequate all the time.

Vicky's hair had grown and she had developed a way of flicking it out of her face as it fell over her eyebrows. It annoyed Sissie as she noticed that it had become a new habit, not seen before her visit to her auntie's house. She let Vicky know by remarking on how grown up she looked, and how she would need to have it cut neatly before starting school. This would be after Easter, after her fifth birthday and it would be the summer term. In fact, several things annoyed her as she recognised the ways Vicky spoke and behaved reflected copies of Emma's little ways. Vicky sighed when things were not happening as she expected them to, and she had a way of wrinkling her nose at Sissie when she used one of her colloquial phrases, whenever she was talking.

Sissie pronounced 'book' and 'look' using the two oo's as in 'you'. It was a typical pronunciation used by Yorkshire locals. At first Vicky laughed, then copied, and then when she realised that her stepmother was genuinely using that pronunciation, she rolled her eyes upwards and tutted, looking at her aunt. Clearly this had been mentioned when the two had been together. Sissie was hurt and embarrassed and noted that this connection between them was going to cause some awkwardness in their relationship if Vicky continued to spend the time with her aunt.

Surely, Emma wasn't trying to set Vicky against her was she? She worried about this later that evening while tucking Vicky into bed, but dismissed it as her imagination - why - the child was only five!

She came down to a tea tray laid with a light supper that sat on a small table in front of the fire.

"I prepared some tea and cake for us, Sissie," said Emma pleasantly. "I thought we deserved it. It's a long time ago since our nursery tea with the little ones. I thought we might have something more." Sissie thanked her, and sank uneasily into her chair, wondering what might be coming next.

"My bus is booked for tomorrow, so before I go, I wanted to give you some advice on Vicky and her development. There won't be time then, so now is best. She's learning fast. She knows her alphabet and can write her own name - in a fashion. Her number work is quite advanced for her age too. Don't forget I teach so I've got the knowledge and I can make a comparison with her and the children in my class."

"That's good, Emma. I know she is a bright 'un. I'm goin' to 'ave a job keepin' up wi' 'er!" smiled Sissie relaxing, her accent more pronounced in the process.

"I do think we have to watch the way we speak as well, though. We don't want her using rough accents do we?" she added, pouring the tea, deliberately avoiding eye contact with her sister- in- law. Sissie coloured slightly. She was upset and irritated by the other woman's patronising tone. She said nothing. She decided that this was the best and only way she would now deal with Emma's presumptuous and bossy manner. She knew she would not speak to her like this, if John were in the room. That was certain!

As Sissie took her teacup from her, she lowered her gaze and said, "My only 'ope for Vicky is for 'er to be 'appy. An' she will be - when 'er Daddie comes home and we are family again."

A silence followed that was not uncomfortable for either of the women as they sipped their tea, but Emma broke it.

"Everything will be fine when John comes back, of course. He's away now, just when his daughter most needs him, and its high time he realised he should be coming home every night to his family. I hope he will. And act on it."

Sissie picked up her knitting. She had no wish to indulge in conversation about her marriage with Emma - or anyone else for that matter. A marriage was between two people and there was no call for anyone to interfere and believe they could get involved.

The sound of a key turning in the lock of the front door prompted them both to sit upright and exchange surprised glances. There could be only one other person who would be letting themselves in at this time in the evening. The morning room door opened and in hobbled John, leaning on a stout wooden walking stick.

"Good evening, ladies. And how are we?"

"John, John you're 'ome already! Oh Lord what 'ave you done to yer'self?" cried Sissie as she leapt from her chair and rushed towards him. Before he could answer, Emma stood up.

"And where exactly have you been, that's what I want to know. Sissie seemed so vague."

"Ahh," replied John with a grin. "That's because I've been on the Road to Damascus!"

"What do you mean by the road to Damascus?" Emma demanded.

"If you don't mind, dearest sister I'll save the stories of my trip for my wife when we've had a good night's sleep," he replied.

"As you wish, John. Only please explain the reason for a stick," she insisted, as Sissie took him by the arm and guided him gently into the room nearer the fire.

"A slight accident on the grassy slopes above Cologne," he explained simply. "Only a sprain but difficult to press my weight on at the moment. Looks more serious than it is. Now than my dearest, how are you?" he asked Sissie as he sat down.

This sounded like a cue to leave them together as they were oblivious to her standing there, so Emma wished them both goodnight and left them to themselves.

"Come here, lass. I have missed you so much," he whispered, leaning towards Sissie who had just put a little more coal on the fire. She was too excited at his unexpected arrival to want to go upstairs to bed yet. She got up from her knees and sat gingerly on his lap.

"Is that alright?" she asked. "I don't want to hurt you."

"Don't be so daft! It's my ankle, that's all and it will be right in no time now I'm back home," he reassured, her putting his arms around her waist.

He noticed she was getting her slimness back, now the baby was growing and the time since the birth was racing ahead so fast.

"Tell us what 'appened and why you're back early," she demanded, looking at him, searching his face for answers.

"It's a long story but as I say, it was a fall. I was stupid to go out walking alone, slipped, fell and had to be carried off the mountain side. As simple as that," he explained. "But I'm back now where I belong and in the company of a very pretty wife and a happy family. That's where I belong" he added.

She cast her eyes downwards, suddenly feeling shy and awkward by his words, but inside the urge to hug him and show her love and devotion to him. She listened to his calm and steady voice and felt him looking lovingly towards her.

"I'm so glad you said that, John. It has felt such a long time without you here. Vicky has been to Emma's and come back with some fancy ways and Emma seems to have even more instructions for me - to do this and not that," she blurted out, but then she smiled at him and rested her head on his shoulder. They remained holding each other, swaying slightly in a comforting rhythm. There was not a lot to say now that wouldn't keep until morning and so eventually they broke apart.

"You go up. I'll turn the lights off," said John tenderly.

The next morning as dawn broke, he hobbled downstairs to light the fire so that the morning room would be warm for everyone when they came down. He could hear the sound of a kettle beginning to boil in the kitchen and realised that Evelyn was already up and on duty, and he smiled contentedly.

"She's a good 'un is that one," he muttered to himself, as he folded a few firelighters to get the fire going.

"Oh, Mr. Bland. Good Morning, sir. You've beaten me to it," Evelyn gasped as she entered the room. "I thought to get t' kettle on first and then here you are doin' me job for me!" she smiled uncertainly.

"Don't you fret, Evelyn. I arrived home last night unexpectedly. It's good to be back," he replied, straightening up on his good leg on which he'd been leaning to sort out the fire.

"I'll be ready for my first morning cuppa though."

Emma peered round the door, her tiny frame looking unusually lost and frail in the grey light coming through the heavy draped curtains.

"Good Morning, all," she announced, nodding approval as Evelyn dipped courteously, "I hope you slept well, John."

They exchanged formalities - of sleeping well in one's own bed and remarking on the chill in the morning air, together with the guessing game regarding the weather. They stopped as they watched the door being pushed open and Vicky appeared.

"My Daddie is here! Hello, Daddie! I am your Vicky and I am here," she sang as she ran towards him, flinging her arms around his neck.

"And I am your favourite, aren't I? And you love me the best!" she added looking at him seriously.

"I am home because I love you and everyone else - all the same," replied John evenly, as he hugged her and put her down gently.

"Be careful with your father. He has hurt his foot," explained Emma, always guaranteed to take the excitement and spontaneity away from such situations.

Vicky jumped back in surprise. She began bombarding him with questions about how he had done it, and declaring that she was going to look after him.

Shaking his head, John flashed a glance of mild disapproval towards Emma who had disturbed a moment of fun and easy chatter between himself and his little girl, whom after all he hadn't seen for some time now. But he decided to say nothing.

Then Sissie arrived, holding the bright eyed and rosy cheeked baby Ronnie who bounced up and down looking for some fuss and attention. John held out his arms in delighted surprise.

"And here's my little boy who has grown so much whilst I've been away. My goodness, you've been eating your Yorkshire puddings lad, haven't you?" he joked.

"He eats everything," said Sissie proudly, giving her son an extra special squeeze and beaming broadly.

Evelyn was quietly, unobtrusively bringing in the breakfast pots and assorted bread and spreads for the table, weaving herself between them all to avoid spilling anything.

"Shall we all sit down? It's rather crowded in here," Emma interrupted imperiously.

With much clatter of chairs and general disorder as everyone settled, Sissie poured tea for the adults and helped the children with their breakfast dishes.

John began to describe the visit to Germany, mentioning that he would like to read the postcards he had sent to her, being a reminder and a record of the city of Cologne and scenes around. He was proud to admit to them that he had remembered some language too, in order to have conversation and went on to remark on how absolutely beautiful the countryside was. He avoided any detail of his fall and the resulting injury. It wasn't important, since he was getting over the inconvenience of it quite quickly and he never had been one to enjoy women's fuss. He spared them the detail of the factory visit. He knew it was quite technical and irrelevant to them both, so he merely summarised, saying that it had been worthwhile and that he had returned with important ways of developing the work they were doing over here in England.

After second cups of tea, Emma rose from the table, gently putting her hand on the top of Vicky's head, saying, "Well, if you will all excuse me, I need to go upstairs to make my bed and to collect all my belongings for going home. I have a big day ahead."

Turning to Vicky, who was licking the marmalade off her fingers, she said gently, "And now then young lady, it won't be long before I see you again, will it?"

She addressed the child but her message was meant for the adults, and John soon responded.

"I'm sure we will all be organising another trip very soon if that is what you would like Vicky." It was said rhetorically. There would be no opportunity for a five-year-old to be saying where, when and what she was going to be doing. Those plans lay in the hands of adults!

Several minutes later, just as Ronnie's face, adorned with missed spoonful of porridge was wiped, the door opened and Emma announced that she would be going. She said she wanted to leave plenty of time to catch her bus to the station. Everyone stood up, and made their way towards the hall where she and Sissie embraced each other stiffly. John smiled, and put his hands on Emma's shoulders and kissed her warmly on both cheeks. It was a charming gesture he felt, and one that he had adopted since he had experienced it as a protocol, back in the Brussels days.

"Bye-bye, Auntie and thank you for having me," Vicky spoke out, who had been primed and rehearsed by her father, just before Emma had come down the stairs.

"You were a good girl, and I enjoyed having you," replied Emma, patting her shoulder and then swiftly, she turned and walked out of the door that Sissie had purposefully opened wide.

Down the garden path she marched, closing the gate firmly behind her without looking back at the family grouped together in the porch ready to wave goodbye. As the gate clicked shut, she turned into the street, her eyes glistening with tears. Oh, how she wished that little girl was coming with her.

*　　*　　*

Snow fell in late February, just after Sissie's birthday, which was fortunate because during the week before, Doris gave birth to a baby daughter, whom they named Mary. Naturally, the family were excited to see mother and baby and to introduce themselves. Snow would have made travel more complicated and it would be less likely that they would leave their homes to visit. A dark haired and dark eyed chubby baby lay swaddled in her crib, the one that Sissie had given away. On the way home John enquired if the crib they had just seen was the one that had belonged to Ronnie. Sissie admitted that it was, and told him that they would have no use of it and Doris had asked her for it so she had given it to her.

"And what if we do have other children?" asked John, knowing full well that after the difficulties with Ronnie's birth it would be unlikely that they would have more.

"Now, John," murmured Sissie, sadly. "We 'ave to accept the facts. I'm not going to be 'avin' any more babies, am I?"

Sissie had needed an emergency hysterectomy, after complications followed when Ronnie was born. After the shock of it, they talked at length and agreed to remain discreet. It had been devastating for them both, and it had taken time before Sissie was feeling fit and well. Their privacy on the matter however, had caused people to wonder why it had taken so long for her to recover and to return to normal. No one asked any questions though, and so it became another of those many events that remained unexplained and in the past.

"We knew that didn't we, John?" she continued, still disappointed that she would never have any more children, now that the subject had been raised. "I thought it'd be nice for our Doris to 'ave it." John sympathised quietly, but was of the opinion that they should move on, grateful that they had a girl and a boy in their family life together. He was particularly annoyed however, that she had not consulted him about giving the cot away. She hadn't even mentioned it, almost as if she was afraid to tell him. He was irritated that Doris had such a control over Sissie. Clearly, the woman was resentful of their comfortable lifestyle, managing the basics only, on Herbert's low wages as a labourer. He made a note to himself to watch that situation, before it got out of hand. He wasn't sure how or if it would develop, but he would have to ensure that Sissie was not burdened by Doris's overbearing ways. It seemed Sissie's gentle and placid temperament was being taken advantage of, by both his sister and her own.

"No, no! As usual, you were being kind hearted and generous, because that's in your nature and that's why I love and admire you. Just don't let her take advantage of you! And - don't forget to tell me everything!" he replied, as he took over the pram pushing - which was awkward with Vicky sitting on top of it on a cushion because she wanted a ride home.

Sissie enjoyed a quiet birthday at home. Vicky had helped Evelyn to make and decorate a chocolate cake for tea and they all sang Happy Birthday to her. John gave her a beautiful solitaire pearl dress ring and Vicky gave her some scented soap that John had purchased for her to give to her stepmother.

He had kept the ring in its little box a secret, because he had once given it to his cherished late Victoria. He then brought it to England from Brussels, at first as a token of his past, but then he realised it would bring some joy to Sissie. No one knew about it, and he felt that there was no need for her to know its origin, so he didn't tell her in case she was hurt or offended. In fact, Sissie was overwhelmed by its delicate prettiness and by John's thoughtfulness and generosity. She gasped, as she opened the navy blue velveteen lid of the box with shaking fingers, and gazed at the ring laying elegantly on its ivory lining.

"Pick it up and put it on," John encouraged her quietly. Gently, she pushed it on the ring finger of her right hand. It fitted her perfectly.

"Thank you," she whispered "It is so beautiful. Thank you, John."

The morning they woke up to a generous covering of snow, there was much excitement in the Bland home, and Vicky was impatient to play in it. Being a Saturday, John was able to snowball with her and to build a snowman who, with coal eyes and carrot nose, stood staring vacantly towards the window of the morning room, positioned in the middle of the lawn.

Then, having found some old wooden slats at the back of the shed, he knocked them together to make a simple toboggan, and they set off after lunch onto the town fields that lay opposite the house, to sledge down the slopes of the extensive parkland.

They wrapped Ronnie in layers with woollen leggings and jackets and, under his cosy bonnet, he was tucked into his pram. Propped up to enjoy the cold, snow filled air, he was able to watch all the boys and girls shrieking, shouting and having fun on similar toboggans, each one hurriedly constructed for the day's snow play.

Back home, they shook themselves, shedding their cold, wet coats and hats, and lined up their boots by the scullery door. Then into the parlour together, they toasted crumpets in front of the open fire which was already roaring, thanks to Evelyn and enjoyed cups of steaming tea and fruit cake.

It had been an eventful and happy family day. One of those they would never forget.

*   *   *

As time went by, John consolidated his General Manager role in the factory. He was regarded as firm, fair and well organised because he knew this industry so thoroughly. Orders for spinning artificial silk were plentiful, ensuring a healthy production line and providing jobs for local people, establishing profit and gaining status that stood for reliability and quality.

Doncaster people talked about the company which was growing and earning a good reputation for its fair pay and conditions which attracted both reliable and mainly female workers.

Those who had family members who worked at the Nuttall's Mintoes factory smiled when he pulled out of his jacket pocket, the familiar boiled sweet. It was wrapped in cream and red waxed paper, and he unscrewed it carefully before popping into his mouth. They were another well-known factory employer in the town for a nationally recognised product.

Every new 'run-off' of twenty or so yards of a new design were shared among the management and from time to time he would bring some of it home for Sissie so that she could have it made into an outfit by a well-known seamstress in town. She had given up protesting and was happy by now, to choose a new style and cut for a dress or blouse for herself.

Sissie was finding it difficult however, to manage the demands of the bright, intelligent and energetic Vicky who, at six years old was becoming even more determined and high spirited. So it seemed, was baby Ronnie. He was prone to screaming until his needs were met, which she found exhausting, and almost always gave into him. During the day, it had become Sissie's routine to go round to Doris's house to share baby time together, a cup of tea and gossip while the little ones tumbled around and entertained each other. She found it reassuring and easier to manage the demands of her son this way and the days passed quickly. Vicky rarely went there however, being either at school or spending time increasingly, with her Auntie Emma who, these days, made it so easy for travel to and fro.

Vicky was learning to play the piano and seemed to have a natural aptitude, so convincing that John and Sissie agreed that they should buy one for her to practise and to play on at home. It was a splendid piece of furniture and a fine sounding instrument in an attractive walnut case and whose ivory keys gleamed invitingly, in the light from the bay window in the parlour. They decided to present it to Vicky as a surprise. So, one afternoon when she returned from school with Sissie, John, who had returned home earlier than usual, for that purpose, greeted her cheerfully at the back door, "Hello there, little girl and how was school today?"

"Daddie! You are home early. Are we going to play?"

She looked up at him with hope sparkling in her eyes. She pulled off her school coat leaving the sleeves inside out, as she shrugged it off onto the floor in her excitement.

"We are going to play, my dear. That's exactly what we are going to do and Mammie and I are going to show you what we are going to play at! We have a little surprise for you."

He led her by the hand and Sissie followed, carrying Ronnie on her hip, and as she slowly opened the parlour door, John issued his instructions,

"Now, close your eyes and I will tell you when to open them." She giggled excitedly doing as she was asked.

"There now! Ready? You can open them." he commanded. She gasped as her eyes focused on a new piano in front of her.

"Is this for me? Can I play it?" she asked, as she scrambled on to the dark green moquette seat of the piano stool.

"I hope you will play it every day until you are a famous concert pianist!" said John laughing, clearly satisfied with the decision to invest in such a thing. It would be right for Vicky now and for Ronnie later on, he hoped. Sissie stood back, enjoying the happy atmosphere and the fact that today, for once, John was home early.

"Let's hear something from you, then," she suggested. And Vicky played her scales up and down before playing a few recognisable notes of 'All Things Bright and Beautiful'. John and Sissie exchanged glances, knowing exactly who had been teaching her a children's hymn.

"I don't know it all. I've only just learned from Auntie Emma," said Vicky apologetically

"It's very good child. You are learning fast and you will play well if you practise. That's the reason why we've bought a piano for you," said John pleasantly, still resting his hand on her shoulder. "Can you play Mammie?" she asked.

"No dear, because we didn't have a piano when I was your age, and my father couldn't afford to pay for lessons for me," she answered self-consciously.

It was at times like this that she felt limited and inadequate.

"Let's get some tea. I think that's probably enough excitement for today," she added, turning to the door. Vicky groaned but she followed her, holding John's hand.

"I'm very happy now," she said, looking at him and speaking in a tone that suggested she might not have been happy before this event.

Apart from a day like today, the days and weeks passed uneventfully and routines set in as they did within most households. Emma continued to invite Vicky to stay and it seemed very obvious that they shared a lot of fun and good time together. Vicky was learning to spell and with help from Auntie she was able to write a short note to accompany a drawing, placed carefully in an envelope ready for postage. A delight to receive, Sissie would wait for John to return home so that they could open it up and read it through together.

Together with Emma's 'progress report' there was another little note written on pale blue paper where pencil lines had been carefully ruled to keep the handwriting level, where someone had written the words and the little girl had traced the familiar outline of the letters in her own young hand.

Dear Daddie,

I like staying with my Auntie.
She is very kind.
I am eating my greens.
We found a baby bird.
It had lost its Mammie.
We fed it and made a bed for it.
It made us happy.

Love from Vicky xx

An awkward silence followed whilst they both stared at the letter, recognising that Sissie had not been mentioned. They began to murmur about how she was developing and how fortunate that she was experiencing so much when suddenly John slammed his hand down on the dining table at which they were sitting. With unexpected anger in his voice, he raised his voice to say,

"And - tell me - WHY is my daughter spending so much time away from her rightful home? Sissie! What are we thinking of? I am missing all this growing up. Do I have a father and daughter closeness? NO! I do not! And why? Because that dratted sister of mine is selfishly wooing her away from us. Sissie don't you see what is happening? She's becoming a stranger to both of us.

Don't you see? We are allowing her to prefer being with her aunt than to be with us because we can't offer her anything! And why? Because we've grown apart from her, and now we have so little in common with her, we don't know how to behave with each other. Where are all the fun times and family times we should be sharing together? Do you know how it feels to me at present? It's like history is repeating itself," his voice choking in emotion.

He continued, "I am so sorry to bring this up my dearest, but it is just like the distance I felt when I left this same little girl with her grandparents in Brussels. It's the same familiar pain and loss as before. This time you and I are together and we MUST do something about it before it's too late. It's all a damn farce and I want it to stop. I do, Sissie, I do," He lowered his voice, growling, "And I want it to stop right now."

He fumbled for Sissie's hand, holding back his tears. Sissie looked down, unable to bear seeing him in such distress. She had felt so unable to express her own similar feelings to him because he was always so busy and so tired when he returned home from work. She had thought she would just be burdening him, and that he would not see the situation himself. She was wrong. He had been aware all along and today the gasket in his emotions had truly blown, and there would be no holding him back now. She looked down

"I know, I know," she said, comforting him gently and with a quiet voice. "We will get her back here and start to change things."

She hoped the uncertainty didn't show in her voice. She had spent many hours wondering how she could gain Vicky's trust and confidence that was so vital for a relationship between stepmother and daughter to develop and perhaps eventually flourish. She couldn't help but feel the competition that would be made to exist between herself and Emma, in terms of what she could offer in raising Vicky and what Emma could, and already did provide. Again, she had to face her own inadequacy and lack of self-confidence and most of all, the experience in raising someone else's child. John expected so much of her and without discussion he seemed to expect that by magic she could become the perfect mother figure. There was no one she could confide in and to share her fears and doubts with, either.

He drew his hand away and rummaged urgently in his trouser pocket for a handkerchief and then quite unexpectedly he wept unconsolably, and it was quite a while before he recovered himself. Sissie was so shocked. This man was always so composed and measured in his reactions in any given situation. This was quite out of character; she had never seen this side of him ever before. Worse, she could not think of anything that would comfort him, so she just sat quietly waiting for the unbearable sounds of his heartache to subside.

Eventually, he looked up and his watery eyes and reddened nose showed the depth of his distress. It was as if the outburst had released the tension and anxiety of all the years of remaining silent. He had always just wanted to get on with the practical matters to survive. All the setbacks and disappointments, sorrow and hardship would be easier to deal with in this way.

He sank back into the hardback dining chair and looked at her, and in the next moment he realised that all that he had ever wanted was a woman to love, to be by his side and to raise his children. He had always hoped to find a challenging and rewarding career. He had wrongly expected her to get on with the wife and mother role that she had accepted when they exchanged their vows on their wedding day, to honour and obey, in sickness and in health, until death do us part. He had been naïve and had under estimated her capacity to match him in sensitivity and sentiment, in practicality and persistence.

Painfully, he began to realise that he had not supported her enough or shown her how to cope. She was young and inexperienced and he'd left her to it, without understanding the challenges that she was facing. He had employed some help, yes, and Evelyn, thank goodness, had made a significant contribution in their home, but that did not address the considerable, complicated and sensitive business of raising a family.

Overwhelmed and embarrassed by his outburst he sank back in his chair and admitted to himself that here it was. He had it all. There was nothing else that he needed to look for in his life. Eventually, he looked at her. Her head was bowed with uncertainty and sadness. He leaned forward gently towards her, tilted her chin towards him and then, holding each of her hands in his, he looked at her tenderly.

"We can do this, my dearest, most precious one. Sissie, we have everything to work for and we will do this together. We will help each other to face the difficult tasks ahead and we will succeed. We have to believe that."

She sighed, knowing the extent and the effort they would both need to succeed in bringing John's daughter back into their arms and for her to draw them both into her heart. Most of all, she wanted to sweep away the sadness so that her dear husband would be fulfilled.

"Yes, John. Don't be sad my dearest. I know that we can come through this together if we try, and then we will make a good family."

Her dark eyelashes were still glistening from her own silent tears as she searched into his eyes and beyond, even to the depths of his soul. Putting her cheek gently onto his hands, she whispered,

"Action not words my, love. Action not words."

Acknowledgements

So many friends and family have supported me in this endeavour to write my first story based on family history. I am grateful to each and every one of them.

Specifically, my thanks go to the following: Trevor Millum for initiating the idea to write the story; Joan Drake for pushing me to write it; Helen Garlick for her inspiring writers' retreat that 'lit the touch paper' and a special thank you to Georgie Boyers ('Creative Concepts') who inspired the synopsis and the cover design.

In particular, I am indebted to Jackie Knight for her enthusiasm, skill and expertise as both a reader and a writer for editing my work with such dedication, energy and fun!

My gratitude would not be complete without a loud shout for my husband Steve Carey for being my sounding board (never bored!) throughout the whole journey.

About the Author

*B*orn in the UK in Yorkshire, living and working in Derbyshire and Lincolnshire, Christine now lives in Brittany, France having moved here with her husband from the UK in 2011. She has taught for 33 years in secondary education, finally in her career as a Principal of two successful schools.

With grown up children and growing grandchildren, who live across the miles, she and her husband are active travellers to be with them all.

Growing up with stories about her ancestors, largely from her own grandmother, she enjoys the historical context of any novel and this, in part, inspired her to write her own.

Embracing the French language and culture has fulfilled a lifelong dream. The family, good friends and gardening focus her energies on an active and absorbing lifestyle. And now writing her own novel has challenged her even further.